Whispers of Truth

A River Falls Novel

Valerie M. Bodden

River Falls Series

Pieces of Forever
Songs of Home
Memories of the Heart
Whispers of Truth
Promises of Mercy

River Falls Christmas Romances

Christmas of Joy

Hope Springs Series

Not Until Forever
Not Until This Moment
Not Until You
Not Until Us
Not Until Christmas Morning
Not Until This Day
Not Until Someday
Not Until Now
Not Until Then
Not Until The End

A Gift for You

Members of my Reader's Club get a FREE book, available exclusively to my subscribers. When you sign up, you'll also be the first to know about new releases, book deals, and giveaways.
Visit www.valeriembodden.com/freebook to join!

River Falls Character Map

If you love the whole Calvano family but need a refresher of who's who, what they do, and which book belongs to each, check out the handy character map at www.valeriembodden.com/rfcharacters

Never will I leave you.
Never will I forsake you.

Hebrews 13:5

Chapter 1

Summer peeled her fingers off the steering wheel, then swiped her palms over her cheeks, wiping the moisture they came away with on her t-shirt. She pulled down the sun visor and flipped up the mirror to assess the damage. Fortunately, she hadn't done her makeup yet, or her face would be a disaster. But she looked bad enough the way it was. A full night of crying had left her with puffy eyes and a red nose, and this fresh round of tears had created great pink splotches on her cheeks. She'd have to tell Mama it was a cold. Or allergies.

She supposed other women might turn to their mothers for comfort after a breakup. But she wasn't other girls. And Mama wasn't other mamas. If she knew Nick had dumped Summer, it would be just one more weapon in the arsenal of insults she could hurl at her daughter.

Taking a shaky breath and letting it out slowly, Summer opened the car door and made herself get out. Instantly, the July humidity pasted itself to her already sticky face. She let herself gaze into the distance for a moment, her eyes roving hungrily over the lush green mountain slopes that ringed the town of River Falls. They always looked so inviting, and more than once as a kid, she had dreamed of running away from Mama and living out there on her own. If it hadn't been for her brother TJ, maybe she would have.

She let out a long breath and moved resolutely to the trunk to unload the groceries, then hurried to the door. She might as well get this over with. She

1

only had a couple of hours before she needed to be in costume and ready to entertain a roomful of giggling girls.

She probably should have saved the shopping for tomorrow and gone to church this morning, but the thought of showing up there all red-faced and puffy-eyed had been less than appealing. Especially knowing that Benjamin would be there, and he would be all sweet and concerned and wonderful—and she couldn't take that right now.

Besides, this way she wouldn't have to do Mama's shopping after the party, when she'd be completely worn out.

She tromped to the stoop and set one of the bags down to fish out her keys, then took another breath and forced herself to unlock the door and step through.

"Good morning, Mama." She didn't bother to try to sound cheerful—that would have made Mama suspicious—but she managed to keep the tears out of her voice.

From her chair in front of the TV, Mama grunted something in Summer's direction. Summer kept going until she reached the kitchen and deposited the packages. She made two more trips to the car, relieved that Mama never once glanced in her direction.

Summer made quick work of unpacking the groceries, then emptied the dishwasher and sorted through the refrigerator for leftovers that had gone bad. She held her breath as she opened the garbage can, hoping against hope that she wouldn't find—

She let the breath out. Sure enough, an empty bottle of whiskey nestled on a bed of beer bottles. Summer tossed the rotten food on top of the pile, her stomach churning. She never bought alcohol for Mama, but somehow it always found its way into the house. Summer suspected that Mama paid a neighbor to pick it up for her.

She did a quick search of the cupboards but didn't find any more. And even if she did find it, she wasn't sure what she would do. The last time she had dumped Mama's stash, her mother's wrath had been intense. Summer had learned to face the fact that if end-stage liver disease wasn't enough to stop Mama's drinking, there was nothing she could do to stop it either.

"Bring me a sandwich," Mama called from the living room.

Summer bit back a reply of, *What's the magic word?* and started putting together a ham and cheese sandwich.

TJ was constantly asking her why she still came over here, why she took care of Mama when Mama had never worried about taking care of them. It was a question Summer had asked herself more than once. And she still didn't have a good answer.

She finished making the sandwich and poured Mama a glass of milk, then carried them both to the living room. "Here you are, Mama."

Mama's eyes flicked from her soap opera to Summer. She took the sandwich but waved the milk away. Summer sighed and set it on the TV tray that lived next to Mama's chair. "It's good for you."

Mama grunted. "I'm not thirsty. What's the matter with you, anyway?"

"Nothing."

"Then why's your face all splotchy and your eyes all puffy?"

Summer wished she could believe that was concern in Mama's voice. "It must be allergies." She sniffed to make the statement convincing.

Mama snorted. "Yeah, and I have a touch of the flu." She turned toward Summer, her yellowed skin gaunt on her cheeks. "Your boyfriend dump you?"

Summer winced even though the comment was exactly what she'd been expecting. She sniffed back the fresh burst of tears that threatened. "He got a job offer in California."

A wave of humiliation rolled over her as she recalled her reaction to his announcement: "I can't move to California."

And his response: "I wasn't asking you to."

But that was nothing Mama needed to know.

"Yeah, well." Mama glanced at her, and Summer couldn't tell if it was her imagination or wishful thinking, but she could have sworn she saw a flash of sympathy in Mama's eyes. Before she could analyze it, it was gone, replaced by Mama's signature cynical expression. "It's like I always told you. A man will amuse himself with you until something better comes along and he realizes he doesn't really want you." Her eyes swung back to the TV.

Summer wondered for the eight-millionth time if Mama would have been like this even if Summer and TJ's father hadn't left the day Summer was born. "Took one look at you and that's the last I ever saw of him," was the way Mama told it, making it abundantly clear that it was some undesirable quality in the newborn baby that had chased him away.

Maybe *that* was why Summer was so driven to take care of Mama—she felt like she had to make it up to her.

"Do you need anything else before I go?" Summer picked up a throw pillow off the floor and tossed it on the worn couch Mama never used.

"What about the laundry?"

Summer checked the time. If she didn't get going, she wouldn't have enough time to get ready for the party. "I can start it. Do you think you can put it in the dryer later?"

"Yeah, sure. Maybe I'll have a dizzy spell and fall down the basement steps and then you won't have to worry about my laundry ever again." Mama's eyes remained glued to the TV the entire time she spoke.

"Don't talk like that." Summer grimaced. "I'll put the laundry in now and then I'll come back after my party to finish it."

"Isn't twenty-two a little old to still believe in fairy tales?" Mama rolled her eyes. "Aren't your tears plenty proof that there's no such thing as a happy ending?"

Summer ignored the questions—Mama was still absorbed in her TV show anyway—and marched to the bedroom to grab the laundry. But just because she hadn't answered out loud, didn't mean the thoughts weren't bouncing around in her head.

Did she believe in fairy tales and happy endings?

Yes, absolutely.

Just because she was unlikely to ever experience one didn't mean she should keep other girls from that dream.

She carried Mama's clothes down to the basement and dumped them into the washer, thinking, as she poured in the detergent, that at least it wouldn't be much of a stretch for her to play Cinderella today. Even if her Prince Charming was some high school kid she'd found through an online ad. He had only one qualification that had gotten him the job: he was the only one who applied.

There was another, a little voice reminded her. But she pushed it away. Benjamin Calvano had only been joking—that man didn't know how to be serious.

And anyway, if there was anyone she *didn't* need to play her Prince Charming right now, it was Benjamin. She could only imagine the havoc *that* would wreak on her heart. Aside from Nick, he was the only other guy she'd dated—and it had turned out that he hadn't wanted her either.

She closed the washer harder than she meant to and pulled her phone out of her pocket as she walked up the stairs. If she left right now, she should be—

She stopped in the middle of the steps, as her eyes fell on the text that had popped onto her screen.

Can't make it today. Sorry.

She didn't recognize the number, but a sick feeling in her stomach told her she already knew who it was from. She clicked over to the string of earlier texts to check. Sure enough, it was her Prince Charming.

She groaned.

She never should have agreed to Mrs. Feldman's request that she provide not only a princess but also a prince for this party. She was a solo act. She'd told Mrs. Feldman that. But the influential woman had insisted, and Summer knew this party had the potential to bring her a bunch more clients looking for princess parties. It seemed like her last chance to finally get her fledgling little business off the ground.

Which was why she couldn't afford for anything to go wrong.

She scanned the dingy stairway, as if a Prince Charming might suddenly materialize.

When none did, she fired back a quick text. *The party starts in two hours. I don't have time to find someone else.* She sent it, even though she already knew it would do no good. The kid hadn't exactly struck her as the reliable type.

She marched up the stairs, calling, "I'll be back in a few hours, Mama," on her way through the living room. Mercifully, Mama's only answer was a light snore.

When Summer got to her car, she checked her phone again, but her text remained unopened. She let out a breath, wracking her brain for a solution. She couldn't show up without a prince, not when she'd promised Mrs. Feldman. It would be the end of her business, for sure.

With a resigned sigh, she tapped her brother's name. TJ had taken his four-year-old son Max fishing after church, but Summer knew her nephew well enough to know he wouldn't last long before getting antsy anyway, and if they left right now, they could get back in time for the party.

Still, she hated to ask TJ to rescue her yet again. He already let her live with him and Max rent-free so that she wouldn't have to live with mama. Sure, she babysat Max while TJ was at work and covered as many other expenses as she could, but that came nowhere near to making it even.

But she didn't see what other choice she had right now. She sent a quick text asking him, then started the car and backed out of the driveway. If she didn't get going, there wouldn't be a princess party at all. Fortunately, the drive through downtown River Falls—where families mingled on the streets in front of the bookstore and the art shop and Daisy's pie shop, and where couples strolled the riverfront walkway, and where everyone's smile seemed to mock Summer's loneliness—took less than ten minutes. The instant she pulled into the driveway, she grabbed her phone and found a reply from TJ.

You know Benjamin offered to do it.

Summer made an annoyed sound. Her brother's obsession with getting the two of them back together was wearing on her. The first thing he'd said when she'd come home crying last night was, "Nick is an idiot. And so are you if you don't know who you should call now."

I'm sure he has to work, she texted back. *And I'd rather go princeless than ask him.*

Ouch, TJ replied. *You better hope I don't tell him that.*

TJ, was her only reply.

Yeah, I'm on it, his text came back a moment later. *Bring the Prince Charming costume with you and send me the address.*

Summer heaved a sigh of relief and sent a *Thank you, thank you, thank you* message.

Then she headed inside, stubbing her toe on one of Max's dinosaur toys. She hobbled toward her bedroom and opened the door of her small closet, smiling as she always did at the gem-colored ball gowns hanging there. It was her five-year-old self's dream come true. Her heart suddenly lighter at the thought of making another little girl's dreams come true, she grabbed the blue dress and prepared to transform into a princess.

Chapter 2

Benjamin pulled his arm back, pumping the football a few times as he waited for his brother Joseph to get open in the makeshift end zone of Dad's front yard. The moment he saw his opening, he let the ball fly, the satisfaction of a perfect spiral coursing through him with the same power as it had at the state championship game he'd led his team to three years in a row in high school.

Joseph caught the ball effortlessly, and Benjamin threw his arms in the air with a cheer. "And that's how the kids do it," he called to his older brothers Zeb and Simeon and his brother-in-law Liam.

"I'm not sure I still qualify as a kid," Asher muttered to him. "But I'll take the win anyway."

Together, the sweaty brothers jostled and laughed their way to the porch where Simeon, Joseph, Asher, and Liam all went instantly to their wives. Zeb, whose wife had died just over a year earlier, scooped Asher and Ireland's little girl, Caroline, off of Dad's lap and kissed her cheek.

Benjamin debated between claiming Ava and Joseph's six-month-old Noah or Simeon and Abigail's little Genevieve, born the same day in the same hospital.

"Ah, I think this guy needs a diaper change," Ava announced, and that decided that.

Benjamin reached for Genevieve, and Abigail handed her over with a smile. The little girl grinned at him, two teeth poking through her gums, and patted his face.

He listened as multiple conversations flew around him, soaking up the sounds of his siblings' chatter as he made faces at Genevieve. The little girl's giggles were contagious.

"So." Abigail looked up at him from the rocking chair. "How are things?"

"Good. Why?"

"Any news on the dating front?" Abigail smiled knowingly.

"Oh. That." Benjamin shrugged. He'd been planning to wait until he saw how things went before he brought it up with his family. Otherwise, they were likely to blow everything out of proportion. As the youngest and the only remaining unmarried sibling—although they hadn't seen Judah in so long that it was entirely possible he was married and had a family they knew nothing about—he was often the victim of unwanted matchmaking. "I have a date tonight." A Sunday night date might seem strange to some people, but Jasmine hadn't batted an eye when he'd mentioned that he had Sunday-Monday and Tuesday-Wednesday off on alternating weeks. As a realtor, her weekends were busy too.

"I know." Abigail grinned, and Benjamin didn't bother to ask how. River Falls was a small town, and he had a big family, so it was pretty much a given that nothing could be kept secret.

"Oh, who is it with?" Ava joined the conversation eagerly.

"Jasmine," Abigail answered for him.

"The real estate agent who sold you the house?" Ireland jumped into the conversation. "She's nice."

"She is," Abigail agreed. "Although I wish you would have asked Summer out. I still don't get what happened there. You're the most impulsive person I know, and you dragged your feet for months on that. And then it was too late."

Benjamin shrugged, even though his heart agreed with his sister-in-law one hundred percent. He had been an idiot not to ask Summer out before that Nick guy got to her.

He'd spent the last four months kicking himself for that. But now it was time to move on. Besides, it wouldn't be bad to have a fresh start with someone who had never broken his heart before.

"Where are you taking her?" Lydia joined the conversation too, and Benjamin rolled his eyes. So much for keeping this under wraps. "The Depot?"

Benjamin snorted. "So all of my coworkers can ogle us? No thanks. I was thinking that pizza place up on the ridge, but I should text her to see if she's okay with that."

He adjusted Genevieve so he could reach into his pocket, but his phone wasn't there. "Where is my . . ." He glanced around. "I must have left it in the house." He planted a big kiss on his niece's cheek and gave her back to Abigail, then traipsed into the house.

His phone was on the kitchen counter, and he swiped a cookie as he picked it up.

A string of texts from his friend TJ lit the screen, and he scrolled through them.

You busy? Summer needs a Prince Charming. 3pm to 5pm.

Benjamin grinned, his eyes flicking to the time. It was 2:15 now. And his date wasn't until 7.

You there? If you don't do it, I'm going to have to. But I think we'd both prefer if it was you. Benjamin stared at that one for a moment, trying to decide if *both* referred to TJ and Benjamin or to TJ and Summer.

Before he could figure it out, another text came through. *I guess you're busy. I'll go. But don't say I didn't give you your opportunity. She and Nick broke up last night, btw.*

Benjamin blinked at the words, his heart racing and breaking at the same time. He hated to think of anything hurting Summer, and yet . . . If she wasn't with Nick—

He stopped himself right there. He had a date with another woman tonight. And anyway, if he and Summer started dating again, chances were good that it would only destroy the friendship with her that he'd worked so hard to rebuild over the past year.

Still . . . Friends helped friends out.

I can do it, he texted TJ.

Three seconds later, TJ texted an address in the foothills on the outskirts of town. Benjamin was going to have to leave right now if he wanted to get there on time. He slid his phone into his pocket and made his way back through the house and out the door.

"So I guess she likes pizza?" Lydia asked with a laugh.

"Huh?" Benjamin halted. "Who likes pizza?"

"Jasmine." Lydia rolled her eyes.

"I don't know. I didn't get a chance to text her."

"Then what were you doing, and why are you grinning like a fool?" Abigail asked.

"Eating cookies." Benjamin grinned back easily. It wasn't a lie. "I gotta take off."

"Where are you going in such a hurry?" Joseph asked. "Don't tell me it's going to take you four hours to get ready for your date."

Everyone laughed, but Benjamin didn't care. "I have to do a favor for a friend first."

Chapter 3

Summer twisted in the seat of her parked car to scan the street behind her again. The little guests would be arriving soon, and she should really be setting up inside. But TJ wasn't there yet, and she couldn't face going to the door and telling Mrs. Feldman that she didn't have a prince after all.

Maybe she should have asked Benjamin. He at least wouldn't have had to worry about getting a four-year-old going.

In the rearview mirror, she saw a car turn onto the street, and she turned again, trying to make out if it was TJ's.

But no, it was too small and . . .

Her heart jumped ahead three beats as she recognized the tiny Gremlin.

Only one person she knew drove a car like that. But what was he doing way out here? The area was entirely residential, so there was no reason to be driving here unless . . .

Her heart skipped another half dozen beats as the car pulled up behind hers. There was no way . . .

She picked up her phone and dashed off a text to TJ. *I thought you said you were coming.*

No. The reply was nearly instant. *I said I'd take care of it. You're welcome.*

Summer clicked the phone off and blew a breath at her suddenly way-too-hot face, her eyes flicking to the mirror to double-check that her makeup hid the puffy eyes and splotchy cheeks. It wasn't perfect, but it would have to do. Anyway, it wasn't like Benjamin had any reason to look that closely.

And it's not like you're here for him, she reminded herself.

A light knock on her window made her jump, and she hastily opened the door, nearly taking Benjamin's legs out before he could jump backwards.

"Sorry," she murmured, lifting the poofy blue dress so she could get out of the car, feeling suddenly self-conscious and ridiculous in the costume. Sweat trickled down her back, but she couldn't have said if it was from the stifling heat or Benjamin's nearness.

His eyes were fixed on her face, his mouth lifted into a wide smile. "I hear you're looking for a Prince Charming."

She shook her head, and Benjamin frowned. "Wrong prince?"

"No." She shook her head harder, trying to get her thoughts straight. "You're the right prince." Benjamin's grin widened, and Summer stumbled to rephrase. "I mean, Prince Charming is the right prince, but I thought TJ was coming."

"Nope," Benjamin said cheerfully. "You're stuck with me. Now where's my costume? I don't want to look like a schlub standing next to this beautiful princess."

Summer rolled her eyes, praying the rosy cheeks she'd painted on earlier hid the blush she felt rising to her face. She opened the back door and ducked inside, grateful for the momentary distance. But it only took a second to grab the Prince Charming costume. She stepped out and passed it to him. He held it up and gave a long, appreciative whistle. "Now this is what I'm talking about."

Summer laughed—he had always had the ability to make her do that—and moved to the trunk to retrieve the large plastic tote of goodies she'd need for the party.

"Here, let me take that." Somehow Benjamin was right there, his arms wrapping around the tote before Summer could process what was happening. His forearm brushed against hers, sending shockwaves all the way up her arm, but he seemed completely unphased.

Of course he was.

It wasn't like he was here because he wanted to spend time with her. He was simply a nice guy doing his friend's sister a favor.

"You weren't at church this morning," he said softly as they started up the driveway toward the large brick house.

She looked at him quickly, but his expression wasn't accusing. Just concerned.

"I heard about Nick," he added. "Are you okay?"

"I'll be fine." She prepared to blink back fresh tears, but to her surprise, none came.

"For what it's worth, you're better off without him."

"Yeah." Summer sighed softly. She was better off without anyone. Being with someone meant wanting them to want you. And when you found out they didn't—well, that was worse than being alone.

Benjamin gave her a look she couldn't read and opened his mouth as if to say something more, but Summer cut him off. "You do know Prince Charming's part in the story, right?"

"Of course." Benjamin grinned, his eyes traveling her dress. "You're Snow White, so—"

"Cinderella," she corrected.

"That's what I meant. Cinderella. She's the one who's locked in the tower, right? I don't think that wig is long enough for me to climb up."

Panic whooshed through Summer. She had a prince who didn't even know the fairy tale he was supposed to be from. "Cinderella is the one with the fairy godmother and the pumpkin carriage and the glass—" She broke off as Benjamin chuckled, her hand swinging out to swat his arm before she could think better of it. "Be serious."

"Who me?" Benjamin made a goofy face. "Never."

She rolled her eyes but couldn't hide the twitch of a smile that threatened to turn her lips.

"There." Benjamin smiled back. "That's better."

Fortunately, the front door burst open, and a little girl with blonde curls, crutches, and a contagious smile stood in front of them. "I can't believe you're really here," she squealed.

"You must be the birthday girl." Summer automatically switched to her soprano Cinderella voice—much higher than her normal speaking voice—and curtsied to the girl, feeling slightly silly with Benjamin watching. But she had a job to do. "I'm Cinderella. And this is my—" She choked a little but forced herself to say it, vowing internally to kill her brother for instigating this. "My husband, Prince Charming."

"M'lady." Benjamin offered a stately bow over the tote he still carried.

"You don't look like a prince." The girl giggled.

"Oh, well—" Summer scrambled for an explanation.

"That's because," Benjamin cut in with a conspiratorial whisper, "I get messy easily, so Cinderella doesn't let me wear my uniform until we get anywhere important. She can wear her dress all the time because she's always neat and beautiful. But I'm—" He looked around as if about to divulge a state secret. "Kind of a slob."

The girl's giggles pealed through the large foyer.

"Does m'lady have a name?" Benjamin asked the girl.

She nodded. "I'm Lily."

"Well, Lady Lily—"

The name elicited another giggle from the girl.

"If you'll but tell me where to change," Benjamin continued, "I shall adorn myself in more princely garb fit for the celebration of your birthday."

Lily blinked at him wide-eyed, and Summer translated in her Cinderella soprano, "Prince Charming needs somewhere to change."

"Oh." Lily grinned. "The bathroom is down there." She pointed down a long hallway.

Benjamin set the tote down and scooped his costume off the top, then bowed and disappeared in the direction Lily had indicated. "I shall return anon."

"I like him," Lily announced. "It must be fun to live with him in your castle."

"I— Um— Yes," was the only answer Summer could muster as she bent to pick up the tote Benjamin had carried in for her. "Now, where should I set up?"

Lily led her to a spacious room that was probably a library but could have easily passed for a fairy-tale ballroom. Twinkle lights crisscrossed the ceiling and pink balloons floated in large clusters throughout the room. A large table held gifts and a magnificent cake, while a couple more tables had been arranged with chairs around them.

"Great, you're here." A blonde woman with soft laugh lines around her eyes set a lollipop bouquet on one of the tables, then hurried toward Summer with her hand outstretched. "I'm Mrs. Feldman. And I know who you are." Her smile was warm and pleasant as she looked from Summer to her daughter. "Lily insisted that she be the one to answer the door. Does everything in here look okay?"

"Oh yes. It's . . . amazing."

"Oh, thanks. I may have gone a little overboard, but . . ." Mrs. Feldman smoothed Lily's hair. "You only get a birthday once a year."

A flash of awe and longing rippled through Summer. The most Mama had ever done for her birthday was say she could have a friend over—an offer Summer had only taken her up on once. That was enough to learn that a drunk mother and a sleepover did not go well together.

"Prince Charming!" Lily's delighted cry pulled Summer's gaze past Mrs. Feldman. Benjamin was striding across the room, resplendent in red pants and an embroidered white tunic with gold epaulets and gold braid and even a gold belt. The costume should have made him look ridiculous. But, combined with his wide smile and twinkling eyes, it made him look like he belonged in a fairy tale.

"Lady Lily." Benjamin held out a hand for a fist bump.

The little girl giggled. "Do princes do fist bumps?"

"Of course. But we have a special, royal fist bump. Shall I teach it to you?"

Lily nodded, eyes wide, and Mrs. Feldman sent Summer an approving look.

Benjamin and Lily giggled and made up new fist bumps as Summer got everything set up. Soon the guests started to filter in, and Summer recognized a couple of the girls who were in her dance class. But in her costume and wig, and with her Cinderella voice, they didn't seem to recognize her.

As soon as Mrs. Feldman said everyone had arrived, Summer gathered the girls and introduced Benjamin, who gave a deep bow. Having him there made her more nervous than usual, but once the party got going, she found herself relaxing into her role. It helped that Benjamin played his part beautifully. He gamely let the girls paint his fingernails during manicure time, made a much-too-small foam crown for himself that dissolved the girls into giggles when he put it on, joined in her storytelling—supplying all the wrong details, which the girls loved correcting—and was pretty much the star of the show.

Summer didn't mind. The girls were having a good time. And so was she. She barely had time to think about Nick, and when she did, it was with an odd sort of detachment, as if he were part of a different world. She could almost imagine she really was in a fairy tale, this home her castle, the little girls her sisters, and Benjamin her—

No. That was where the fairy tale had to end. She could not afford to think of Benjamin as her prince.

"I got you some cake." Benjamin strode across the room, two plates of cake in his hands. He held the plate with one slice out to her. "Unless you want two?" He thrust the other one in her direction instead.

She laughed and shook her head. "One is plenty."

He shrugged and handed her the first plate. "One might be plenty, but two is better." He shoved a large, very un-prince-like bite into his mouth. "So what's next?" He nodded toward the girls, who were eating their cake as Lily opened her gifts.

"Um . . ." Summer's cake turned to sand in her mouth. This was the part she'd been dreading all day.

"What?" Benjamin raised an eyebrow at her. "Do I have to juggle swords or something?"

"Not exactly." Summer swallowed. "We have to dance."

Benjamin scrutinized her. "And that's a problem because . . ."

Summer shook her head. He knew why it was a problem.

"It's not a problem," she murmured, just to get his eyes off of her.

Before he could say anything else, she gathered up the length of her skirt and whisked over to the girls, who had finished their cake and presents.

"Okay, everyone." She clapped her hands together and used her most excited princess voice. "It's the moment you've all been waiting for."

"The Royal Ball," Lily squealed, her smile so large that Summer wished she had a camera to capture the moment for her website.

"That's right." She directed them all to take a seat, then made her way nervously back toward Benjamin, who had polished off his cake. He held out a hand, but she swept past him to start the music. The strains of "So This Is Love" filled the space, and Summer nearly groaned out loud. When she'd told Mrs. Feldman she could conclude with a Royal Ball, she hadn't fathomed that she'd be dancing to this song with Benjamin, of all people.

When she turned back, his hand was still out, palm up. She took a breath and, not quite brave enough to look at him, set her hand in his.

"Do you know how to waltz?" she whispered as he led her to the middle of the floor.

"I guess we'll find out." His smile rang through his voice, but Summer still couldn't bring herself to look at him.

In the middle of the floor, he stopped and spun her toward him, curling one arm decisively around her waist and shifting his other hand to lift hers between them. She barely had time to grasp her long dress in her free hand, and then he was stepping off in perfect time to the music.

Summer lifted her head in surprise, her gaze going from the sparkling blue of his eyes to the playful lift of his lips—which wore a fine coat of red frosting on one side. She let her dress fall to tap her own lip. "You have a little frosting on your . . ."

Benjamin grinned sheepishly, his tongue darting out to clear it away. "Did I get it?"

"No." Without thinking, Summer lifted her hand to wipe it away, as if he were Max. An instant before her fingers made contact, she realized her mistake. Her hand hovered in the air between them for a moment, and she turned the movement into an awkward sort of point. "Right there." She dropped her arm as Benjamin brought the back of his hand up to swipe at it.

"My Mama would be so embarrassed. Fortunately, I don't embarrass easily. Which is why I can do this." He cinched her closer, then dipped her backwards.

The sudden movement drew a small shriek from Summer, but the girls all cheered.

Benjamin's firm arm held her like that for a moment, and then he pulled her upright, the taut muscles of his arm flexing against her back.

"Don't do that again," she gasped, struggling to get her breath back.

"Sorry." Benjamin's grin said he was anything but.

"Where did you learn how to waltz?" Summer asked to keep herself from focusing on his nearness.

Benjamin didn't answer for a moment, then said quietly, "Would you laugh at me if I said my mama?"

Summer laughed but shook her head. "No."

"You just did," Benjamin pointed out, but he was grinning too.

"Only because I think it's sweet."

"I didn't at the time." He made a face. "But now I'm glad she did." He snugged Summer a little closer to him.

A hint of citrus and fresh, sweet herbs drifted from him, and Summer had to remind herself not to rest her head on his shoulder.

"So have I done okay as a prince?" he asked.

She let her eyes meet his. She owed him big for how well the day had gone. "More than okay. You were a hit with all the girls."

"All of them?" He raised an eyebrow.

Summer pretended not to catch his meaning. "I think little Dory was afraid of you at first, but she warmed up."

"Yeah." Benjamin kept his eyes on hers but didn't say anything further.

"Kiss her," a little girl's voice called, startling Summer. She'd almost forgotten they weren't alone.

"Kiss her," another voice echoed.

Benjamin glanced over his shoulder toward the girls, and suddenly they were all chanting in time to the music, "Kiss her. Kiss her."

Benjamin's head swiveled back to Summer, his look questioning.

She shook her head. "That's not part of the package."

But Benjamin's feet slowed and then stopped altogether. The hand on her waist tugged her closer, and he gazed down at her with an expression that made her heart jump from waltz to tango.

"Benj— Prince Charming," she said weakly.

His smile gallant, he let go of her waist, took a step backwards, and swept her hand to his lips, brushing a light kiss over her knuckles.

Chapter 4

Benjamin said one last goodbye to the girls, then slipped out the front door, his Prince Charming suit draped over his arm. He'd almost hated to change out of it. It was stiff and sweltering—but it also seemed to have worked some kind of fairy-tale magic between him and Summer.

He jogged down the driveway toward the street, where Summer stood leaning against her car. She had slipped out of her dress to reveal a white tank top and pink athletic shorts. She'd shed the wig and was unwinding the dark braids coiled around her head.

"I just ran into Mrs. Feldman," Benjamin announced the moment he reached her.

"Did she say anything?" Summer darted a glance at the house.

"Only that she's going to be recommending you to everyone she knows," he said nonchalantly. He didn't add that Mrs. Feldman had also said the two of them had great chemistry.

"Really?" Summer's huge smile almost beckoned Benjamin forward to hug her, but then he remembered that they weren't Cinderella and Prince Charming anymore. They were Summer and Benjamin. Friends.

He wasn't sure yet if they were friends who hugged.

"Did she say anything else?" Summer asked, combing her fingers through her hair so that it tumbled in wild waves down her back.

Benjamin swallowed, remembering how soft those waves had been. "Uh, no. Not really. Just that, you know, she liked the double act. So you might have more requests for those in the future."

Summer frowned. "I'll have to find a new prince then. I can't be calling you up every time I need one."

Benjamin shrugged. "I don't see why not. I had fun."

She gave him a skeptical look.

"What? I did. And besides, my nails have never looked better." He held up a hand and waved his pink fingernails. "Plus, it was fun to see you like this."

Summer lifted surprised eyes to his. "Like what?"

He shrugged, trying to figure out how to put words to it. "Like . . . happy, I guess? Like you're doing something you really love. You're really great with those kids, you know. Mrs. Feldman told me she hasn't seen Lily smile this much since her dad left."

Summer waved a hand dismissively. "That was mostly you."

But he wasn't going to let her duck out of the compliment. "You gave that girl something she has always dreamed of. Do you realize how big that is?"

Summer's eyes snapped to his and then away—but not before he saw the emotion in them.

"We should go," she said after a moment. "I'm sure the girls' parents will be here to pick them up soon, and we don't want them to see that Cinderella and Prince Charming are only Summer and Benjamin."

Benjamin shrugged. "I don't know. I think they might like Summer and Benjamin too."

He was pretty sure her cheeks grew rosier than her makeup, but she kept her head down and opened an envelope in her hand. She fanned through something inside, then held up three $50 bills. She held them out to him. "Here's your half."

Benjamin shook his head, the smile melting off his lips. "I don't need that." He wasn't rich or anything, but he was doing fine. And he certainly hadn't done this for the money.

"Of course you do. You worked just as hard as I did to earn it."

"I'm not going to take it." Benjamin folded his arms in front of him.

She blinked from him to the money and back again. "Benjamin." She sounded annoyed.

"Summer." He could sound just as irritated.

"Fine." She shoved the money back into the envelope with a sigh. "At least let me buy you dinner or something. I mean—" She looked up, her eyes suddenly panicked. "As a thank you."

Benjamin's heart jumped—and then crashed back down.

He couldn't.

"I would love to. But I have a—" Why didn't he want to tell her he had a date? "Other plans." For half a second, he considered canceling those plans. But that wouldn't be fair to Jasmine. And besides, Summer was only asking as a friend. He couldn't let himself get caught up in thinking of her as more again.

Summer's smile bobbled but then fixed back into place. "No problem. Have a good night. And thank you again."

"You're welcome again." Benjamin sought desperately for a way to salvage the situation. "You know who to call the next time you need a prince."

"I guess I do." Summer's smile was thin as she got into her car. Benjamin watched her drive away, then made his way to his Gremlin, trying to tug himself out of the fairy tale of the past few hours.

Chapter 5

"Beautiful work today, girls." Summer held out her hand to high-five her beginner ballet students. "Work those pliés at home."

"How's Prince Charming?" Nadia asked slyly as she reached Summer.

Summer tried not to let her surprise register on her face. She'd been so sure none of her students at the party the other day recognized her. She prided herself on keeping her real identity a mystery whenever she did princess parties. It added to the illusion that the fairy tale was real. Which was exactly why she'd had to take her costume off as soon as she'd gotten out of the Feldman's house—she needed to break that illusion for herself after the way Benjamin had held her in his arms and kissed her hand.

"Prince Charming?" She pretended to be confused. "I don't know any Prince Charmings."

"It's okay," Nadia whispered, gesturing for Summer to bend closer as if to let her in on a secret. "I know you have to wear this disguise to teach ballet. Otherwise, people would flock here to see a princess, and you'd never get any teaching done."

"That's true," Summer whispered back, fighting to keep a straight face. "Will you help me keep my secret?"

The girl nodded and mimed zipping her lips and throwing away the key.

"Thank you. I'll see you next week."

Nadia kept her lips pressed tight but made a sound that Summer assumed was supposed to be "goodbye" and scurried off to her mom.

Summer allowed herself a chuckle as she moved around the room, collecting hula hoops off the floor from the game they'd played at the end of class.

But now that Nadia had turned her mind to Prince Charming, she couldn't turn it away. Not that she'd really stopped thinking about him all week.

She'd tried. Valiantly.

But with little success. It had occurred to her that Nick was the one she should be dwelling on. But somehow that afternoon with Benjamin kept coming back to her.

It wasn't only the dancing or the kiss either. It was the smiles and the laughs and the easy way he had about everything. And most of all, though she hated to admit it to herself, it was wondering if his "other plans" had been a date.

It shouldn't matter to her. She'd told herself a hundred times that it *didn't* matter. She'd already decided she was done with dating. She just had to find a way to get the memo to her heart.

She hung the hula hoops on their peg, then moved the portable barres to the side of the room. By the time she was done, the children and their parents had all left, and Summer gathered up her own things to head home. If she hurried, she should be able to say goodnight to Max before he went to bed.

"Oh good, you're still here." Danica, Summer's boss—and the closest thing she had to a friend, though they never spent time together outside of work—glanced around the room as if looking for something. Although Danica was nearly three decades older than Summer, she usually moved with such a youthful energy that people guessed she was in her thirties. But today her movements seemed slow and weighted.

"Is everything all right?" Summer asked.

Danica sighed. "It is, and it isn't."

Summer waited as her boss adjusted her sleek blonde bun. She had learned over the years that Danica put as much care into her words as into her dance.

"You know my daughter in Colorado just had a baby?"

Summer nodded. It would have been hard not to know, given that Danica had decorated the studio with pink streamers for the occasion.

Danica smiled as if touched that Summer had remembered. "Well, her husband decided that now would be a good time to up and leave her." Danica's usually serene features transformed with indignation. "She didn't see it coming at all, and she's going through postpartum depression and now with this on top of it . . ."

Summer nodded sympathetically.

"I just feel like I need to be with her," Danica concluded.

"Of course. It might take a little juggling, but I'm sure I can cover your classes. How long do you think—"

She cut off at Danica's head shake. "I don't mean a trip. I mean we're going to move there."

Summer stared at her. "Oh," was the only word she could get out.

"We've been thinking about it for a while anyway. Bill has always wanted to live in the mountains, and with our grandchildren there . . ." Danica went on. "To be honest, the main reason I resisted for so long was that I didn't want to pull the rug out from under you. But I can't bear to see my daughter go through this alone."

Summer nodded numbly, trying to picture her own mama dropping everything to help her. But the image was too absurd to even conjure.

"When— Um— When do you plan to go?"

Danica bit her lip. "Bill is going to stay here and pack up, but I'm going to head out this weekend."

"And the studio?" Summer almost couldn't bring herself to ask it.

"I have to let it go," Danica said softly. "I'm going to tell the families tomorrow. I thought, maybe, if you want to cover one more week of lessons, we could do that. But then Bill is going to sell off our few assets. He's already talked to the building owners, and he has another business that wants to move into the space, so he'll let us out of the lease."

"Another dance studio?" Summer asked hopefully.

Danica shook her head. "I'm sorry. I never planned for things to happen so quickly. But sometimes God's plans are different from ours."

Summer nodded numbly, trying to trust that God actually had a plan. But right now, if he did, it seemed to be to let her life fall apart, one piece at a time.

"You'll be all right, won't you?" Danica looked worried. "I'll give you a wonderful reference, of course. And anything else I can do."

Summer swallowed and made herself say, "I'll be all right."

Danica studied her for a moment, then nodded, as if convinced.

Good.

Now all Summer had to do was convince herself.

Chapter 6

"Order up!" Benjamin gave himself a moment to bask in the satisfaction of a dozen dishes, all plated at the same time, as the wait staff pulled them off the line. He'd have to give his cooks an extra thank you at the end of the night.

"The church ladies are asking for you, Chef," a long-time waitress named Vicki grinned at him. "Every Thursday night, like clockwork."

Benjamin glanced over his shoulder at his sous chef, Chloe.

But she made a face. "I've got the kitchen under control. You go."

Benjamin laughed. "You know they don't bite."

"No. Worse. They matchmake."

Benjamin waved off the comment. "You just have to know how to handle them."

He pulled his apron off and hung it up, then pushed through the kitchen doors and strode down the short hallway to The Depot's dining room. He paused a moment at the edge of the large space, letting his eyes wander over the tables filled with laughing, talking people, all enjoying his food. He recognized at least half of them.

When he'd first left River Falls for culinary school, it had been with grand aspirations of going off and making a name for himself as a chef somewhere else—preferably somewhere that people wouldn't constantly be comparing him to his older brothers. He loved them all dearly, but they were hard names to live up to, especially in a town this small, where everyone knew everyone.

But when John, his sister-in-law Ireland's brother, had offered him the head chef position at The Depot, it was too good to turn down. It was unheard of for someone so young to become a head chef—a role Benjamin would have to wait years for otherwise. He'd reasoned that after a few years of experience here, he could move on to bigger and better things. But the truth was, he wasn't even sure he wanted that anymore. He *liked* running into people he knew every day. He *liked* being close to his family. He even *liked* the church ladies and their sweet—if meddlesome—comments about his love life.

He made his way toward them, stopping at a few other tables on the way to greet his customers. He knew some chefs hated this part of the job, but he loved it. His mama had always said he was born talking and had never stopped.

"There he is." Mrs. Richter waved her fork at him, her wrinkled cheeks crinkling with her smile. "We were starting to think you'd forgotten about us."

"Never." Benjamin smiled around the table of six women who had attended Beautiful Savior since well before he was born and never missed Thursday night's lamb chop special. "I was saving the best for last."

"Oh, you're a charmer." Mrs. Alpine wiped her mouth with her napkin, her eyes sparkling. "It's a wonder you're still single." She leaned closer. "How old are you now?"

"I turned twenty-three a few weeks ago," Benjamin answered patiently, though he was sure they knew that already.

"He has plenty of time yet," Mrs. Richter told her friends. "Kids these days don't settle down so early, you know."

Benjamin nodded appreciatively.

"Oh, but I have a feeling he'll be settling down soon," Mrs. Simmons practically shouted from the far end of the table. "You've been seeing that pretty real estate girl, haven't you? My daughter saw you two bowling last night."

"I— Uh—" Benjamin prided himself on rarely being at a loss for words, but he wasn't sure two dates qualified as seeing someone—and certainly not as being about to settle down. Still, if he said yes, it would shut down any potential matchmaking attempts. "We've been on a couple of dates," he finally admitted.

Mrs. Simmons looked satisfied, and the other ladies nodded their approval.

Benjamin subtly changed the subject by asking them about their children and grandchildren, then excused himself to return to the kitchen, promising to send out a special dessert.

When he got back to the kitchen, he let out a long breath and slipped his apron back over his head.

Chloe chuckled. "They finally got to you?"

"Nah." Benjamin grabbed a spoon to taste the sauce she was stirring. "Apparently Mrs. Simmons's daughter saw me bowling with Jasmine, so they're convinced we're seeing each other."

"Well, you are, aren't you?" Chloe reached for some basil, but Benjamin held up a hand.

"It's perfect as it is." He left her question unanswered, and she didn't press, so he figured it must have been rhetorical.

He moved around the kitchen, checking dishes, making adjustments, putting in the order for the church ladies' dessert.

But all the while, he tried to figure out why it bothered him that the church ladies thought he was seeing Jasmine. He'd been on two dates with her, and he'd had a nice enough time on both. Jasmine was sweet and smart.

She told interesting stories about the houses she'd sold and the clients she'd met. She was reliable and compassionate. And the church ladies were right that she was pretty. But Benjamin couldn't help but feel that something between them was missing.

It didn't help that ever since that party he'd helped at, Summer had climbed into his head and refused to budge. He'd tried to push her out. After all, just because she'd felt perfect in his arms as they'd danced together, and just because she'd looked somewhere between hopeful and terrified when the girls had chanted for them to kiss, and just because the brush of his lips across her knuckles had sent a jolt through him ten times as powerful as a lightning strike didn't mean he should ask her out.

For one thing, she had already broken up with him once.

And for another, she might be single again. But he wasn't. Apparently, he was *seeing* Jasmine.

He turned that phrase over in his mind and decided it was apt. They were *seeing* if they were compatible with each other. Maybe the more time they spent together, the more his feelings would grow.

Yes, he was sure they would.

He approved the plated desserts and sent them on their way. He would text Jasmine as soon as he got home to see if she wanted to go out again. And to prove to himself that he was determined to give their relationship a chance, he'd bring her to dinner here.

Chapter 7

"One more story?" Little Max gazed at Summer with the pleading look she could never resist.

But she shook her head firmly, checking her watch yet again. "Time for nuh-night. We can read more stories tomorrow."

"I want to wait for Daddy." Tears bubbled out of Max's eyes.

"I know, little man." Summer bent to kiss his forehead and smooth his hair. "Dad will kiss you when he gets home."

"One more story. Please, Aunt Sunny," Max sobbed, using the nickname TJ had given her long ago.

Summer sighed and sank back onto the edge of the bed, trying not to be annoyed that her brother was late. It would be nice if he had called—or at least responded to her texts—but he'd probably just stopped at that little restaurant he liked up in the hills on the way home from his trail run. She checked the time again, even though no more than thirty seconds could have gone by, trying to shake the little niggle of worry that said TJ would never miss bedtime without at least calling to say goodnight to his son. And that even getting dinner wouldn't make him this late.

Maybe he'd twisted his ankle. Maybe he'd had car trouble. Maybe, maybe, maybe . . .

The word thrummed in her head as she began to read *Danny and the Dinosaur* for the eight-thousandth time since Max was born.

She knew the story so well that she barely needed to pay attention to the page, and her mind continued to rove over the possible reasons her brother was late, all the while trying to push the darker possibilities aside.

Maybe she should text Benjamin to see if he'd heard from TJ. Or at least knew exactly which trail he would have taken. She knew for a fact that Benjamin hadn't gone along on the run because when she'd oh-so-casually asked her brother if Benjamin was going with him, he'd shaken his head and said, "He bailed on me. Said he had other plans."

She hadn't been able to keep the words from popping out of her mouth: "What other plans?"

TJ had looked at her, sighed, and said, "I think a date. I'm sorry."

She'd waved off the apology. "There's nothing to be sorry about. You're the one who wants us to get together, not me."

TJ had given her that look that said he thought he knew her better than she knew herself, and she'd told him to shut up and get going and that was the last she'd heard from him.

Please don't let anything bad happen to him, she prayed as she kept reading.

They might drive each other crazy at times, but TJ was the only person in the world who had always been there for her.

She heard a soft snore and glanced down to find Max's eyes closed, tears still shining on his cheeks.

Carefully, she eased herself off the bed and pulled the covers up over him. Then she kissed him and turned off the light.

As soon as she was in the hallway, she texted her brother one more time, deciding that if he didn't get back to her within the next thirty minutes, she would contact Benjamin. Or the police.

"Thanks for dinner." Jasmine slipped through the door Benjamin held open for her. "It was nice to meet your coworkers."

Benjamin chuckled, shaking his head at the setting sun. "I think *be harassed by* my coworkers is more accurate." In the course of the evening, every single server had somehow managed to make a trip past their table, and even Chloe had popped her head out of the kitchen, sending him a thumbs-up before ducking back inside. "Thanks for being such a good sport."

Jasmine laughed, tucking her glossy blonde hair behind her ear. "I think it's sweet. They all clearly love working with you."

Benjamin shrugged. "What can I say? I'm a lovable guy."

Jasmine laughed again, and Benjamin tried to get his heart to jump at the sound. It was light and pleasant and came easily—even at his dumbest jokes—and yet, every time he heard it, he couldn't help but think of Summer's laugh, deeper, slower, harder to win—but all the more rewarding for it.

"So now what?" Jasmine asked as Benjamin opened the passenger door of his Gremlin for her.

He glanced at his watch. "Well, it's almost nine p.m. on a Sunday, so this town is pretty much asleep . . ."

"What about a walk in the park?" Jasmine suggested. "It's a beautiful night, and the stars should be coming out soon."

"Sure. That sounds nice." Benjamin told himself that it did sound nice. He liked the park, he liked stars, and he liked Jasmine.

And anyway, putting off the end of their date meant he could put off the decision of whether or not to kiss her for the first time at least a little longer.

It wasn't that he dreaded the thought of kissing her or anything. It was just that he didn't have a burning desire to kiss her—not like the desire he'd had to kiss Summer the other week. That desire had been . . . overwhelming and overpowering and all-consuming.

"The gazebo looks so pretty at night," Jasmine gushed as Benjamin pulled into the parking lot at Founder's Park, and he guiltily pulled his thoughts back to her.

"Yeah, it does." Benjamin stared at the gazebo, the soft white lights draped around its edges giving it a perfect romantic glow.

They got out of the car and walked silently toward it. The night was warm but not sticky, and crickets chirped from within the soft beds of flowers.

Benjamin tried to suck up some morsel of romance from the setting. But all he could think about was bringing Summer here.

And that was when he realized he couldn't keep doing this. Even if he and Summer never got together, it wasn't fair to Jasmine to keep seeing her when he was thinking about someone else.

"Listen." He stopped at the bottom of the gazebo steps.

Jasmine gave him a questioning look, and Benjamin swallowed. He didn't want to hurt her. "I don't know how to say this, but—"

His phone dinged and then dinged again. And again.

Jasmine raised an eyebrow, and he fumbled for it. "Sorry. It's probably the restaurant. I just need to . . ."

His mouth went dry as he spotted Summer's name on his screen. His first instinct was to stuff his phone hurriedly back into his pocket. He could read it *after* he did this.

But his phone dinged again, and this time his screen lit up with her message. *I'm starting to get worried.*

"Sorry," he mumbled again to Jasmine as he turned on the phone and tapped to go to the beginning of the string of texts from Summer.

TJ hasn't come home yet.

Do you know where he went running?

He isn't answering his phone or opening any of my texts.

I'm starting to get worried.

Benjamin's eyes flicked from the time on his phone to the darkened sky. TJ had been planning to leave for his run right after church. Which meant he should have been home at least a couple of hours ago.

I'm sure he's fine, he texted back quickly, careful not to mention all of the dangers that could befall a solo runner out on the trail. *But I'll check with my brothers. Hold tight.*

He quickly scrolled to Zeb's number.

"Is everything all right?" Jasmine's voice jerked Benjamin's head up. He'd almost forgotten she was there.

"Yeah. Sorry. My friend went for a run in the mountains today, and he should have been home hours ago, but his sister said he hasn't returned and he's not answering her texts. I just need to call my—" He cut off as his brother answered on the other end of the phone.

"Benjamin?"

"Zeb, hey. Are you busy right now?"

"I'm on patrol. Why?"

"TJ went for a trail run this afternoon, and Summer just called to say he hasn't come home yet. You haven't had any reports of any—" He didn't even want to say the word, not after what Zeb had been through last year.

"No accidents." Zeb didn't seem to struggle with the word. "Everything has been quiet around here today."

"That's a relief." Benjamin tried to let out a breath, but that still didn't explain what had happened to TJ.

"How late is he?" Zeb asked.

"He should have been home a couple of hours ago."

"That's not necessarily cause for alarm. Maybe he went out for a drink or something."

Benjamin shook his head. "He's not that kind of guy, Zeb."

Zeb didn't answer, and Benjamin knew his older brother was thinking that he was being naive.

"Look, can you ask around? See if there are any reports of car trouble or anything like that?"

"Yeah, I can do that. You might want to check with Asher too."

"He's my next call." Benjamin hung up and immediately dialed Asher's number.

As he waited for the phone to ring, he glanced around to apologize to Jasmine again, but she had wandered to sit on the gazebo steps.

"What's up, bro?" Asher sounded relaxed, but Benjamin found himself pacing with pent-up energy.

"Have you heard any reports of trouble in the mountains today?"

"No. Why?" His brother's voice took on a sudden alertness. Asher was a park ranger, and even when he wasn't on duty, he usually knew of any major events in the Smokies.

"You know my friend TJ? He went for a trail run earlier today, and he hasn't come back yet."

"He went alone?" Asher asked sharply.

Benjamin swallowed. "He wanted me to go, but I had plans."

Asher didn't say anything for a moment, and Benjamin tried not to let his mind dwell on all of the possibilities he hadn't mentioned to Summer.

The Smokies were a beautiful place. But they were filled with hazards too. Benjamin should have gone along with TJ.

"I haven't heard anything," Asher finally said. "Let me call in. Do you know where he went?"

Benjamin shook his head. "We usually take the Grayback Trail. But sometimes the Grizzly. I know he wanted to do fifteen miles today, so maybe the Draco Ridge?" He should have insisted that TJ leave his route with someone before he left.

Asher let out a low whistle. "That's a tough run."

"Yeah. But he was up for it." At least Benjamin prayed he was.

"All right. Let me do some checking, and I'll get back to you."

"Thanks, man." Benjamin hung up and tried to call TJ. When the call went to voice mail, he sent a text, just in case Summer's hadn't gone through for some reason. *Where are you? People here are starting to get worried. If you're hurt, text me your location, and we'll get help to you. If you're lost, then you're not the human compass you claim to be. But text me, and we'll come find you.*

Afterward, he stood staring at his phone, trying to figure what else he could do. Was there anyone else he could call? Anywhere else he should go? Maybe up into the mountains to look for TJ himself?

"Any news?" Jasmine's voice was soft, but it made Benjamin jump. He'd almost forgotten her again.

He moved toward where she still sat on the gazebo steps. "No. Not yet."

"Do you want to go?" She stood as she spoke.

"Would you mind terribly? I feel like I should do . . . something." He only wished he knew what.

"Of course."

They started down the path silently, Benjamin's thoughts caught up in what could have happened to TJ.

"What you were going to say before . . ." Jasmine broke into the quiet.

"Oh." Benjamin sighed heavily. That felt like hours ago.

"It was that this isn't working, right?" Jasmine sounded wistful, maybe, but not upset.

Benjamin nodded. "Yeah. I'm sorry. It's not you. It's—"

"No need to apologize." Jasmine stopped him. "I feel that way too. I wanted it to work. But sometimes it just . . . doesn't."

"True." Benjamin's thoughts went to Summer, sitting at home, worrying. Things between them may not have worked out—might never work out—but that didn't mean he wasn't going to be there for her. It was what TJ would want, if nothing else.

He took Jasmine home, and she promised to keep TJ in her prayers.

Benjamin thanked her and then pulled out of her driveway and headed to the place he knew he needed to be.

Chapter 8

Summer paced the living room, dodging around a pile of Max's dinosaurs, and checked her phone yet again. It had been almost half an hour since Benjamin had said he would contact his brothers, and still she hadn't heard back from him. She couldn't decide if that was a good thing or a bad thing.

She reached the wall at the end of the small living room and spun back in the other direction just in time to see the swivel of headlights turning into the driveway.

Her breath left her in a solid brick, and she rushed to the door. TJ had better have one very good explanation for scaring her half to death, or she was going to— Well, she didn't know what she'd do, but she'd figure it out after she hugged him.

She yanked the door open. "Where in the world have—"

But that wasn't TJ's boxy old sedan in the driveway. It was Benjamin's tiny Gremlin. And he was marching toward her, his face covered by the shadows of the night.

Summer let out a small sound of protest and sagged against the door frame. Benjamin wouldn't be here if everything was fine.

"It's all right." His voice was as cheerful as ever, and his footsteps picked up speed as he got closer. Light from the house spilled onto his face, and he gave her his usual easy smile. "I don't have any news yet, but Zeb and Asher are both checking."

"So what are you . . ." Summer's voice felt weak and shaky, and she tried again. "Why are you here?"

He shrugged. "TJ keeps bragging about this new video game he got." He grinned and slipped through the door as if this were one of the thousands of times he'd hung out and gamed with her brother. "I figure now is my chance to get in some practice before he makes me play it with him."

"Oh." Summer considered pushing him for the real reason, but she was afraid she couldn't handle the answer. "Are you hungry? We have some . . ." She actually had no idea what kind of food they had. She'd made herself and Max a box of macaroni and cheese for dinner, but other than that, the cupboards were pretty bare.

"Nah." Benjamin grabbed the TV remote, along with two game controllers, and plopped onto the couch, setting his phone next to him. "I had dinner at the restaurant."

"Oh, I didn't realize you were working, or I wouldn't have—"

"I wasn't working." Benjamin waved off her concern.

And Summer suddenly remembered what TJ had told her earlier. Benjamin had a date tonight. She clapped a hand over her mouth. "Benjamin."

He turned to her in surprise.

"I interrupted your date."

He shrugged and turned back to the TV. "Don't worry about it."

She shook her head. "You should go find her." She resisted the overwhelming urge to ask who *her* was. "I'll be fine. Text me if you hear from your brothers."

Benjamin clicked on the TV and the gaming console. "I'm not going anywhere, Summer. Now, are you going to play with me or not?"

Her laugh was half exasperated, half relieved. "When have I ever gamed with you?"

"Then it's about time you learned." He held out the controller to her. "Think how you can hustle TJ."

Summer sighed and reluctantly took the remote. "Don't think I don't know what you're doing." She settled onto the couch, careful to leave a full cushion between them so she wouldn't drop her head onto his shoulder and fall apart.

Up went his eyebrow again. "Beating you, hopefully."

He gave her some instructions she didn't follow at all, then turned the game on.

"So," he said as she randomly pressed buttons on the control, "have you gotten any more requests for a prince at your parties?"

Summer's character on the screen fell down a hole. "Uh, yeah. A couple."

"Really?" Benjamin grinned as his character expertly dodged an obstacle. "When are they? I'll make sure I have off."

"Uh, well, there's one in two weeks. But I already posted an ad for a prince." Not that finding a prince through an ad had been successful last time.

"What?" Benjamin's character died, and he turned to her. "Did I not prove myself worthy to be your Prince Charming?"

Summer felt her face warm, but she rolled her eyes to cover it. "I need Aladdin this time."

"I can do Aladdin." Benjamin grinned and crossed his arms in front of him. "You have three wishes."

Summer laughed in spite of herself. "I think you need to review your fairy tales. Aladdin doesn't grant wishes. He makes them."

"I can do that too. I *wish* you would let me do this. Please?" He gave her the same pleading look Max had used earlier.

44

"I— Maybe." It sure would be easier than finding a stranger to do it. Plus, he had already proved he was good with kids. "But only if you accept half of the payment," she added.

Benjamin opened his mouth—to argue, she assumed—but his phone buzzed. He picked it up, read it, and frowned, his eyes going dark as he tapped an answer.

Summer's stomach heaved. For a couple of minutes, he'd managed to distract her from why he'd really come.

"What is it?" Her breath barely made it across her vocal cords.

"They found TJ's car at the head of the Draco Ridge trail." His voice was strained. "It doesn't look like he ever came back to it."

"Oh no." Summer couldn't say anything else. Couldn't move. Couldn't think.

"There could be a lot of reasons." Benjamin scooted onto the empty couch cushion and scooped her hands into his. She stared at the cocoon his fingers made around hers, but she couldn't feel anything.

"He might have twisted an ankle or gotten turned around," Benjamin continued. "Asher said they're setting up a search party. They'll find him." He gave her hands a little shake, and she lifted her head to him. "They'll find him," he said firmly.

She nodded, but her heart refused to beat. "I don't— I think I need—" She tried to stand, but her legs refused to support her, and Benjamin eased her back to the couch.

"What do you need?"

She closed her eyes and shook her head. "I don't know," she whispered.

"I know." Benjamin wrapped his hands around hers again. "Please be with TJ, Lord. Please watch over him, wherever he is at this moment."

It took Summer a moment to realize that Benjamin was praying. She clung to his hands and to his words.

"Please protect him," Benjamin continued. "Please help the search crews find him quickly and get him whatever help he needs. Please bring him home safely. And please give us strength and comfort and trust in you as we wait. In Jesus' name we pray. Amen."

Summer tried to murmur *Amen* too, but the word got stuck in her chest.

"Now what?" she whispered instead.

"It's up to you." Benjamin's fingers were still wrapped around hers, and his thumbs painted little circles onto the back of her hands. "We can just sit here. We can watch TV. We can play that game. You can go to sleep, and I'll wake you when I hear something. Whatever you need."

She shook her head. She had no idea what she needed. Except for him to stop being so sweet and so supportive and so wonderful. That was only going to make her lose the thin grasp she currently had on her emotions.

She pulled her hands out of his. "You should have gone with him." The words weren't loud, but she could see their effect on Benjamin instantly.

His face paled, his mouth dropped, and his eyes flooded with guilt. "I know."

She pressed a hand to her lips. "I'm sorry. I didn't mean that. I'm just—"

"I know," he said again. "It's okay. I wish I had gone."

They sat in silence a while longer, and eventually Benjamin picked up the gaming controls again. He held one out to her, but she shook her head.

He set it down and began playing by himself, although even as inexperienced as she was with video games, she could tell he was doing horribly.

Minutes passed into an hour. And then two. She stared at the TV screen blindly, unable to think, unable to pray. The only thing she could do was remember. Remember how TJ used to play pranks on her when they were kids, and she would get so mad. Remember the way he would stand up for her to Mama. Remember the way he had always taken care of her, always guarded and protected her. And now he was missing, maybe hurt, maybe—

She gulped down the sob rising in her chest and pushed to her feet.

"Summer, where are you—"

Benjamin's phone rang, making them both nearly hit the ceiling.

Benjamin grabbed at the phone, but not before Summer saw Asher's name on the screen. She sank woozily back onto the couch.

He was calling to say they'd found TJ and he was okay and Summer could ream him out when he got home—that had to be it.

But she could tell from the way Benjamin turned away from her and dropped his head to his hand that it wasn't.

"Thanks," he said finally. He hung up the phone but didn't turn to her.

She was too weak to ask what he'd learned. She didn't want to know. If she didn't know, she could go on telling herself that everything would be fine, that TJ would—

She choked on her breath as Benjamin finally turned to her, his eyes red-rimmed and serious.

"No." She shook her head. "No. Don't say it."

He slid closer to her and reached his arms around her, pulling her against him. "They found him on the trail." His voice cracked. "He's gone, Summer."

"No." She shook her head harder, trying to shove him away, but he held on tighter, pressing her head into his shoulder.

"They'll have to do an autopsy, but he was on the right trail and had no obvious injuries. They think it might have been his heart."

"It can't be." Summer torqued her body sharply so that Benjamin would have to let go. "He's twenty-six. They have the wrong person, that's all. Call them back and tell them it's not—" Her voice broke as a sob shook her whole body. "Tell them it's not him," she insisted through the tears.

"Zeb's on his way with a picture for you to ID." Benjamin reached for her again, but she lurched off the couch. He kept talking. "But Asher and Zeb both recognized him."

She shook her head wildly, stumbling around the room like a mad woman, barely noticing when she kicked one of Max's blocks and almost fell over.

She tried to keep going—where she didn't know—but Benjamin's arms wrapped around her, and this time she let him pull her close as they cried together.

Chapter 9

Numbly, Benjamin pushed himself off the couch to answer the door. The only indication that Summer noticed was a tiny whimper that almost pulled him back to the couch. But he had to keep going so Zeb wouldn't knock and wake Max up. The little he and Summer had spoken in the past hour had revolved around when to tell the boy, and they'd both agreed it was best to wait until the morning. Nausea rolled through Benjamin every time he thought about it.

He opened the door and stepped outside, expecting to find a pitch-black veil over the whole world. But a full moon gleamed overhead, and the sky shone with a blanket of stars. A warm breeze stirred the leaves, and the same crickets that had been singing earlier still sang on.

It seemed wrong somehow that everything went on as it always had.

The door of Zeb's police cruiser opened, and his brother got out, closing it silently behind him. His footsteps were strong and certain as he came up the driveway, and Benjamin again admired his brother's strength after everything he'd been through.

Zeb took the steps two at a time, and then his arms swallowed Benjamin in a bear hug. "I'm so sorry." His gruff voice held a deep compassion, and Benjamin had to clench his jaw to keep from dissolving into tears again. He and his brothers were close, but he'd always hated crying in front of them because it made him feel every bit his position as the baby of the family.

"Come in," he said as Zeb released him. "Summer is . . ." He had no idea how to finish that sentence, but Zeb nodded like he knew.

Benjamin opened the door and led the way inside. Summer's spot on the couch was empty. He scanned the room, but there was no sign of where she'd gone.

"Summer?" he called softly.

The only answer was a muted clatter from the kitchen. He glanced at his brother, who nodded, and they both made their way toward the sound.

In the kitchen, the bitter smell of coffee hung in the air, and Summer had lined up three mugs next to a bag of sour cream and onion chips and a couple of overripe bananas. Benjamin exchanged another look with his brother, then moved toward her as Zeb hung back.

"Summer." He said her name quietly, but she jumped anyway. "What are you doing?"

"We don't have much food," she said briskly. "But you've been here all night, and your brother is probably hungry, and I was going to make tea, but we didn't have any because I was supposed to go to the store, but TJ—" The moment his name came out of her mouth, her face crumpled, and she sagged into the counter.

Benjamin moved quickly to her side and took her arm. "It's okay. We're not hungry. Come on, let's go sit down."

To his relief, she let him lead her to the table and help her into a chair.

"You remember Zeb, right?" Benjamin took the chair next to her as Zeb pulled out a seat across the table.

Summer nodded but refused to look at Benjamin's brother.

"I'm sorry to ask this," Zeb said gently, and Summer shook her head.

But Zeb kept going. "When you're ready, could you look at this picture?" He set his phone on the table upside down. Summer's head kept shaking, and Benjamin wanted to tell Zeb to stop—to take whatever was on his phone out of here and never mention it again. But he knew his brother had to do his job.

"I need to confirm that it's TJ," Zeb continued, his voice calm and soothing. "He didn't have ID on him, but . . ."

The words seemed to pump new life into Summer. "It isn't him," she said with certainty, her hand darting to flip Zeb's phone over before Benjamin could stop her.

He groaned as his eyes fell on the picture, and Summer recoiled as if she'd been bitten by a snake.

Her head started shaking again, and her whole body trembled.

"It's him?" Zeb asked gently.

But Summer's only response was a wrenching sob.

"It's him." Benjamin pressed his hand to Summer's shoulder, swallowing over and over again.

Summer sat suddenly upright, wiped at her eyes, and pulled in a couple of gasping breaths. "What happens now? With Max and the house and I have to tell Mama and TJ's boss and—"

"Summer, hey." Benjamin rubbed her arm. "Slow down. There's time to figure all of that out—"

"Time?" Summer yanked away from him. "Max is going to wake up in a few hours and I have to tell him—" She broke off with a shuddering breath.

"Let me call Child Services," Zeb said. "I'm sure there will be no problem with you taking temporary guardianship of Max until a hearing can be held to decide on a permanent placement." He slid his chair back and picked up his phone, swiping away the image of TJ before stepping into the other room.

"What does he mean temporary guardianship?" Summer wheeled on Benjamin. "And a permanent placement?"

"I don't know," Benjamin answered honestly. "We'll ask him when he comes back."

"Max has to stay with me, Benjamin," Summer said desperately. "What if they send him to someone else, like Mama or— Or— Stacy?"

Benjamin shook his head. "Your mama is sick, right?"

Summer looked surprised that he knew but nodded.

"And who even knows where Stacy is?" Max's mother hadn't even wanted to carry her pregnancy to term. The only reason she'd agreed to it was that TJ had promised to take full responsibility for the baby. The moment Stacy had been discharged from the hospital after Max's birth, she'd left town and never returned. As far as Benjamin knew, she'd never so much as sent her son a birthday card.

"A stranger then," Summer worried. "Foster parents."

Benjamin caught her waving hands. "That's not going to happen. Why would they give him to a stranger when his aunt who has helped care for him since he was a baby is right here?"

"I don't know," Summer whispered, but the fear in her eyes eased a little. She tugged her hands out of his as Zeb returned to the room.

"Child Services says you are good to go with temporary guardianship. If you want it to be permanent, you'll need to go to the courthouse to file a petition for guardianship."

"But it will go through, right?" Benjamin said. "They'll give him to her?"

Zeb leaned against the table. "Do you know if TJ had a will?"

Summer stared at him blankly. "I— Not that he ever mentioned."

Zeb nodded, and Benjamin caught the grim set of his mouth. "You might want to look around. See if you can find one. It will make things a lot easier."

Summer slid her chair back, and Benjamin looked at her in surprise. "It doesn't have to be right now. You need some sleep."

"I have to go tell Mama." Dread and exhaustion clung to her words.

"I can tell her," Zeb offered, and Benjamin looked at his brother gratefully. He'd never really considered the heavy burden Zeb's job put on him. He hoped Zeb didn't often have to tell a parent of their child's death.

"Thanks." Summer stood. "But I should do it." She took three steps, then froze. "Oh. But Max."

"I'll stay with him," Benjamin volunteered, "if you really want to go. But I think you should let Zeb—"

She shook her head.

"At least let him go with you," Benjamin insisted. "Or let me come, and he'll stay with Max." He looked to his brother for confirmation, and Zeb nodded.

"No." Summer's voice was stronger than it had been all night. "I have to do this alone."

❧

Summer drew a shaky breath as she stood on the doorstep of Mama's house, trying fruitlessly to gulp strength from the empty night air. Maybe she should have let Benjamin come with her. Or at least Zeb.

But she could never guarantee how Mama was going to be, and she couldn't bear the thought of those two men from that perfect family seeing her shame.

The key trembled in her hand as she finally lifted it to the lock, and it took her a few attempts before she managed to turn it and let herself silently inside. She closed the door and then just stood there, telling herself she needed to let her eyes adjust, although plenty of moonlight streamed in through the window.

The TV droned from Mama's room, and Summer couldn't decide if she hoped that Mama was still awake or that she was asleep.

She had no idea how to expect Mama to react to the news, but a thousand scenarios had played through her head on the drive over. In some of them, Mama laughed hysterically; in others, she sobbed uncontrollably; but in most, she was indifferent, and Summer knew that would be the hardest to take.

Finally, she had to confess to herself that she could see every outline in the room and had run out of excuses to stall. She tiptoed through the space so she wouldn't startle Mama, but when she was nearly across the living room, she tripped over a shoe in the middle of the floor. She managed to remain upright, but her other foot came down with a heavy thud.

"Who's there?" Mama's voice called, more angry than fearful.

"It's just me, Mama." Summer tried to sound natural as she hurried down the short hall to Mama's room.

"What are you doing prowling around here in the middle of the night? Stealing from me?" Mama was half sitting up, her head propped on three pillows, the TV remote in her hand.

"No." Summer summoned all of her patience. "I wouldn't steal from you."

"Good thing too," Mama said sarcastically. "The racket you make. I thought dancers were supposed to be graceful."

Summer ignored the comment. Mama's words couldn't sting her, not when everything inside of her was already broken.

"Mama." Summer surprised herself by moving closer and taking Mama's hand.

Apparently, she surprised Mama too because she jerked her gaze to Summer's, something vulnerable and afraid darkening her eyes.

It only lasted a moment before Mama pulled her hand away. "Well, spit it out. What's so important that you had to barge in here at midnight? I'm sure it could have waited until—"

"Mama." Summer cut her off more sharply than she meant to. But she needed to do this before she lost her nerve. "TJ went for a trail run earlier today, and when he wasn't home after dark, I got worried and called the police."

"The police? Leave it to you to overreact. Did they tell you that you were crazy?"

Summer swallowed and told herself that Mama was only trying to protect herself from what was coming.

"They set up a search," she said softly, but then she couldn't go on.

"Well," Mama said when Summer didn't say more. "I don't know what you want me to do about it. I'm sure they'll find—"

"They already found him." Summer's voice came back, quiet but firm. "He's dead." It was the first time she had said the word out loud, and it disturbed her how easily it came out of her mouth.

"What do you mean dead?" Accusation punctuated Mama's words.

Summer blinked at her. "What do you mean, what do I mean? He's gone, Mama."

"How?" Mama's eyes narrowed as if she suspected Summer of making the whole thing up.

"They'll have to do an autopsy. But they think it might have been his heart."

Mama stared at her as if she didn't comprehend, and Summer didn't blame her. She couldn't comprehend any of this either.

"I have to get back to Max soon," she said, feeling a sudden bond with Mama over their shared loss. "But I can stay with you for a little while. If you want me to."

Mama's head shook back and forth against her pillow. "You can leave." She unstacked the pillows and lowered herself to lie on them, her back to Summer. "Lock the door on your way out."

Summer stared at her mother's still form for a moment, then got up silently and left the house.

After she locked the door, she stood on the stoop a moment, marveling at how wrong she had been before. It turned out that even in her brokenness, Mama's words could still sting her.

Chapter 10

Benjamin stared at the ceiling with bleary eyes as a gray dawn began to creep into the living room of TJ's house.

Except it wasn't TJ's house anymore.

TJ was gone.

Benjamin rubbed at his chest, but the ache that had installed itself there last night had only grown worse as the hours went by.

Why hadn't he gone with his friend? TJ had been there for Benjamin through his mama's death and Carly's and Abigail's accident and even through his breakup with Summer. But the one time his friend had needed him, Benjamin had bailed on him. And for what? A date he knew wasn't going to work out anyway?

He sat up impatiently. He needed to move, needed to do something. But nothing he did could bring TJ back. The only thing he could do now was make sure he was here for Max and Summer. He knew in his gut it was what TJ would want.

Which was why when Summer had tried to force him to go home last night after she got home from her mama's, he'd flat-out refused. She hadn't argued much, but Benjamin was pretty sure she had only relented because she was too tired to fight. He'd finally convinced her to go to bed around three a.m., but he doubted that she'd gotten any more sleep than he had.

Once or twice, he'd been tempted to go check on her, to see if she was awake and they could just sit together. But he hadn't, and the past three hours felt like the longest of his life.

He scrubbed his hands over his face and stood. At least now that the sun was coming up, he could make some coffee.

He was halfway to the kitchen when a cheerful cry sounded from down the hallway. "Daddy, can I wake up now?"

The words simultaneously made Benjamin laugh and demolished his heart.

As long as Max slept, he'd been protected from the awful truth that his daddy would never wake him up again. Would never tickle him or read him a story or rock him to sleep.

Lord, give me strength, Benjamin prayed as he hurried down the hallway before Max could wake Summer.

But he was too late. She emerged from her room, still in the same clothes as last night, her eyes swollen and red, cheeks blotchy, hair disheveled.

She looked startled to find him still there, and a sudden longing to take her in his arms and shield her from all of this swept over him. But she crossed her arms in front of her and stepped past him. "I've got this. You can go home now."

Benjamin ignored the comment and followed her to Max's room.

She paused with her hand on the doorknob, eyes closed.

"Go back to bed," Benjamin whispered. "I'll do it."

She shook her head, her knuckles whitening on the doorknob. "I have to tell him."

He heard the tears in her voice, but they didn't fall to her cheeks as she pushed the door open.

She stepped inside, not protesting when Benjamin followed close behind.

"Benji!" Max's face lit up, and Benjamin tried his hardest to smile at the boy, but he felt the moisture gathering behind his eyelids. TJ had given him that nickname when Max couldn't pronounce his full name.

"Hey, Maxerooni." He managed to keep his voice from breaking. The boy giggled at Benjamin's nickname for him. "You're up early."

"I'm hungry," Max announced. "Where's Daddy?"

"Max, sweetie." Summer eased herself onto the edge of Max's bed. "Daddy—" She choked and looked away from the boy, burying her face in her hands.

"What's wrong, Aunt Sunny?"

Summer shook her head, but she couldn't seem to say anything, and Max's wide eyes came to Benjamin.

He moved closer and squatted in front of the bed, resting one hand on Max's knee and the other on Summer's.

"Do you remember at Sunday school," Benjamin asked Max, "when you talked about Jesus going to heaven and how he's going to bring us all to heaven someday too?"

Max nodded. "Yes. Miss Ava said it's going to be the best place we've ever been. Even better than the zoo."

Summer snuffled, and Benjamin squeezed her knee.

"That's right, buddy. And your daddy—" He cleared his throat and had to look away from the earnest young eyes. But he made himself turn back to Max before he finished the sentence. "Jesus brought him to heaven yesterday."

Max blinked at Benjamin. "Without me?" he asked. "When is he coming back?"

"Oh, buddy." Summer wrapped her arms around the boy and kissed the top of his head.

"He can't come back." Benjamin swallowed hard. "But someday, you'll get to go there to see him again."

"But he'll be lonely," Max protested. "He likes to be with me."

"I know he does, buddy." Benjamin had to work hard to get the words out past the egg-shaped lump in his throat. "But he won't be lonely. My mama is there. And my sister-in-law. And Jesus."

Summer shot Benjamin a look he couldn't decipher, but Max seemed to think about what he'd said. "But I need my daddy to take care of me," he finally said.

"I'll take care of you." A fierceness Benjamin had never heard from her entered Summer's voice. "Always."

"Okay," Max said, slowly nodding. "But do we have to have macaroni and cheese every day?"

Summer's laugh was soft. "No, probably not *every* day."

"Good." Max wriggled out of the bed. "Can we have breakfast now?"

Benjamin met Summer's eyes over Max's head. He could tell she was wondering the same thing he was—had Max really understood what they'd told him?

Summer nodded subtly, and Benjamin stood and held out his hand to the boy. "Sure. How about pancakes?"

Max stuck his hand in Benjamin's, his little grip trusting. "Boy oh boy! Pancakes are my favorite!"

Benjamin laughed sadly—the boy had picked up that saying from his father—and met Summer's eyes again. Fresh tears slipped down her cheeks, and he was torn between going with Max to make breakfast and staying here to comfort her.

"I'll be there in a minute," she said, deciding for him.

"Why don't you go back to bed for a little while?" he offered. "Max and I have breakfast under control."

She shook her head. "I won't be able to sleep anyway. But maybe I'll go grab a quick shower if you don't mind watching Max for a few minutes? Unless you have to go. I'm sure you—"

"Take as long as you need," Benjamin interrupted her. "I'm not going anywhere."

"But—"

Benjamin shook his head at whatever she was going to protest. "I'm not going anywhere," he repeated. "Go shower, and then we'll have breakfast and figure out what we need to do next."

She opened her mouth, and Benjamin prepared to cut her off, whatever argument she might make. But she snapped it shut again and turned to the bathroom without another word.

Chapter 11

Summer pulled her wet hair back into a bun and snatched her phone off the bathroom countertop, quickly jotting down a list of the fifty million things she'd thought of in the shower that she needed to do today. Call TJ's boss. Text Danica to let her know that she couldn't teach a final week after all. Check on Mama. Find TJ's will. Go to the courthouse.

And before all of that: convince Benjamin to go home.

She didn't want to, not really. But he'd already done more than enough. And he had his own life to get back to. A life in which she likely wouldn't see him very often, since he would no longer come over to hang out with TJ.

The thought nearly made her fall apart again. But she couldn't afford to. She had things to do. And a nephew to take care of. On her own.

She marched herself out of the bathroom and into the kitchen, where Benjamin was pouring syrup over a mile-high stack of pancakes on Max's plate.

"Hey." Benjamin looked up with a gentle smile, although the new seriousness she'd noticed in his eyes last night lingered. "Come have a seat."

She shook her head, but her feet pulled her to the table anyway. Even though she'd been sure she could never eat again, her stomach rumbled eagerly.

Benjamin set a plate stacked as high as Max's in front of her, then added one for himself before taking a seat on the far side of the table. They'd left the spot where TJ usually sat open.

"We should pray," Benjamin murmured.

Max's hands were already folded. "It's my turn," the boy announced, and Summer nodded. For the past few months, Max and TJ had been taking turns to say the breakfast prayer. They'd invited Summer to join them as well, but she preferred to listen silently.

"Dear Jesus." Max's little boy voice sounded as trusting and confident as always. "Thank you for pancakes. And thank you for letting Daddy hang out with you in heaven."

Summer sucked in a breath as the tears darted through her closed eyelids.

"Could you please tell him that I miss him and I hope he has a good time there and he's not lonely without me? Amen."

Summer swiped at her cheeks before she opened her eyes.

"That was a good prayer, Maxerooni." Benjamin's voice was as thick as Summer's throat felt.

The three of them ate silently, and Summer felt as if she were betraying her brother by enjoying the food.

When Max finished eating, Benjamin wiped the boy's hands and face with a wet cloth, then led him into the living room to turn on a movie.

By the time he came back, Summer had finished too and was clearing the table.

"Hopefully that will keep him occupied while we look for a will," he said quietly.

Summer shook her head. "I have some calls to make first. You should get going. I'm sure you have things—"

"Summer." Benjamin took the plate from her hand and set it on the counter. "Listen to me. I said I'm not going anywhere, and I'm not. You go make your calls, and I'll start looking for a will. Where do you think it would be?"

Summer shook her head, but she didn't have the energy to argue. "He has a small filing cabinet in his bedroom where he keeps important papers."

"Then I'll start there." Benjamin nodded, and she appreciated that he didn't correct her use of present tense verbs. She couldn't bear the thought of talking about her brother in the past tense.

She led him to TJ's bedroom. The bed was rumpled, the covers shoved aside as if her brother had slept in it last night. Summer knew that was because he never made his bed, but still the image drew her up short, as if he was going to come walking out of his closet and smile and say it had all been a big, stupid prank that he and Benjamin had played on her.

But the closet door remained closed. "It feels like he should be sleeping right here." Benjamin echoed her thoughts.

She nodded silently, something inside her easing to know that he felt the same way.

She pointed out the filing cabinet, then retreated to her own room to make the necessary calls.

By the time she was done, she wanted to collapse into her bed and never come out again. Even though everyone she'd spoken with was sympathetic—she was pretty sure TJ's boss had been crying—explaining what had happened over and over again had taken all of her energy and then some. Every time she said that TJ was dead felt more unreal than the last, until Summer had almost convinced herself that she had fallen asleep, and this was all one terrible dream.

But when she returned to TJ's room to help Benjamin search for a will, his grim expression said it was all too real. If she were dreaming, he would be smiling.

"You didn't find one?" she asked.

Benjamin shook his head. "No, but I found these." His voice was hard, almost angry, and he held out a stack of papers.

Summer took them slowly, afraid to look at whatever it was that had the power to make the always-smiling Benjamin Calvano sound like that. "What is it?"

"Credit card bills." Benjamin's voice hadn't lost its hardness, and Summer glanced at him in surprise. It wasn't a crime to use a credit card.

"Look at the amounts," he prompted.

Summer obeyed, and she couldn't stifle a gasp. "He owes six thousand on this one." She flipped a page. "And four thousand." She hesitated before flipping another page, but Benjamin nodded for her to do it. "Eight thousand." She was going to be sick. "What could he have . . ." But she already knew. She'd thought he was better. Thought he'd stopped when Max was born.

Her eyes went to the itemized list of charges. More than half had words like *Play* or *Bet* in their names.

"He was gambling." The hardness still clung to Benjamin's words, and Summer bristled, but all she could do was nod.

"You knew?" he asked.

"Not this time, no."

Benjamin stared at her. "This time."

"It's an addiction," she defended her brother, careful not to add that it ran in the family, though she imagined he'd heard the rumors about Mama. "He thought he beat it, but I guess . . . I'm sure he was trying to take care of Max and me," she finished lamely.

Benjamin made a sound that could have been disagreement or even disgust, and Summer realized yet again that her family was worlds apart from his perfect one.

"Where else can we look for a will?" Benjamin asked, and Summer was grateful that he'd let the matter drop. What difference did TJ's gambling make now anyway?

"What about the closet?" He stepped around her and pulled open the door. "Oh, man." He breathed out heavily, and Summer turned to see him staring at her brother's collection of superhero t-shirts. Summer had made fun of her brother a million times for them—but the truth was, she'd always thought them fitting since he had been her superhero.

Benjamin reached for a Superman shirt and held it up, then shook his head. "How is he never going to wear this again?"

Summer shook her head too, her own grief tempered at seeing his. Her hand went to his shoulder before she could stop it.

Benjamin turned to her with a wry smile. "Sorry. This isn't helping, is it?"

"It is," she whispered. "It makes me feel less alone."

"You're not alone." Benjamin pulled her into a sudden, fierce hug. She clutched at him for a moment, longing to sink her head into his shoulder and let him tell her everything would be okay. But she couldn't do that.

Because she *was* alone. Sure, Benjamin was here now. But as soon as all of this was settled, as soon as TJ was buried, Benjamin would be gone. He'd be back out there dating other women and living his own life. As he should be.

She pulled away brusquely. "You check the top shelf, and I'll check these boxes." She gestured to a couple of plastic bins on the floor.

The small space was so cramped that it was hard not to run into each other as they worked, but fortunately it took only a few minutes to dig through every inch of the closet. Again they came up empty-handed.

"What about a bank?" Benjamin asked. "Maybe a safe deposit box?"

"He doesn't have one," she answered confidently, but then added, "That I know of," as she remembered the pile of credit card debt she hadn't known about.

"I'll call the bank and ask." Benjamin left the room, and Summer moved to TJ's bed, carefully pulling the covers up so that it was neat and tidy—and so unlike her brother that it only made her heart ache harder. She sat on the edge of it and massaged her fingers into her temples. How could all of this be happening? And how was she ever going to find her way through it without TJ to lean on?

Her phone blared, and she frowned at the unfamiliar number. But then, she'd had to face a lot of unfamiliar things today.

"Hello?" She put the phone on speaker so she wouldn't have to go through the effort of lifting it to her ear.

"Miss Ellis?" A crisp but not unfriendly woman's voice filled the room. "I'm Kimberly Parish, the Fuller County medical examiner. First, let me say how sorry I am for your loss."

"Oh." Summer gripped the comforter she had just pulled up so neatly.

The woman hesitated, and Summer realized she probably should have said thank you, but the words caught in her throat. Was this woman going to be able to give her some answers about her brother's death? And did she want them?

"I have completed the autopsy on TJ Ellis," Kimberly finally went on. Though her tone was gentle, it seemed to bore a hole right through Summer's heart. She clutched at her chest, trying to remember how to breathe.

"The results are inconclusive," the medical examiner went on. "He appears to have died of heart failure, but—"

"I don't understand," Summer interrupted. "He was healthy. He ran miles every day. He . . ." She petered off. It wasn't as if any of these things could change the facts.

"I'm sorry." The woman seemed unruffled by Summer's protests. "I can't tell you more than that at the moment. The underlying causes are unclear from the physical examination. It's possible he had an undiagnosed condition. Which is actually why I'm calling. I wanted to speak to you about a new pilot program that involves genetic testing in the case of sudden death in people under the age of forty. This can help us gain a better understanding of underlying causes, genetic variants, undiagnosed conditions, and such. Is this something you'd be interested in?"

"I— Um—" Summer tried to get her mind to catch up with all of those words, but her brain felt like one giant mass of fog. "Sure."

"Great. I'll send the authorization form over. You can sign that and send it back to me, and we'll take care of everything else from our end. You should get a preliminary report from us based on the physical autopsy within a few days and then the results of the genetic testing in a couple of months. I'm so sorry again for your loss."

This time, Summer managed to murmur, "Thank you." She sat staring at her phone after the line went dead.

"Summer?" Benjamin's voice startled her. "Are you okay?" But the moment he asked, he shook his head. "Sorry. Dumb question."

"Yeah." She shook her head too. "That was the medical examiner's office. They said it was his heart, but they don't know why. They have to do some testing. I have to sign a form." At least that was what she thought she'd gotten from the conversation.

"Okay." He let out a heavy breath. "There's no safe deposit box."

Summer nodded. She had figured as much.

She forced herself to stand, but Benjamin blocked her path out of the room. She didn't dare try to squeeze past him for fear he might try to hug her again—and that this time she wouldn't let go.

"I need to go check on Mama," she said instead, hoping he'd take the hint that she needed to leave the room. "And then get to the courthouse." The one-hour drive to the county seat in Brampton suddenly felt as daunting as a trip to the moon.

"You're exhausted." Benjamin didn't budge. "I'll drive."

"You don't have a car seat for Max in your car. And anyway, you should really—"

"Don't tell me to go home again." Benjamin's command was close to a growl. "I'm coming with you. We can either take the car seat out of yours and put it in mine, or I can drive your car. Your choice."

"You can drive mine," she answered meekly. "Even Max wouldn't fit into the back seat of your car."

She waited for Benjamin's retort that his little car was perfect, but it didn't come. Instead, he only nodded—and that was enough to remind her that everything was different now.

Chapter 12

Benjamin sat in Summer's car, parked in her mama's driveway. He stared out the windshield at the faded gray siding of the house she'd grown up in. He'd never been inside even though he and TJ had been friends since sixth grade. Even during the brief time he and Summer had dated, she had always been waiting outside for him when he came to pick her up. Neither TJ nor Summer had ever said much about their parents, but he knew their dad had left when Summer was a baby. And it was hard not to hear the rumors about their mother.

He wondered if that was the real reason Summer had asked him to stay in the car with Max while she checked on her mama—though the excuse she'd given was that Max might fray her mama's already frazzled nerves.

Benjamin glanced to the back seat, where Max was quietly paging through a book on dinosaurs. He didn't look like he'd frazzle anyone's nerves at the moment, although Benjamin knew from experience that he could throw a tantrum with the best of them.

He turned back to the front, trying to figure out how to reconcile the TJ he knew with the pile of debts he'd found this morning. But if the rumors about Summer's mama were true, he supposed it made sense that TJ struggled with addiction too. Why hadn't he ever said anything to Benjamin? Maybe he could have helped—or at least helped him find someone who could. His brother Simeon was a Christian counselor, for goodness' sake.

Benjamin wasn't exactly sure what happened when someone died in debt, but he prayed that TJ's mistake wouldn't end up costing Summer and Max. That was the last thing his friend would have wanted. Those two were everything to TJ.

A heavy weight of responsibility descended on Benjamin's shoulders. He owed it to his friend to make sure Summer and Max were okay, no matter what.

"How are you doing, Max?" he asked, turning to really look at the boy.

"I'm hot," Max complained.

Benjamin nodded. It *was* hot in the car, though they had all of the windows open. Maybe he should unbuckle Max and play with him in the yard.

But before he could unfasten his own seat belt, the front door of the house opened, and Summer emerged. She hurried toward the car, her head down, and dropped into the passenger seat.

"How is your mama taking it?" Benjamin asked.

Summer clicked her seat belt into place. "She's . . . fine." She averted her face to stare out the window, but not before he noticed the fresh tear tracks on her cheeks. "We should get going."

Benjamin wanted to press more, to ask how he could help with whatever was going on with her mama, but something held him back. Clearly, Summer didn't want him involved in that part of her life.

He backed the car out of the driveway. Next to him, Summer pulled the rubber band off of her severe bun and shook out her hair, running her fingers through it with a sigh.

Benjamin locked his fingers on the steering wheel so he wouldn't be tempted to smooth his hand over the sleek strands. Whatever feelings he'd once had—or still had—for Summer had to be put aside now. She was much too vulnerable. It was his job to protect her. Not to confuse her by trying to bring a relationship into the picture.

She leaned her head back on the seat and closed her eyes, and Benjamin drove in silence, until Max announced, "I have to go potty."

Benjamin groaned to himself. But to the boy he said, "It's only a little longer."

That wasn't exactly the truth. They had at least half an hour until they reached Brampton.

"I can't wait," Max whined.

"I forgot to have him go before we left," Summer muttered, her eyes still closed. Louder, she said, "You can hold it, Max. You're a big boy."

But Max started to cry. "I want my daddy. I want to go potty."

"Okay. Shh." Summer's eyes opened, and she reached into the back seat to pat Max's leg. "We'll find somewhere to go potty." She turned to Benjamin. "Is there a gas station coming up?"

"Not until the outskirts of Brampton."

Max cried harder. "Daddy," he called. "Daddy, please come back. I have to go potty."

The words sliced at Benjamin, but he forced himself to lift his voice over them. "Hey, Maxerooni, what's that song you love so much? The one with the dinosaurs?"

"One Hundred Little Dinosaurs?" Max asked.

"Yeah. That's right. Can you teach it to me?"

Max gave a long-suffering sigh. "*Then* can I go potty?"

"Yes," Summer promised.

"Fine." Max started to sing. "One little dinosaur, wishing for a friend. Along came another and then there were two."

"A songwriter, my brother was not," Summer mumbled, but she joined in on the next line. "Two little dinosaurs, wishing for a friend. Along came another and then there were three."

"But he sure could count," Benjamin murmured back, gratified by the brief smile it brought to Summer's face. He joined in the song too, and by the time they got to one hundred dinosaurs, they had reached the outskirts of Brampton.

He pulled into the first gas station he spotted.

"I have to go potty," Max said, as if he'd just remembered.

"Yep. I'll take you." Benjamin got out of the car and opened the back door, then leaned in to unbuckle the boy. But nothing happened when he pressed the car seat's harness release.

Summer leaned in from the other side. "You have to press here and here." Her fingers accidentally brushed Benjamin's as she showed him, and she stilled for a moment, her eyes closing. Benjamin's heart lurched.

Get it together, he commanded himself, unfastening the buckle the rest of the way. *She needs you as a friend. Don't do anything to make her push you away.*

He pulled Max out of the car and led him into the gas station's restroom. Fortunately, Max had been potty trained long enough that he didn't need help with anything except reaching the paper towels.

When they came out, Summer was stepping out of the checkout line. She handed Max a chocolate bar, then gave Benjamin a chocolate peanut butter cup.

"Do you still like these?" Her question was almost shy.

"I do." The fact that she'd remembered shot a beam of joy into his heart, but he quickly squelched it. It didn't change anything. "Thank you."

In the car, Summer buckled Max back into his car seat, then climbed into the front seat next to Benjamin.

"What did you get yourself?" he asked as he pulled out of the gas station's parking lot. "Wait, don't tell me. Taffy. No, sour worms. No, strawberry hard candy." He'd always teased her that she was the only girl he knew who didn't love chocolate.

She held up a bag of candy corn, and he made a face. "You know that's probably from last Halloween, right?"

She shrugged and popped a handful into her mouth. "It will serve its purpose."

"What purpose is that? To kill your taste buds?"

She laughed a little, the sound so perfectly normal that for a moment Benjamin was sure nothing had happened to TJ. That this was simply a pleasant day out.

But then the courthouse loomed in front of them, and their mission became all too real again.

It was busier than he'd expected on a Monday morning, and he had to circle the area a few times before he found a place to park.

When he finally did, he turned off the car, and he and Summer just sat, as if neither of them could face what came next.

"Get out?" Max asked from the back seat.

"Yep, Maxerooni. That's what we need to do." Benjamin unfastened his seat belt and opened his door. When Summer still didn't move, Benjamin extracted Max from his car seat. Then, together, they moved to open Summer's door.

She got out slowly, as if every inch cost her something.

As they started toward the courthouse, Max slipped one of his hands into each of theirs.

"Swing me," he cried.

Benjamin looked at Summer, and she didn't protest, so he counted down. "Three, two, one." He and Summer both lifted together, and the boy's feet swung into the air, rising alongside his shrieking giggle.

A woman walking toward them smiled. "Enjoy your son while he's young," she called. "They grow up too fast."

Benjamin exchanged a quick glance with Summer, but neither of them had the heart to tell the woman that they weren't one big, happy family. They were just three broken people trying to figure out how to get through loss together.

⸎

Summer's head spun as the clerk handed her yet another form.

"This one is a petition for guardianship. You need to fill it out and attach all of the required tax forms, proof of income, etcetera. And then you'll need to send notices to any of the boy's other relatives." The clerk sounded matter of fact, as if people came in needing to take guardianship of their dead brother's kids all the time.

Who knew? Maybe they did. Maybe this was routine for the woman. But it wasn't for Summer.

"His other relatives?" she asked numbly. Did that include people who were so far out of the boy's life that they didn't even know he existed? Like his mother, who hadn't seen the boy since the day after he was born, when she'd left the hospital without her son? "What if I don't know where to find them?"

"You can serve them by publication. Your lawyer will be able to handle all of that."

"My lawyer?" Summer gaped at the woman. It wasn't like she kept a lawyer on retainer for such situations. "Do I need a lawyer?"

75

"In a case without a will?" The woman eyed her sharply over the top of her glasses, as if it were Summer's fault that her brother hadn't written a will. "I would get one."

"Oh." In her mind, Summer had thought this would be so much easier. Like she would simply sign a piece of paper that said she would take care of her nephew and that would be that.

"I read about a case recently," the clerk continued, apparently warming up to the subject. "A woman wanted guardianship of her soon-to-be stepson after her fiancé died, but there wasn't a will and she didn't have a lawyer, and the kid ended up going into foster care because the stepmom didn't have the income to support the kid."

"Oh." Summer swallowed roughly. Did she have the income to support Max?

It didn't matter to her. She would give every last penny to the boy. But would the court see it that way?

"And then there was a case where—"

"Is there anything else we need to do?" Benjamin interjected, quelling the woman's story.

The clerk frowned, clearly not appreciating the interruption. "You have the forms for the estate and probate and the guardianship. You return that all here when you're done, and then they'll name an executor of the estate, and a hearing will be set up for the guardianship."

"Thank you." Benjamin took Summer's arm and steered her toward the door, grabbing Max's hand with his free one. "Come on, Maxerooni, time to go home."

Summer managed to hold it together until they reached the steps. Then she whirled on Benjamin.

"A lawyer? I have to get a lawyer? I can't afford that. They're going to take Max from me, and there's nothing I can do to stop them." She managed to catch the sob in her chest before it escaped.

"It's going to be okay." Benjamin squeezed her elbow.

"How?" she demanded. "How is it possibly going to be okay?"

Benjamin's forehead wrinkled uncharacteristically, and she could tell he was worried too. But he said, "My dad has a friend who's a lawyer. We can call him as soon as we get home."

Summer shook her head. "I can't pay him. I'll have to figure it out on my own."

"I'll pay him," Benjamin said firmly. "You can't risk doing this on your own. What if something goes wrong and you lose him?" Benjamin tilted his head toward Max, who had stopped to examine an ant.

Summer shook her head desperately. He was right that she couldn't risk losing Max. But she also couldn't take his money.

"I'll pay you back," she finally offered feebly. Though where she'd ever get the money to do that, she didn't know.

Benjamin didn't say anything, and she knew him well enough to know that was his way of disagreeing, but they could argue about it later. For now, she needed to focus on getting guardianship of Max. Once that was figured out, she could worry about everything else.

When they got to the car, Benjamin opened her door, and she fell into her seat before remembering that she needed to buckle Max in too.

She blew her hair out of her face and darted a look around as if a judge might be watching her every move this very moment, deciding whether she would be a fit guardian.

But Benjamin was already leaning into the back seat and settling Max into his car seat. She watched as he snapped the clips together, then ruffled the boy's hair, a sudden wish that he would always be there to help them almost overpowering her.

She spun around and settled back into her seat, fastening her own seat belt and then leaning her head back and closing her eyes.

She hadn't slept even a minute last night, and heaviness weighed her eyelids down so that she couldn't open them even when she heard Benjamin get in and start the car. She felt him lean closer as he turned to back out of the parking spot. His subtle citrus-herb scent made her feel safe, and she let herself drift into sleep.

Chapter 13

"Thanks, Dad." Benjamin walked out the door with his father, who had come over to Summer's to help with the funeral plans.

The sun had tucked itself behind the surrounding mountains, and Benjamin wasn't sure whether he was relieved that this long day was over or afraid it would only usher in an even longer night.

"Of course." Dad stopped and rested a hand on Benjamin's shoulder. "I'm so sorry you're going through this. But I'm proud of the way you're handling it."

Benjamin shook his head. It didn't feel like he was handling it well at all, at least not on the inside, where doubts and fears and worries had swirled all day.

"Listen, does Don still practice law? It looks like Summer is going to need a lawyer to help her get guardianship of Max."

Dad nodded. "He does. Do you want me to give him a call?"

"Nah. Give me his number and I'll call."

Dad pulled out his phone and sent Benjamin the number. "And this is why I'm proud of you." Dad eyed Benjamin. "You're stepping up and helping Summer and Max through this, taking care of details men twice your age often haven't had to take care of yet."

Benjamin swallowed. He would give anything not to have to take care of these kinds of details either. But not if it meant putting them back on Summer.

"Make sure you take care of yourself too." Dad stepped forward and pulled him into a hard hug. "I'm so sorry about TJ."

Benjamin nodded, hugging his dad back. He wanted to pretend he was six years old again and a hug from his dad could fix everything.

When Dad finally let go, Benjamin got up the nerve to ask, "Do you think it would be okay— I mean, would it be wrong if I stayed here with them a couple more nights? I'll obviously sleep on the couch and—" Ah, man, he felt suddenly like a teenager again, asking if he could have a later curfew. "I just don't want to leave them alone right now," he finished desperately.

"I think that would be a good idea," Dad said with quick reassurance. "I'm not sure Summer is quite over the shock yet."

Benjamin nodded. When he'd woken her after the drive from the courthouse, she'd hit him with such a smile that his heart jumped—and then he saw everything come crashing back in on her, as if she'd just learned of TJ's death for the first time all over again.

She'd barely said a word throughout the funeral planning, deferring most of the decisions to Benjamin and Dad. The only thing she insisted on was that the casket be closed for Max's sake.

Benjamin stood on the porch for a minute after Dad left, waiting for . . . he didn't know what. Peace would be nice. Or comfort. Or some kind of certainty about what he was supposed to do next.

When none of those came, he went back into the house. Summer had been tucking Max in, and he headed down the hallway to see if she needed any help with that. But Max's bedroom door was already closed, the faint glow of a night light peeking through the crack under it.

Benjamin nudged the door open just enough to see Max snuggled under the covers, already asleep. Sorrow and determination collided in his chest.

He was going to make sure this little guy got to stay with his aunt, no matter what.

Silently, he pulled the door closed. Summer's bedroom door was open, the lights off. So was TJ's, although Benjamin couldn't bring himself to look inside.

He moved to the kitchen to let Summer know he was going to run home and get some clothes and then be right back, but she wasn't there. He glanced around the space, as if she must be hiding. It wasn't a large house, and if she wasn't in the bedrooms or the living room or the kitchen, he didn't know where she could be.

His eyes fell on the patio door that led to the backyard. It was dark out there, and he couldn't make out any figures, but he opened it anyway and stepped out onto the deck.

"Summer?" he called softly into the dark, scanning the small yard.

"Yes?"

It took a moment for him to realize the voice came from a hammock that stood in the yard, next to the stairs that led off of the deck.

He treaded softly down the steps and stood next to it. She didn't turn her head toward him but seemed to be focused on the sky.

"What are you doing out here?" he asked.

She blinked but still didn't look at him. "Trying not to think, I guess."

He puffed out a breath. "Let me know how that goes."

"Not well." She sat up and swung her legs to the ground, turning sideways so that she was sitting on the hammock more like it was a chair. "Want to sit?"

Benjamin eyed the contraption dubiously. It was faded and worn through in spots, and he had his doubts that it could support the weight of two people.

But Summer looked so alone and small sitting there . . .

He sat carefully, leaving enough room between them that their skin wouldn't brush, even though he wanted nothing more than to pull her into his arms and promise he would protect her.

The hammock swayed a little but held up, and Benjamin let himself lean into it so that it supported his back.

If it weren't for the circumstances, this could be a perfect night. The air was still but not oppressive. The tree frogs and crickets sang in harmony, and a million stars blinked down at them.

He shook his head, making the hammock rock lightly.

"What?" Summer asked. He felt her turn toward him, but he kept his eyes on the stars.

"I was just thinking this would be a beautiful night, if it weren't for . . ."

"Yeah." Summer sighed softly. "I'm not sure if there will ever be another beautiful night again."

"I'm sorry." The words that had been suffocating his heart all day whispered out. "I should have gone with him. If I had been there—"

Summer's fingertips brushed his arm, the touch so light and fleeting that he would have thought it was the breeze if there were one.

"It's not your fault." Her whisper floated between them. "I shouldn't have said that yesterday. I don't blame you. I blame . . . God, I guess."

Benjamin swallowed. He felt like he should say something about that, something profound and deep and encouraging. But the truth was, he blamed God a little bit too.

But that seemed too awful to admit. He was a Calvano, a pastor's son. He wasn't supposed to have doubts.

"Anyway," Summer continued softly, "you've been nothing but helpful. So thank you."

"You're welcome." Slowly, carefully, he slid his hand into hers, holding his breath until her fingers closed around his. He prayed the connection brought her as much comfort as it did him.

"I used to think," she said quietly, "that TJ was the one person who would always be there for me. No matter what else happened or who else didn't want me, he always would."

"I know." Benjamin tightened his grip on her hand. "But I'm going to be there for you now. And for Max."

"Benjamin—" Summer started, but he wasn't going to let her argue the point.

"It's the least I can do for TJ," he added.

Summer's exhale filled the space between them, but she fell silent, and Benjamin felt like he'd won that point at least.

"You know," she said after a while, "I don't think I ever knew you had a serious side before."

Benjamin snorted. "Yeah, well, don't let word get out. It would ruin my reputation."

Summer's laugh was quiet but genuine, and he wanted it to continue, so he pushed his feet against the ground to set the hammock swinging.

"Ah, Benjamin, don't," Summer shrieked, but the movement had achieved the desired effect of extending her laughter.

"Don't what?" he asked innocently.

"It's going to—"

But Summer's words were lost as the fabric of the hammock gave way, spilling them onto the ground in a tangled heap.

"Break," she finished, her face so close to Benjamin's that he could see the barely visible freckles that dotted her nose.

The situation was so absurd that a laugh burst out of him.

"So much for your serious side." Summer's laugh mingled with his, and they lay there in the moonlight, laughing until they were both gasping for breath.

When they finally fell silent, they both stared up at the sky, and Benjamin couldn't help but think that maybe everything would be okay after all.

Chapter 14

Summer tapped her toes against the tile floor of the lawyer's office. The intensity with which Don was examining the paperwork she'd spent all day yesterday filling out was making her nervous.

She glanced at Benjamin, who sat forward in his seat, his hands pressed to his knees, staring as intently at the white-haired lawyer as Don stared at the paperwork. As if he felt her watching him, Benjamin turned to her with a quick smile, but she saw the way the muscle in his jaw jumped with his nerves.

When he turned away, her eyes went to his hands. Those hands had held hers last night, and they'd felt like such a lifeline that she was tempted to reach out and clutch them again.

"All right." Don tapped the edge of the stack of papers against his desk, the sound sharp enough to make Summer wince. "Based on this, I don't see any problem with you being named executor of the estate. As soon as that goes through, you can sell your brother's house and—"

"Sell TJ's house?" Summer interrupted. "It's my house too."

Don looked at her in surprise. "Is your name on the deed too? That changes things." He reshuffled the papers.

"No," Summer answered quietly. "TJ paid for it. I mean, I live there too. And Max."

"Ah." Don nodded sympathetically, setting the papers back down. "I'm afraid there's no way for you to hold on to it. It's going to need to be liquidated to pay off TJ's debts. Fortunately, the market is pretty good right now, so . . ." Don cleared his throat. "As far as the guardianship, that might be a little trickier."

"Trickier how?" Benjamin demanded before Summer could say a word. "Summer has been like a mother to Max since he was born. You won't find anyone who loves him more."

Don pulled off his glasses and laid them on top of the papers. "It's not a question of whether she loves him enough," he said calmly. "It's a question of financial ability." He turned to Summer. "I know you just lost your job."

Summer winced as Benjamin looked at her in surprise. With everything that had happened, she hadn't even thought to mention that to him.

"But even before that," Don continued, "you were only working part time."

"That was so I could help take care of Max," Summer said defensively, tears gathering behind her lids. She had never dreamed that could be used against her.

"And the judge will take that into consideration," Don said, still sickeningly calm. "But the fact is that you have next to no savings, no job . . . No way to support a child."

"I'll get a job," she promised.

"And then what about childcare?" Don asked.

Summer threw her hands in the air, then buried her face in them. "I can't win here, can I?"

"What if I offered to help?" Benjamin asked before Don could answer, and Summer's head shot up.

"Benj—"

But he kept going. "Could you put me down as a, I don't know, benefactor or something? I don't have a lot saved because I just put a down payment on my house, but I could give them a monthly amount, enough to cover their living expenses. I can submit my finances so the judge can see—"

"Benjamin." This time Summer succeeded in cutting him off. "I am not going to take your money."

"Fine. Can I give Max an allowance then?" he asked the lawyer.

Don shook his head with a sad smile. "I'm afraid it doesn't work that way. If the two of you were married, sure, we could report your income. But short of that . . ."

"What will happen to him if I don't get guardianship?" Summer could barely force the words out.

"He'll go to another family member if there is one—"

"There's not," Summer said flatly.

"Then he'd likely go to a group home or a foster family."

Summer closed her eyes.

"Listen, I'm not saying it's hopeless," Don said gently. "We'll fill out the paperwork, submit the documents, publish the notice, and then wait and see what the judge says. There's a chance he will decide that the stability of being with a familiar adult is more important than your financial situation." He didn't sound at all certain, but Summer clung to the possibility.

Don stood, and it was clear that their meeting was over. Benjamin stood too and held out a hand as the older man came around the desk. "Thanks for your help."

Summer pried herself out of her seat too. "Thank you," she murmured, more out of politeness than any real gratitude. She knew he was only being honest with her, but still she felt as if he had single-handedly pulverized her world.

Don ushered them to the door, promising to contact them as soon as a date for the guardianship hearing was set.

The moment they stepped outside, every last bit of strength Summer had left seemed to give out, and she felt herself sag. Benjamin's arm was instantly around her back, and even though she knew she should pull away, she leaned into him.

"What am I going to do?" She didn't realize she'd said the words out loud until Benjamin said, "God's got this."

Summer pulled away and stared up at him. "How, Benjamin? How does God got this? I don't see him standing here offering any brilliant solutions, do you?"

Benjamin didn't answer, and she couldn't decide whether it was satisfaction or disappointment she felt over that.

They walked silently to her car, and Benjamin let her into the passenger seat, then took up what had become his spot in the driver's seat.

But he didn't start the car.

"We have to get Max," she reminded him. He had arranged for his eighteen-year-old niece Mia to watch the boy while they met with the lawyer, but Summer had promised they'd be back before lunch.

Benjamin nodded but still didn't move.

"I'm not going to let you lose him, you know." He turned to her, and his eyes held a wild determination.

"I'm not sure you can stop it." Her head felt like it weighed a thousand pounds, and she leaned it back on the seat and closed her eyes.

"Marry me."

Summer snorted softly without opening her eyes. "Be serious, Benjamin."

He didn't answer, and she let herself settle deeper into the seat. All she wanted was to sleep. When she slept, her heart couldn't hurt so badly.

"I *am* serious," Benjamin said quietly.

Summer peeked her eyes open and looked at him without turning her head. He was staring out the windshield, his hands grabbing the steering wheel even though the engine remained silent. There wasn't a hint of goofiness in his demeanor.

But that didn't mean he really meant what he said. He was just . . . Well, she didn't know what he was. But he clearly wasn't in his right mind.

He turned to her suddenly. "You heard what Don said. If we were married, you could include my income on the forms. That would be more than enough to take care of you and Max."

She shook her head. "You don't want to marry me." That much she knew was true. He was on a date with another woman just the other night. "And I don't want to marry you."

Had she let herself dream about it once upon a time? Sure.

But she wasn't going to marry someone who didn't want her—who didn't love her.

"I told you last night that I would do whatever it took to take care of you and Max."

Yeah. He'd also said it was the least he could do for *TJ*. And she was pretty sure even TJ would think this was taking things a little too far. "That doesn't mean marrying me."

"But what if it does?" Benjamin's voice was low, his eyes earnest, and Summer had to turn away.

"Stop it, Benjamin." Her voice wobbled with the effort of holding back her tears, though she couldn't say exactly why his offer made her want to cry. "You're being ridiculous. We're not getting married, and that's final."

She felt Benjamin's eyes on her, but she refused to look toward him, and after a moment, he silently started the car.

Summer closed her eyes so he wouldn't bring the subject up again. But he didn't say a word all the way back to River Falls. And Summer couldn't figure out why that upset her even more than his ridiculous proposal had.

Chapter 15

"Come on, Max. It's time to go inside." Benjamin's voice was hoarse, and he wondered if the boy could even hear it over the sound of the church bells. They'd come out here half an hour ago when Max had grown restless greeting the long line of mourners who had come to pay their respects before the funeral. It had nearly ripped Benjamin's heart out to leave Summer's side, but it was either that or risk Max throwing an all-out tantrum at his daddy's funeral—and that wasn't a memory Benjamin wanted for the boy.

Max looked up from the handful of sticks he'd been collecting. "Can I bring these in?"

Benjamin laughed a little in spite of the ache in his middle. "I think we'd better leave them out here."

"What if someone steals them?" Max's eyes filled with tears, and Benjamin almost relented. Until he pictured Max wielding the sticks like swords during the service.

"How about we hide them behind this bush?" Benjamin pushed aside some branches on a bush next to the church to make a little hiding spot. "Then you can get them after church, okay?"

Max nodded reluctantly and stashed the pile. Then he stuck his hand into Benjamin's and looked up with such trusting eyes—eyes that looked so much like TJ's—that Benjamin had to swallow hard. He really would do anything for this kid.

91

Even if it meant convincing Summer to marry him.

He'd spent the past two days thinking about it, and it was still the best solution he could come up with, although he'd refrained from saying anything more about it to Summer. Once they got past the funeral, he could sit down with Dad, make all the arrangements, and then she would see that everything would work out.

"Be very quiet," he whispered to Max as he pulled open the church door for the boy.

But instead of the solemn hymn music he expected, there appeared to be some sort of commotion at the front of the church.

Benjamin hurried Max forward, and his eyes fell on Summer and her mama, both standing in the aisle near the front pew. Summer's face was pale and mortified, her mama's twisted and angry as she said something Benjamin couldn't hear. Benjamin's feet carried him swiftly toward them, Max running alongside to keep up.

Benjamin had noticed the faint smell of liquor on Summer's mother when they'd picked her up earlier, but she'd seemed fine—if a little surly—in the receiving line before Benjamin left to take Max outside.

Dad reached Summer and her mother from the front of the church at the same time that Benjamin reached them from the back. He stood as close as he could to Summer without touching her, though everything in him wanted to shield her from whatever this was.

"Let me help you to your seat, Mrs. Ellis," Dad offered.

Summer's mother sneered at him. "I see the way you all are judging me. Wondering what kind of mother I must be to come here like this."

"I think you're a mother who is hurting," Dad said quietly.

Mrs. Ellis made a strange choking sound at the back of her throat that may have been a strangled laugh. "He wouldn't even talk to me, did you know that? Six months and not a word. From my own son."

Benjamin winced. It had been years since Benjamin's brother Judah had talked to Dad. But Dad's expression didn't falter.

"Mama," Summer started.

"And you." Mrs. Ellis whirled on her daughter. "Doing all of this without me?" She waved her hands wildly as if to encompass the whole room, and Benjamin's jaw tightened. Both Summer and his father had asked Mrs. Ellis to be part of the planning, but she had refused.

"You think I wanted all these people here?" Mrs. Ellis's voice rose. "You think any of them cared about my son?"

"I think we all cared about your son very much," Benjamin said firmly, and Summer shot him a look that could have been gratitude—or reproach.

Mrs. Ellis eyed him but didn't say anything for a moment, and Dad used the opportunity to say, "If you'd like to take your seat, we'll begin the service."

Mrs. Ellis shook her head. "You all go ahead and have your service. Summer, take me home."

"Mama." Anguish twisted Summer's plea, but Mrs. Ellis ignored it and started down the aisle.

"I'll take her," Benjamin murmured, though the thought of leaving Summer and Max to go through the funeral alone knifed at his insides.

He squeezed Summer's arm, then tucked Max's hand into hers and followed Mrs. Ellis toward the lobby. As he passed his family's pew a few rows behind Summer, his siblings stirred. He glanced over his shoulder to see them shuffling out of their pew and filing in to surround Summer and Max, and his heart swelled into a great lump that seemed to lodge in his throat.

The only one who didn't sit was Zeb, who followed Benjamin instead.

"I'll take her home," Zeb said as soon as they reached the lobby. "You go back inside."

Benjamin hesitated, watching Mrs. Ellis struggle with the outside door.

"You need to be in there," Zeb insisted. "Summer and Max need you." He strode toward Mrs. Ellis, making the decision for Benjamin.

Zeb said something in a low voice to Mrs. Ellis, who shook her head adamantly. But Zeb spoke again and then opened the door for her. She stumbled a little as she stepped through, and he caught her arm, holding it as he steered her toward the parking lot.

Benjamin let out a breath, thankful that Zeb was the one taking her home. He wasn't sure he would have been able to hold his tongue after the way Mrs. Ellis had spoken to Summer.

He slipped back into the sanctuary and debated sitting behind Summer, since his family had packed the pew around her, but Joseph glanced up at Benjamin's approach. He nudged Ava, who held little Noah, and the three of them slipped into the pew behind them.

Benjamin slid into the space they had left and moved as close as he could to Summer. Max climbed from her lap to his, and he wrapped one arm around the boy and one around Summer, who trembled against him.

"Where's Mama?" she whispered, her eyes clouded with wariness.

"Zeb is taking her home," he whispered back.

She nodded, and they both turned to listen to the service. Dad was reading from 2 Timothy 4:7. Benjamin recognized the verse because it was one he and TJ had studied before their last trail run together. "I have fought the good fight, I have finished the race, I have kept the faith. Now there is in store for me the crown of righteousness, which the Lord, the righteous Judge, will award to me on that day—and not only to me, but also to all who have longed for his appearing."

Benjamin's jaw clenched. Just a few weeks ago, those words had seemed to hold such promise. But now— Now he couldn't help resenting God just a little for ending TJ's race so early.

Summer stared into the side view mirror until the cemetery disappeared behind a bend in the road. If it weren't for Mama's humiliating outburst, the day would have been . . . not pleasant, but nice.

"Do you want to check on your mama?" Benjamin's question was carefully neutral, and Summer rubbed at her achy eyes.

"Not right now." She'd have to check on Mama later, but not with Benjamin. What must he and his whole family be thinking after her stunt?

The only good thing about it was that now Summer didn't have to worry about Benjamin repeating that ridiculous proposal from the other day. There was no way he'd want to join himself—and his perfect family—to a family like hers.

"How long has she . . ." Benjamin glanced in the rearview mirror, and Summer knew he was checking if Max was listening. She glanced over her shoulder too, but Max's eyes were closed, his head tipped to the side in sleep, the sticks Benjamin had helped him collect from church clutched in his fingers.

"As long as I remember," she answered quietly, and Benjamin nodded, his jaw hardening.

"I'm sorry."

She shrugged. "She went to rehab once. When I was maybe eight. She came home and told us she was all better and we were going to plan a trip to the zoo. TJ said he didn't believe her, but I did." She shook her head. "He was right."

Benjamin's hand reached for hers, and she closed her eyes. The way his fingers wrapped around hers, the way his arm had held her tight at church, the way he had been there with her and Max every day—she wanted all of that to last forever.

But it couldn't.

Still, she couldn't quite bring herself to pull her hand out of his. Surely it couldn't hurt to let herself indulge in this little comfort until they got home.

But the drive went much too quickly, and when they got back, Benjamin unbuckled the still-sleeping Max and carried him to his room for a nap.

Summer dropped onto the couch and used the whole time he was in Max's room to convince herself to do what she knew she had to do. But when Benjamin strode into the living room, his eyes sad but his expression kind, almost tender, she nearly lost her resolve.

"We should talk." Benjamin settled on the couch next to her and reached for her hands, and Summer was suddenly on high alert. She absolutely couldn't let him repeat the proposal he'd made the other day.

"I was thinking that too." She tugged her hands from his. "I appreciate everything you've done for us. I don't know how I would have gotten through the past few days without you. But I think you should go now."

His brow wrinkled. "Go where?"

"Home." She almost couldn't push the word out.

"Oh."

The single syllable held too much, and Summer forced herself to go on.

"You need to get back to your life. And your work. And your—" She couldn't bring herself to say *girlfriend*. "House. And I need to figure all of this out."

"You don't need to figure it out on your own." Benjamin's voice registered somewhere between a growl and a plea. "Have you thought about—"

But Summer wasn't going to let him go there. "I need to figure it out," she repeated firmly. "Max and I will be fine." The panic slashing through her gut said she didn't believe her own words. But she only needed Benjamin to believe them.

"This is really what you want?" Benjamin's frown nearly undid her, but she forced herself to nod.

"I'm going to come by to check on you, you know." His look dared her to contradict him. "And I'm going to help with the guardianship fight and figuring out all of the estate stuff. So don't think you can keep me away."

Summer nodded, wondering how long it would take before he got too busy with work and . . . other things to follow through on that.

Which she knew wasn't fair to him. He'd stuck with her and Max all week.

But still, he had a life of his own.

"At least let me make you dinner before I go," Benjamin bargained.

But Summer shook her head. She needed to do this now, or she never would.

"Okay." Benjamin's voice was soft and defeated. "Promise you'll call me if you need anything."

Summer nodded obediently.

"I'll stop by tomorrow before work." His gaze rested on hers for a moment, and he lifted his hand as if he were going to touch her. But then he let it fall and disappeared out the door.

Chapter 16

Benjamin tapped his fingers restlessly on the steering wheel of his Gremlin as he headed for Dad's house. He was glad he'd gone to church this morning, and yet the comfort and peace he'd expected to feel still eluded him. He couldn't explain it.

He'd watched his siblings walk through trial after trial—and not one of them had ever questioned God's love. His own faith had never really been put to the test before, and he'd sometimes wondered if that was because God knew he'd fail. Which he seemed to be proving right now.

He tried to pray, but the only thing he could think was, *It's not fair, God,* so he gave up on that.

Fortunately, Dad's house was just ahead. He hadn't been planning on coming today—he wanted to get to Summer and Max's as soon as he could, since he hadn't been able to convince Summer to come to church with him. But she'd said they would be at her Mama's. And he had to work in a couple of hours.

He sighed. It was only two days ago that he'd promised he'd check on them every day. It felt like he was already failing them—and TJ.

He parked his car behind Simeon's SUV in Dad's long driveway. The air was heavy and oppressive as he walked toward the house, gray clouds hanging low and threatening to unleash a torrent.

But the moment he opened the door, the usual family chatter spilled out, and his heart lightened. *This* was what he needed.

He stepped inside and headed straight for the kitchen, where he knew everyone would be gathered. A spread of food covered the countertop, and his siblings were in various stages of filling their plates, tending their babies, and chatting.

"Let's pray before y'all scatter to eat," Dad called over the hullabaloo.

Benjamin folded his hands along with everyone else, ducking his head and hoping that this, at last, would give him peace.

"Gracious Father," Dad began. "We ask for your comfort for all who mourn TJ's death."

A hand gripped Benjamin's shoulder, and he knew it must be Asher, who had been standing right next to him.

"Let us rest in the promise of his victory in you, Lord," Dad continued. "And let us remember that all of our days are in your hands. Lead us to use them to your glory. In Jesus' name we ask it. Amen."

Benjamin opened his eyes, and Asher patted his shoulder. "You doing okay, man?"

Benjamin nodded, the knot in his chest a little looser after Dad's prayer.

"You know it's fine if you need to take a few more days off of work." Ireland shifted Caroline to her other hip. "John understands."

Benjamin shook his head. He knew her brother, who owned The Depot, understood, and so did the rest of the staff, but if he was going to have the money to support Summer and Max, he needed to get back to work.

"I'm going in today," he insisted.

Ireland nodded. "I told John you'd say that."

The simple comment lifted Benjamin's heart. He liked having a family who knew him so well.

"I heard this year's Trail Classic is going to be run in TJ's memory," Asher said.

Benjamin nodded. TJ had been involved in trail running a lot longer than he had and even helped to get the race started.

"So we were thinking," Asher added. "What if we all ran it together?"

Benjamin blinked at him. "Who all?"

Asher rolled his eyes. "*We* all. Your brothers."

"I— Really?" Benjamin felt a lump form in his throat at the same time a smile pulled on his lips. He had been dreading the thought of running without TJ.

"You might have to carry some of us over the finish line," Liam called from the table.

"Speak for yourself, old man," Joseph joked back, filling his plate. "I, for one, intend to win the race." He added a cupcake to his pile of food. "For energy." He grinned.

"I can set up a training schedule," Zeb offered.

"Make sure it doesn't start at four a.m.," Simeon retorted.

Benjamin shook his head as he moved to fill his own plate. *This family.* He only wished Summer could be here to experience their love. He hated the thought of her all alone, dealing with her mama.

"How's Summer doing?" Ava asked as he pulled out a seat at the table next to her. She spooned a scoop of peas into Noah's mouth, and the baby made a face, letting them dribble down his chin.

"Doing as well as she can be, I guess." Benjamin used his napkin to wipe Noah's face. "She's worried she won't get guardianship of Max."

"Why wouldn't she?" Abigail sat across from him, trying to keep Genevieve's fingers out of her food. "She brings him into the bookstore all the time, and it's clear they adore each other."

"I know." Benjamin's chest tightened again at the unfairness of it all. "But apparently that's not the only consideration. She has to prove that she can support him financially, and she just lost her job, and she doesn't really have any savings, and—" He cut off, reluctant to expose TJ's gambling. "And it's not looking good," he finished.

"Isn't there anything else she can do?" Simeon asked. He and Abigail had faced their own uphill battle in adopting a child, and Benjamin was trying to hold on to their story as a sign of hope for Summer.

He shrugged. "If you know of any job openings . . ."

"The restaurant," Ireland said instantly.

But Benjamin shook his head. "I offered that, but our hours won't work for her. She needs to be home in the afternoons and evenings for Max. If I had more savings, I would give it to them, but it all went into my down payment on the house. I asked the lawyer if I could give them a monthly allowance or stipend or something, but he said we'd have to be married for that."

"I can just see that proposal." Joseph chuckled. "I know I'm dating someone else right now, but will you marry me?"

Everyone laughed, but Benjamin jumped in. "Jasmine and I aren't seeing each other anymore." He could at least clear that up.

Abigail's eyes widened. "Because of this?"

Benjamin shook his head. "No. That happened before this. It just didn't work out."

Abigail studied him a moment longer, and Benjamin forced himself to dig into his food, though he didn't taste a single bite.

A rattling clap of thunder followed by the onslaught of a downpour pulled everyone's attention off of Benjamin, and he focused on wolfing down his food. Then he searched out Dad and asked for a private word.

"Of course." Dad led him to the small home office that always smelled like coffee and books. Benjamin used to love sitting in here, pretending he was important, just like his father.

Dad leaned against the edge of his desk, and Benjamin shuffled from foot to foot, trying to figure out what to do with his hands. Finally, he shoved them in his pockets.

Dad didn't say anything, and Benjamin knew that was to give him the space to start when he was ready. At last, he let out a breath and took the plunge. "I asked Summer to marry me."

Dad's expression remained neutral, and Benjamin wondered if that was from his years of parenting or his years of pastoring.

"You asked her to marry you," he repeated.

Benjamin wasn't sure if it was a question, but he nodded anyway.

"I assume this has to do with what Don said about the money."

"Yes, but—"

"Benjamin." Dad spoke slowly and deliberately, as if Benjamin were three years old. "Do you really think—"

"That I can convince her?" Benjamin shrugged. "I'm going to try."

Dad shook his head. "That's not what I was going to ask."

"Yeah, but if I can convince her," Benjamin rushed on, before Dad could make whatever objections he was going to make. "Will you marry us? Soon? The hearing will be scheduled in a few weeks, and I want to make sure there's plenty of time to get my paperwork in, and for them to do whatever they need to do."

"Benjamin." Dad crossed his arms in front of him, his expression somber. "You've always been compassionate. It's one of your gifts. But you're also young and impulsive."

Benjamin opened his mouth to argue that his age had nothing to do with it, but Dad pushed on. "You can't marry Summer just so that she'll get guardianship of Max. That isn't fair to any of you."

"Why not?" Benjamin felt his jaw tighten. It wouldn't matter if he was twenty-three or forty-three or sixty-three. He'd still want to help Summer.

"Do you love her? Does she love you?"

"Do you think I would be willing to do this if I didn't love her?" He ignored the second part of the question. It didn't matter if Summer loved him. What mattered was that this was how he could take care of her and Max.

"I think," Dad said slowly, "that guilt can be a powerful but misguided motivator."

"I'm not doing this because of guilt." But the words burned against Benjamin's throat, and the ache that he hadn't been there for TJ hit him again. "Anyway, is that a yes or a no? Will you marry us?"

Dad let out a weighted breath. "I don't know," he finally said.

"Is it wrong?" Benjamin asked defiantly. "People in the Bible got married for all kinds of reasons, you know. It wasn't just love. Marriages were arranged by families without the couple ever meeting. Or they were to form family alliances or political alliances or—"

Dad held up a hand to halt him. "I'm not saying it's necessarily wrong, but I also don't think it's necessarily wise. Marriage isn't only a promise to each other. It's a promise to God."

"I know that. And it's not a promise I would break."

"I know you think that now." Dad's voice was overly gentle, and Benjamin couldn't help thinking of all the times his father had pulled him onto his knee and explained that he couldn't do all the things his brothers did because he wasn't big enough yet. "But suddenly becoming a husband *and* a father. That would be a lot for anyone."

"So you won't do it." Benjamin strode to the window and stared out at the rain.

"Not right this minute, no. Maybe in a few months. After we have time to go through some premarital counseling. You might want to go on a date or two as well, make sure she even likes you." A teasing note crept through Dad's voice, but Benjamin was not amused.

"We don't have that much time." His frustration bled through the words. He turned to Dad in desperation. "I don't know what else to do."

"You do know," Dad said gently. "Trust it to the Lord."

Benjamin let out a long, slow breath. "That's hard."

Dad chuckled a little. "It sure is. But he knows what he's doing."

"I know." But the words felt hollow. Benjamin had never doubted that God had a plan before. But right now . . . "I should get to work," he mumbled.

He started toward the door, but Dad intercepted him with a hug. "I'm praying for all of you. And I'm here anytime you want to talk."

Benjamin nodded, then headed for the door.

Chapter 17

"Do we *have* to go to Grandma's?" Max whined from the back seat, and Summer gritted her teeth as she backed the car out of their driveway.

"It will only be for a little while," she promised. She didn't want to see her mother any more than Max did, and she'd avoided her all day yesterday, but she couldn't just leave Mama to fend for herself in her condition.

Besides, there was something she needed to ask Mama. She'd gone around and around with herself about it. But she couldn't see any other way. She needed money to prove to the court that she could care for Max. She knew Mama didn't have a lot, but she must have *some* . . .

"Is it Sunday?" Max interrupted her thoughts as they drove past the empty parking lot at Beautiful Savior.

"Yes." One week since TJ's death. The realization shot through her, and she wondered if that was how she would always mark time now.

"Why didn't we go to church?" Max's voice pitched toward a whine again. "Daddy always said church is the most 'portant thing."

Summer exhaled hard. Benjamin had spent yesterday trying to convince her to join him at church this morning, but she didn't know how she was ever supposed to step foot in that building again, after the humiliation of Mama's behavior at TJ's funeral. But she promised, "We'll go next week."

"I don't wanna go next week, I wanna go today," Max insisted. "I don't wanna go to Grandma's. Daddy never made me go to Grandma's."

"Well, that's what we're doing," Summer snapped, instantly regretting her harsh tone. She let out a rough breath. "I'm sorry, Max." She glanced in the rearview mirror. "Church is already over anyway, so we can't go even if we want to. But you can play outside at Grandma's. And then we can get some pie when we're done."

"Can I have whipped cream on mine?" Max brightened.

Summer chuckled. She'd give him a whole tub of whipped cream if it could make him smile like that.

"Whipped cream *and* hot cocoa," she pledged.

"Boy oh boy!" Max clapped his hands. "Can Benji come too?"

Summer's heart dipped. "He has to work today."

It was the first day since TJ's death that she wouldn't see Benjamin, and it was her own doing—she could have timed her visit to Mama's so he could still come over. But she had to start getting used to the fact that he wouldn't always be there.

Not to mention that every time she saw him now, she was terrified that he'd bring up his ridiculous scheme to marry her so she could get guardianship of Max.

It had been an offhand, flippant comment, one she knew he didn't mean. But she also knew Benjamin well enough to know that he often carried his crazy ideas to fruition. Buying a Gremlin had started out as a joke—and now he drove that thing everywhere.

Summer turned her own, much more practical, sedan onto Mama's street, her whole body tightening as if someone had cinched a rope around her. She considered driving right past Mama's and going straight to Daisy's for pie, but muscle memory turned the car into the driveway.

Slowly, she got out of her seat. Slowly helped Max out of his, slowly led him to the front door. "Come in and say hi, and then you can go play in the backyard." It was fenced, so she wouldn't have to worry about him out there.

Summer stuck her key in the lock and shoved the door open. And then she and Max stood on the threshold, as if neither wanted to be the first through.

"You trying to cost me money?" Mama called from her chair. "Come in and shut the door already."

Summer sighed and laid a hand on Max's shoulder, and they stepped through together.

"Hi, Mama," Summer called, mostly as a model for Max. If he weren't here, she wouldn't have spoken to Mama at all.

"Hi, Grandma," Max obediently mimicked.

Mama grunted, and Summer nodded to Max to let him know he could go play. He rocketed through the living room and into the kitchen, and half a second later the back door banged shut.

Silently, Summer gathered up the dirty dishes accumulated on the TV tray next to Mama and started toward the kitchen.

"I suppose those Calvanos are happy, kicking me out of my own son's funeral." Resentment dripped from Mama's words, and Summer froze.

She opened her mouth, but no sound came out. She'd known it was too much to hope for an apology, but this was beyond what she'd thought even Mama capable of.

"I suppose they talked about me all day too. Bunch of hypocrites, that's what they are."

"Mama!" Shock loosened Summer's tongue. "No one kicked you out. You chose to leave. And no one was talking about you. The day wasn't about you. It was about TJ." She spun on her heel and rushed headlong to the kitchen, tossing the dishes on the counter with a loud clatter.

She had to take a few minutes to just breathe before she could start washing them. She could see Max out the kitchen window, boring little holes in the dirt with a stick. Normally, she would stop him, but today it gave her a little flash of vindictive pleasure to see him wrecking the yard. And it wasn't like Mama ever went outside anyway.

When the dishes were done, she moved around the kitchen, taking out the garbage, wiping counters, taking inventory of the pantry, but mostly giving herself more time away from Mama.

Finally, there was nothing else to do. She threw together a sandwich and cut up some carrots for Mama's dinner, then stuck them on a plate in the fridge.

She took a couple of fortifying breaths and made her way to the living room. As much as she wanted to leave, she couldn't go without asking for the money.

Mama was half dozing in front of the TV, and Summer clicked it off.

Mama's eyes shot open. "I was watching that."

Summer ignored her. "There's something I need to talk to you about."

Mama waved her away from in front of the TV. "I got a letter from your attorney yesterday."

"About the guardianship?" Summer blinked in surprise. She hadn't realized Don would get those out so quickly.

"Obviously." Mama rolled her eyes. "Unless I should be expecting more news from your lawyer that you could have told me yourself."

"The letter is a legal requirement." Summer tried to keep a grip on her patience. "It has to go to all of Max's relatives. I guess I didn't say anything because I assumed you'd realize I planned to be his guardian."

"You're sure you want to throw your life away over your brother's mistake?" The way Mama said it, not snarky, not barbed, but as if it were a legitimate question, knocked the air out of Summer.

"Max isn't a mistake." Somehow, Summer's voice was calm and controlled.

Mama shrugged. "Back in the day, that's what we called it when someone got knocked up without intending to. Believe me, I should know."

Summer swallowed back a wrathful response. She wasn't going to rise to the bait. Anyway, it wasn't as if Mama's words were a revelation. She'd never hidden the fact that TJ had been a mistake and Summer unwanted.

"If you ask me, you should send Max to his mama. Let her deal with her own mess." Mama waved Summer away from the TV again.

But Summer held her ground. "Stacy never wanted Max, Mama."

Mama shrugged. "Doesn't mean she shouldn't take care of her own problems."

"She doesn't even *know* him," Summer insisted. She didn't know why it mattered so much to her that Mama acknowledge that she would be the best choice for Max's guardian. "TJ wouldn't want him to go to her." Her brother had always said he was glad Stacy had left rather than stick around and resent Max the way Mama had resented them.

"TJ is dead," Mama said flatly. "Doesn't matter what he wants."

"You know what, Mama? Forget it." Summer turned the TV on and slammed the remote onto the arm of Mama's chair.

Mama looked at her, mouth open slightly, as if Summer had taken her by surprise. "You don't have to get all huffy. It's just the truth."

"It might be true that TJ is dead." Summer's voice cracked on the word. "But it's not true that it doesn't matter what he would want. Max is his *son*. And he loved that boy more than anything. I'm going to get guardianship of him with or without your help."

Mama blinked at her. "I don't see how you think I could help anyway."

Summer let out a breath. This was what she'd come here to talk about. But after all Mama had said, Summer wasn't sure she even *wanted* her money. Still, for Max's sake, she had to ask.

She forced herself to swallow her pride—and her anger. "The lawyer says that the court might think I'm not able to provide for Max. Financially. Danica had to close the dance studio." She hadn't told Mama that yet, and she rushed past it now so Mama couldn't add her insults. "I'm going to look for another job this week, but it would help if I had some money in the bank. I would pay you back," she finished desperately.

"Sell TJ's house."

"I'm going to." Summer swallowed painfully. For some reason, she'd wanted to keep this part from Mama. "But TJ had a lot of debts. The money from the house will have to go to those."

If Summer wasn't mistaken, a flash of sadness went through Mama's eyes. "He was gambling again?"

Summer nodded.

"Well." Mama shook her head. "I told him gambling would destroy him faster than drinking." The words were harsh, but something about Mama's tone of voice caught at Summer. Maybe, in her own way, Mama had understood, and even loved, TJ.

"So will you help me?" she whispered, letting her hope lift a little.

Mama blinked twice, then turned back to the TV. "I can't say whether I would if I could, but I can't, so it doesn't matter."

"What do you mean, you can't?" Summer asked.

"What does it sound like I mean?" Mama turned up the volume on the TV. "I don't have anything to give you. Why don't you go ask that Calvano family you like so much. Wasn't one of them friends with TJ?"

Summer closed her eyes. Benjamin had been best friends with TJ since middle school. How could Mama not even know his name?

"Benjamin offered." She didn't know why she felt compelled to say it—only that she wanted Mama to see that someone cared, even if she didn't. "But the lawyer said that would only work if we were married." She wondered if Mama even remembered that she and Benjamin had once dated.

"There you go then." Mama smirked. "Go ahead and marry him. He'll either leave you or resent you, but if you really want Max that badly, what does it matter?"

A desire to contradict Mama's prediction seethed through Summer, but she couldn't. Because she knew that was exactly what would happen. If she did marry Benjamin, he would only end up hating her for ruining his life. Weren't her parents living proof of it?

"I have to go, Mama." Summer stalked to the backyard to get Max, who cheered that it was time for pie. But Summer had a feeling she wouldn't taste a bite of it.

Chapter 18

"What a night." Benjamin groaned as he held The Depot's door open for Chloe.

"I thought you liked busy nights." Chloe eyed him as they stepped into the thick, still night air. Even the cricket's songs seemed stifled, and the dark forms of the mountains in the distance only seemed to trap the heat in the valley. "School must be starting soon. We always get our worst heat wave then."

"Yeah. Max starts the day after tomorrow." He'd learned that from the boy when he'd stopped over this morning—in the twenty minutes he'd had with Max before Summer had practically shoved Benjamin out the door, claiming she and Max had to finish school shopping. When Benjamin had offered to help, Summer had mumbled some lame excuse about how they might have to drive to Cypresswood to get some things and she didn't want to make him late for work.

Benjamin hadn't called her out on the flimsy excuse—which wasn't even the flimsiest she'd used over the past two weeks. Every day, it seemed she wanted less and less to spend time with him.

Well, she could fight it all she wanted, but he wasn't about to go back on his promise to take care of her and Max.

"Hello? Are you still here?" Chloe's voice penetrated through Benjamin's thoughts.

"What? Sorry. Did you say something?" Benjamin pulled his gaze off of the mountains.

"I asked how your finger is."

"Oh." Benjamin shifted the bag of leftover prime rib to his right hand and lifted his left. Blood had nearly soaked through the bandage on his index finger. "Rookie move."

"Distracted move," Chloe corrected.

Benjamin sighed. "Yeah. I guess."

"It will get better." Chloe patted his arm. "Give it time."

Benjamin nodded and said goodnight, then dropped into his car, every one of his muscles protesting from the training regimen Zeb had them all running. He let himself sink back into the Gremlin's restored seats.

Time was the one thing he didn't have. Max's guardianship hearing had been set for four weeks from now. And still Summer hadn't found a job, TJ's house wasn't ready to sell, and everything felt less certain than ever.

Trust in the Lord. Dad's advice had been rolling through Benjamin's head for the past two weeks, and he was trying. He really was. But sometimes he felt like if God didn't do something soon, Benjamin was going to have to take matters into his own hands.

And do what, he didn't know.

Maybe not marry her. He'd come to realize that Dad was probably right about that being a bad idea. But surely there must be *something* he could do.

He scrubbed his hands over his face and started the car. The time on the dashboard flipped over to midnight. He had to get to bed. He planned to be at Summer's bright and early tomorrow. It was Max's last day off before he started preschool, and Benjamin planned to make it a good one for all of them—no matter how much Summer protested. Max needed to remember what fun felt like. So did Summer. And so did he, for that matter.

The three weeks since TJ's death had felt like one long, somber unrelenting march through grief.

Tomorrow, they were going to smile and laugh and remember what it was to be alive. He was determined.

When he pulled into his driveway, everything was dark—he kept forgetting to leave the light above the door on for himself. Inside, he kept the lights off, navigating the spartan space easily. The living room boasted only a second-hand couch and a TV, and he hadn't had time yet to purchase a dining room table. But the bar stool at the kitchen island worked fine for one person.

After a quick shower to wash off the smells of the kitchen that always clung to him after work, he dropped into bed, sighing as the comfortable mattress he'd splurged on cradled his sore muscles. He set his alarm, then closed his eyes, looking forward to letting sleep take him. But he had just started to doze when his phone dinged. He pried his eyes open and snatched it up in case Summer needed something.

But the text was from Ian, one of his buddies from culinary school.

Got a proposition for you.

Benjamin set the phone down. Ian always had some wild plan or another. He could wait until morning to find out what it was this time.

But his phone dinged again. And then again.

Benjamin sighed and picked it up.

Kalibre is opening a second location, the first text read.

They asked for my recommendation for a chef. I gave them your name.

Benjamin blinked at the words. Kalibre was the hottest new restaurant in New Orleans, owned by Kendra Hill, a friend of Ian's who also happened to be a YouTube sensation who credited her success to Ian. She'd started

Kalibre as a thank you to him, although neither of them had anticipated how quickly it would take off.

They're opening a location in River Falls? Benjamin texted back, his curiosity getting the better of his exhaustion. It seemed an unlikely spot for a second location. The Depot did well, but Kalibre was much trendier, much more big city than small mountain town.

A laughing emoji greeted his comment.

Atlanta.

Benjamin stared at the screen for a moment. *As in Georgia?*

Obviously. He could practically hear Ian's dry response. *What do you think?*

Benjamin shook his head against his pillow. It was what he'd thought he wanted once—the acclaim of working for one of the hottest restaurants. And it would allow him a lot more culinary creativity than The Depot's steakhouse menu.

But he had responsibilities in River Falls. A house. A job. His family. And Summer and Max.

Even if he wasn't going to marry Summer, he *was* going to stay put to make sure they were cared for.

Thanks, man. But I can't.

He laid his phone down, telling himself to ignore it when it dinged with a reply.

But Ian was nothing if not persistent.

Three dings later, Benjamin relented again.

This is a once in a lifetime opportunity. You have to at least see the place.

I'm going in a few weeks. I'll buy you a ticket too.

And cover your hotel room.

Benjamin rolled his eyes. *What part of no do you not understand?*

The return text was quick. *Come on. If you say no after that, I'll stop bugging you. Besides, you know you want to see me.*

Benjamin set his phone down without replying. He already knew it would do no good.

Chapter 19

Mechanically, Summer went through the motions of getting Max ready for the day. She fed him breakfast, sent him to get dressed, timed him as he brushed his teeth. All of it felt so pointless.

She'd thought grief was supposed to lessen with time, but it had been three weeks, and her heart still ached as much as it had the day TJ died. The only good news was that the probate court had approved her as executor of TJ's estate. Which meant she could inventory his assets and get the house ready to sell. Where she and Max would go after that, she had no idea. She needed to find a job fast if they didn't want to end up homeless—or have to live with Mama, which might be worse.

But between taking care of Max and Mama, going through TJ's paperwork, and trying to keep herself from sinking under the surface of her own grief, she hadn't had much time or energy left for a job search.

Once Max started school tomorrow, she would start job hunting in earnest, she promised herself as she cleared the breakfast dishes. And looking for a small apartment. And—

"Benji is here!" Max called joyfully from the living room, and Summer's heart gave a forbidden leap. Sometimes it felt like his visits were the only bright spots in her days—which was why she had started cutting them shorter and shorter. She allowed him just enough time to play with Max while she showered, then talked to him for a few minutes about how the inventory was going or his training with his brothers or how her Mama was doing, then came up with some pretext or another for why she and Max had to get going.

She supposed he was probably on to her—but he always left without protest.

And never once had he even hinted that he intended to renew the proposal he'd made the day they'd spoken to the lawyer.

Because it wasn't real, she reminded herself. And she needed to stop wishing it was. Benjamin wasn't going to marry her and ride off into the sunset with her and take care of her and Max forever. She might like acting out fairy tales. But she didn't live in one.

His proposal had been him grasping at straws, trying to help her keep Max. Trying to fulfill what he felt was his duty to TJ.

Which was the same reason he kept visiting now.

But one day he would feel like he had fulfilled that duty in its entirety and stop coming.

Which would be for the best. Another thing she had to keep reminding herself, even though it left her with an empty feeling in her middle every time.

The Gremlin's engine shut off, but Summer waited for Benjamin's knock before she opened the door. No reason to let him think she had been anticipating his arrival.

"Hey, Maxerooni." He always greeted the boy first, and Summer wondered if that was to make sure she didn't get any mistaken ideas about why he was here. "Sunny." He'd taken to using Max's nickname for her, and Summer made a face. It was fine when her nephew said it, but when Benjamin did, it sounded ridiculous. It was bad enough that she had always felt like the very opposite of the name Summer. When someone pictured a girl named Summer, they pictured a shiny-haired blonde, all bubbles and sunshine. And they were inevitably disappointed when they instead found a reserved brunette.

Ignoring her look, Benjamin held up a paper bag with The Depot's logo. "I brought prime rib."

"Thank you." Summer took the bag gratefully. The leftovers he'd been bringing from work were a large part of the reason her grocery budget had stretched so far. She headed for the kitchen to put the food in the fridge while Benjamin dropped to the floor to play dinosaurs with Max.

"I'll be out in fifteen minutes," she said as she passed back through the living room on the way to the bathroom to grab a quick shower.

"Great. And then I thought we'd go to the petting zoo in Brampton."

"Sounds— Wait. What?" She stopped and spun toward him as Max shouted, "Boy oh boy! The zoo!"

Benjamin grinned, although she could see the traces of gravity his eyes had worn since TJ's death. "I thought we should do something special for Max's last day of summer."

"I don't know, Benjamin," Summer hedged. "I should really—"

But Benjamin set down the dinosaur he'd been holding and clasped his hands in front of him, begging, "Please, Sunny. Please, please, please." He nudged Max, who joined in with his own, "Please, please, please. I want to feed the goats."

"Me too!" Benjamin's eyes sparkled enough to almost hide the seriousness under the plea. "Don't deny it—you want to feed the goats too."

Summer shook her head, but she already knew she was defeated.

"Fine," she relented. "But only for a little while. We need to be home by lunchtime." She couldn't afford to take Max out to eat today.

Benjamin shook his head. "Not gonna happen. I packed a picnic."

Max's belly laugh rang out across the whole petting zoo as a goat nibbled his t-shirt, and Benjamin smiled down at Summer, who squatted next to him, petting a baby goat. Her answering smile lifted his heart about a million miles into the air.

It had been killing him to see how much more worn and tired she seemed every day, and he had wanted so badly to lift the burden for her. He felt like this trip to the zoo was doing the trick—at least for a little while. He only wished he could make it last.

Though the heat was as oppressive as ever, a welcome breeze stirred the air and lifted a strand of Summer's dark hair. The baby goat jumped to nibble at it.

Summer shrieked in surprise, grabbed at Benjamin's arm, and pulled herself up.

He chuckled. "Don't tell me you're afraid of a little goat."

"One that thinks it's a barber? Yes." Her hand was still on his arm, and she was standing close enough that he could smell the enticing apricot scent of her shampoo. No wonder the goat had wanted to nibble it.

"Thank you for this," she said quietly. "It was a good idea."

"And it didn't even hurt you to say that," Benjamin teased.

"Well, not that much," Summer conceded, her hair lifting again. A wisp brushed against Benjamin's arm, sending all kinds of sparks shooting through him. Without thinking, he brushed it back from her face, his eyes traveling to her lips, which opened in a little O.

She snatched her hand off his arm and backed away. "We should probably get some lunch. I'm sure Max is hungry. I'll go get the picnic basket from the car." Her cheeks were red, her movements jerky, and Benjamin tried to make himself regret flustering her. But he couldn't help but grin as she took off for the car. Maybe she had felt that electricity too.

Chapter 20

A strange chirping sound kept poking at Summer's ears, and she tried to force it away so she could pay attention to Benjamin. He was standing close to her, holding her hand and saying something that she couldn't really make out but that sounded soothing anyway.

But the incessant chirping drove her eyes open, and she had to blink a few times before she realized she wasn't holding anyone's hand—and she wasn't even standing. She was lying on the hill at the petting zoo, where they'd had their picnic, and the chirping was her phone.

She sat up, casting a panicked gaze around her, trying to figure out why she was alone, but her eyes quickly picked out Benjamin and Max feeding the goats in the pen at the bottom of the hill. Benjamin's hand rested on Max's shoulder, and a pang of longing went through Summer. She'd almost thought for a moment earlier that Benjamin wanted to—

But no. She couldn't let herself start wanting that. Couldn't let herself start wanting him to want her. She knew better.

Her phone continued its chirping, and she scooped it off the blanket. Don's name lit up her screen, and Summer swiped her sweaty palms on her shorts before answering.

"Hello?" Her greeting came out on a laugh as she watched Benjamin nudge his head into Max's arm, pretending, she supposed, to be a goat.

"Miss Ellis? This is Don Davis, the lawyer."

She pushed herself upright. "Yes?"

"I wanted to let you know that I sent out the notices of your petition for guardianship, as is required."

"Yes." She already knew that. He had emailed her the information the day after she met with him. Her eyes tracked to Benjamin and Max again. Their heads were bent close together, and both were smiling. Benjamin suddenly looked up and met her eyes, and her heart jumped toward him the same way the baby goat had jumped toward her hair earlier. He said something to Max, and then they both started toward her, wearing identical grins.

"I just got off the phone with a Stacy Pierce." Don's voice was grim, and Summer felt the smile melt off her face. She clutched at the phone.

"Max's mom," Don added, as if Summer didn't already know that.

"Yes?" Summer's voice was wispier than the silvery threads of cloud that barely brushed the sky. "What does—" She couldn't get enough air to finish the question.

"She plans to challenge the guardianship." Don's tone was compassionate, but the words slammed against Summer's solar plexus, and she felt herself physically wince.

"I don't— How can— She's never—" Summer fought to form a coherent thought.

Benjamin and Max were waving and making goofy faces at her, and Summer felt her lips tremble. *She* loved Max. *Benjamin* loved Max. Stacy didn't even know Max.

"Anyone has a legal right to challenge a guardianship," Don said calmly. "And she is the boy's mother, so—"

"She's as much his mother as I am the queen," Summer shot back, her anger suddenly firing her voice. "She's never even seen him. She dumped him in my brother's arms and never looked back."

"And the judge will take that into account."

Summer let out a breath. "So I don't have to worry?"

Don didn't say anything, and Summer gripped the phone tighter as Benjamin and Max reached her. Benjamin crouched in front of her, his brow lined with worry. *What's wrong?* he mouthed.

But she could only shake her head as Don spoke again. "It's hard to say. In most cases, judges prefer to keep parents and children together."

"She's never been—" Summer started again.

"I know," Don cut her off. "But it depends on whether the judge puts more emphasis on being with a familiar relative or on financial stability. I did some digging, and it looks like Stacy has a stable job. She owns a house. Doesn't have any debt to speak of."

Yeah, Summer wanted to shout, *because she hadn't spent a dime to help care for her son. She hadn't worked herself ragged like TJ had. Hadn't sat up with Max half the night when he was sick. Hadn't scrimped and saved to take him to the dinosaur exhibition at the museum.*

But Max had settled onto the blanket, and Summer wasn't about to say all of that in front of him.

"So what can I do?" she whispered.

Benjamin's hand wrapped around hers, and she knew she should pull away, but she couldn't. She needed his strength right now because she had completely run out of her own.

"There's not much else to do," Don said. "Keep looking for a job. Keep taking care of Max. And pray."

Summer grimaced. That didn't sound very promising. But she said, "Thank you," and hung up.

"What's going on?" Benjamin's hand still clutched hers, and she gave a halfhearted try to pull it away, but he didn't let go.

She eyed Max.

"Hey, Max." Benjamin's voice held a lightness that wasn't reflected in his serious eyes. "You can roll down the hill now if you want to."

"Really?" Max jumped up. "Boy oh boy! This is going to be fun!"

"He wanted to before," Benjamin explained. "But I told him he had to wait until you woke up. I didn't figure we wanted him doing that right after he ate."

"Good thinking." Summer attempted to smile but failed.

The moment Max started his roly-poly tumble down the hill, Benjamin turned to Summer. "What happened?"

She exhaled roughly. "Stacy is going to contest the guardianship."

"Stacy?" Benjamin's face darkened to an expression Summer had never seen on him before. "Did you tell Don that she's never even seen her son?"

"I did. He said the judge will take that into account. But apparently she has more financial stability. Plus she's his actual mom. I'm just his aunt."

Benjamin's hand tightened. "You're just the person who has loved him and cared for him since the day he was born," he said fiercely. "You know TJ would want you to be the one to raise him."

"I know." Summer dropped her head to her knees, trying to catch her breath. But the air felt too heavy, the fear too oppressive.

"We could get married." The whisper floated over her. She told herself it was the wind, or maybe a hallucination born out of her desperation.

But when she lifted her head, Benjamin was watching her, a question in his eyes.

Chapter 21

Benjamin's heart thudded slowly—too slowly—against his chest as he watched Summer's expression. Confusion. Fear. Doubt. Hope.

He seized on the last one. "It's the only way, Summer. We can provide for Max. Give him a happy home." And they would be happy together too, although he didn't add that. He knew Summer's only thought right now was for Max.

She dropped her eyes to the blanket, and Benjamin's resolve wobbled.

Trust in the Lord, Dad had urged.

But he *had* trusted. And the Lord hadn't seemed moved to do anything.

So now it was Benjamin's turn to step up. Before it was too late and Summer lost Max forever.

Besides, who was to say this wasn't how the Lord would take care of Max and Summer?

"Did you see me?" Max's little legs scampered back up the hill. He grinned around the puffs of his breath. "I went fast."

"You sure did, Maxerooni. Do it again, and I'll time you." Benjamin held up his left wrist to set his fitness watch. Max loved the stopwatch on it.

"Boy oh boy." Max clapped his hands. "I'm going to go super-fast."

"Be careful, Max." Summer's voice was shaky.

As soon as the boy started rolling again, Benjamin turned to Summer. "So? What do you say?"

She pressed her lips together. "You don't really mean it."

126

"I do." Benjamin reached for her hand. "You know I would do anything for Max." He so badly wanted to add, *and for you*, but he was afraid that would only spook her. It was better if she thought this was all for Max. There would be plenty of time for her to fall in love with him once they were married.

And if she never did . . . Well, he could live with that. As long as she got to keep Max.

Summer slid her palm out of his. "I don't know."

"Do you have a better idea?" He switched tactics.

She shook her head slowly.

He grabbed both of her hands this time and waited for her to look at him. "Summer, we can do this. For Max. And for TJ."

"How long was that?" Max burst back up the hill, and Benjamin checked his stopwatch.

"Thirty seconds."

Max cheered. "Time me again."

Benjamin started the watch, and Max tucked himself over the side of the hill.

"You can't lose him." Benjamin's eyes were still on Max, but his hands gripped Summer's tighter.

"I know," she whispered. And then, "Okay."

"Okay?" Benjamin turned to her with one eyebrow raised, trying to figure out if that meant what he thought it meant.

"Okay." Summer nodded. "Let's do it. Let's get married." Her face was somber, as if she'd just agreed to a business proposal rather than a marriage proposal. But a thousand pounds seemed to lift off of Benjamin's heart.

"Okay," he agreed, allowing himself the tiniest grin.

They stared at each other for a moment, and then Benjamin jumped to his feet.

"Come on." He held out a hand to help Summer up.

"Now?" The word was more of a gasp than a question.

Benjamin nodded. "The courthouse is just down the road, and Tennessee doesn't have a waiting period for a marriage license." One of the many things he'd researched after the first time he'd asked her.

"The courthouse?" Summer's forehead creased, and she didn't take his still-outstretched hand. "Don't you want your dad to do it?"

Benjamin averted his eyes.

Dad had made it clear that he didn't think this was a good idea. Benjamin hated the thought of going against his father's wishes. And yet, he felt like this was the right thing to do—and he was an adult, after all. He could make his own decisions.

"He has a lot going on." Benjamin waved off Summer's question. "He probably couldn't fit us in anyway. I'm sure he'll understand why we did it at the courthouse." He said it as much to convince himself as to convince her, but he couldn't help seeing a flash of his estranged brother Judah.

A low roll of anxiety went through him. What if this caused a rift between him and his family?

Well, then it caused a rift, he decided. He had to do what he felt was right, even if his family might not approve.

"Benjamin." Summer gave him a searching look, but Max reappeared before she could say anything else.

"Are you going to roll, Benji?" the boy asked eagerly.

"Sure, Maxerooni. And then we're going to go. We have to make one more quick stop on the way home." He snorted to himself. It wasn't like he'd ever really fantasized about his wedding. But he'd always thought it would be more than a "quick stop" in his day.

"For ice cream?" Max's eyes lit up.

"Nope." Benjamin was pretty sure his own eyes were more eager than the boy's. "Something better."

Chapter 22

This was all going so fast. It had only taken five minutes to drive to the courthouse. Another twenty to fill out the marriage application. Ten for them to process it.

And now here she was, walking into a sparsely appointed courtroom next to Benjamin, who was carrying Max.

Summer had spent hours—sometimes entire days—as a child dreaming about her future wedding. She had imagined herself in a dress fit for a princess, her hair swept off her neck, a gorgeous bouquet of flowers in her hands—and her very own Prince Charming beaming at her from the end of the aisle.

Instead, she was standing here in cutoff shorts, sweat matting her hair to her neck, her fingers clutching the paperwork they'd been given. Sure, the face of her imaginary Prince Charming had been awfully similar to Benjamin's face. But in all of her dreams, he had married her because he *wanted* her. Because he loved her. Not out of necessity.

But it didn't matter. They weren't doing this for love. They were doing it for Max. He was the only thing that mattered.

"Benjamin Calvano and Summer Ellis?" a judge with silver hair and glasses called from his bench at the front of the room, and Summer nearly turned and bolted.

But Benjamin grabbed her hand and called, "That's us."

They reached the bench, and the judge looked from one to the other of them, then to Max.

"And is this young fella your best man?" he asked Benjamin.

"Absolutely." Benjamin grinned at the judge as if getting married was something he did every day.

"All right. I see that you don't have rings?"

"Not yet," Benjamin said before Summer could answer.

"And have you written your own vows?"

"Uh no." This time Benjamin seemed a little uncertain. "Coming here today was kind of a spur of the moment thing."

The judge looked at both of them over the top of his glasses, and Benjamin pulled Summer closer, as if trying to convince him that they were really in love.

"I see. Well, then—" The judge took off his glasses. "This should be quick and easy."

Summer let out a shaky breath.

"It's nothing to be nervous about," the judge reassured her. "Are you ready to begin?"

"Let's do this," Benjamin said cheerfully, and Summer managed a mute nod.

The judge picked up a piece of paper and read, "Marriage is a legally binding contract that must be entered with mutual consent." He lifted his head and turned to Benjamin. "Do you, Benjamin Calvano, take Summer Ellis to be your lawfully wedded wife?"

"I do." Benjamin's voice was strong and sure, and it flipped Summer's heart upside down, even though she knew it wasn't real.

"And do you, Summer Ellis, take Benjamin Calvano to be your lawfully wedded husband?"

"I do." The words came out as the faintest whisper, but apparently that was good enough for the judge.

"Please repeat after me." He was facing Benjamin again. "I, Benjamin Calvano, take you Summer Ellis to be my wife."

"I, Benjamin Calvano, take you Summer Ellis—" Benjamin turned toward her, and Summer caught her breath as his eyes met hers. "Take you Summer Ellis to be my wife."

Oh, she wanted this to be real more than she'd wanted nearly anything in her life.

"To have and to hold from this day forward," the judge continued, and Benjamin repeated it.

"For better, for worse, for richer, for poorer, in sickness and in health, to love and to cherish, for as long as we both shall live." Benjamin repeated the rest of the vow, his gaze so serious and unwavering that Summer had to look down.

"Repeat after me, please, Summer." The judge said the first line, but Summer couldn't make her lips move. She couldn't do this to Benjamin. She knew he was willing to do anything for Max. But what would it mean for his life?

Benjamin squeezed her hand and offered her a reassuring smile.

The judge repeated the words, and Max squirmed to get down from Benjamin's arm, where he'd been waiting so patiently, and suddenly Summer knew what she had to do.

For Max.

"I, Summer Ellis," she repeated the judge's words, her voice only shaking a little. "Take you Benjamin Calvano, to be my husband."

She recited the rest of the vows without stumbling, until she got to the final words. She hesitated, then said, "for as long as we both shall live."

She swallowed roughly as the judge said, "Please join hands. Ah, you already did." He smiled indulgently, as if they really were newlyweds. "By virtue of the authority vested in me and in accordance with the laws of the state of Tennessee, I pronounce you husband and wife. Congratulations."

Summer blinked from the judge to Benjamin. "That's it?"

"You can kiss if you want," the judge said with a chuckle.

"Oh." Summer felt all of the blood in her body rush to her face. That wasn't what she'd meant. She'd only meant to ask if their wedding was really done—if they were really married—after less than five minutes.

But Benjamin waggled his eyebrows at her and stepped closer.

She had time only for a nervous, breathless laugh before his arms curved around her waist and his lips brushed against hers, light and gentle and so . . . perfect.

It was over almost before it had begun, and Summer accidentally sighed as he pulled away.

"My turn!" Max cried, and Summer bent over to let her nephew give her a sloppy kiss that entirely erased the feel of Benjamin's lips from hers.

Which was probably for the best.

"All right, I just need your signatures on the marriage license, and you'll be all set." He handed Benjamin a pen, and he signed it with a flourish, then passed it to Summer.

She quickly scratched her name onto the license, then dropped the pen as if it were on fire. The full weight of what she had just done crashed over her.

The judge signed his name to the certificate as well. "And it's official. You are free to go."

"Thank you." Benjamin scooped Max into one arm, then crooked the other, as if waiting for her to take hold of it.

She rolled her eyes. It wasn't like this was a church, or even a real wedding—but she took his arm anyway. And they exited the courtroom as husband and wife.

Chapter 23

Benjamin darted another glance at Summer, who sat in the passenger seat, chewing her lip and twining her fingers together.

He wanted to reach across the seat and grab her hand or . . . or *something* to mark this new phase of their relationship.

He nearly snorted out loud. New phase. They had just gotten *married*.

He still wasn't sure it had sunk in. Or maybe it had, given the joyful-nervous-surreal-terrified acceleration of his blood through his veins.

He was a husband now. And Summer was his *wife*.

He tried to picture introducing her that way: *This is my wife, Summer.*

The words sounded foreign. And yet . . . They sounded rather nice too.

Or they would if she looked more pleased about the situation.

He'd thought, when he'd kissed her in the courthouse, that maybe things were going to be easy. Maybe they were going to walk out of there and suddenly everything would fall into place, and they would be a genuine married couple.

But judging from the silent car ride—and he was as much to blame for that as she was—that wasn't going to happen.

Oh Lord, tell me I didn't just make the biggest mistake of my life, Benjamin prayed.

Then he forced himself to open his mouth. "Hey." He kept his volume low so he wouldn't wake Max, who had fallen asleep in the back seat, but Summer jumped as if his voice were a crack of thunder. "We should probably tell our families."

"Probably." Summer's voice was strained, her expression tense.

"Do you want to tell your Mama first or my family?"

"Your family," Summer answered without hesitation.

Benjamin's stomach sloshed with sudden nerves, but he nodded and pulled off onto a side road to send a quick text to the family chat, asking everyone to meet at Dad's after dinner.

The second half of the drive was quieter than the first, if that was possible.

When they got to River Falls, Benjamin hesitated. Which house should they go to, TJ's or his? He glanced at Summer, but she was staring out the window, lost to her own thoughts.

He turned toward TJ's house. All of Max's and Summer's things were there, so they'd all stay there for now, until they had it ready to sell. He could stop at his house—*their* house—to get some clothes on the way home from Dad's later.

When he turned into the driveway at TJ's house, Summer looked at him in surprise, as if not sure how they'd gotten there. Silently, she got out of the car.

They both leaned into the back seat at the same time from opposite sides, and Benjamin smiled at her. Her responding smile was small, but it was enough to ease Benjamin's fears just a little.

Together, they unbuckled Max, who cracked his eyes open sleepily as Benjamin carried him to the house.

He settled the boy on the couch, then looked around, suddenly at a loss.

"Now what?" Summer echoed his thoughts.

Benjamin exhaled. "I have no idea."

"At least that makes two of us."

Benjamin laughed, wishing suddenly that they could have a honeymoon and everything that a wedding usually included.

And then he had an idea. "I'm going to make a cake," he announced.

Summer blinked at him. "A cake?"

"A wedding cake," Benjamin specified. "To celebrate."

And, he thought but didn't say aloud, *to butter up his family.*

<hr/>

"Boy oh boy! Look at all the cars!" Max's enthusiasm only made Summer's heart slam harder against her throat as Benjamin steered her car into his dad's driveway.

"One. Two. Three. Four. Five," Max counted. "Plus us. That makes six."

"Good job, Maxerooni." Benjamin's voice vibrated with a tension Summer had never heard from him before. He was nervous—and that only made *her* more nervous.

What had they done? What would his family say? Would they hate her? Would they disown him?

Question after question whipped through her head.

"Is that the river back there?" Max asked as Benjamin parked behind a black SUV and turned off the engine.

Summer peered out the windshield, but it wasn't the soft pink reflection of the setting sun on the river behind the house that caught her eye. It was the house itself. It wasn't large or grand, but something about it, situated in the middle of the big, green lawn, with cheerful flowers lining the walk to the front door, made it feel just right. Like a *home.*

Like the kind of place she had never belonged.

"Ready?"

She could feel Benjamin's eyes on her, but she couldn't look at him. She shook her head.

"I'm ready," Max called eagerly. "Can we go swimming in the river?"

"Not today. But we'll come here lots," Benjamin promised. "And we can swim and fish and skip rocks."

"Boy oh boy!" Max's shout nearly rocked the car, and Summer's chest loosened a little, thinking of Max having that kind of life.

Benjamin opened his door, and Summer followed suit.

"I'll grab Max if you want to carry the cake," Benjamin offered.

Summer nodded and retrieved the delicacy Benjamin had somehow managed to conjure into existence this afternoon. She'd watched him for a little while, fascinated by the ease and certainty with which he combined ingredients. But she'd made her escape when he offered to teach her how to pipe on the scalloped edges of the frosting using an improvised piping bag.

That would have required them to get too close. Maybe even to touch.

And *that*, in turn, would have led her to want this marriage to be real. It would have led her to want *him* to want her as his wife. And that, she knew from painful experience, was the surest way to heartache.

She carried the cake around the car, meeting Benjamin on the other side. He had boosted Max onto his shoulders, and the giggling boy called, "Giddy-up, dino."

"Roar," Benjamin offered.

And then they were walking toward the house side by side.

She wanted to ask Benjamin what they were going to say, how she should act, if they could maybe just turn around and go home without telling anyone.

But the front door opened, and his brother Joseph stepped out. Of all of Benjamin's siblings, he was probably the one she knew best, since he was the closest in age to Benjamin, although she was pretty sure there was still a five- or six-year age gap between them.

"It's about—" Joseph started, but then his eyes landed on Summer and widened. She wondered if Benjamin had already said something to his family in his text. But Joseph said, "Is that a cake?"

A relieved giggle slipped between her lips, and Benjamin grinned from her to his brother. "As a matter of fact, it is."

"Good. Mrs. Kerigan's dog needed emergency surgery this afternoon—managed to eat five golf balls." He shook his head. "I didn't even have time to eat dinner before Ava whisked me over here." He jogged down the steps past them, calling over his shoulder, "I have to grab the diaper bag from the car. Don't start eating that without me."

"No promises," Benjamin called back, his voice close to normal. "Come on." He swung Max down from his shoulders, taking the boy's hand in one of his and resting the other lightly on Summer's back. A thrill traveled up her spine, but she ignored it. He was only trying to make their marriage look genuine for the sake of his family.

When they reached the top of the porch steps, he let his hand fall, exhaled quickly, sent her a weak smile, and opened the door.

A tumult of conversation and laughter filtered out into the night, and Summer hesitated. Benjamin nodded her through, but Max scrambled past her.

"Well, who do we have here?" a voice she recognized as Pastor Calvano's asked warmly.

Summer made herself step through behind her nephew. The living room was crowded with men and women and babies, all of them turning their eyes toward the newcomers. Their smiles were warm and inviting, but still Summer would have turned and fled if it weren't for Benjamin's solid presence behind her.

"It's me, Max," Max said cheerfully. "I love your house. Benji said we can swim and fish and skip rocks in your river."

"Well, it's not my river." Pastor Calvano smiled at Max, but Summer caught the questioning look he directed at Benjamin, who seemed to shift uncomfortably. "But you sure are welcome to come and do all of those things anytime."

Benjamin cleared his throat. "I think you all know Summer. TJ's sister."

There were sympathetic nods and murmurs and hellos, but all Summer could do in response was stand there, clutching the cake.

"But she may not know who *we* all are." A dark-haired woman smiled at Summer. "There are a lot of us. I'm Ireland. Asher's wife." She laid a hand comfortably on the knee of the man sitting with his arm around her.

Summer smiled weakly. She knew Asher was the park ranger who had put together the search for TJ.

"And that's our daughter, Caroline." Ireland pointed to an infant who was snuggled on Zeb's lap, chewing on a board book. Zeb nodded to her, and Summer nodded back. She still needed to thank him for the night he had come over and walked her through the next steps after TJ's death.

The door behind them opened, and Benjamin gently nudged her forward to make room.

"Oh good, you didn't eat it yet," Joseph said as he came in. "What are we waiting for?"

"We're doing introductions," a red-haired woman holding a baby boy answered. "I'm Ava, Joseph's wife." She stood and passed the baby to her husband. "And this little guy is Noah."

"I'm going to go change him. No cake without me," Joseph warned again.

As he disappeared with the baby, another woman spoke up. "I'm Lydia."

Summer nodded. It would be hard not to know who Lydia St. Peter was. Her music was everywhere. "And this is my husband Liam. Our daughter Mia babysat Max a few weeks ago."

"Max said Mia was his favorite babysitter ever." It was the first time Summer had spoken since arriving, and her voice came out rather croaky, but no one seemed to mind. Benjamin shot her an approving look.

"She was," Max confirmed. "I hope she can babysit again. It's way better than going to Grandma's."

Summer felt her face fire red. She only left Max with Mama on rare occasions, and only for a few minutes at a time in an emergency. Still, after Mama's stunt at the funeral, she could only imagine what this family would think about her letting him have any contact with his grandmother at all.

But Lydia only smiled at Max. "I'm sure she'd love that."

"And we're Simeon and Abigail," a woman on the couch said, nodding to the man next to her, who held a baby girl against his shoulder and rubbed her back gently. "And our daughter Genevieve. You won't believe this, but I was actually going to get your number from Benjamin so I could call you tonight."

Summer stared at her blankly. "Why?"

After the word came out, she realized it probably sounded rude, but before she could fix it, Abigail was gushing, "I work part time at the Book Den downtown." Summer nodded. She had seen Abigail there when she'd brought Max in for story time. And she'd also seen the table promoting Abigail's forthcoming book, *Memories of the Heart*, which she had preordered a copy of.

"Anyway," Abigail went on, "one of the girls who was working there for the summer is leaving for college this weekend, and she kind of forgot to tell us until today. Our owner, Ruth, was about to put an ad up for the job, but I told her I already had the perfect candidate."

Summer nodded. That was nice. But what did it have to do with her?

"She means you," Benjamin prompted with a low chuckle.

"Me?" Summer stared. How had Benjamin's sister-in-law even known she needed a job?

"Yes," Abigail went on, her cheeks glowing. "The hours are totally flexible, and the store isn't open nights, so you'll be able to be home for Max. And the pay is decent. Anyway, Ruth says the job is yours if you want it."

"I— Well—" Amazement swallowed Summer's words.

"You don't have to decide right now," Abigail offered. "I know it's probably not exactly what you were looking for. But I just thought I'd mention it."

"No. I mean, yes. I'll take it." She wasn't in any position to turn down a job offer.

"Great." Abigail smiled as if they were old friends. "Come by the store sometime, and I'll introduce you to Ruth, and you two can work everything out. You're going to love her."

"Love who?" Joseph strode back into the room, flying his little boy in front of him like an airplane.

"Ruth," Abigail answered.

"She's a character." Joseph grinned. "Her cats have her wrapped around their tails. Now, are we going to eat that cake or what?"

Benjamin nodded and sent Summer a look that she was pretty sure was supposed to be reassuring but that instead set every nerve in her body on edge.

He took the cake from her hands, and she felt suddenly as if she'd lost a shield.

He started toward a hallway that led off of the living room, and Summer followed him, barely hearing as Max chatted with one of Benjamin's siblings as they all followed.

Too soon, they reached a cheerful kitchen with a large island and an even larger dining table. Benjamin set the cake on the counter and pulled off the cover.

"Wow, Benjamin," Ava gasped. "That's beautiful. Did you make it?"

"What's the occasion?" a male voice questioned, but Summer couldn't place which of the brothers said it.

"Who cares? Let's eat it." Joseph strode forward eagerly.

"Actually." Benjamin held up a hand, and Joseph's eager expression fell. "There's something I—we—have to tell you first."

He moved closer to Summer but didn't touch her. "We— Uh—" He cleared his throat. Then he turned and looked at Summer, as if she was the one he was telling. "We got married today."

Chapter 24

The kitchen had fallen eerily silent, but Benjamin couldn't take his eyes off of Summer. He needed her to know that no matter what his family said, no matter how they reacted, it wasn't going to change his mind. That had been locked since the moment he said, *I do.*

"Wow, I don't think I've ever heard this family this quiet." Joseph's joke broke the silence, and then everyone was talking at once.

Summer's eyes widened, and Benjamin caught her hand, fearing suddenly that if he didn't anchor her in place, she would flee.

"You're kidding, right?" A coherent voice finally broke through the chaos. "This is one of your crazy pranks."

Benjamin glared at Joseph. He knew the comment was meant as a joke, but Summer didn't.

"I'm not kidding," he said quietly.

"But y'all are so young," Joseph protested.

"Carly and I were younger than they are when we got married," the usually quiet Zeb spoke up. Benjamin sent him a grateful look. He'd always known Zeb was his favorite sibling.

"You and Carly were dating from the time you were babies," Simeon pointed out.

"Why so suddenly?" Lydia looked hurt, and Benjamin's heart gave a pang. He may have only met his oldest sibling two years ago, but they had become close almost immediately.

He toed the tiles. "I'm sorry we didn't invite y'all. It was kind of a spur-of-the-moment thing." At least here his reputation as the young and impulsive one should serve him well. He thought about adding an explanation about Max's guardianship and Stacy and why it had been an emergency, but he didn't want to get into that with Max standing right here. Besides, it didn't matter how he and Summer had come to be married. It only mattered that they *were*.

"You two are so sneaky." Ireland waved a finger at them that baby Caroline tried to catch. "I didn't even know you were back together. I thought—"

Benjamin sent her a look, and she broke off. "Congratulations!" She launched herself forward and hugged first Benjamin and then Summer.

The rest of his siblings followed, some looking stunned, some pleased, some uncertain.

Dad hung back, and Benjamin watched him anxiously. He was sure at least some of his siblings suspected the motive for their quick marriage—but dad *knew*. And had advised against it.

Finally he approached, smiling softly, though Benjamin could see the worry in his eyes. He turned to Summer first. "Welcome to the family. I hope you know what you've gotten yourself into." The words were light-hearted, sparking a sprinkle of laughter, yet underneath them, Benjamin could hear his admonition from their last conversation—that marriage was a promise before God.

Dad turned to Benjamin with a solemn look and shook his hand. "Congratulations, son. I trust that you'll be a good husband. And father."

"Yes, sir." Benjamin swallowed sharply. He had exactly zero idea how to do that. But he trusted he would figure it out.

"Not to be that guy," Joseph called. "But do you think we can eat that cake now? I'm starved."

"All right. Let's have a prayer first," Dad replied.

Across the room, every head bowed, and Benjamin kept his hand wrapped around Summer's. Max, who had been playing peek-a-boo with baby Genevieve stopped and folded his hands. Benjamin grinned at the boy, then closed his eyes as Dad began to pray. "Lord God, you have made man for woman and woman for man. Bless Summer and Benjamin in their marriage. Lead them to support and love and cherish one another all of their days. Help them, Lord, to build each other up and encourage one another in your love. Be at the center of their marriage always, and guide them to serve you together day by day. In Jesus' name we pray. Amen."

"Amen," the others all murmured, and then there was a surge toward the island. Benjamin cut the cake, and Summer passed out the pieces, and his heart soared with renewed hope. They made a good team. Handing out cake. Leading princess parties. And now, as husband and wife.

Summer's cheeks had taken on a soft pink glow, and she was even smiling a little as her eyes swept over the commotion in the room.

"Did we get everyone?" he asked.

"I think so." Summer handed him a plate and took one for herself. "Wait. Where's your dad?"

Benjamin scanned the room, but there was no sign of Dad. His stomach dropped. Dad rarely left in the middle of a family gathering—unless something was wrong.

"I should go find him," he said quietly. "Will you be okay in here by yourself?"

"I don't think I'll exactly be by myself." Summer nodded toward the full room. "But, yes, I'll be okay."

Benjamin gave her arm a quick squeeze—resisting the urge to brush a kiss over her temple too—and ducked out of the room. In the hallway, he took a few deep breaths, then edged toward Dad's office, his stomach knotting the same way it had when he was ten and Mama had sent him to tell his father that she had caught him saying a bad word.

Dad didn't get angry.

He got disappointed.

Which was so much worse.

And Benjamin could only imagine how disappointed he must be right now. Benjamin had deliberately disregarded Dad's wishes.

The office door was open, and Dad must have heard Benjamin coming because he called, "Come in, son," even though his back was to the door as he faced the window that looked out over the river.

"Dad." Benjamin didn't know what else to say.

Dad turned toward him. "Sorry. I just needed a minute."

Benjamin swallowed. "I know you're upset. But Summer found out that Max's mom is going to challenge her guardianship. And Don thought Summer might lose. And I know TJ wouldn't want that." The words came out in a tumbling rush. He had to make Dad understand. "I thought about calling you, but I knew you would try to talk us out of it." He dared to look up and meet Dad's eyes. "And I really think it was the right thing to do."

Dad didn't say anything for a moment. Then he shook his head and crossed the room, planting a hand on Benjamin's shoulder. "I'm not upset. Or disappointed," he added, as if he realized that was what Benjamin feared most. "I only hope you understand how serious your marriage vows are."

"I told you—" Benjamin's voice was firm. "It's not a vow I intend to break."

"And Summer?" Dad asked quietly. "She plans to keep her vows too?"

"Of course." Benjamin brushed off the trace of doubt the question raised deep down in his gut. Just because Summer wasn't in love with him didn't mean she hadn't been sincere in her vows. "Come on. You have to try the cake."

As he led Dad to the kitchen, Benjamin solidified his resolve to make his wife fall in love with him.

Now all he had to do was figure out how.

Chapter 25

The air clung to Summer like a second skin as she sat in the dark on the deck steps. But she couldn't bring herself to retreat into the air-conditioned house. Benjamin had offered to tuck Max in, as if he'd sensed that she needed some time to herself after returning from his dad's, and she'd gratefully hugged Max and made her escape out here.

The crickets trilled loud and fast, but clouds blotted out the stars over the mountains, and Summer wondered if they were in for a storm. Because there sure was one going on inside of her right now.

She shouldn't have married Benjamin. But she'd *had* to marry Benjamin.

Except.

Maybe she hadn't. Not if it was true that his sister-in-law had found a job for her.

Which meant that she had trapped him for no reason.

Unless . . .

She pulled out her phone and searched for the term "annulment."

She tapped on the first result and started to read, but before she'd gotten to the grounds for an annulment, she heard the patio door open behind her.

Quickly, she clicked the phone off and set it down. There was no reason to hide it from Benjamin—she had a feeling he would be relieved—but guilt coiled in her stomach all the same.

His footsteps fell lightly on the deck, and then he lowered himself next to her. Though the steps weren't wide, he managed to leave enough space between them that not even their sleeves brushed.

"This has been quite a day." He sounded half amused, half uncertain, and Summer felt her lips lift at the absurdity of it all.

"Sorry if my family was overwhelming," he added. "You'll get used to them after a while."

"They weren't overwhelming."

Benjamin snorted. "Liar."

Summer couldn't help the laugh. "Maybe a little overwhelming. In a good way." She'd never experienced family life like that before. They'd all been so warm and welcoming, so loud and joking, so open and encompassing, that it had felt a bit surreal. Like she'd been picked up and dropped in someone else's life. It seemed like a good life—possibly a wonderful life—but it wasn't her life.

"I feel bad that we didn't tell your mama yet," Benjamin said.

Summer slid her right hand over her left, but then realized she was rubbing the spot where she'd be wearing a wedding ring if this were a real marriage and stopped.

"It's better if we wait until the morning." Summer didn't add that there was less chance that Mama would be drunk then, but Benjamin's nod said he understood.

"Your dad doesn't approve, does he?" she asked quietly.

Benjamin sighed. "It's not that he doesn't approve." He seemed to be choosing his words carefully. "He just wants to make sure we understand what marriage means. That it's a commitment. He's afraid we rushed into it too quickly."

"Maybe we did." Summer could barely lift her voice above a whisper, but even with the space between them, she felt Benjamin stiffen. "If we had waited just a couple of hours," she pressed on, "I would have known about the job at the bookstore, and then you wouldn't have had to . . ." She exhaled, letting the rest of the sentence hang unspoken.

Benjamin didn't say anything for a while, and she desperately wanted to know what he was thinking. But she wasn't brave enough to ask. Maybe he would bring up the idea of an annulment himself.

Finally, he said, "Even if we had waited, we can't know that it would be enough. Especially with Stacy in the picture."

"So you don't think we made a mistake?"

"No." This time his answer was immediate. Then, slower, he asked, "Do you?"

Summer hesitated. In some ways, today felt like the best thing that had ever happened to her. But she also knew it was all an illusion. And she was afraid that the longer it went on, the more it was going to hurt that it wasn't real.

She could feel Benjamin watching her, and finally she whispered, "No. I guess not."

"Ouch." On its surface, Benjamin's chuckle was lighthearted, but she could hear the note of regret under it, and she resolved to do some more research on annulment for his sake.

"Do you want to watch a movie or something?" he asked, sounding like his old cheerful self.

Summer suddenly had a vision of snuggling on the couch in her new husband's arms.

"I—" Her mouth had gone dry, and she had to swallow before she could try again. "I think I'm going to go to bed. It's been a long day."

"Okay." If Benjamin minded, he didn't let on. He stood, and then his hand was dangling in her face, and she realized he wanted to help her up.

They'd held hands enough over the past few weeks, as they were united in grief, that it should have been natural to place her hand in his. But that had been as friends. Now they were husband and wife.

Did he intend to . . . do other husband and wife things?

Slowly, she raised her hand to his and let him tug her upward. The momentum of his pull nearly sent her tumbling down the steps, and he wrapped a hand around her arm to catch her.

His eyes held hers, and they were close enough that he could have lowered his lips to hers if he wanted to.

Summer suddenly forgot to breathe.

"Summer." His whisper unfroze her, and she sprang out of his grip and up the steps.

"Goodnight," she called over her shoulder. "Thanks for everything." She rolled her eyes at herself. She was thanking him as if he'd helped carry her groceries into the house—not like he'd given up his whole life to marry her.

"Goodnight." Benjamin's reply sounded far away, as if he were still at the far edge of the deck.

But Summer wasn't brave enough to look back.

Chapter 26

Benjamin stuck his face into the flowers he'd set in the middle of the table, pulling in a deep breath of the lightly sweet hibiscus blossoms, then stepped back and surveyed them with a critical eye. He suddenly wished his mama were here, both so she could advise him on the flowers and so she could see him all grown up and married.

He snorted to himself as he hurried back to the stove to flip the omelet crackling there. Being married might make him feel all grown up. But wishing for his mama sure didn't.

Still, he would have liked her to know that he was a husband now. Not that last night had gone how he'd ever imagined his wedding night would go. Standing out there on the deck in the dark, he had yearned to kiss Summer properly, something more substantial than the light brush of their lips at the courthouse—although, truth be told, even that had set his heart on fire.

But she wasn't ready. She'd made that much clear with her hasty escape. Benjamin had tried to watch a movie by himself, but eventually he'd given up and decided to go to bed. In the hallway, he'd stood staring at her closed bedroom door for a full five minutes, wondering if they'd ever share a bedroom. And then he'd turned and gone into TJ's room, reminding himself that they had all the time in the world for their relationship to grow—after all, they'd just vowed to stay together as long as they both lived.

Benjamin flipped the omelet onto a plate and added salt to the hash browns, trying to banish the question that had autoplayed through his sleepless brain last night: *Do you think we made a mistake?* It had been Summer's question, and yet, in his head, he heard it not only in her voice but in Dad's and his siblings' and even his own.

He didn't think they'd made a mistake. But he had a feeling he might be the only one.

"Boy oh boy! It sure smells good in here!" Max bounded into the kitchen, his enthusiasm pulling Benjamin out of his worries.

"Thanks, Maxerooni. Happy first day of school."

The boy had already dressed himself in a pair of shorts and a misbuttoned plaid shirt. "You're looking sharp." Benjamin brought the eggs and hash browns to the table, where he'd already set out cut fruit and orange juice. Then he knelt in front of Max. "Here. Let's tweak this a little." He redid the buttons, then ruffled the boy's hair and stood, startling to find Summer in the room. He couldn't exactly identify the expression on her face—surprise, or maybe hope—but he liked it.

"Good morning." He smiled at her and pulled out a seat at the table. "Breakfast is served."

"Oh boy!" Max climbed into the chair Benjamin held.

Benjamin looked at Summer, shrugged, and then pulled out another chair for her, rejoicing in the sprinkle of her slight laugh.

"You didn't have to do all of this," she murmured as she sat.

"Of course I did. Max needs a good breakfast for his first day of school. Hibiscuses are still your favorite flowers, right?"

Summer nodded, and this time he was certain of the look in her eyes: delight. "Where did you even find them this early in the morning?"

"There's a hibiscus bush in my backyard." It was one of the things that had drawn him to the house. "You're going to love it."

He dished out food for everyone, then sat across from Summer and Max and folded his hands. They did the same, and a whoosh of nerves suddenly coursed through Benjamin. He'd prayed with both of them plenty of times, but somehow this felt different. He'd never prayed as the head of an actual family before.

"Dear Jesus," he began, "we want to thank you for this new day, for Max's new school year, and for our new marriage." He had to stop for a second as the enormity of the word hit him. "Please bless us in the ways that you know are best. Help us to trust in you—" He faltered as he suddenly wondered if marrying Summer had shown a lack of trust, but then pushed aside the thought. "And help us to give you glory in all things. In Jesus' name. Amen."

Max's exuberant "Amen" almost drowned out Summer's quiet one, but Benjamin had lifted his head in time to see her lips move with the word.

"Can I have some orange juice?" Max's eager question tugged Benjamin's eyes from Summer just as the boy pushed onto his knees and reached for the juice pitcher.

"Careful, Max—" But before Benjamin could finish his sentence, Max lost his grip on the pitcher. It hit the table with a crash and a great cascade of juice.

Both Summer and Benjamin shoved their chairs back from the table as juice poured onto their laps, but Max seemed to be frozen in place, juice soaking into his shirt.

Benjamin raced for the paper towels and tossed a handful to Summer, who had scooped Max away from the table. She started to blot at the boy while Benjamin attempted to rescue the food, but both the omelets and the hash browns were soaked in orange juice.

"Maybe ask for help next time, okay, Maxerooni?" Benjamin said as he tossed the ruined breakfast.

A loud wail made him spin back toward the table.

"I didn't mean to," Max cried, burying his head in Summer's shoulder.

"I know, sweetie." Summer rubbed her hand over Max's back, sending Benjamin a reproachful look.

He gazed back helplessly. He hadn't been trying to upset the boy. Just to remind him to ask for help.

"It's okay, Max," he tried again. "Let's all go change out of our wet clothes, and then we should have time to eat some cereal before we go."

"I don't want to change." Max's voice was muffled by Summer's shoulder. "Daddy bought me this shirt for the first day of school."

Oh man. Benjamin swiped at his own wet clothes. If Max's were half as wet as his, there was no way he could wear them to school.

He raised his eyebrows toward Summer, but she responded with an uncertain shrug.

"Okay, well . . ." Benjamin searched his mind, but he'd never been a parent before, and he had no idea what to do.

If TJ was here, he would have a simple solution. Benjamin had seen that man head off many a meltdown when it came to Max. But TJ wasn't here. It was up to Benjamin and Summer to figure out what to do.

"What if you wore one of your dad's shirts?" he asked, patting himself on the back for the flash of insight.

"Really?" Max lifted his tear-streaked face.

"They would all be way too big." Summer's tone said that Benjamin had only made the problem worse. "He'd trip over them."

"What about that Batman one that shrank in the wash?" Though TJ had been disappointed, he'd gotten a good laugh out of it and said he planned to give it to Max one day. "Does he still have that one?" He kept himself from correcting his use of the present tense.

"Maybe," Summer said slowly. "I haven't had a chance to go through his clothes yet."

"We'll go look for it. You go get changed, and we'll meet you out here in a few minutes." He held out his hand to Max, who took it with a little sniffle. "I'm sorry, Benji."

Benjamin squatted in front of the boy, planting his hands on Max's shoulders, the same way Dad had always done with him. "It was an accident, Max. And I forgive you. You don't need to worry about it anymore, okay?"

Max nodded solemnly, and Benjamin pulled him into a quick hug, closing his eyes at the feel of the small, trusting arms around his neck.

It only took a few minutes to find the shrunken t-shirt in TJ's closet. Though it hung to Max's knees, at least it had brought a smile back to the boy's face. Benjamin sent him back to the kitchen, where he could hear Summer pulling out bowls and cereal. He quickly changed out of his own orange juice-soaked clothes, shaking his head at himself—his first day as a husband and father was off to a rocky start. But at least it could only go up from here.

Chapter 27

Summer was pretty sure she was more nervous than Max as they approached the school. She wasn't worried that Max wouldn't be able to handle saying goodbye—she was worried that *she* wouldn't. Her nephew raced ahead of her and Benjamin, and she reminded herself that school was only half a day.

"Maybe that shirt wasn't my best idea ever," Benjamin said with a rueful chuckle as the long t-shirt flapped around Max's knees.

But Summer shook her head. Benjamin had been an absolute hero, coming up with that solution. "TJ would like it." She reached to pull her hair, damp and sweaty from the humid morning, into a quick ponytail.

Max was already at the school door, and he gestured them forward impatiently.

Benjamin touched a hand to Summer's back to guide her through first, and a ripple of goosebumps traveled up her arm. She stepped through quickly, leaving his hand behind and telling herself that the goosebumps were from the sudden chill of the air conditioning in the school.

"Wow." Benjamin sounded awed as he stepped through the door. "Everything looks so different."

Summer nodded. The school had been renovated several years ago, and she barely recognized it from the days when she went there. They followed a sign that pointed toward the preschool classroom. Inside, the room sported four different colored walls. A few children had already arrived and were busy exploring the space. A woman dressed even more vibrantly than the room approached them with a wide smile, her friendly eyes sparkling behind purple glasses. "Good morning. What's your name?" Her voice was as cheerful as her clothes.

"I'm Max." Max shuffled back into Summer a little bit.

"It's nice to meet you Max." The woman held out a hand to Max, who shook it dutifully. "I'm Mrs. Rayburn. I like your shirt."

"It was my dad's," Max announced proudly. "But it shrank in the wash."

Mrs. Rayburn smiled, her eyes going to Benjamin, then Summer. "And is this your mom and dad?"

"Nope. My dad is in heaven," Max answered before Summer could get past her mortification enough to explain. All of the phone calls she'd made over the past few weeks, and somehow it hadn't occurred to her to call Max's teacher.

"Oh my goodness. I'm so sorry." Despite the sympathy in her voice, Mrs. Rayburn's smile didn't falter. "So you must be . . ." She turned to Summer.

"This is my Aunt Sunny," Max introduced her. "And my Benji."

"I— Oh." Mrs. Rayburn's smile still didn't budge, though Summer could see her confusion through it.

"I'm Summer." She held out a hand to the teacher. "Max's aunt. I have temporary guardianship of Max, and hopefully permanent guardianship soon. And this is my . . ." She couldn't quite get the word husband to roll off her tongue. "This is Benjamin."

She watched Benjamin's hand land in Mrs. Rayburn's but didn't have the courage to look at his face.

"It's so nice to meet you both." Mrs. Rayburn was still smiling away. "Would you like me to take a picture of the three of you, and then you two can be on your way and we can get to having some fun?"

"Yes," Max said definitively. "Do we get to play with those dinosaurs?" He pointed to a bin in the corner of the room.

"Oh yes. Sometimes."

Max shot an arm in the air, yelling, "Boy oh boy! I like school!"

"Calm down, Max," Summer murmured, but the teacher didn't seem in the least bothered by his enthusiasm.

Mrs. Rayburn took the phone Benjamin held out to her and glided a few steps backwards. "Get close to each other," she called.

Before Summer could move, a strong arm wrapped around her waist, and she sucked in a breath as Benjamin snugged her close to him. His other hand rested on Max's shoulder in front of him.

"Say preschool," Mrs. Rayburn called.

Max and Benjamin both repeated the word obediently, but Summer couldn't speak past the breath she was holding.

"Can I play now?" Max asked as Mrs. Rayburn passed the phone back to Benjamin.

With Mrs. Rayburn's cheerful, "Yes," he took off without a backward glance.

"Pickup is at noon." Mrs. Rayburn smiled them to the door. "Y'all have a good morning, and we'll see you then." She disappeared back into the classroom, and Summer let out a breath.

"You okay?" Benjamin was studying her a little too closely, and Summer let herself take one last peek through the door, but Max must have gone straight for the corner with the dinosaurs.

She nodded. "That was easier than I thought it would be. And harder."

Benjamin nodded too. "Are you ready to go?"

"No." But she started toward the exit.

Benjamin held the door open for her, and then they were back out in the bright, stifling heat. It was the kind of day TJ would have said licked you in the face.

Benjamin was unusually quiet on the walk home, and Summer's mind kept going back to the question she knew she should ask him: Did he want to get an annulment?

He'd said last night that he didn't think they'd made a mistake. But now that he'd had the whole night to think about it, maybe he'd changed his mind.

Somehow, she couldn't bring herself to ask. Because she knew what he had said last night was right—even the part-time job at the bookstore might not be enough to win her guardianship of Max over Stacy. She and Benjamin would need to stay married until after the hearing. And then they could visit the topic of an annulment.

She'd done some more research in bed last night, and as long as they didn't consummate their marriage, an annulment was still a possibility. Given that they hadn't even kissed, aside from at the courthouse, she was pretty confident that wasn't going to be a problem.

A little cavity opened in the middle of her chest, filling her with the desire for this to be more, but she stuffed it full of reminders that she was doing this for Max, not for herself.

"Next stop?" Benjamin asked as they walked up the driveway at TJ's house.

Summer grimaced. "I still think I should go by myself."

"We're going together." His tone didn't leave room for argument, and Summer didn't try.

The truth was, even though she didn't want Benjamin to come along, she was pretty sure she needed him there for this.

"We'll bring some cake," he said cheerfully. "No one can be upset when there's cake involved."

Summer nodded. But she knew it was going to take a lot more than cake to make telling Mama go smoothly.

Benjamin could feel the anxiety radiating off of Summer from the other side of the car. He wanted to reach over and take her hand, but she clutched the plastic container holding the leftover pieces of cake so tightly that he wouldn't have been able to get a finger in edgewise.

He wished he could tell her that they didn't have to do this.

But she couldn't exactly go through life without telling her mama she was married.

Then again, it had sure seemed like not telling people was Summer's plan at school this morning. He hadn't missed the way she'd stopped short of calling him her husband to Mrs. Rayburn. Who that sweet, smiling teacher thought he was, was anyone's guess.

He pulled into the driveway and parked the car. They both sat for a moment, and he offered a quick prayer that this would go well, for Summer's sake. After the way her mama had behaved at TJ's funeral, Benjamin didn't much care if she approved of this marriage or not—but he didn't want things to be any harder for Summer than they already were.

"Come on." He touched a hand lightly to Summer's, though what he really wanted to do was pull her close and protect her from whatever they were about to face. "Let's do this. And then it will be done."

She nodded, and they got out of the car and started toward the house. At the door, Summer hesitated, then lifted her hand as if she was about to knock. Then she dropped it and instead fished a key out of her purse. She unlocked the door, knocking as she opened it. "It's just me, Mama," she called.

"Of course it's you. Who else would it be? Stop letting all the cold air out." Mrs. Ellis's voice was none too welcoming, but Benjamin stepped in behind Summer, who shot him an apologetic look.

Her mama sat in a worn recliner on the other side of the room, near a large television. She didn't bother to look away from it as she called, "Grass is getting long. You here to mow?"

Indignation clawed at Benjamin's chest. He already knew Summer did the shopping and the cleaning for her mama, besides taking her to all of her doctor appointments. But she did the yard work too?

"I'll mow it." His offer seemed to startle both Summer and her mother, who finally pulled her eyes off the TV. They widened as her gaze fell on him, and her mouth twisted into an expression that may have been a smile—if a smile could be hard and cold. Without pausing to consider whether it was wise, Benjamin slid an arm around Summer's waist. She stiffened but didn't pull away, and her mama's smile grew harder.

"And why would you mow my lawn?" she asked.

"Mama." It was probably good that Summer cut in before Benjamin could reply. "You know my— You know Benjamin Calvano."

"I know him." Mrs. Ellis's words were as hard as her smile. "I don't know why he's here."

"I— Well, we—" Summer stammered.

"There's something we wanted to tell you," Benjamin said for her.

"So go ahead and tell me. I'm not getting any younger sitting here."

"We got married yesterday." Summer dashed out the words so quickly that Benjamin barely understood them, but they seemed to register with her mama immediately.

Her hard smile fell away, replaced by a complete lack of expression.

Summer's eyes flicked to Benjamin, then back to her mama. "Did you hear me, Mama?"

"Of course I heard you," Mrs. Ellis snapped. She gazed at them another moment, then shook her head and turned back to the TV.

Summer held utterly still for a moment, then gave a shuddering sigh. Benjamin hugged her closer, then took the plastic container from her hands. "We brought cake," he said, approaching Mrs. Ellis.

Her eyes flicked to him, then back to the TV. But when he held the container out to her, she took it.

"I'll go get started on the lawn."

She grunted, but he could almost convince himself he saw a slight softening in her eyes. He'd count that as a win.

"I think she likes me," he whispered to Summer when he returned to her side.

She rolled her eyes, but a light smile dusted her lips. He considered brushing a quick kiss there—but then decided that he didn't want their first kiss since their wedding to be in front of her mama.

Chapter 28

"Goodbye. And thank you again." Summer waved over her shoulder as she pulled open the door of the Book Den.

Ruth, the bookstore's owner, who was every bit as sweet as Abigail had said, smiled back. "See you tomorrow morning. Have a good night."

Summer had come into the bookstore this afternoon, after she and Benjamin had left Mama's and picked Max up from school. She'd expected to fill out an application, maybe answer some interview questions, but instead Ruth had pulled her behind the counter and set immediately to training her, acting as if Summer were doing her a favor instead of the other way around.

"I think that went well."

Summer startled at the voice. She hadn't expected Abigail to wait for her. "Did you like it?"

"I did," Summer answered honestly. They started toward their cars, heat radiating up from the pavement even though the sun was sinking behind the mountains to the west. Its last rays rested lightly on the river that wound beyond the parking lot.

"I'm so glad. Although you and Benjamin could have taken a little time for a honeymoon before you started working." Abigail's tone was teasing, but Summer felt her face warm. She had assumed that all of Benjamin's family realized their marriage wasn't real—but maybe not. She didn't know if that made her feel better or worse.

"It was Max's first day of school anyway," she answered feebly. She felt bad that Benjamin had to spend his afternoon off watching her nephew, but he'd insisted that he wanted to. And anyway, they were going to have to get used to adjusting their schedules so that one of them would always be home for Max.

"I still can't believe y'all are married," Abigail gushed. "But then again, I guess I shouldn't be surprised. When those Calvano boys want something, they will pursue it until they get it." She laughed, and Summer tried to force herself to make a sound that could pass for a chuckle.

But her heart knifed. Benjamin might be a Calvano. But he hadn't pursued her. Nor did he want her. Her eyes roved over the couples who strolled the riverwalk hand in hand despite the heat. They all wanted each other.

"I'm off tomorrow," Abigail said when they reached their vehicles. "But I'll see you Friday? And you and Benjamin and Max have to come over for dinner sometime. Don't worry, Benjamin gave me cooking lessons, so the food will be good." She laughed, waved, and then got into her car, leaving Summer astounded once again by this family. Were they for real? And how must her mama look to Benjamin in comparison?

Fortunately, Mama had been on decently good behavior this morning, but still, Summer had felt the tension in Benjamin's arm when he'd wrapped it around her, and she'd known it was as much for Mama's sake as for hers that he did it. She also knew she should have moved away from him, but some part of her had wanted Mama to see that not everyone thought she was worthless.

Mama didn't need to know it wasn't real.

But the moment Benjamin had gone outside to mow the lawn, Mama had turned off the TV. "So you got him to do it then."

Summer had frozen in the act of picking up Mama's dirty dishes and lifted her head defiantly.

But instead of the sneer she expected, Mama's face looked almost . . . sad. And that stole all of Summer's strength.

"What else was I supposed to do?" She resumed picking up the dishes. "Stacy is going to contest the guardianship."

"Stacy?" This time Mama did scoff. "So let her. Max should have been her problem all along."

"He's not a problem, Mama," Summer repeated wearily. "He's your grandson."

"Well, you'd better hope he's worth all the trouble. I have a feeling you and Benjamin are going to end up regretting this."

Summer had ignored her and gone about her work silently, but those words had played through her head all afternoon.

And they echoed loudly now as she started the car and headed home. She didn't regret marrying Benjamin—not really, not if it meant she got to keep Max. But how could Benjamin not regret it, if not now, then eventually, when he realized everything he had given up for her?

She let the worries chase her all the way home, and by the time she pulled into the driveway, she knew what she had to do. They couldn't get an annulment yet, since she couldn't risk the guardianship. But she could keep herself and Max from getting too close to Benjamin so they wouldn't be hurt when things ended. And they had to end—she couldn't let Benjamin give up his whole future for them.

Resolved, she marched herself to the door. But the moment she opened it, she was hit by two things: the tantalizing scent of something warm and garlicky, and the sound of a giant belly laugh.

An uninvited smile lifted her lips at the thought of coming home to this every day. She tried to flatten it as she closed the door quietly behind her.

This didn't change anything. In fact, it only made it more important that she stick to her resolution.

She followed the giggles—and the delicious smells—to the kitchen.

Max stood on a chair at the dining table, and Benjamin stood close by him with one hand on the boy's back. They were both leaning over something on the table, and Max giggled wildly.

Though Summer didn't make a sound, Benjamin looked over his shoulder as if he'd somehow known she was there. His smile seemed to welcome her home, and a dangerous little flutter in her middle said she liked that.

"What on earth are y'all doing?" She moved to Max's other side.

"Making a volcano!" Max said exuberantly, spooning baking soda into what looked like a cup of water. An empty soda bottle sat on the table behind it, along with a jug of vinegar.

"You're just in time." Benjamin took the baking soda box. "All right, Maxerooni, stir up the cup and then we'll pour it into the bottle and see what happens."

Max stirred gleefully, but Summer couldn't help looking past him to Benjamin, who looked as excited as the boy.

"Now?" Max asked.

"Now." Benjamin nodded and took the cup from Max. "Ready." He held the cup over the top of the bottle. "Set." He tilted it a little. "Go." He poured the water out quickly, then stepped back.

A milky geyser shot into the air, and Summer jumped backwards as it came at her. But she was too slow.

She gasped as the concoction hit her square in the face. Warm liquid soaked through her shirt.

She wiped at her eyes and found both Benjamin and Max staring at her, mouths open.

"Oh no," Benjamin said. But he couldn't keep a straight face. Max clapped his hands and chortled. "Aunt Sunny got volcanoed."

"I'm so sorry." But Benjamin was laughing so hard that there was no way to take his apology sincerely.

"You sound really sorry." Summer tried to glare at him, but his and Max's laughs combined were infectious.

"You should have seen your face," Benjamin burst out around his peals of laughter.

And Summer broke, laughing harder than either of them, until tears joined the "lava" on her face. She had a feeling her response might be from the craziness of the last two days, more than the hilarity of the moment.

Still, it felt good.

When their giggles were finally under control, Benjamin turned to her. "You go get changed, and I'll get this cleaned up and have supper on the table by the time you get back."

"Don't think you can buy me off with a little bit of food," Summer warned. "I will get you back for this."

"I'm counting on it." Benjamin lifted a hand and slid it across Summer's cheek before she realized what was happening.

"A water drop," he explained. But his hand lingered for a moment, and Summer swallowed roughly and backed away, suddenly remembering her earlier resolve.

She couldn't let herself get sucked into believing this was real—no matter how badly she wanted it to be.

Benjamin sighed and leaned back into the couch. All in all, it had been a good day. Even telling Summer's mama hadn't been as bad as he'd anticipated. And now that he knew the extent of the chores Summer took care of for her, he could help out. He'd already told Mrs. Ellis that he'd swing by to clean out her gutters sometime next week. He wasn't sure it had exactly endeared him to his new mother-in-law, but at least it would ease Summer's burden.

He peered toward the hallway, searching for his wife, but there was no sign of movement. She'd ducked into her room the moment they'd finished putting Max to bed, but he had assumed she would be back out. It was only 8:30.

Unless she was avoiding him . . .

He dropped his head back on the couch and stared at the ceiling. Maybe he shouldn't have touched her cheek before. It had felt natural enough—more than natural, it had felt wonderful—but he'd seen the look of panic in her eyes as she'd backed away. And when she'd returned to the kitchen after changing into a pair of athletic shorts that showed off her long dancer's legs and a sleeveless shirt that made Benjamin want to run his hands over her arms, up her shoulders, and into her hair, she'd seemed determined to keep as much distance between them as possible. Even in Max's small room, she'd managed to avoid getting within more than a few feet of Benjamin.

Meanwhile, the only thing he could think about was finally kissing her for real.

Patience, he reminded himself. She was still grieving. Still vulnerable. Still coming to grips with their new reality.

Or maybe she didn't want to kiss him. Maybe she was still caught up on Nick and wished he was the one she had married instead.

Benjamin pushed the thought aside. She hadn't mentioned Nick to him once since TJ's death. And besides, Nick wasn't here, offering to take care of her. Benjamin was.

"Sorry. I didn't mean to bother you." Summer's quiet apology shot Benjamin upright.

She stood in the doorway, her dark hair hanging loose around her shoulders, her expression caught between apologetic and uncertain.

"You're not bothering me." He patted the couch next to him. "I was waiting for you."

Summer gave him a quizzical look but didn't step closer. "For what?"

"I thought we could play a game. Or watch a movie. Or talk."

Or kiss. But he kept that one to himself.

Summer hesitated, then moved toward the cabinet next to the TV. "What game?"

"Monopoly?"

She shot a caustic look in his direction.

He held up his hands. "Just kidding. I haven't forgotten how much you hate that game. How about Scrabble?"

"Only if you promise not to make up words."

"I've never made up a word," he protested. "An ai is a three-toed sloth. We looked it up."

Summer rolled her eyes. "You didn't know that when you put the letters down."

Benjamin chuckled. "If I remember correctly, you won anyway."

"That's not the point." Summer squatted in front of the cabinet and pulled out the game.

"No?" Benjamin asked, losing track of the conversation as she walked toward him, the barest hint of a smile dancing against her lips.

"No," she said firmly, dropping the game onto the coffee table. "The point is, you can't just make things up. There are rules."

"Okay," Benjamin agreed, moving over so that she could sit next to him. But she crossed the room and dragged a small armchair to the other side of the coffee table.

"Can't risk you cheating," she said lightly, but Benjamin had a feeling there was more to it than that.

They drew tiles, and Benjamin chuckled at his selection.

"What?" Summer demanded.

"You'll see." He rearranged the letters on his tray. "Do you want to go first?"

She shook her head. "And deny you whatever you're giggling about?"

"I'm not giggling," he corrected. "I'm cackling. But since you insist . . ." He laid down the letters: A-X-O-L-O-T-L.

"Benjamin," Summer sputtered. "You just promised you wouldn't make things up."

"I didn't." Benjamin couldn't stop grinning. "It's a kind of salamander. Look it up. If you dare."

Summer still looked skeptical, but she shook her head. "I believe you. Against my better judgment."

"What a lovely thing for a wife to say to her husband." Benjamin tested the words on his tongue. And decided he liked how they felt.

Summer's face took on a light pink flush, but she silently laid her tiles on the board.

"Laugh," Benjamin read her word. "Not bad. Not as good as axolotl, but not bad."

Summer laughed quietly, and Benjamin smiled. The word may not be worth a lot of points, but he sure liked how it sounded on her.

"So . . ." he finally worked up the nerve to say as they continued to build off of each other's words. "We should talk about moving. To my place. Our place."

Summer didn't say anything as she spelled the word *joy*.

"Thirteen points." She looked up from the board. "I guess we should. I can call a moving company.

Benjamin waved off the comment. "I don't have such a big family for nothing. They'll help."

"I couldn't ask them to do that," Summer protested.

"You don't have to." Benjamin added his own word to the board: *always*. "I'll do it right now." He pulled out his phone to send a quick text but was distracted by a string of texts from Ian that he hadn't heard come in.

He tapped on the notification.

Going to be in Atlanta September 18-19.

Sending your ticket.

Hotel and car are covered too.

So you have no excuses.

Benjamin snorted in exasperation. "Unbelievable."

"What's unbelievable?" Summer put down the word *amuse*.

Benjamin clicked off his phone. "A friend of mine from culinary school wants me to check out his new restaurant in Atlanta next month. I already told him I couldn't, but he booked me a plane ticket and hotel anyway." He shook his head, though he shouldn't have been surprised. Ian had always been dauntless.

"Why can't you go?" Summer looked up from the board.

He stared at her. Why couldn't he go? He wasn't going to get married to her and then up and leave. Unless . . .

"Do you and Max want to go?"

Something like wistfulness crossed Summer's face but was instantly replaced by that guarded look she wore so often. "I have to take care of Mama. Plus, Max will have school."

"Oh. Right." He probably shouldn't have forgotten that already.

"But you should still go," Summer insisted.

"I'm not going to—"

"Yes, you are." Her eyes darted determination. "Or— Or I'll knock the Scrabble board off the table."

"You wouldn't." Benjamin clutched at his chest in mock horror. "I'm winning."

"Try me." Summer raised her eyebrows in an adorable challenge that made him want to lean across the table and kiss her.

Benjamin forced himself to drop his eyes from her lips. "Fine. You win. I'll go."

"Good." Summer sounded satisfied. "It's your turn."

Chapter 29

Summer shielded her eyes against the sun as Benjamin steered her car into the nearly full parking lot at Beautiful Savior. Nerves crunched her stomach, and she had to fight the temptation to ask Benjamin to turn the car around and take her home.

She hadn't been able to face coming to church since TJ's funeral, and she had her doubts about coming today. But Benjamin had seemed to take it for granted that they would all go this morning. And he was a pastor's son. What would it look like if his wife didn't show up?

"Look, there's Aunt Ava and Uncle Joseph," Max yelled enthusiastically. "They're waving to us."

Summer forced herself to wave back. All of Benjamin's siblings had insisted the other night that Max be allowed to call them aunt and uncle, and the boy had been tickled to think that he'd gone from having one aunt to having a dozen aunts and uncles. Summer loved the thought of so much love being lavished on her nephew, but she'd have to be careful not to let him get too close to Benjamin's family. She didn't want it to be any harder on the boy than necessary when this was all over.

Why does it ever have to be over? the insidious little voice that had been getting louder over the past few days asked.

But Summer shoved it away. It knew as well as she did why this couldn't last.

"Ready?" Benjamin reached over and squeezed her hand, and Summer tried desperately to ignore the zaps it sent through her. They'd been married for five days now, and in that time, Summer was pretty sure they'd touched less than at any time in the previous few weeks, when his hugs had been generous, and he'd held her hands through the hardest days of her life.

But it was as if their wedding had put up a wall between them.

It wasn't the wedding that put up the wall. It was you, the accusing little whisper hissed. Summer didn't even try to deny it. Of course she had put up a wall. It was the only way to keep herself from wanting this to be more than it was.

But she did miss the way Benjamin had held her and comforted her as a friend, and it hurt to think that was all over now.

"Ready." She pulled her hand out of his, her need for space making her response more definitive than she felt. She got out of the car and waited for Benjamin to unbuckle Max.

Her eyes traveled to the tall steeple at the top of the church. She still remembered the first time she had attended a service here. It must have been nine or ten years ago now. Benjamin had invited TJ, and TJ had insisted that she come too. Summer had never admitted to her brother that the only reason she'd agreed was to see Benjamin. When they'd gotten here, he came over to say hi, and even though she knew he didn't see her as anything more than TJ's little sister, the way he had smiled at her—Summer was pretty sure she had fallen a little in love with him right that moment.

"It's beautiful, isn't it?" Benjamin came up next to her, craning his head skyward.

She nodded mutely, and they joined the other families walking toward the church. They'd only gone a few steps when she felt something brush against her hand. It took her a moment to realize it was Benjamin's fingers threading through hers.

She sneaked a look at him, but he was talking to Max, who held his hand on the other side.

Summer should pull her hand away, but there were so many people around. What would they think if Summer was unwilling to hold her new husband's hand?

Fortunately, when they reached the church, Benjamin had to let go to open the door. She took the opportunity to cross her arms in front of her, which not only kept him from taking her hand again but also made her feel like she was wearing a protective shield against the crowded lobby.

Benjamin stepped next to her, wrapping an arm around her waist, and she realized her fatal mistake in keeping him from holding her hand. Her heart raced ahead of her feet as he steered her toward the cluster of his family.

"Aw, look at y'all. You are just the sweetest couple." Ava clasped her hands to her heart as if the sight of them made her rapturously happy.

"Yeah. We know." Benjamin grinned and squeezed her closer, but it took all of Summer's willpower to force out a painful smile as Ava's comment brought back mocking words spoken five years ago, just before Benjamin was supposed to leave for culinary school.

"Don't you and Benjamin just make the sweetest couple," Christine West had said, clasping her hands to her heart.

"I— Um— Thank you," had been Summer's stammered reply. Christine was part of the popular crowd and had never spoken to her before.

"And to think, *I'm* the one he wanted to go to prom with," Christine had added. "He was so disappointed when he found out that I was already going with Darren. So I told him to ask you. It was supposed to be a joke. I never dreamed he'd actually date you after that. But I suppose he felt like he had to, after everyone saw you kiss him." She'd sighed with an evil little laugh. "I know *I* wouldn't want a boyfriend who didn't actually want me, but I'm glad you're happy with it."

Summer had always regretted not replying to her. But what was she supposed to say? Christine was right about the fact that she had impulsively kissed Benjamin in front of everyone—the only bold thing she'd ever done in her life, at least until she'd *married* him.

"Summer?"

She pushed the memory away and tried to focus on what Lydia was saying.

"Sorry, what was that?"

"I was just asking if you want me to bring any boxes this afternoon. We have a bunch, if you're not completely packed yet."

Summer shook her head. She'd barely started, but Benjamin's siblings had all offered to come over and help after church. "Boxes would be great. Thanks."

She slipped out of Benjamin's hold, his arm around her waist too much of a reminder that she was in the exact same position now as she had been when she and Benjamin were dating. He hadn't chosen her then—and he hadn't chosen her now.

She and Lydia talked for another minute, Summer working valiantly to keep her attention on the conversation, and then the Calvanos started to file into the church.

Benjamin appeared at her side again. "Are you okay?" he leaned over to whisper as they made their way down the aisle Summer had always dreamed she would walk down one day in a beautiful dress, holding a beautiful bouquet—and with a groom who actually wanted to marry her.

"I'm fine." She followed Ava into the pew, grateful when Max settled himself between her and Benjamin, creating a safety zone.

As the service began, Summer tried to follow along, tried to keep her mind on the readings and hymns and prayers, but a thousand other thoughts kept pushing their way to the front.

When Pastor Calvano moved to the pulpit, Summer blinked in surprise. Was it really time for the sermon already? She worked to refocus her attention as the pastor—her father-in-law, she realized with a start—began to speak.

"All right, y'all, I have a confession to make." Pastor Calvano leaned forward and rubbed his hands together, as if nervous. "Sometimes, when my wife and I were just sitting together and not really saying anything, she would ask me that question wives are so great at asking: 'What are you thinking about?'"

He paused, making a deer-in-the-headlights face, and swiveled his head as if panicked. "Uh . . . You, of course, honey." He batted his eyes. "What else would a loving husband be thinking about?"

A laugh shook the church—and especially the pews filled with Pastor Calvano's children. Summer could pick out the sound of Benjamin's above the rest, and she couldn't help looking at him out of the corner of her eye. His mama had died not long after they'd broken up. But she should have been there for him, the way he was there for her now. He caught her looking and smiled, and she snatched her gaze away.

"Now, when we were newlyweds, my wife seemed to accept that answer," Pastor Calvano continued. "I got away with it for a couple of years even. But I can still remember the first time she called me out. Our oldest had just been born, and we had put him to bed and were sitting on the couch, completely exhausted. And she asked the question. My mind had been wandering. I can't even remember what I was thinking about anymore—probably about how much I missed sleep—but I gave my default answer. 'I was thinking about how wonderful you are.' And she looked at me and said, 'Abe, I love you. But you're a terrible liar. There's no way your mind can possibly be on me every time I ask.'"

In front of Summer, Liam wrapped his arm around Lydia and whispered something in her ear that made her look to him with a smile.

A stab of longing went through Summer, but she quashed it. She couldn't go wanting that kind of relationship with Benjamin.

"Now that I've admitted I was a less than perfect husband," Pastor Calvano said, "you'd probably like me to get to the point." He grinned. "And it's this: My mind may not have always been on my wife. But God's mind is always on you and me." He picked up a Bible and paged through it for a moment, then read, "My God, my God, why have you forsaken me? Why are you so far from saving me, so far from my cries of anguish? My God, I cry out by day, but you do not answer, by night, but I find no rest."

Summer shifted in her seat and looked around. Was she missing something? Whoever wrote that didn't really sound as if they thought they were always on God's mind. They sounded more like Summer felt—like God had completely forgotten them.

Pastor Calvano looked up. "All right, y'all. Go on and admit it. You're thinking I need to put my glasses on and find the right verse. Surely that wasn't the one I meant to read."

He smiled. "I said what I meant, and I meant what I said. God always has us on his mind. . . . But we don't always feel like he does. The words of this Psalm are best known from when Jesus cried them on the cross. But let's back up a thousand years to when they were written by King David. Now, here was a guy who should have known that God's mind was always on him. After all, God had taken him, a mere shepherd boy, sought him out, and made him king. He had given him the ability to defeat Goliath, to win great battles, to expand the kingdom of Israel to nearly its greatest extent. He'd given David wealth and fame and riches. But even David went through some tough times. And when I say tough times, I mean *really* tough times. He was hunted by King Saul, his son died as a result of David's sin, another son led a rebellion against him and was killed by David's own men."

Pastor Calvano shook his head. "Again and again in the Psalms, David cried out to the Lord. Sometimes in confidence. But often in despair. In Psalm 13, he cries, 'How long, Lord? Will you forget me forever?' In Psalm 10, 'Why, Lord, do you stand far off? Why do you hide yourself in times of trouble?' And maybe the most desperate cry of all, right here, 'Why have you forsaken me?' David felt forsaken. Alone. Forgotten by God. And he's not the only one." Pastor Calvano lifted his head, and Summer felt like he could see right through her. Like he could see that she felt the same way as David.

"We face tough times too. Sometimes *really* tough times," Pastor Calvano continued. "Job loss. Relationship troubles. Bills to pay. People to take care of. Loved ones dying."

A burning started at the back of Summer's throat, and she clenched her fists in her lap. She felt a stir next to her and glanced over to see Benjamin shift Max to his lap and then slide closer to her. His hand landed on hers and squeezed tight. She sniffed to keep the tears back.

"And when we see these things, when we go through them, it's hard not to feel forsaken by God. Hard not to feel like he's completely forgotten us. Hard not to wonder how long we are going to have to cry out before he answers us—if he ever will."

Pastor Calvano paused, his eyes roaming over the congregation. "But he has already answered," he said quietly. "Right here, in his Word." He held up his Bible. "Where he tells us about One who really was forsaken: Jesus. When our Savior cried out, 'My God, my God, why have you forsaken me?' he didn't only *feel* forsaken. He *was* forsaken. By God, his Father. That's the price of sin—of our sin. And Jesus took that sin on himself, he suffered the excruciating agony of being forsaken by God, so that we would never have to. So that we would never be forsaken, not even for a moment. So that we would know that God always has us on his mind—and the things he has in mind for us are always for our good. So that we could rejoice, like King David, even through our suffering, even through our trials, even through those times when we *feel* forsaken, that we are not, for God sees us and knows us and watches over us. 'Never will I leave you,' he promises. 'Never will I forsake you.'"

Summer exhaled shakily. She had heard that verse before, of course. But sometimes she wondered if it was really true.

"But what about us?" Pastor Calvano asked. "God always has us on his mind, but do we always have him on ours? Or are we more like me with my wife—claiming to always be thinking about her, but really having my mind somewhere else?" He flipped through the Bible still in his hands. "God tells us, 'Since, then, you have been raised with Christ, set your hearts on things above, where Christ is, seated at the right hand of God.' And yet—" Pastor Calvano set the Bible down. "How often do we set our minds on everything *but* things above?"

Summer thought guiltily of all the distractions that had pulled her thoughts from the service.

"We're so often caught up in the here and now, on our temporary situation instead of our eternal promise," Pastor Calvano continued. "But the good news is that when Jesus died on the cross, when he was forsaken by God, he took even this sin on himself. He forgives us for it. And he urges us again and again back to his Word, where he reminds us again and again that we are always on his mind. Though we at times feel forsaken, we are not. And we never will be. So we can proclaim, with David, 'Praise the Lord, my soul; all my inmost being praise his holy name. Praise the Lord, my soul—and forget not all his benefits—who forgives all your sins and heals all your diseases, who redeems your life from the pit and crowns you with love and compassion.' Amen."

It wasn't until Benjamin gently tugged her upward that Summer realized the sermon was over.

Benjamin wrapped his arm around her as Pastor Calvano led them in prayer. Summer closed her eyes and fought against the desire for this to last forever. Because right at this moment, she didn't feel quite so forsaken.

Chapter 30

"Thanks, y'all." Benjamin waved to the last of his siblings as they headed out into the twilight. Then he turned back to the house, swiping at the sweat on his brow. The heat still hadn't broken, but that hadn't slowed his family down as they'd moved Summer's and Max's things across town.

Inside, he looked around, his heart full to see that his spartan little house was spartan no more. Two chairs and the coffee table from TJ's house filled out the living room, and there was even a table in the dining room now, complete with space for the large family he hoped he and Summer would have one day, although the likelihood seemed low at the moment, given that the walls she put up between them seemed to grow higher every day.

But she hadn't pulled away when he'd slid his arm around her in church this morning, which he took as a sign of progress.

He headed down the hallway to see how she and Max were coming on setting up his room. Their backs were to the door as they organized a shelf with Max's toys, and Benjamin let himself pause for a moment to watch them, emotion pressing against his throat as he considered how happy it would make TJ to see them here.

"It looks great in here, Maxerooni." Benjamin stepped into the room, and Max spun around with a grin.

"It's the same as my old room. See, we put the bed here and the books here and the toys here." He pointed toward the spot where Summer remained absorbed in organizing dinosaurs on a shelf.

Benjamin moved farther into the room so that he was standing right behind her. "You shouldn't put the Triceratops by the T. Rex," he teased. "That's a recipe for disaster."

Summer didn't look up, but he heard the tiny chuckle low in her throat, and she moved the T. Rex farther down the shelf. Then she stood, apparently not realizing how close Benjamin stood behind her because when she turned around, she startled and took a step backwards—right into the shelf. All of her carefully arranged dinosaurs went tumbling.

She sighed and bent to pick them up at the same time he did, her silky hair brushing lightly over his arm. He swallowed and picked up a dinosaur to pass to her, intentionally letting his fingers brush over hers in the hand-off. He heard her light inhale, but she didn't say anything.

When they were done cleaning up the dinosaurs, he made himself ask the question he hadn't wanted to bring up while his family was here. "Do you want me to— I mean, would you prefer—" He couldn't seem to get a grip on his suddenly flustered tongue. "Should I set up your bed in the spare bedroom, or . . ."

He couldn't quite give voice to the rest of the question: *Or do you want to share my bed?*

He knew which he'd prefer. But he wasn't going to push her.

"Oh." Summer looked startled. "Um. I guess— It would probably be better— If you don't mind—"

Benjamin realized he was holding his breath as he waited for one of these sentences to end.

"I guess it would be best to set up my bed. If it's not too much trouble," she finally completed the thought, and the air seeped out of Benjamin's lungs, along with the hope that had been building.

But he worked hard to keep his disappointment off his face. "No trouble at all," he said, heading straight for the door. "I'll go do it right now."

Chapter 31

Summer woke well before her alarm clanged and lay in the dark, disoriented for a moment until her eyes fell on the window, where she could just make out the beautiful hibiscus plant in the dim moonlight. She had woken up in her own bed. At Benjamin's house. Just as she had for over a week now.

She tried to figure out what had woken her, and then remembered. She'd been dreaming about lying in Benjamin's bed, with his arms around her. She remembered feeling pure bliss, until his eyes suddenly opened and his face twisted as he said, "Oh, it's you." And then he pulled his arms away from her and sort of faded away and she'd woken up, wanting him to come back but knowing he wouldn't.

Summer sighed and sat up. As long as she was awake, she might as well do something productive. She pulled out her phone and typed *River Falls real estate agent* into the search bar. She'd spent the past week and a half cleaning TJ's house, selling off or donating the items they'd chosen not to move over here. Benjamin and his brothers had done some minor repairs so that it would be ready to sell. It had hurt to see the house nearly empty yesterday, but the sooner she sold it, the sooner she could stop worrying about all of TJ's debts. And maybe have enough left over to help support Max.

A long list of results came up in response to her search, but Summer liked the friendly smile of the first woman. And her name was Jasmine—which happened to be one of Summer's favorite princesses.

She clicked on the contact button, then filled out the short form and sent it off.

"Now what?" she asked herself. It was still too early to get Max up and ready for school.

Through the wall that separated her room from Benjamin's she heard a soft snore that made her giggle. A longing that she couldn't block rose in her chest as she wondered what it would be like to wake up in his arms. But then her dream came back to her.

Besides, she hadn't missed how hesitant he had been when he'd asked whether she wanted to sleep in his room.

In fact, he hadn't actually asked her to sleep in his bed at all. What he'd asked was if she wanted to sleep in *hers*. Any implication that the alternative was to sleep with him had come solely from her imagination.

Summer's phone buzzed in her hand, and she glanced down, surprised to see a reply from the real estate agent already.

I'm so sorry for your loss. I'd be happy to take a look at your brother's house and help you list it for sale. I have some time around 1 pm today, if that works for you. Jasmine

She heard an alarm from Benjamin's room, followed by a light groan and then the sound of drawers opening. She knew he was getting up so early so he could run with his brothers, just as he had nearly every morning. She still couldn't believe they were *all* running the race in TJ's honor. But she supposed she shouldn't be surprised by anything this perfect family did.

She should ask Benjamin if one o'clock would work for him. He had already bought a house, so he would know more about what to do than she did.

She wove her hair into a quick braid, swung her legs out of the bed, and padded to the door. In the dark hallway, she hesitated. Should she go out to the kitchen and wait for him there? Or knock on his door and ask if he had a second?

Before she could decide, the door opened, and he walked straight into her. She gasped, her arms flailing as she fought to regain her balance. They got caught in another pair of arms, and then she was upright and pressed against his bare chest. She could hear his heart thudding wildly under her ear.

"Are you okay?" His whisper brushed across the top of her hair, and she eased herself backwards, but that was a mistake because her eyes were adjusted enough to the dark to see the outline of the muscles carved into his skin.

"I'm fine." She sounded breathless, and she forced her eyes off of him, gulping in as much air as she could to get her voice back under control.

"What are you doing up already?" he whispered. "Did my alarm wake you?"

She shook her head. "I couldn't sleep, so I emailed a real estate agent. She can meet today at one. I was just coming to see if that worked for you. I know it's your day off, so if there's something else you were planning on doing, I can handle it myself, but I really have no idea about anything having to do with real estate and you just bought a house so—"

"Relax, Summer." Benjamin's muffled laugh made her look up. "I don't need the hard sell. If you want me to be there, I'll be there."

She swallowed, knowing she needed to tear her eyes away from him but unable to. "Thank you."

"You're welcome." His words seemed to enfold her, and he took a step closer, gently brushing a strand of hair that had escaped her braid. "You're so beautiful."

Summer wanted to melt into his arms.

But she couldn't let herself do that—couldn't even let herself want it.

"I should let you get going." She took a step backwards. "Your brothers will give you a hard time if you're late."

"Yeah." Benjamin's voice was dull, and she saw the flash of frustration in his eyes. He slipped past her toward the bathroom, and Summer let out a long breath as the door closed behind him.

Do not start wanting him to want you, she ordered herself.

But as if in defiance of the warning, she let herself glance toward the rumpled bed in his room. Then she returned to her own room so she wouldn't run into him again before he left.

Chapter 32

"Look who finally decided to show up." Simeon mocked lightly as Benjamin climbed out of his Gremlin at the head of the trail that wound through the foothills on the outskirts of River Falls. The actual trail race would be higher in the Smokies, but for training purposes, this one was close enough to town that they could all get to it on a regular basis.

"Give him a break." Joseph grinned. "He's a newlywed."

Benjamin's face heated as his brothers all laughed. He worked to force a laugh too.

"Remember when we were little," Asher said, "and Mama made us sleep in the same bed on vacation because she was afraid you'd fall out otherwise? You swore you'd never share a bed with anyone when you grew up." He chuckled. "I guess you got over that."

"True." Benjamin swallowed painfully and tried to keep a bright expression.

"To be fair," Joseph cut in, "Summer probably doesn't kick and snore as much as you do."

Again Benjamin made himself laugh along with his brothers. He sure wished he knew *how* she slept. The way she'd felt pressed close against him in the dark hallway this morning—he wanted to feel that all night every night.

"All right. Let's run." Zeb fiddled with his fitness watch. "It's going to get hot out here soon."

The sun was peeking over the easternmost mountains, sending a spill of gold over the trees there, but in the foothills, everything was still cloaked in shadows. Even so, the air was already growing warm and sticky.

They all started off down the trail in a pack, but soon Joseph and Liam fell back, while Zeb and Asher pushed ahead. Benjamin could have joined them, but instead he kept pace with Simeon. His brother eyed him but didn't say anything, and Benjamin didn't either, instead focusing on the songs of the waking birds and the chatter of the squirrels. With every breath, he pulled in the earthy scent of the woods, and something close to peace settled over him.

Until Simeon asked, "Something you want to talk about?"

Benjamin concentrated on his footfalls. "Nothing in particular."

Simeon gave him a side eye, clearly seeing through the lie, just as Benjamin had known he would. They ran in silence, their steady breaths mingling with the sounds of the forest.

"Can I ask you something?" Simeon finally cut into the quiet.

Benjamin's only answer was an inhale and exhale.

Simeon apparently took that as a yes. "Is the reason you two got married so quickly to get guardianship of Max?"

Benjamin breathed in and out again, wrestling with himself. Simeon was a Christian counselor. But did that mean he'd understand or that he'd rebuke Benjamin, tell him he was crazy and stupid and young and impulsive?

"That's part of the reason," he finally said. He made himself look at Simeon to see his reaction, but there wasn't one.

"But it's not a fake marriage," he added quickly. "It's just as real as yours and Abigail's or anyone else's."

"I believe you." Simeon took a few more breaths, then asked, "How are things going?"

"Great. Really great," Benjamin answered, maybe too quickly, because Simeon eyed him again.

But his brother nodded and let another quarter of a mile pass. Then he said, "Because it would be understandable if it took a while to adjust. I mean, that's true even if you spend years planning for a wedding."

Benjamin ran on, keeping a neutral expression. Was it possible his brother had deduced that he and Summer were living more like roommates than husband and wife?

"I guess what I'm saying," Simeon added around deep breaths as they climbed a rise in the trail. "Is to be patient. She's still grieving. And dealing with the stress of TJ's estate and what's going to happen to Max. Plus, y'all are young."

Benjamin started to protest, but Simeon held up a hand. "I'm not saying it as an insult. It's just a fact. I would guess marriage wasn't on her mind any more than it was on yours. Wasn't she dating someone else up until a few weeks ago?"

"He wasn't the right guy for her," Benjamin growled.

"I'm not saying he was." Simeon's voice remained calm. "Just that it's a lot for one person to take in all of that change at once. So it wouldn't really be a surprise if things were a little rocky at first."

Benjamin thought about denying it again. But Simeon was too good at his job to buy it.

"So what do I do?" he asked finally.

Simeon seemed to be thinking, and Benjamin tried not to be impatient. If his brother had any ideas for how to fix his broken two-week-old marriage, he wanted to hear them.

After a while, Simeon said, "I imagine Summer feels a lot like Abigail did when she woke up and learned she was married to me—like she was dropped right into the middle of a relationship without building the foundation first. You might need to take things slowly. Start at the beginning."

Benjamin considered that as he swiped at the sweat running into his eyes. "I can do that," he said at last.

Chapter 33

Summer did a double take as she turned onto Mama's street after dropping Max off at school. There was a small blue car parked in the driveway. Was she finally going to catch the culprit who brought Mama alcohol?

Grimly, she pulled in behind the car, blocking its owner from making a quick escape. She only hoped she'd have the courage to confront the offender and give them a piece of her mind. Her habit of shrinking from conflict was a problem—she knew that. But it had also helped her survive two decades with Mama.

She opened her car door and took a deep breath of the hot, sticky air to steel herself. Before she could chicken out, she marched up the driveway and shoved open the front door—harder than she meant to. It careened into the house and bounced against the door stop that jutted out from the wall beyond it.

From her recliner, Mama's head lifted in sour surprise. "Who put a hornet in your pants?"

A man sat in a chair near Mama with his back to the door, and when he turned around, Summer barely managed to stifle a gasp. "Pastor Calvano. What are you doing here?"

"That's a nice way to greet your father-in-law." Mama smirked, and Summer couldn't quite tell if the remark was meant to be cutting or humorous.

"Sorry." She closed the door behind her. "I wasn't expecting— What are you doing here?" she repeated.

Pastor Calvano smiled kindly. "Since we're all family now, I thought it would be good to get to know your mother better."

Summer nearly groaned out loud. The last thing she wanted was for Pastor Calvano to get to know Mama better.

"The pastor thinks I need more Jesus," Mama added.

Summer closed her eyes helplessly, but Pastor Calvano chuckled. "We *all* need more Jesus. I hope you don't mind if I drop by again."

Summer held her breath. Mama was going to make some kind of awful reply, and then Pastor Calvano would regret ever coming.

But Mama just shrugged. "Suit yourself."

Pastor Calvano smiled and put his chair back, then headed for the door, where Summer still stood dumbly. She scrambled out of his way, but he stopped and patted her arm. "I'll see you soon."

She nodded mutely. It wasn't until he was out the door that she realized her car was still blocking him in.

She hurried outside, fishing her keys out of her purse. "Sorry about that," she called. "I'll move my car for you."

"It's no problem." Pastor Calvano waited outside his car door, and Summer wished he'd get in the vehicle before she reached him so it wouldn't be so awkward.

But instead of ducking into the car, he stepped away from it, blocking her path. She had no choice but to stop.

"How is everything?" he asked gently. "Benjamin treating you all right?"

"Yes sir." Her lips curved into an involuntary smile. "Too good, really."

Pastor Calvano's smile seemed to relax. "That's what I like to hear." He nodded toward the house. "Your mama's pretty sick?"

Summer nodded. "Yes. End-stage liver disease. The doctor says it's hard to know how much longer she has." She didn't add that it would be longer if Mama stopped drinking. Her mother seemed to be blessedly sober today, and Summer didn't need her father-in-law knowing what she could really be like.

"I'm sorry." Compassion shone from Pastor Calvano's eyes. "I'll try to stop over often. Maybe she'll let me do a devotion with her."

Summer had to stop herself from laughing in his face. Mama had made her feelings about religion clear when Summer and TJ started attending Beautiful Savior.

"You don't have to do that," she said. "I'm afraid Mama's not really interested in Jesus."

"Well," Pastor Calvano said cheerfully, "Jesus is still interested in her." With that, he moved out of Summer's way and got into his car. "See you later. Love you."

Summer startled. He'd said that the other night when they were leaving his house too, but she'd assumed he was talking to Benjamin. After all, he had no reason to love Summer.

Even so, the words chased her back to her car, and she couldn't shake the warm, disconcerted feeling they left her with the rest of the morning as she cleaned up Mama's house, then went to pick up Max, fed him a quick lunch, and headed over to TJ's to meet the real estate agent.

She and Max got there right at one o'clock, and a red car was already parked in the driveway. She sure hoped the car belonged to the real estate agent. She wasn't sure she could handle another surprise today.

By the time she unbuckled Max and pulled him out of the car, a pretty blonde woman Summer recognized from the pictures online stood behind her vehicle, waiting for them.

She held out her hand to Summer with a warm, sympathetic smile. "I'm so sorry we couldn't meet under better circumstances. I'm Jasmine."

Summer introduced herself and Max. "My, um— My husband—" The word stumbled out of her mouth. "Should be here soon."

Jasmine's smile was friendly and set Summer at ease. "Do you want to get started or wait for him?"

"Um. I guess we can get started."

"Great. Why don't you give me the tour, and I'll take some notes and ask questions, and we'll go from there. You've got great curb appeal."

"Oh. Thanks." Summer had planted some of the flowers out front herself.

As she led the real estate agent through the house, Summer suddenly saw every little flaw and defect, but Jasmine kept up a steady stream of friendly chatter, simultaneously making notes on her tablet.

They moved into TJ's room, which still held his bed, since there wasn't room at Benjamin's for it, and Summer hadn't been able to bear selling it. They had talked about putting it in storage so it could be Max's bed someday.

Summer heard the front door open.

"Sorry I'm late," Benjamin's voice called, and Summer's heart leaped higher than even her best jete.

"Benji," Max cheered and ran out of the room.

Jasmine paused in the middle of making a note on her tablet and smiled widely. "Someone's happy to see his daddy."

"Oh. No," Summer stammered. "My brother TJ was his daddy. Benjamin is his— Is my—" She stumbled over the word again. "He's my husband."

"Of course. I'm so sorry. I didn't mean to—"

"It's okay," Summer said quickly.

"Look what Benji brought." Max reappeared in the doorway, his face a wreath of smiles as he hugged a dinosaur stuffed animal in one arm and a koala in the other. "This one is for you." Max held the koala out to Summer.

"For me?" She stared at it, as Max thrust it into her arms. She instinctively lifted it to her face and slid its silky fur against her cheek. She couldn't believe he'd remembered. They weren't even dating yet when she'd told him years ago that koalas were her favorite animal. Or, more likely, he hadn't remembered. It was only a coincidence.

She was about to ask Max where Benjamin had gone after delivering the gifts when he appeared suddenly in the doorway behind the boy. His eyes went instantly to Summer's, and the way his face lit up when he saw her cuddling with the koala made her heart stutter. Was it possible he really had remembered?

Summer quickly dropped the toy from her face. "Benjamin." She stepped to the side. "This is our real estate agent—"

"Jasmine?" Benjamin's expression registered surprise—and something else Summer couldn't identify.

"Benjamin?" Jasmine sounded equally astonished.

"You know each other?" It shouldn't bother Summer that Benjamin already knew the beautiful woman selling TJ's house for them.

"Jasmine is the one who sold me my house." Benjamin's expression returned to his usual easy smile.

"I did," Jasmine replied, her voice slightly cooler than it had been when she'd talked to Summer alone. "But I didn't realize you were getting married. I would have taken some other things into consideration if I had."

Benjamin shifted, and though his smile remained in place, Summer thought he looked slightly uncomfortable. Maybe Jasmine hadn't been such a great realtor, after all. Summer should have consulted Benjamin before she just chose a random person online.

"We weren't—ah—married at the time," Summer said, trying to ease whatever this strange tension was. "We've only been married for two weeks. And I love the house you sold him."

"Oh." Jasmine looked like she had more questions, but she ducked her head back to her tablet and made a few more notes.

As they moved on to the rest of the house, she didn't chat nearly as much as she had before. But when the tour was finished, she turned to them with a bright smile. "I'll go over everything and put together some numbers for you by tomorrow. If you're happy with them, there's no reason we can't have this place on the market by the end of the week." She held out a hand to shake Summer's, then Benjamin's, and whatever weirdness Summer had thought she sensed between them seemed to be gone.

Still, as soon as Jasmine had left, Summer turned to Benjamin. "I'm sorry. I should have talked to you before I called her. I didn't realize she was your agent. Were you not happy with the job she did?"

Benjamin looked surprised. "No, she did a great job. Why?"

Summer studied him for a moment, then shrugged. "Y'all just didn't seem to really . . . click."

Benjamin shook his head. "I was just surprised to see her here, that's all. But she'll do a great job for us. Now, I have something to ask you." His expression became boyish and a little mischievous.

Summer tilted her head, narrowing her eyes. "What?" she asked cautiously.

"Will you go out to dinner with me tonight?"

"Boy oh boy! Can we go to Murf's?" Max's voice broke in.

Summer didn't even know where he had come from, but she was grate-ful for the distraction. And the reminder that Benjamin wasn't asking her on a *date*. He was asking if they could all go out to dinner.

But Benjamin shook his head. "Sorry, Maxerooni. This time it's just going to be me and Sunny."

"That's not fair." Max pouted, but Benjamin laughed.

"Maybe you'll think it's fair when I tell you that Mia is going to watch you, and she said she'd take you to Daisy's for pie."

"Oh boy!" Max lost his pout. "Yes, I think that's fair."

Summer's eyes darted between Benjamin and Max. "Do I get a say in this?"

"Sure." Benjamin's boyish grin teased her. "As long as your say is yes."

Chapter 34

"Wow." Benjamin tried to whistle, but Summer had stolen his breath. "You look fantastic."

She wore a light pink sundress that flowed loosely and yet still managed to highlight her curves. The waves of her hair tumbled over her shoulders and down her back, and her mouth wavered in a nervous smile.

Her cheeks matched the pink of her dress, but she waved off the compliment. "Not really."

"You really do," said Mia from her spot on the floor, where Max had recruited her to play dinosaurs the moment she walked in the door ten minutes ago.

"Thank you." Benjamin grinned at his niece for providing backup, grateful she had decided to stay in town and attend the local community college, especially since he had big plans to take Summer on lots more of these dates.

"Max's bedtime is eight o'clock," Benjamin reminded Mia.

"But we'll be home by then," Summer quickly added.

"No," Benjamin said firmly. "We will not."

"Benjamin," Summer protested.

But he shook his head. "Max wants Mia to tuck him in anyway, don't you Max?"

Max nodded the head of his stuffed dinosaur up and down. "Yes, I do," he said in a deep voice punctuated by a giggle.

"There you have it. The dino has spoken." Benjamin crossed the room to give Max a hug. "Behave for your cousin."

"I will." Max's dinosaur nodded again.

Benjamin stepped out of the way so Summer could hug Max too.

His phone dinged, and he pulled it out of his pocket. It was a text from Jasmine. He'd texted her after their earlier meeting to explain the whole situation.

You don't owe me any explanations, her reply read. *But thank you for telling me. I'll keep y'all in my prayers.*

He clicked off the phone and tucked it back into his pocket, feeling more relieved than he'd expected to. He didn't want her to think he'd been dating her while he was planning to marry Summer. And now that she knew, things wouldn't be so awkward the next time they met.

"Come on." He reached for Summer's arm and tugged her away from Max. "It's time to go."

She let him pull her toward the door, and he used the opportunity to slip his hand into hers. She didn't pull away, but as soon as they were outside, she murmured, "I'm not so sure this is a good idea."

"It's not." Benjamin led her to the Gremlin—the same car he'd driven for their very first date. "It's a *fantastic* idea."

She laughed, though the sound held more anxiety than amusement.

At the car, he stopped and turned to her. "Relax. This is going to be fun. I promise." He leaned forward and brushed a kiss across her forehead, then quickly opened her car door, before he could be tempted to let his lips travel to her mouth.

Once she was in, he took a deep breath, then circled to the driver's side.

"Where are we going?" Summer asked as he started the car.

"You'll see." He couldn't suppress a playful grin.

"Benjamin, you know I don't like surprises."

"I know." His grin grew. "But I love them." He reached across the tiny space between them and threaded his fingers through hers.

She made a sound that he assumed was meant to convey annoyance, but he didn't buy it. Not with the soft way her lips lifted, nor with the way her fingers closed around his.

They chatted easily as Benjamin drove—about the unrelenting heat, and about the picture of a dinosaur Max had painted at school, and about how things were going at the bookstore and the restaurant.

When Benjamin slowed the car to pull into a parking lot, Summer laughed. "I think I might be a little overdressed for Murf's."

"Nope. You're perfect."

Summer dipped her head but didn't say anything.

"I thought about taking you to The Depot," he added as he pulled into a parking spot. "But my coworkers would have harassed you endlessly, and tonight I want you all to myself."

Something wistful and fleeting passed across Summer's face but disappeared so quickly that Benjamin told himself he'd imagined it. He got out of the car and ran around to open her door, a thrill running up his arm as she let him take her hand again.

The burger shop was packed full, and Benjamin wrapped an arm around Summer's waist to keep her close as they waited in line. Her head swiveled toward him, and for a moment he was sure she was going to pull away. When she instead leaned into him a little, he nearly cheered out loud.

Simeon was a genius. Starting this relationship from the beginning was exactly what they needed.

They placed their order, then carried their food to a small table in a corner since it was too hot to eat at the picnic tables outside. Benjamin's only regret as they ate was that Murf's burgers were too big to eat with one hand, which meant he had to let go of Summer's for a little while.

They lingered over the meal longer than he had planned, until Benjamin suddenly realized that if they didn't get going, they were going to be late for the next part of their date.

"Now where are we going?" Summer asked as he took her hand and led her toward the door.

"You know I'm not going to tell you that," he teased.

"What if I refuse to go with you unless you tell me?" Summer stopped in the middle of the crowded restaurant, flattening her lips—but her eyes sparkled playfully.

"Then I guess I'll have to pick you up and carry you," he retorted, stepping close and squatting a little to circle his arms around her legs and lift.

"Benjamin, put me down," she gasp-shrieked, and heads around the room turned.

Undaunted, Benjamin asked, "Are you going to come with me, no questions asked?"

"Yes, yes," she promised. "Put me down."

He complied, and she swatted at his shoulder the moment her feet were on the ground. "I can't believe you did that."

He gave her a cheeky grin. "Really?"

She relented with a laugh. "Well, I *can* believe it. But I wish I couldn't."

"Now would you stop wasting time? We're going to be late." Benjamin took her hand and tugged her toward the door, ignoring her splutters.

The final credits scrolled across the movie screen, and still Summer didn't want to move. Somehow, Benjamin had managed to get the owner of the town's small movie theater—which was usually only open on weekends—to not only open on a Wednesday night but also to play Summer's favorite princess movie: *Beauty and the Beast*. Benjamin had kept her laughing through the beginning of the movie, with his commentary on the villain Gaston, but halfway through, when Belle and the Beast started to fall in love, he'd quieted and wrapped his arm around her back. After a while, she'd relaxed enough to rest her head on his shoulder.

They still sat like that now as the credits came to an end. She felt Benjamin shift a little, and her eyes closed as he pressed a kiss to the top of her head.

"Did you like it?" he whispered.

She nodded, though she didn't know whether he was asking about the movie or the kiss.

"Good. And now it's time for the next part of our evening." He slowly slid his arm out from behind her, his fingers tracing lightly over her skin and leaving tingles in their wake.

"The next part?" Reluctantly, she sat up. "I think this was enough already. We should probably get home."

But Benjamin shook his head stubbornly. "Not yet."

"Are you at least going to tell me what the next part is?"

"Of course not."

It was the answer she'd expected, and despite her earlier claim that she didn't like surprises, she found herself enjoying the anticipation of what Benjamin might have planned for her.

They headed out to the small lobby, where Benjamin thanked the theater owner—who reminded him that he'd be looking forward to moving to the top of the reservation list at The Depot.

"Benjamin," Summer protested. "Isn't that a bribe?"

He chuckled. "He has a standing reservation, so no. He's good friends with John."

"And John is the owner of The Depot, right? And Ireland's brother?" Summer felt like it would take a lifetime to get a grasp on all of the Calvanos and their connections. They seemed to know everyone in town.

"Correct." Benjamin opened the door for her, and Summer stepped out into the night, bracing for the sudden wave of heat. But a cool, refreshing breeze caressed her skin, and the sidewalks glistened with rainwater in the streetlights.

"I didn't realize it rained while we were in there," she said.

"I didn't realize there was anywhere other than the inside of the movie theater while we were in there." Benjamin's arm slipped across her shoulders and drew her close.

Before she could figure out how—and whether—to respond, he led her toward the Gremlin. He tucked her inside, then got in himself. But instead of starting the vehicle, he turned to her, his expression earnest. "Are you having fun?"

"I am." She was startled into answering honestly.

He chuckled. "You don't have to sound so surprised about it."

"Sorry." Summer laughed too. "I'm not— It's just—"

"I know." Benjamin's expression went suddenly serious as he reached for her hand. "It's been a lot."

She nodded, swallowing roughly. "It has."

His gaze was still on her, and her pulse began to throb against her neck so hard that she wondered if he could see it. The car was so small that their faces were only inches apart. If he wanted to, he could lean forward and—

"We should go," Benjamin turned abruptly to the steering wheel, his Adam's apple bobbing. "Daisy's is only open until ten."

"Aha," Summer said, but her voice lacked the triumph she was going for. "Now I know where we're going."

Benjamin mock groaned. "You got me that time."

The drive to Daisy's took less than five minutes, and Benjamin kept up a steady stream of conversation, as if nothing had happened.

Because nothing did, she reminded herself.

Clearly kissing was the farthest thing from his mind.

And from hers.

The moment Benjamin pulled into a parking spot and turned off the vehicle, he jumped out. Summer blinked at his empty seat for a moment, then reached for her own door, but it was already open.

She got out slowly, careful to keep some distance between herself and Benjamin. But he reached for her hand and pulled her closer with a smile. Summer swallowed and ordered herself not to look at his lips.

Inside, Benjamin ordered a slice of coconut cream pie for himself, then turned to her. "Caramel apple?"

Summer nodded, telling herself that the fact that he still remembered her favorite pie flavor shouldn't make her heart skip a beat. It was a common enough flavor.

"Could we get those to go?" Benjamin asked the girl at the counter.

"To go?" Summer glanced around the nearly empty restaurant. There were plenty of places to sit here. "Where are we going?"

"I'm not sure yet." Benjamin's grin was impish. "You ruined my surprise by figuring out we were coming here. So I'm improvising."

"*I* didn't ruin your surprise," Summer argued. "You *told* me. I can't help it if you can't keep a secret."

Benjamin stood close enough that his arm brushed hers. "Yes, but you're the one who distracted me."

"Distracted you?" Summer attempted a scoff. "How did I distract you?"

"You made me want—"

"Here y'all are." The girl behind the counter interrupted Benjamin's whispered response, and Summer exhaled shakily as he moved away from her to take the bag. What had he been about to say?

She scurried ahead of him to open the door. It was better if she didn't know anyway. Maybe he was going to say that she made him want pie.

Outside, she headed straight for his car, but he called her back. "We're not going anywhere."

Summer looked around dubiously. "We're going to eat pie in the parking lot?"

He shook his head. "We're not going *far*," he amended. "Come on." He held out his hand, and despite her better judgment, she took it.

He led her toward the riverwalk that led behind the downtown shops, stopping at a bench under the soft glow of an old-fashioned streetlamp. "How's this?"

"Um . . ." Summer didn't want to rain on his plans, but— "It's kind of wet."

"True." Benjamin frowned, then handed her the Daisy's bag and started unbuttoning his shirt.

"Benjamin, what are you . . ." The white t-shirt he wore under his button down did nothing to conceal his muscles, and Summer had a sudden flash of being pressed against his chest in the hallway this morning.

He pulled his button-down shirt off all the way and balled it up. Before Summer could protest, he was running it over the bench like a towel.

"There." He looked up, clearly satisfied with himself. "Now it's dry."

Summer shook her head with a wry laugh. "But your shirt's not."

He shrugged. "It's worth it."

He dropped onto the bench and beckoned Summer to sit next to him. Still shaking her head, she obeyed. He took the Daisy's bag from her, opened it, and fished out two clamshell containers and two forks.

"Close your eyes," he ordered suddenly.

"I— What?" Summer blinked at him.

"Close your eyes," he repeated.

"Benjamin," she objected with a confused laugh. "What are you going to do?"

"Just trust me. Or no pie."

Summer rolled her eyes. "I want it noted that I'm doing this under protest."

"So noted."

Summer sighed and closed her eyes, a dance troupe's worth of nerves suddenly leaping through her middle.

Was he going to kiss her?

She heard the crunch of a clamshell opening and let out a breath. Pie had never felt like such a disappointment before.

"That had better not be coconut," she warned.

"Trust me," Benjamin repeated.

A hand slid against her cheek, and she inhaled sharply, but then a fork touched her lips. Instinctively, her mouth opened, and the tart sweetness of apple and caramel mingled on her tongue.

"How is it?" Benjamin asked.

"Mmm." She sighed, opening her eyes slowly to find his gaze on her lips. She licked them quickly to catch any crumbs. "But why did I have to close my eyes?"

Benjamin's gaze moved from her lips to her eyes. "So I could do this," he whispered, both of his hands coming to her face as he leaned toward her.

Summer's breath caught in her chest.

Benjamin hesitated, his eyes questioning, and Summer knew she should stop him. Tell him this was a bad idea. But she nodded, letting her eyes fall closed again.

His lips brushed hers with a caress softer than the breeze, and Summer sighed the same sound she'd made when she tasted the pie.

Benjamin chuckled low in his throat and deepened the kiss.

Oh, Summer shouldn't want more of this, but she did.

She slid closer and brought her hands to his shoulders.

But her knee bumped into his, and the sound of something hitting the ground pulled them apart.

"Oh no." Summer had barely enough breath to get the words out. She stared at the two clamshells and their contents spilled on the ground. "I'm sorry."

"I'm not." Benjamin's finger grazed her cheek. "I found something much more delicious than pie." He grinned and brought his lips to hers again.

Chapter 35

"Boy oh boy! Caramel apples!" Max shouted, tugging Benjamin toward a table covered in the golden goodies.

Benjamin tightened his other hand around Summer's so he wouldn't lose her in the crowd of people enjoying the September Daze festival at Founder's Park. He had always thought it was an oddly named celebration, but this year it felt appropriate. He seemed to have spent the past week and a half in a happy daze. He and Summer had both had to work plenty, but they spent every moment they weren't at work together—taking Max to the park, hanging out with his family, hosting another princess party, doing chores for her Mama, and—his favorite—kissing. Even though they still slept in separate rooms, he at last had hope that this relationship was blossoming into a real marriage.

They reached the caramel apple table, and Benjamin ordered three of them, grinning as he passed one to Summer. Her pink cheeks and soft smile said that the treat reminded her of the flavor of their first kiss too. Ignoring the crowds around them, Benjamin dropped a quick kiss onto her lips.

"Benjamin," she protested, but she was laughing.

"What?" He raised his eyebrows. "Can't a guy kiss his wife in public?" He really loved calling her that.

They walked through the booths of crafts and artwork as they ate their apples, stopping to linger over a display of Ava's photography.

"Hey, y'all," Ava greeted them warmly. She bent to hug Max, then hugged Benjamin and Summer, who stepped right into her embrace. Contentment swelled in Benjamin's heart as he watched the two women chat like sisters. His earlier desire for Summer to experience the real love of a family was being fulfilled right in front of him.

A loudspeaker announced that there would be a magic show on the stage in thirty minutes.

"Oh boy!" Max waved his half-gnawed caramel apple in the air. "Can we go?"

"You and Summer can, Maxerooni. But I have to get to work," Benjamin said regretfully. They'd driven two cars over for exactly this reason, but he was still sorely tempted to call in sick. But he would never do that to Chloe.

"Chef Benjamin." An older woman whose voice could have been heard three counties away bustled into the booth. "Don't tell me you're not working today. I was counting on one of your delicious porterhouses tonight."

"Don't worry, Mrs. Simmons. I'm on my way now. I haven't seen you at The Depot in so long that I thought maybe you didn't like my food anymore," he teased.

"Don't be silly. Didn't the other ladies tell you? I've been in Europe for the past seven weeks. My son and his family live there. I told the ladies to tell you."

"Oh yes, I remember now." Benjamin grinned, and Mrs. Simmons smacked his arm.

"Always a joker, aren't you?'

"You know me well." Benjamin smiled at Summer over Mrs. Simmons's shoulder. His wife looked thoroughly amused by the conversation.

"And how is that girlfriend of yours?" Mrs. Simmons's voice seemed to echo off of the stands holding Ava's pictures. "The nice real estate lady. Jasmine, right?"

Benjamin's eyes were still on Summer's face, so he saw the moment her smile wilted and all the color drained out of her cheeks.

"Actually," Benjamin choked, stepping past Mrs. Simmons to take Summer's arm. He half dragged her the two steps to Mrs. Simmons's side. "I'd like you to meet my wife. Summer."

Mrs. Simmons squinted between them. "Summer? Is that some kind of nickname?"

"No." Summer's voice was faint. "It's my name."

"Why did I think it was Jasmine?" Mrs. Simmons looked perplexed. "Getting too old to trust my own memory. But you *are* in real estate?"

"Mrs. Simmons," Ava jumped in smoothly. "Is your daughter here? I have a picture I think she's going to want to see." She shot Benjamin a look that said, *Go*, and he didn't have to be told twice.

"We'd better get going," he said. "I'll see you tonight at The Depot, Mrs. Simmons."

As he ushered Max and Summer away from the booth, he could hear Mrs. Simmons say to Ava, "I'm usually so good with names. But whatever her name is, they sure did get married fast, didn't they?"

Judging from Summer's stiff walk, she heard it too.

"Summer," he started, but she shook her head.

"It's fine, Benjamin. You need to get to work."

"I know." He caught her arm and pulled her to a stop. "But I don't want to leave you like this."

"Like what?" She shrugged and maneuvered her arm out of his grasp. "Everything is fine."

He sighed. Everything clearly was *not* fine. "I should have told you Jasmine was—"

"I don't want Max to miss the magic show," she cut him off. "We'll see you when you get home.

"Summer," he tried again. But she had already grabbed Max's hand and was marching him toward the stage.

Benjamin let out a long breath, his happy daze draining away with it.

Slowly, he made his way toward his car. It looked like he was going to have to start from square one again.

∞

"How did he do that?" Max cheered wildly as the magician stood on the stage with a bird perched on his finger.

Summer shook herself and tried to focus on her nephew. But she could no more explain where the bird had come from than how Benjamin had made her drop her guard. Made her forget that he had only married her for Max's sake. That he had been dating someone else right up until they got married. Not just someone else. *Jasmine*. Sweet, perky, upbeat Jasmine—his perfect counterpart.

Summer had never had the courage to ask who he'd been dating before. And he had never volunteered the information—even when she'd hired Jasmine as her realtor. The surprise she'd sensed from Jasmine when she'd learned Summer and Benjamin were married suddenly made perfect sense. What must the other woman think of her? Would she let it affect the job she did for Summer?

And what about Benjamin? Why hadn't he mentioned that he and Jasmine had dated? Was it possible that he was still seeing her on the side?

The thought made Summer queasy, but she quickly dismissed it. She knew Benjamin well enough to know he wasn't that kind of guy. Most likely, he hadn't told Summer because he didn't want her to feel bad about what he'd had to give up to marry her.

Well, he wouldn't have to give it up for much longer. The guardianship hearing was in a week, and after that, whatever the outcome, she could let him off the hook, and he could go back to the woman he really wanted.

A fresh wave of nausea went through her. Well, that was what came of letting herself want him to want her.

"Aunt Sunny." Max was tapping her shoulder impatiently. "I'm hungry."

Summer nodded, noticing dully that the magic show was done, and people were scattering in every direction. She led Max to a hot dog cart.

They were still in line when Ava rushed over. "I'm so glad you're still here. I'm so sorry about Mrs. Simmons." She looked around and lowered her voice. "She can be a bit of a busybody."

It took every muscle in her face, but somehow Summer managed a smile that she hoped didn't look as painful as it felt. "It's really fine," she reassured Ava. "It was just a misunderstanding."

"Do you want to eat with us, Aunt Ava?" Max asked eagerly. "I'm going to get a chili dog."

"Yum." Ava patted Max's head. "I'd love to."

"Actually, we have to get ours to go," Summer said quickly. As much as she liked Ava, she had to get out of here.

"Oh, well, next time," Ava said cheerfully. She chatted with Max about school as they waited for their turn in line, but Summer noticed the concerned glances Ava kept shooting in her direction. Thankfully, all of Summer's experience at smiling for hours on end at princess parties had trained her well, and she kept her smile cemented in place.

When they finally reached the front of the line, Summer ordered a chili dog for Max and a plain hot dog for herself, even though she knew she wouldn't be able to eat it.

They said goodbye to Ava and headed for the parking lot. Halfway there, Summer's phone buzzed, and she pulled it out of her pocket, steeling herself for whatever sweet words Benjamin was going to say. She couldn't let herself be lulled by them again.

But when she tapped on the screen, she was staring at Jasmine's name. She shook her head, making an ironic huff at the back of her throat. She stuffed the phone back in her pocket. But after another two steps, she pulled it out again. Whatever the history between Jasmine and Benjamin, she was still Summer's realtor, and she might need something for the house.

Summer opened the notification, her feet jerking to a stop as she read it.

We have an offer!!!! $10,000 over asking! Do you have time to meet so we can discuss it?

Summer could only stare at that number. She hadn't expected to even get asking price for the house. And now someone wanted to give her $10,000 more? That would be enough to pay off the mortgage, cover TJ's debts, and have a little left over for Max.

She looked up to find Max still loping toward the parking lot.

"Max," she called. "Hold up a second."

The boy stopped, and she sent off a quick text agreeing to meet Jasmine at TJ's house in ten minutes.

When they got there, Jasmine's car was already in the driveway. Summer let out a long, slow breath as she pulled in behind her. She couldn't let what she had learned this morning bother her. In fact, it would probably be best to pretend she still didn't know. It would make things less awkward for both of them.

Satisfied with her decision, she grabbed the hot dog bag, got out of the car, and unbuckled Max, who raced ahead of her to the front door.

Anxiety tightened her stomach as Max knocked and Jasmine opened the door with a smile. All she could think was that it could have been Benjamin's door Jasmine was opening if Summer hadn't gotten in the way of their relationship.

"It's great news, isn't it?" Jasmine said, her smile perking up even more.

"Yes," Summer managed to croak. "It happened so fast. Is there— I mean, is it for real?"

Jasmine's smile turned to understanding. "It's for real. We've had a lot of interest, so the buyer wanted to put in a strong offer. They're moving from out of state, and they really love the house."

Summer nodded numbly and stepped inside. Jasmine led her to the kitchen counter, where several papers were spread.

"Did you want to wait for Benjamin?" Jasmine's smile didn't falter even a little, but Summer felt like the other woman had kicked her in the gut.

"He's at work," she managed. "I'll take care of everything."

"Okay. Great." Jasmine didn't flinch, but Summer wondered if she meant she thought it was great because it meant she wouldn't have to be reminded of what Summer had stolen from her.

While Max ate his chili dog, Jasmine went over everything with Summer, pointing out the various places she needed to sign to accept the offer.

When they were done, Jasmine turned to Summer with an outstretched hand and an enormous smile. "Congratulations. You've just sold your house."

"Thank you." The words felt inadequate. "You don't know what a huge burden this is off my mind."

"I'm glad I could help." Jasmine squeezed her arm. "I'm sure this has been a hard time."

She looked so sincere, so sympathetic, so *nice* that Summer couldn't pretend any longer. "I'm sorry about everything with Benjamin," she blurted.

Jasmine looked at her in surprise.

"It must have been a shock to find out that we were married," Summer rushed on. "I know you two had been dating, and I never meant to get in the way of that."

Jasmine's kind expression didn't change. "There's nothing to be sorry about," she said easily. "Benjamin explained everything. I think it's really great what he did. Very noble. The world could use more men like him." She gathered her paperwork. "I'm going to get all of this to the buyer's realtor, and we'll get things rolling for the appraisal and inspection. I'll be in touch as we get things scheduled." She called goodbye to Max on her way to the front door, pausing to wave cheerfully to Summer before she disappeared outside.

Summer let out a long breath, the word *noble* echoing in her head. That was exactly what Benjamin was. Exactly why he had married her.

And exactly why she couldn't let herself give in to the illusion that he wanted her.

Chapter 36

Benjamin filled two mugs with coffee, then added the tiniest drop of cream and half a spoonful of sugar to one—just the way Summer liked it. His hand shook a little as he stirred it, and he ordered his nerves to hold steady. Summer needed him to be strong today, whether she would admit it or not.

He took a sip from his own mug, then carried hers past the dining room table with its centerpiece of half-wilted flowers that he'd brought home for Summer after work last Saturday. She'd been in her room—asleep, he assumed, though he couldn't be sure—when he'd gotten home, so his apology for not telling her about Jasmine had had to wait until the next morning. She'd received it graciously, insisting that she wasn't upset.

And yet, all week she'd been cool and distant. She still accepted his kisses, but her response to them was lukewarm at best, and she didn't seek out opportunities to hug him and hold his hand the way she had been starting to do after their date.

Benjamin sighed, telling himself that things would be better after today.

But his stomach tightened at the possibility that things might not go their way. That they might be coming home without Max.

Don't think like that, he ordered himself as he knocked softly on Summer's door.

There was no reply, and he waited a moment, then knocked a little harder. "Summer? Are you up?"

"No," a voice called, and he chuckled quietly.

"I'm coming in," he warned, reaching for the doorknob. "I have coffee."

She didn't protest, so he opened the door slowly.

She was still in bed, the covers pulled up to her chin, her cheeks tear streaked.

"Ah, Summer." He hurried across the room and set the coffee on the bedside table.

"I can't do this," she sobbed as he sat on the edge of the bed. "I can't lose him."

"You're not going to lose him." Benjamin's words were quiet but fierce, and he bent to gather her in his arms.

"You can't know that," Summer argued, clutching at his back.

He couldn't answer at first, the truth of her words closing off his throat.

But after a moment, he pulled back and looked into her eyes. "What I do know," he said, "is that whatever happens we'll get through it together. Okay?"

The fear and uncertainty remained in her eyes, but she slowly nodded.

"Good." Benjamin couldn't resist pressing a kiss to her forehead. And then to each of her cheeks. And then to her lips.

She stiffened, but then let out a soft breath and drew him closer, her lips yielding to his.

Relief powerful enough to knock him over coursed through Benjamin, and when they parted, he slid his hands over her cheeks to wipe away the fresh tears.

"It's going to be okay," he promised her with one more kiss. Then he reluctantly got up so she could get dressed.

"I'll get Max ready," he offered. "You don't worry about anything."

"Benjamin," Summer called when he reached the door.

"Yeah?" He turned to look at her over his shoulder.

"Thank you." She smiled weakly, but it might as well have been the full noonday sun for the joy it brought him.

"Always."

Her smile wavered a little, but she nodded.

He stepped into the hallway and closed the door, then made his way to Max's room.

He paused at the door to pray. *Please Lord, let us get the guardianship. Let us be a family always. Amen.*

⁓

Summer stared around the courtroom, trying to process all of the faces she saw. She had assumed it would only be her and Benjamin and Max and Don, along with a social worker and Stacy and possibly Stacy's lawyer. But the room was packed with nearly Benjamin's entire family.

She pressed a hand to her mouth. "What are they—" She had to stop to choke back a sob. "Why is everyone here?"

"They're our family," Benjamin said lightly, as if it were the most obvious thing in the world. He wrapped an arm snugly around her back as they made their way to the seats at the front of the room.

Summer knew she should pull away—just like she should have pulled away from his kiss earlier—but she didn't have the strength right now.

Benjamin slid out a seat for her, and Summer scanned the room again as Max climbed onto the chair on her other side. Every member of Benjamin's family looked hopeful and confident, and several sent her smiles and thumbs-ups. Summer tried to smile in return, but she was pretty sure her lips had forgotten how to do that.

"Wait." Summer ran her eyes over the room again. "She's not here."

"Your mama?" Benjamin asked in surprise.

Summer shook her head. She had been worried that if Mama came, she would make a scene, but she hadn't really expected her to show up.

"Stacy."

"What?" Benjamin turned in his seat and scanned the room as well. "You're right."

Before Summer could ask Don what that meant, the judge was calling the room to order.

"This is a guardianship hearing for Max Ellis," she announced, "in response to a petition by Benjamin and Summer Calvano." Summer's heart jumped a little every time she heard their names paired like that. "Before I hear statements from the petitioners and the child, is there anyone who would like to contest the petition?"

The courtroom was silent, and the judge's eyes tracked to the people gathered behind Summer and Benjamin. Summer tensed, resisting the urge to turn around. What if Stacy had come in at the last second and was even now raising her hand?

But after another moment, the judge smiled, and said, "All right then, this should be pretty straightforward."

The hearing raced by, with the judge asking first her, then Benjamin, a series of questions. Then the judge called Max and the social worker into her chambers. Even though Don had warned them that this would be part of the proceedings, it was still unsettling. But not as unsettling as the fact that Stacy hadn't shown up.

Summer leaned closer to Don. "I thought Stacy was going to contest the guardianship."

Don shrugged. "That was the last I heard. I guess she changed her mind. It's good news for you. I don't see any reason why you wouldn't get guardianship now."

Summer nodded, biting her tongue against the question that had been needling her through the whole hearing—since Stacy hadn't shown up, could she have gotten guardianship without Benjamin? Had he married her for nothing?

The time ticked by slowly, the courtroom eerily silent, and Summer focused all of her attention on praying that Don was right. That the judge would come out here and say that Max could stay with her forever.

Benjamin had folded his hands in his lap, and his head was bowed, so she knew he was doing the same.

The sound of a door opening cracked through the courtroom, and Benjamin lifted his head quickly.

The judge reentered the room, but Max and the social worker weren't with her.

Summer's breath caught sharp against her ribs. Benjamin's arm was instantly around her, his lips pressed to the top of her head. "It's going to be okay," he whispered hoarsely into her hair.

The judge took her seat. "That Max is a delightful boy," she said easily. "He found some magnet blocks in my chambers and asked if he could keep playing with them while I came back to the boring courtroom." She laughed lightly, and Summer heard the nervous chuckles from behind her, but she couldn't let out enough air to laugh.

"It's also clear that he adores the two of you," the judge continued, and Summer felt Benjamin's tension ease, but she couldn't bring herself to relax.

"And as you have the means and the desire to raise him," the judge said, "I am happy to grant permanent guardianship of the minor Max Ellis to you, Benjamin and Summer Calvano."

A giant sob of relief escaped Summer as Benjamin's arms engulfed her and the courtroom burst into a clamor of applause and cheers.

Summer buried her head in Benjamin's chest as he stroked her hair. After a moment, he let go of her, and his arms were replaced by those of her in-laws.

Summer finally had her tears under control when Max came sauntering into the courtroom, his eyes going wide at the noise but a grin on his lips.

Benjamin stooped to pick him up and hug him tight, and Summer's tears poured down again.

"What's wrong, Aunt Sunny?" Max's little face wrinkled with worry.

"Nothing is wrong." Summer quickly wiped her eyes. "I'm just happy."

"The judge said we all get to stay together," Benjamin explained to the boy.

Max smiled. "That's what I told her to say. Can we get some magnet blocks?"

"Yes." Benjamin kissed Max's cheek with a loud smack that made the boy giggle. "I think we can definitely get some magnet blocks."

He looked at Summer with shining eyes and held out his arm so she could join their hug. As soon as she did, he leaned over and kissed her cheek as loudly as he had kissed Max's.

Chapter 37

"Are you okay?" Benjamin eyed Summer, who had curled into a ball on the couch the moment they'd gotten home from a celebratory lunch at Dad's. She'd grown quieter and quieter as the day went on. Not that Benjamin blamed her. After the weeks of stress and wondering what would happen to Max, finally having the answer they'd been praying for was overwhelming.

Summer looked up with a start. "Where's Max?" she asked quietly.

"Playing in his room. I told him we could all go to the park in a little bit, but I can take him by myself if you don't feel up to it."

Summer shook her head, but he wasn't sure if that meant no, she didn't feel up to it, or no, she would go along.

"It's been an overwhelming day." He lowered himself to the couch next to her, resting his hand lightly on her leg. "It's okay to need some time to process it."

"Stacy didn't come," she whispered.

"I know." He brushed at a stray hair hanging over her cheek. "It was an answer to our prayers."

But she shook her head. "We got married because Stacy was going to contest the guardianship. But she didn't."

"I know," Benjamin said patiently. Clearly Summer was trying to work through something. "God worked everything out." He had been a fool to ever doubt that God had things in his control.

225

Summer shook her head harder. "No. Don't you see? We wouldn't have had to get married at all. I could have gotten the guardianship myself, and you would have been free to—"

"You don't know that," Benjamin interrupted. "Even before we knew Stacy planned to contest it, Don said he wasn't sure you'd be able to get guardianship on your own. That's why I asked you to marry me in the first place. You were just too stubborn to say yes until Stacy came along," he teased.

But instead of easing into a smile, Summer's frown deepened. "I have guardianship now," she said, her voice oddly detached.

"*We* have guardianship," Benjamin corrected, his stomach suddenly tightening.

"But we don't have to be married to keep it." Her voice was barely louder than a whisper, but it lashed at Benjamin.

"What are you saying?" He was pretty sure he didn't want to know the answer, but he couldn't keep himself from asking.

"I'm saying." Her lips trembled, but she didn't look at him. "That we can still get an annulment, since we haven't . . ."

Benjamin reared back. Was this why she had kept her distance from him, so she could use him and then leave him?

"When I said, 'for as long as we both shall live,' I meant it." He had to work to keep his voice under control. "Did you?"

"I'm not going to hold you to that." She finally turned to him, but her eyes were too guarded for him to read anything in them.

"Hold me to it?" Benjamin grabbed her arms. "It's not something you're holding me to. It's a vow I made before God."

"I think he would understand," she said, "given the circumstances."

"The circ—" Benjamin got up and paced to the window. "For heaven's sake, Summer, do you even hear yourself right now?"

A blast of sound made them both jump, and Summer snatched her phone up off the coffee table.

Her face went chalk white as she looked at the screen.

"What's wrong?" He strode toward her.

"It says Fuller County," she whispered. "You don't think Stacy decided to contest it now?"

Benjamin shook his head. "I'm sure it's only a follow-up call. Everything has already been decided. They can't change it."

Summer swallowed and nodded, but her voice shook as she said, "Hello?" She paused a moment, then said, "This is Summer Ellis."

Benjamin flinched a little at her use of her maiden name.

The silence stretched as Summer listened, sinking deeper into herself and biting her lip. Benjamin retook his seat on the couch next to her. She reached for his hand and gripped it, and a little knot of fear worked its way through him. He stared at the phone as if that would make the unintelligible sounds he heard from the other end arrange themselves into words.

"Today?" Summer finally asked. She listened again. "Okay. Yes. I'll be there. Thank you." She closed her eyes and sat with the phone still pressed to her ear, though there were no longer sounds coming from the other end.

"What is it?" It took all of his strength not to let impatience leak into his voice.

Summer lifted her head but seemed to be looking through him. "It was the medical examiner's office. I forgot that I agreed for them to do postmortem genetic testing on TJ. It was some sort of pilot program or something . . ."

"And . . ." Benjamin squeezed her hand, and she seemed to shake herself, withdrawing her hand from his.

"And they want me to come in to discuss some of the findings, that's all."

"What kind of findings?" The knot of fear in his gut cinched tighter. He'd never mentioned to her the research he'd done into sudden heart failure after TJ's death because he hadn't wanted to scare her. But if the genetic testing had found something . . .

Summer looked away. "They didn't really say. But they can see me today at four, so if I leave now, I should be able to get there on time."

"Should we bring Max?" Benjamin asked. "Or do you want me to call Mia to see if we can drop him off on the way?"

"Mia has class on Friday afternoons," Summer reminded him. "You stay here with him, and I'll go."

"You're not going alone." Benjamin had already pulled his phone out and sent a quick message to the family chat.

"I'll be fine," Summer argued. "Really."

"I'm coming. Really." His phone buzzed, and he quickly read the replies to his message. "Lydia says she can watch Max. Let's go."

Chapter 38

Summer kept her hands in her lap as Benjamin steered them to the same government complex they had left only a few hours before. His hand grasped her knee, and she desperately wanted to cling to it for dear life, but she couldn't let herself do that. Whatever they learned at the medical examiner's office wouldn't change anything. She still needed to let him go.

The way he'd looked when she'd mentioned the annulment, though, as if she'd punched him in the stomach, maybe it meant—

No, it didn't. She knew it didn't.

He hadn't said he loved her. Hadn't said he wanted to be with her. He'd said that he made a vow before God. *That* was why he didn't want to annul their marriage.

Because he was too *noble*.

There was that word again.

But that didn't mean he should have to be chained forever to a woman he didn't love.

Benjamin pulled into a parking spot and turned the car off but didn't make a move to get out.

"We should go inside," she said quietly. "It's almost four o'clock." When he still didn't move, she added, "You can wait in the car, if you want."

A muscle in his cheek jumped, but he shook his head, let out a hard breath, and opened his car door. Summer did the same, and when they met at the back of the car, he took her hand. His grip was firm and reassuring as he led her to the building next to the courthouse where they'd been celebrating only this morning.

Inside, a kind but somber looking receptionist invited them to take a seat. The waiting area was softer and more welcoming than Summer had expected, and Benjamin led them to a small sofa. He sat next to her and leaned forward, bracing his elbows on his knees and resting his head in his hands. He looked so defeated that Summer couldn't keep herself from resting a hand on his shoulder. His muscles twitched under her fingertips, and he reached to cover her hand with his.

"Miss Ellis?" A middle-aged woman with a kind smile poked her head through a door Summer hadn't even noticed.

She let out a breath and stood. Next to her, Benjamin did the same, his fingers slipping silently into hers.

"Thanks for coming in on such short notice." The woman held out a slender hand, and Summer had to let go of Benjamin's to shake it.

"I'm Dr. Ramstadt. I'm a genetic counselor who consults with the county in cases of postmortem genetic testing."

"Nice to meet you," Summer murmured.

"And you must be . . ." The woman held her hand out to Benjamin as well.

"Benjamin Calvano. Summer's husband," he answered.

"I'm glad you could make it too." Dr. Ramstadt's expression turned serious, though her voice remained cheerful. "Why don't y'all come on back, and we'll talk about a few things."

She led them across the hall to an office that could have been a tropical rainforest, with plants covering nearly every open space—the desk, the shelves, the windowsill. Summer wondered vaguely if this was how Dr. Ramstadt handled dealing with death all day—by surrounding herself with living things.

The doctor gestured for them to sit in two cushioned chairs that were pulled up to a low coffee table covered with orchids. She took a seat across from them.

"As you know," the woman began, folding her hands over her lap as if they'd gotten together for a casual chat, "your brother experienced sudden cardiac death."

Even though she had known this for weeks, Summer winced.

"But because the cause of his cardiac event was undetermined through standard autopsy, we submitted his samples for further testing," the woman continued, and Summer wanted to stop her right there.

TJ wasn't some kind of lab specimen. He was a real, live human being. Or he *had* been.

"Were you able to determine the cause?" Benjamin leaned forward, and Summer could see the ripple of tension in the muscles of his forearm.

"We were." Dr. Ramstadt's voice softened, and she glanced at them both with sympathy. "TJ had something we call dilated cardiomyopathy."

Summer stared at her blankly. "I don't know what that means."

"Cardiomyopathy is a form of heart disease that makes it harder for the heart to pump blood through the body. In the case of dilated cardiomyopathy, this results from a dilation, or enlargement, of one of the heart's chambers, and a thinning or weakening of the heart muscle in that area."

"But he—" Summer tried to grasp what the woman was saying. It made no sense. "He could run for miles and miles and miles." She turned desperately to Benjamin. "Tell her how far y'all ran."

Benjamin opened his mouth, but before he could speak, Dr. Ramstadt cut in. "Patients often don't have any symptoms. That's probably why he was never diagnosed."

"And cardiomyopathy is a genetic condition?" Benjamin asked quietly.

"Not always," Dr. Ramstadt answered. "But in TJ's case, yes. It was caused by a rare genetic variant."

Benjamin reached for Summer's hand, gripping it tightly, and she looked from him to the doctor. Had she missed something?

"Does that mean . . ." Benjamin's face went gray, and his lips stretched into a sharp line.

"Mean what?" Summer had never wished more that she had paid better attention in biology class.

"It means," the doctor said gently. "That everyone in the family should be tested."

"Tested?" Summer felt like her mind was moving through tar. Like everyone else was three steps ahead of her. "For . . ."

"Because it's a genetic disorder," Dr. Ramstadt said, "there's a chance others in the family may also have this variant."

"I— So— You mean Max might—" Summer's brain rebelled against finishing the sentence.

"Max is TJ's son, correct?" the doctor asked.

Summer nodded mutely as Benjamin said, "Yes."

"Then possibly," the woman said. "But TJ had a recessive gene variant. That means both of your parents had the gene mutation. There's a good chance Max's mother didn't have it, and if that's the case, Max couldn't have inherited the disorder." The woman paused, her eyes settling gently on Summer. "It's much more likely that you did."

Benjamin's hand jerked, and his eyes closed as his chin fell toward his chest.

He said something to the doctor, but suddenly the only thing Summer could hear was her heart beating in her ears. She had the odd sensation that it might stop at any moment.

Benjamin talked to Dr. Ramstadt for a few more minutes, but Summer could think of only one thing: She'd promised just this morning that she would take care of Max until he was an adult.

But what if she didn't have the chance?

Chapter 39

Benjamin sat on the couch in the half-dark, listening to the incessant ringing on the other end of his phone. When it kicked to voicemail, he hung up. He'd already left three messages on Judah's office voicemail today. He knew it was pointless to be surprised that his brother hadn't responded—but that didn't stop the disappointment and desperation from burning through him. Dr. Ramstadt had given them referrals to a cardiologist and a geneticist in Brampton. But Benjamin wanted Summer and Max to have the best doctor—and that was his brother.

He shuffled through the paperwork from the medical examiner. He should have called the doctors she'd recommended right away this afternoon rather than waiting on the unrealistic dream that Judah could put aside whatever it was that had driven him to separate himself from the family. Now they'd have to wait until Monday to even get on the schedule. And who knew how long it would be before they could actually be seen.

Benjamin dropped the papers wearily back onto the table and rubbed at his eyes. Summer had gone to bed almost immediately after they'd tucked Max in—but not before withdrawing into that shell she kept pulling up around herself every time they got close.

He let out a heavy breath, the feeling that he was failing at every point of his role as a husband and father hanging heavily from his shoulders.

They have to be okay, Lord. They have to be. He had been repeating the same prayer all day. He knew he should add, "Your will be done." But he didn't want to. He wouldn't. If God's will was to take them from him, then he didn't want God's will to be done. Not now. Not ever.

His phone blared suddenly into the quiet, and he snatched it up and silenced it before the sound could wake Max or Summer. He expected it to be Dad or one of his siblings. He'd texted them earlier with a short summary of what had happened since the hearing this morning—though he'd carefully left out the part where Summer had announced she wanted an annulment—and they'd been calling and texting all evening to offer their prayers.

But the name on the screen read Cleveland Clinic.

Benjamin hit answer. "Judah?"

"Benjamin? Sorry I couldn't call sooner. I was in surgery."

It had been nearly ten years since Benjamin had heard his brother's voice, but something in Judah's tone set him at ease. He didn't hold the same animosity toward his second-oldest brother as some of his other siblings, probably because he'd been so young when Judah stopped coming home that his brother had always seemed like some mysterious, enigmatic figure to him. For a while, he'd been convinced that Judah must be a spy. He'd been terribly disappointed when Dad told him Judah was a cardiologist.

He wasn't disappointed anymore.

"So you're married?" Judah asked.

"Yeah. It was kind of— I guess we eloped. None of the family was there." He wasn't sure why he bothered with the explanation. Judah hadn't sounded the least bit hurt that he hadn't been invited to his baby brother's wedding.

"And your wife's brother died of cardiomyopathy?"

"Yes." Benjamin gave Judah all the details he knew, his brother breaking in a few times to ask questions Benjamin couldn't answer.

Finally, Judah said, "And you're sure you want to bring them here? The insurance is going to be a mess."

"I have good insurance." That was one thing John had seen to from the beginning. "And I'll pay for it out of my pocket if I have to. I want them to see *you*."

"All right. I'll have my office contact you on Monday with a date. It might be a while before I have an opening," he warned. "But I'll make sure they know it's urgent."

Benjamin wanted to argue. Wanted to tell him he should clear his calendar for this. But instead, he said, "That's fine. Is there anything they should do or not do in the meantime?"

"Nothing that I wouldn't recommend for everyone. Healthy food, exercise, all of the usual."

"Okay." Benjamin tried to figure out what else to say. "How— Uh— How are you?" It felt like a stupid question, but he barely knew his brother.

"Tired," Judah answered. "I've been in surgery for the past twelve hours."

"Right." Benjamin could take a hint. "I'll let you go. But thank you again."

They hung up, and Benjamin sat for a few minutes, his eyes roving the once-bare living room that now held little touches of Max and Summer everywhere. Max's dinosaurs in the corner. Summer's book on the table. A bowl from Max's snack on the floor. One of Summer's hair ties on the arm of the couch.

A pang seared his chest at the thought of going back to a life without them here. He stood and turned out the light.

He wasn't going to let that happen. Not by an annulment. And certainly not by death.

He made his way down the dark hall, pausing to peek in on Max. The soft glow of a night light illuminated the boy, who slept on his stomach, his new dinosaur clutched in his arms.

Love for the boy ached through Benjamin as he closed the door.

He turned to his own room, but his heart went to Summer's. He needed to see her one more time before he went to sleep. Needed to reassure himself that she was still there. That she was still okay.

He moved down the hall to her door and eased it open.

She lay with her back to him, her hair fanned across the pillow behind her, her body tucked in under the blankets, which moved in soft rustles with her breaths.

He let out his own breath and blew a silent kiss in her direction, then started to pull the door closed again.

"Benjamin?" Her whisper slipped through the dark, sliding right into place in his heart.

"It's me," he whispered back. "Just wanted to make sure you were okay."

"I'm okay." The blankets rustled, and then she was facing him, and an overwhelming need swept over him.

"Can I—" He hesitated. "I think I just really need to hold you right now."

Chapter 40

She should say no. Tell him to go back to his own bed.

But instead, Summer found herself sliding to the far side of the bed, at the same time lowering the blankets to invite him in.

She heard his ragged exhale, and then, in three strides, he was across the room and climbing into the bed, his arms pulling her immediately into a fierce hug. He buried his face in her hair, and she buried hers in his shoulder, his earthy herbal scent sending a wave of peace that calmed the turbulence of her heart.

"I've got you," he whispered.

She tried to nod, but his hug was too tight to allow for movement.

"You're suffocating me a little," she spoke into his shoulder.

"Sorry." His grip eased a fraction, but his arms still encircled her.

She slid her head back a little so that they were face-to-face on her pillow. "I'm sorry," she whispered into the dark.

"For what?" His hands splayed across her back like a safety net.

"For trapping you."

Benjamin chuckled, his arms tightening again. "In case you haven't noticed, I'm the one who has you trapped at the moment."

But Summer couldn't laugh. "I'm serious, Benjamin. I meant what I said before about not holding you to your vows, but now—"

"Now nothing has changed," Benjamin said firmly. "I'm not going anywhere. I'm sorry, but *you're* the one who's stuck with *me*." His smile was soft but also hopeful, as if he were waiting for her to agree. But how could she?

"If something happens to me—" she started, but Benjamin cut her off with a raspy growl.

"It won't."

"But if it does," she persisted. "You're going to be stuck raising Max on your own."

"Summer." Benjamin lifted a hand off her back and pressed it gently to her cheek. "I love that boy. I would do anything for him. You know that."

She nodded. She did know that. It was how they had ended up here in the first place.

"And I would do anything for you too," he whispered.

She closed her eyes. She fully believed that. He was too noble to do anything less.

"I finally got ahold of Judah." His fingers moved into her hair, rubbing soft circles into her scalp. "He said he'll get us the soonest appointment he can."

"I still don't think that's necessary." She tried to open her eyes, but his hands in her hair felt too good. "The doctors here are fine."

"It's necessary," Benjamin insisted. "He's one of the foremost heart experts in the country."

"But won't it be awkward for you?" According to Benjamin, it had been almost ten years since Judah had cut off most contact with the family. It was hard to believe that even the perfect Calvano family had a black sheep—if one of the nation's best heart doctors could be considered a black sheep.

"Maybe." Benjamin's fingers moved from her hair to her shoulders, and Summer shivered and let herself snuggle in a little closer to him. "But it's not like I have a problem with him, and I don't see why he should have one with me."

"Who *does* he have a problem with?"

"Honestly, I'm not really sure. I was young when he left for college, and he just slowly stopped coming home. I used to think it was because he was a spy."

Summer laughed softly, resting her face against his chest.

"I think the biggest thing was he had a lot of professors and classmates who were telling him that the faith he'd grown up with was foolish. Simeon said that the last time he came home, he and Dad had a big fight. And after that, he just stopped coming home."

Drowsiness pulled at Summer, but she liked listening to Benjamin talk. She liked feeling the low rumble of his voice in his chest as she pressed her face into him. "Is your family going to be mad?" she murmured sleepily.

"Nope." Benjamin kissed the top of her head. "And who knows? Maybe we can convince him to come home with us."

"Mmm." Summer felt herself drifting off to sleep, the word "home" echoing pleasantly in her dreams.

Chapter 41

Benjamin sat in the church pew with one arm wrapped firmly around Summer, the other holding the hymnal they shared. He'd been terrified to open his eyes yesterday morning, afraid he had only dreamed that he'd held her all night. But when he'd finally found the courage to open them, she was right there, in his arms. And waking up with her in the same place this morning—well, he was ruined for life. He never wanted to wake up without her again.

Please, Lord, he prayed as the hymn ended. *Don't let me lose her.*

A plastic dinosaur landed on Benjamin's knee, and he smiled down at Max. *Him either, Lord.*

He had checked his phone a million times yesterday and this morning, even though he knew it was unlikely that Judah's office would get back to him over the weekend. But it was driving him crazy that there was nothing he could do for these two people he loved other than wait and pray.

As Pastor Cooper, Beautiful Savior's youth pastor, moved to the pulpit for the sermon, Benjamin's knee bounced, and Summer's hand fell softly onto it. He stilled, turning to find her smiling gently at him.

"Sorry," he whispered, and she nodded and rested her head on his shoulder just long enough for him to drop a kiss on her hair.

"Well, y'all," Pastor Cooper began. "When I was a kid and people would ask me what my favorite part of school was, I always had a ready answer:

recess." He grinned as the congregation laughed. Benjamin smiled. He always enjoyed the youth pastor's light sense of humor.

"I mean, of course it was. It was easy, right?" Pastor Cooper went on. "And fun. And I was really, really good at it. But—" The pastor held up a finger. "I had an equally quick answer for my least favorite part of school: tests. Because they were the exact opposite of recess. Hard. Not fun. And I was really, really bad at them. It could be a test on a subject I had down cold, something I'd studied for hours, but the moment the teacher put that test in front of me, I froze. You want to know one of my favorite parts of being a grown-up?" He grinned. "No more tests."

The congregation laughed, but Pastor Cooper's grin faded. "Or are there?" He paused and scanned the congregation. "Only these tests are harder. They're not on paper. They're in our hearts. In our lives. I've gone through them, and so have you. Trials and hurts and heartaches of every kind imaginable." He shook his head. "I'd list them, but the list is pretty much endless, isn't it? And they're worse than any test we ever took in school. Because these tests—they're not about a grade. They're about our lives."

Benjamin's eyes traveled the pews that held his family. Between them, they'd been through more than their share of tests like that. And they'd all handled them with grace and faith. All except Benjamin. He felt like he'd messed up every single test of faith he'd been given over the past two months.

"And if I'm completely honest," Pastor Cooper continued. "I like these tests even less than school tests. And I feel like I do worse on them too. I freeze up. I ask, 'Lord, why is this happening to me?' I cry, 'Lord, why aren't you doing anything?' I accuse, 'Lord, you must not love me.' And then," he sighed dramatically and shook his head. "I try to take matters into my own hands. Instead of trusting in the Lord."

Benjamin stared at the pulpit, realization slowly stabbing into his conscience. What Pastor Cooper was describing—that was exactly what he'd done when he'd married Summer. He had been sure that God wouldn't—maybe couldn't—take care of the situation, so he'd taken things into his own hands, followed his own ways.

"Well," Pastor Cooper said, turning cheerful. "My mama always told me the best way to be prepared for a test is to study." He tapped the Bible that rested on the pulpit. "And I can't think of a better book to prepare us for our tests of faith than this one. Lots of people in here faced tests of their faith. I mean, we could go back and start at the beginning, right? Adam and Eve in the garden. Their faith was tested when God forbade them to eat from one single tree in the garden. One tree out of hundreds, maybe thousands, was off limits. And they— Oh hold on. They're not a good example. They failed the test. Okay, skip them. Let's go to Abraham. There's a guy who was tested many a time. God asked him to leave his home and everything he knew and travel to a distant land. And Abraham faithfully went. He brought his wife Sarah with him—and was afraid that Pharaoh might kill him so that he could take Sarah as his own wife. He didn't think God had taken that into account. So Abraham pretended that Sarah was his sist— Oh wait, hold on. He failed the test too, didn't he?"

Pastor Cooper rubbed at his hair, as if thinking, then held up a finger. "Okay, I've got one. Peter. Surely if ever there was an example of someone who passed the test, it must be Peter. He eagerly followed Jesus. He was the first to speak up whenever anyone had a problem with the message of his Lord. He boldly declared that he would die before he would betray Jesus. And then . . . He denied knowing Jesus three times in one night." Pastor Cooper hung his head and sighed. "This is sounding kind of bleak, isn't it? Is there no one who can pass the test?"

He lifted his head again, his brow wrinkled but his smile wide. "Only one. And you know who it is. Jesus. He passed *all* the tests for us. He kept God's law perfectly. He never once messed up. Never once let fear or worries or hardships lead him astray. He remained perfectly in God's will always."

Benjamin leaned forward, restlessness prickling his soul as Pastor Cooper continued, "The thing is, as much as we know that, it doesn't always make going through the tests any easier. We'd rather skip them altogether. Is there any point to them anyway? James 1:2-4 tells us, 'Consider it pure joy, my brothers and sisters, whenever you face trials of many kinds, because you know that the testing of your faith produces perseverance. Let perseverance finish its work so that you may be mature and complete, not lacking anything.' And 1 Peter 1:6-7 says, 'In all this you greatly rejoice, though now for a little while you may have to suffer grief in all kinds of trials. These have come so that the proven genuineness of your faith—of greater worth than gold, which perishes even though refined by fire—may result in praise, glory and honor when Jesus Christ is revealed.'"

The pastor looked up. "So yeah, there's a point. A pretty big one. These tests refine our faith—our most precious possession. They teach us to persevere—not in ourselves, but in the Lord and his ways, so that our faith may become mature and lacking nothing."

The pastor let his gaze sweep over the congregation. "Passing the test doesn't mean having all the right answers. It means surrendering to God and trusting that he does." He paused, looking thoughtful. "You know, there's another person who faced some pretty enormous tests who I didn't mention earlier. Job. I don't think any of us ever want to be tested the way he was. And Job didn't really want to be either. He tried to argue with God, to tell him how things should be. But in the end, Job had to confess, 'Surely I spoke of things I did not understand, things too wonderful for me to know.' He couldn't make that confession on his own. He could only make it after God reminded him who he was—and who God is."

Pastor Cooper smiled. "We can't make that confession on our own either. Left to our own devices, we'll fall and fail just as badly as Adam and Eve, as Abraham, as Peter. But Jesus promises that he forgives us for those failures. That's the whole reason he passed every test. So he could take that perfection to the cross, where he gave it up for you and for me. He exchanged his perfection for our sin. Which means that when God looks at you, he sees an A+ on every one of your tests. He sees Christ's perfect score written on your paper. And because of that, he promises that with every trial, 'you are receiving the end result of your faith, the salvation of your souls.' Amen."

Benjamin let out a breath he hadn't realized he was holding.

Summer turned to him. "Are you okay?" she whispered.

He nodded. He thought he was now.

Pastor Cooper led the congregation in prayer, and Benjamin bowed his head to add his own plea. *Forgive me for doubting and blaming you, Lord, for not trusting in you. Please show me how to surrender to you. How to trust that you have the answers for Summer and Max and their health.* He paused, wrestling with himself for a moment, then added, *Let your will be done. Whatever it may be. Amen.*

After the service, they chatted with his family for a while, all of whom promised to keep Summer and Max in their prayers. On the way out to the parking lot, Benjamin pulled his phone out of his pocket to check it, mostly out of habit. But the notification from Judah set his heart racing. *All right, Lord,* he admitted silently. *You do know what you're doing.*

He held it out to Summer, and her eyes widened. "This Wednesday? We can't. You're supposed to fly out to Atlanta."

"I'll cancel." In all the commotion of the last few days, he'd almost forgotten he was supposed to see Ian, but there was no way he was going to delay getting Summer and Max to Cleveland.

"Benjamin, you can't. Your friend already bought the tickets, and—"

"He'll understand," Benjamin reassured her. Actually, he wasn't at all sure that was true, but he didn't care.

"What about Mama?" Summer asked.

"I'll mow her lawn this afternoon while you get her groceries. Then I'll make a few meals to stick in her freezer, and Dad can stop by to check on her."

"But—"

"Summer." Benjamin grabbed her arm as they reached the car. "We're going."

She watched him a moment, then nodded.

"Good." He caught her lips in a quick kiss. Then he moved to open her door and Max's.

"You want to take a trip, Maxerooni?" he asked the boy.

And Max gave exactly the response he was waiting for: "Boy oh boy!"

Chapter 42

"Oh boy! Look at those buildings! They're bigger than dinosaurs!" Max exclaimed.

"They sure are." Summer tried to keep the nerves out of her voice as Benjamin steered the car out of the hotel parking lot, following his phone's directions toward the hospital.

Max had fallen asleep before they'd reached Cleveland late last night, and Benjamin had carried him up to their room, carefully tucking him into one of the beds before he and Summer had fallen, exhausted, into the other. He had cocooned her against him in the dark, his arms a protective circle she never wanted to leave. She had tried to convince herself not to want that—not to want this to last—but she was so tired of fighting her feelings. And maybe, just maybe he *would* want her. Maybe he *did* want her.

Why else would he have driven her and Max all the way to Cleveland to see his estranged brother?

She let herself glance at him from under her lashes. His grip on the steering wheel was tight, and his left leg jounced against his seat.

"Are you nervous?" she asked quietly.

Benjamin's eyes flicked to her, and he laughed with a light smile. "I think I should be asking you that. I'm not the one who's about to get poked and prodded."

But she knew him well enough to catch the apprehension underneath the words.

"The procedures will be fine," she assured him. "I meant, are you nervous about seeing your brother?"

He shrugged. "What's there to be nervous about? I'm everyone's favorite brother anyway." He shot a lopsided grin at her, and she reached suddenly across the space between them to take his hand.

His eyes came to hers, shining with surprise.

"Thank you for doing this for us." Her heart was too full to say more, but Benjamin squeezed her hand.

"I would walk to the ends of the earth for you two. A little drive to Cleveland? That's nothing."

But it *wasn't* nothing. Not to Summer.

They reached the hospital's campus, and Benjamin followed a series of signs that led to a parking garage.

"Are we in a cave?" Max asked, awe in his voice.

"Something like that." Summer laughed, but Benjamin had gone silent.

He pulled into a parking spot and shut off the car, then turned to her, gripping both of her hands. "Whatever we find out," he whispered, "you have to promise me we're in this together."

Summer hesitated. She so badly wanted to agree to that. But how could she, when she knew it meant asking him to give up everything?

"Summer." The urgency in the word made her nod.

"Good." He leaned forward and kissed her tenderly, as if it might be their last kiss ever, then got out of the car.

Summer forced herself to take a shaky breath and do the same, dread of what they might learn today suddenly hitting her and nearly driving her back into the car.

"Come on." Benjamin was at her side with Max in one arm. He wrapped the other around her, the solidity of his nearness giving her the strength to move her feet. They made their way into the hospital and followed the signs to the cardiology department, where a receptionist invited them to have a seat.

But they hadn't been there for two minutes when Max announced that he needed to use the bathroom. Benjamin got up to take him, and Summer was left to herself just as a nurse popped into the waiting room and called for her and Max.

Summer stood. "My— Uh— My husband"—the word was coming easier lately—"just took him to the restroom."

"That's okay." The nurse's smile was warm. "I'll take you back and then come out here and get them."

Summer nodded, though she wanted to argue that she'd rather wait for them. She followed the nurse through the door and down a brightly lit hallway with doors on either side. Finally, the nurse stopped at one and rapped twice.

"Come in," a male voice that sounded almost familiar called.

"Dr. Calvano will meet with you folks in his office first to go over the procedures and get a thorough history, and then we'll get everything going." The nurse pushed the door open and ushered Summer through. "I'll go get Max and your husband and be right back."

And then the nurse was gone, and Summer was staring at a man who looked remarkably like a cross between Benjamin and his brother Zeb.

"You must be Summer." He came around the desk with his hand outstretched.

Summer shook it, at a complete loss for words.

"I'm Dr. Calvano," he added. "Judah."

"Benjamin's brother," she said dumbly, though he obviously knew that.

He chuckled, the sound deeper than Benjamin's light, easy laugh. "Yes. Benjamin's brother. And I hear you're his wife."

"I— Um. Well, yes."

"Congratulations." He gestured to a couch in the corner of the room. "Have a seat."

Summer obeyed, searching desperately for something else to say. But before she could come up with anything, there was another knock on the door, and Max came charging in, followed more slowly by Benjamin.

"Are you my uncle Judah?" Max asked eagerly.

Judah's mouth opened, and he looked to Benjamin, who appeared to be sizing him up.

"I guess I am," Judah said slowly, holding out a hand to Max. "It's nice to meet you."

Max shook the outstretched hand enthusiastically, and Judah grinned the same grin Summer had seen on Benjamin a thousand times.

"Is that a dinosaur?" he asked Max.

"Yep. Benji gave it to me. He said I could bring it with me today. Is that true?"

Judah nodded. "It sure is."

"Good." Max tromped over to the couch and climbed up next to Summer, but her eyes were still on Benjamin and Judah.

"It's good to see you, Benjamin." Judah held out a hand.

"Yeah. You too." Benjamin stuck his hand in his brother's then stepped forward and pulled him into a hug. "Thanks for getting us in so quickly."

From her vantage point, Summer had a perfect view of the shock on Judah's face, but he raised a hand to awkwardly pat Benjamin's back before he pulled away. He cleared his throat and gestured toward the couch where Summer and Max sat. "Have a seat."

Judah spent the next hour asking questions about her family's health history, but she couldn't tell him much since she'd never known her father, and Mama hadn't said much about her grandparents, who had died when Summer was a little girl. Then he asked questions about TJ's health and his death, and she managed to only break down once while she answered them with Benjamin's help.

Finally, Judah announced that a nurse would take them to the lab for their blood draw, which would be followed by an EKG, stress test, and other procedures Summer couldn't remember.

"Before that," Benjamin wrapped both of Summer's hands in his. "Could we pray?"

"Of course." Judah stepped toward the door. "I'll give you some privacy."

"Actually—" Benjamin stopped him. "We'd like you to join us. If you're willing."

Summer held her breath as she felt the tension radiating through Benjamin's grip and saw the same tension in the set of Judah's jaw.

But after a moment, Judah nodded curtly. "Sure."

If possible, Benjamin's hands tightened even more around Summer's as they all bowed their heads.

"God, you are the Author of all life." Benjamin's voice wavered a little, as if he were nervous. Summer wondered if that was because of the upcoming tests or because of Judah's presence. Benjamin had told her how much he hoped this would be the start of a renewed relationship between Judah and their family—and between Judah and God.

"We ask for your protection over Max and Summer," he continued, his voice stronger. "We thank you for Judah and his team who will care for them, and we ask that you would bless them with wisdom and guidance. Most of all, we ask that you would help us all to trust in you and in your promises, whatever comes next. In Jesus' name we pray. Amen."

Summer whispered, "Amen" at the same time that Max practically shouted it. She opened her eyes to see Judah lifting his head, his jaw locked tight.

There was a knock at the door, and Judah opened it, looking relieved as the nurse smiled and said she was ready for them.

"You can go with them," Judah said to Benjamin. "Or you're welcome to hang out in the waiting room. I have back-to-back patients all morning, but I'll be back to see you before you leave."

"I'm going with them," Benjamin announced, as if daring his brother to contradict him.

But Judah nodded. "I had no doubt."

Chapter 43

Benjamin was going to lose his mind. It had been a long day, and Summer's head rested on his shoulder. Max was curled into a sleepy ball on the chair next to him. Even so, it felt like the tests they'd undergone had been the easy part.

Sitting here, waiting for Judah to give them the results—that was the hard part. They'd been sitting in the waiting room for nearly half an hour, and if he had to sit still any longer, he might explode.

His leg bounced, and Summer rested a hand on it.

"Sorry." He kissed the top of her head. "I'm not good at waiting."

"Really?" She feigned surprise. "I hadn't noticed."

He chuckled and resisted the need to bounce his leg again, instead focusing his energy on yet another prayer. *Let the results be good, Lord. Let Summer and Max be okay, Lord. Let your will be done.*

It may not be getting easier to wait, but it was getting at least a little bit easier to add that last part.

The door to the waiting room opened, and the same nurse from earlier popped out, smiling as warmly as she had at the beginning of the day. "Dr. Calvano is ready for you."

Benjamin exhaled heavily. But suddenly he wasn't ready for this. What if his brother said something was wrong with Summer? Or Max? How would he possibly handle that?

With them, he reminded himself. *And with the Lord.*

He pushed to his feet and scooped Max into his arms, then took Summer's hand in his. The nurse led them to Judah's office. The moment they stepped inside, Benjamin tried to read his brother's expression. Did the small smile he greeted them with convey good news or sympathy? With any of his other siblings, Benjamin would have known instantly. But he barely knew Judah anymore.

Judah gestured them to the chairs in front of his desk, and Benjamin's heart buckled. Did it mean something that he wanted them to sit in the chairs instead of on the couch they'd sat on before? Was this where he delivered bad news?

"How are y'all holding up?" Judah asked as he took his own seat on the other side of the desk.

"I'm tired." Max punctuated his statement with an enormous yawn that shook his little body.

"I think we all are." Benjamin made himself sit, settling Max on his lap and reaching for Summer's hand the moment she lowered herself to her chair.

Judah nodded. "I'll keep this short then." He clicked a few keys on the keyboard that perched on his desk. Then he swiveled his large computer monitor so that they could see it too. "These are the images we took of Max's heart." He clicked a couple more keys. "And these are Summer's."

Benjamin stared at the images. "Were they— Are they—"

"Everything looks completely normal." Judah's smile grew.

"So they're . . ." Benjamin hardly dared to breathe.

"Their EKGs and stress tests were normal too," Judah added.

"So that means . . ." Benjamin leaned forward, and Max cried out that he was squishing him. "Sorry, Maxerooni." He readjusted his position but kept his eyes on Judah.

"It means I see no cause for concern at the moment."

"At the moment?" Summer's voice was small, and Benjamin gripped her hand tighter.

"Cardiomyopathy often doesn't present with physical changes to the heart right away. The only way to rule it out completely is through genetic testing. My colleague Dr. Fowler will get those results to me in a few weeks. Maybe sooner."

"And if the tests show that they have the gene?" Benjamin could barely force his lips to move, but he had to know. "What then?"

"Then we continue with routine screening like we did today. If the disease progresses, there are medicines and treatments that we can use to reduce the risks. I have several patients with cardiomyopathy who are doing quite well." Though Judah's tone remained serious, Benjamin found it reassuring. His brother knew what he was talking about.

Finally, he felt like he could breathe again. But it took a moment before he could speak past the relief washing over him.

"Thank you," he managed at last. "You have no idea how much this means to us."

"Of course." Judah stood, and Benjamin realized he probably had other patients to get to.

He stood as well, hefting Max to his shoulder, then reached for Summer and pulled her into a bear hug, Max sandwiched between them. He never wanted to let go, but after a moment, Summer gently nudged him back.

"We should let your brother get back to work." She turned to Judah, who had come out from behind his desk. "Thank you so much for everything." Then she lunged at Judah and threw her arms around him in a hug that caught Benjamin as much by surprise as it looked like it did his brother. But he found himself grinning when Judah awkwardly returned the gesture.

"It was nice to meet you," Judah said as Summer let him go. "You seem to be good for my brother."

"She is." Benjamin shifted Max so that he could shake Judah's hand. "Thank you again." He glanced at Summer, who nodded her encouragement, but a ridiculous swoop of nerves went through him. Still, he made himself ask, "If you're free tonight, we'd love to take you out to dinner or something."

Judah looked startled by the invitation. "Oh. Uh. I'm sorry, but I can't." He didn't elaborate, and Benjamin worked to squelch his disappointment. He hadn't really expected his brother to accept the invitation.

"No problem." Benjamin led Summer to the door.

"Say hi to everyone for me." Judah's voice was quiet, but it stopped Benjamin.

He turned to his brother. "I think they'd rather hear it from you." When Judah didn't say anything, he added, "But I'll tell them."

Judah nodded, his expression unreadable. "I'll let you know as soon as we receive the results of the genetic tests."

Benjamin thanked him, then ushered his little family out of the hospital. Right now, his priority was to get Max and Summer some rest. So they would be ready for his surprise tomorrow.

Chapter 44

Summer opened her eyes groggily as she heard a car door close. It took her a minute to realize they were at a gas station. Benjamin stood at the pump, his back to her, and she took a moment to thank God for the way he had taken care of her and Max on this trip. He hadn't left their side once at the hospital yesterday, and though he'd woken them early this morning so they could start the long drive home, the moment they were in the car, he'd handed Summer one of his rolled-up sweatshirts to use as a pillow and told her to go back to sleep. Which she had apparently done.

She sat up straighter and turned to check on Max in the back seat. His eyes were closed, and his head lolled against the side of his car seat. Another of Benjamin's sweatshirts was draped over him like a blanket.

Summer watched her nephew sleep for a moment, her heart welling again with the knowledge that Judah hadn't found anything wrong with him.

After a moment, she pulled out her phone to check the time. It was almost one p.m. Which would explain why her stomach was rumbling. She wondered vaguely where they were, but she didn't see any signs to indicate their location.

Benjamin finished pumping the gas, then slid silently back into the car, his face lighting with a giant smile that made her heart pirouette a few times.

"You're awake."

"Yeah. Sorry I dozed off."

He laughed. "You didn't doze off. You full-on passed out. But I'm glad. You needed some sleep."

"Where are we?" A sleepy Max voice came from the back seat.

Benjamin turned to look at the boy over his shoulder. "At a gas station. Are you hungry?"

"Yes," Summer answered before Max could.

"Good." Benjamin turned to her with a grin. "I was starting to think that if y'all didn't wake up soon, I'd have to snack on the steering wheel."

Max giggled. "The steering wheel isn't food."

"That's what you think." Benjamin pretended to take a bite out of it.

Summer could only shake her head. It was good to see him back to his goofball self after how worried he'd been ever since they'd learned about TJ's cause of death.

Ever since he learned you and Max might be in danger, a little voice in her head insisted. Instead of pushing it away, Summer savored the knowledge.

"Should we find a restaurant or get some food here for the road?" Benjamin asked.

"How far do we have to go yet?" Summer scanned their surroundings for any familiar landmarks but found none.

"Maybe four hours? A little more?" Benjamin's hand hovered over the door handle.

"Let's get some food here and eat on the way." After the past couple of exhausting days, she wouldn't mind getting home to her own bed—*their* own bed.

They headed into the gas station and grabbed a few sandwiches, some drinks, and a treat for each of them. While Benjamin paid, Summer scanned a rack of tourist brochures near the door. Someday maybe the three of them could take a vacation just for fun. The thought filled her with an unfamiliar kind of hope, and she reached for a brochure for a cave. If they were only four hours from home, this might be a good place to visit. She flipped it over to read the details, frowning as her eyes fell on the address. This place was in Illinois. She put the brochure back and selected one for a botanical garden. But it was also in Illinois. The next one she grabbed was in Wisconsin.

"Ready?" Benjamin and Max strode over, carrying their purchases.

"Why are all of these brochures for places in Illinois and Wisconsin?" she asked as she stepped out the door Benjamin held open for her.

"Are they? Strange." But Benjamin did a terrible job of hiding his sly grin.

"What's going on?" Summer demanded, grabbing Max's hand and rushing to keep up with Benjamin as he scurried to the car.

"What's going on is we're eating lunch on the road so that we can get to our destination sooner. It was your idea, if you recall." He opened her car door and gestured her in, then handed her the bag of food.

He closed the door and started to buckle Max into the back seat.

"What destination?" Summer asked.

"*Our* destination."

"Which is . . ." Summer craned her neck to pin him with her gaze, but he snapped Max's buckle and ducked out of the back seat.

The moment he got into the driver's seat, she repeated, "What destination?"

Grinning at her, Benjamin started the car, then said, "Should we pray before we eat?"

"Benjamin!"

But he had already closed his eyes and bowed his head.

With an exasperated sigh, she did the same.

"Dear Lord," Benjamin began, his voice full of a lightness and joy that made Summer smile in spite of herself. "We come before you in humble thanksgiving that you have given us safety on this trip and good news. Please bless the results of the genetic tests as you know is best. And please bless our time together on the rest of this trip." He paused, then added in a tone brimming with mischief. "And please help Summer not to be mad when she finds out. In Jesus' name. Amen."

Summer opened her eyes, spluttering. "When she finds out what?"

"Can I have my food, Aunt Sunny?" Max interrupted.

Summer pulled out his sandwich and drink and passed them back to him, never taking her eyes off of Benjamin, who was grinning at the road.

"Where are we?" she demanded.

Grin never faltering, Benjamin nodded out the window.

Summer spun her head in time to read a sign that said, *Chicago 30 miles.*

"Chicago . . ." Summer stared at the sign until they were past it. "That's not on the way home."

"Nope." Benjamin's grin grew.

"Then why are we going there?"

"We're not. Can I have my sandwich, please?" he asked innocently.

She opened her window and held his food up to it. "Not until you tell me what's going on."

He chortled. "Wow, you really want to know, huh?"

"I really want to know."

"Okay, okay. Put the food back inside, and I'll tell you."

"Tell me first."

Benjamin looked at her, his eyes dancing. "You promise you won't throw it out the window, even if you don't like the answer?"

She considered. "I make no such promise."

He snorted. "Fine. You win. We're going to Hope Springs. Wisconsin."

"What?" The answer was so unexpected that Summer was startled into lowering his food to her lap. He snatched for it and eagerly opened his sandwich.

"When Grace heard we were going to Cleveland, she invited us. She wants to meet you."

"She already knows me," Summer pointed out. His sister Grace had been Summer's youth leader at vacation Bible school for years when they were kids.

"Not as my wife." Benjamin set his sandwich on his lap and reached to squeeze her hand. Summer almost gave in. But then the impossibility of it all hit her.

"But I'm supposed to work tomorrow. And the next day."

"Abigail is taking your shifts. She cleared it with Ruth."

"But Max has school."

"I emailed his teacher." Benjamin looked smug.

"But Mama—"

"Dad's going to keep checking in on her. And before you ask, Chloe is covering for me at the restaurant."

"But—" Summer stammered, trying to think of what else he hadn't considered. "But we don't have enough clothes packed." There, let him argue with that one.

"I packed extra for everyone."

Summer stared at him. "You did not."

He nodded. "I most certainly did. Now are you done arguing?"

"But," Summer said weakly.

"Sorry." Benjamin shook his head. "You've used up your quota of buts for the day."

From the back seat, Max giggled and repeated, "Buts."

Benjamin laughed, then turned to Summer, his expression suddenly earnest. "It will be fun. I promise. The town is beautiful. And Max will love the lake. And Grace has a cabin that's just sitting empty, so we'll be doing her a favor."

Summer bit her lip, but not hard enough to keep a smile from escaping. "In that case, I guess we'll have to go."

Benjamin smiled and lifted her hand to his lips. "I guess we will."

Summer settled back in her seat and opened her own sandwich, her eyes eagerly devouring the new scenery around them. The drive brought them alongside Lake Michigan, and Summer couldn't believe how big it was, stretching mile after mile, its waters rolling endlessly against the shore. In places trees blocked the view, and Summer marveled at those too, their leaves dotted with the hues of autumn.

They spent the drive talking and laughing, and Summer could almost feel the cares of the last two months sliding off of her.

As the sun began to set, Benjamin held up a finger. "Get ready."

Summer glanced at him. "For what?" The lake had disappeared from sight a while ago, and all she saw on either side of the car was trees.

"Almost . . ." The car crested a hill, passing a sign that said, *Welcome to Hope Springs*, and then Benjamin pointed out the window. "And . . . now!"

"Wow," Summer gasped as Max yelled, "Oh boy!"

Below them, the waves of Lake Michigan danced in the overflow of gold and pink that spilled from the sky into the water. Gulls swooped low, skimming the surface and then wheeling back into the sky.

"Look at all the boats!" Max exclaimed.

Summer's eyes went to the marina at the bottom of another hill to their left. Colorful masts bobbed up and down along the docks, while beyond them waves sprayed against a barrier of rocks.

Benjamin slowed as they came into a little town, passing a fudge shop and a bakery and an antique store.

"It feels like home," she said. "Only with a lake instead of mountains."

"So this was a good idea?" Benjamin prompted.

Summer laughed. "So far, yes."

"That's all I wanted to hear." Benjamin squeezed her hand. A few miles outside of town, he slowed and turned into a driveway lined by trees.

"The Heather House Inn," Summer read the sign. "Named after your mama?"

Benjamin nodded.

"That's sweet." Summer tried to imagine wanting to name anything after her own mama, but then pushed away the image. She wasn't going to let even the thought of Mama ruin this trip.

Benjamin pulled the car up in front of a large Victorian-style home with tall windows, a wraparound porch, and even a tower.

"I feel like I just stepped into a fairy tale." Summer hadn't meant to say it out loud, but Benjamin smiled at her.

"Good. Because you deserve to feel like a princess. Wait right there." He opened his door and sprang out, running around to her side and bowing low as he opened her door. He held out a hand to her, as if he were a footman. "*My* princess."

"You're ridiculous." But Summer set her hand in his and let him help her out of the vehicle.

The moment she was out, he drew her close and brought his lips to hers. Summer sank into the kiss, wondering how he knew it was exactly what she wanted.

"It looks like the newlyweds are here," a light, laughing voice called.

Summer giggled and pulled back from Benjamin. In five weeks of being married, she had never felt like a newlywed, but at this moment, she really did.

She looked toward the house to find Grace rushing down the porch steps, followed by a man with dark hair and a big smile.

"Who is that?" Max asked, and Summer looked down in surprise to find the boy standing next to her.

"How did you get out of your car seat?" She hadn't seen Benjamin duck inside to unbuckle him.

"You and Benji were too busy kissing, so I did it myself," Max announced, as if it were something he did every day.

Before Summer could respond, she was tackled in a giant hug that almost knocked the breath out of her.

"I'm so glad you're here." Grace squeezed her tight.

"Don't break my wife," Benjamin warned his sister.

"Your wife." Grace seemed to be laughing and crying at the same time. "I'm so happy for you two." She relinquished her hold on Summer and tackled Benjamin next.

"Hey, sis." He lifted Grace off the ground, making her squeal.

The dark-haired man laughed. "Don't break my wife either." He held out a hand to Summer as Benjamin put Grace down. "I'm Levi."

Summer nodded as she shook his hand. "I figured. Benjamin mentions you all the time." She lowered her voice in a poor imitation of Benjamin's. "Did I tell you that my brother-in-law used to play for the Titans?"

"Hey." Benjamin nudged her. "You weren't supposed to tell him that."

"That's okay." Levi winked at her and whispered as if revealing a secret, "He talks about you all the time too."

"Oh." Summer couldn't think of anything else to say as a wave of warmth went through her. Did Benjamin really talk about her to his brother-in-law? What did he say?

"Guilty as charged." Benjamin moved closer to wrap an arm around her.

Grace smiled as she squatted in front of Max. "And you must be Max. Do you like dinosaurs?"

Max's eyes widened as he nodded. "They're my favorite animal."

"That's good to hear." Grace straightened. "Because I put you in the dinosaur cabin. It has all kinds of dinosaur books and toys."

An unexpected prickle of tears came to Summer's eyes as Max yelled, "Oh boy!"

She would never be able to repay this family for all they had done for Max. And for her.

"Come on." Grace grinned and held out a hand to the boy, who eagerly accepted. "Let's go get y'all settled."

Chapter 45

"You're going to be good for your aunt Grace and uncle Levi, right?" Benjamin knelt in front of Max, zipping up the boy's sweatshirt.

Max nodded eagerly, and Benjamin glanced over his shoulder and out the large French doors to make sure that Summer was still sitting on the deck, her back to the cabin as she watched the waves and sipped her coffee.

"I know you will." Benjamin pulled the boy into a hug, then stood to open the front door, where Grace and Levi stood, grinning.

"Does she know?" Grace peered past him.

Benjamin shook his head. "Not a clue."

Since it was the off season, Grace and Levi had been free to spend some time with Benjamin and Max and Summer yesterday. They'd hiked and picked apples and shopped and gotten ice cream at the Chocolate Chicken and even met some of Grace and Levi's friends. Then they'd stayed up late playing board games and talking.

But today, Grace and Levi were helping Benjamin with a different plan.

Grace reached for Max's hand. "Come on, Max. Do you like horses?"

Max's eyes lit up. "Boy oh boy! Really? Horses?"

"Lots of horses." Levi took the bag Benjamin held out to him, and the three of them started down the driveway toward the main bed and breakfast where Grace and Levi lived.

Grace turned and called over her shoulder, "You two have fun."

"We will." A whole day—and night—alone with his wife? How could he not enjoy that?

But as Benjamin made his way through the house to the deck, a wave of uncertainty swept over him. Would Summer enjoy it? Over the past few days, it had felt like she was finally, finally letting go of whatever barriers she'd put up between them ever since their wedding day. But what if now that they were alone, she built them higher than ever?

Then you'll break them down again, one step at a time, he told himself as he opened the door and stepped outside. A bank of clouds had built over the lake, but a shaft of sunlight managed to break its way through and seemed to shine right on Summer, stealing Benjamin's breath.

Thank you for her, Lord.

A brisk wind blew in from the lake, covering the sound of Benjamin's footsteps as he crossed the deck and stopped behind Summer's chair. He let his hands come to rest on her shoulders, and she leaned back into him, as if she'd been waiting for just this moment. Benjamin let out a breath.

"Is Max ready?"

"Uh. Sort of." Fresh nerves tore through Benjamin, and his heart crashed in his ears, louder than the waves against the shore.

Summer turned to him with a puzzled smile. "What does that mean?"

"It means he's ready, but he's not here."

Alarm crossed Summer's face, and Benjamin realized he should have phrased that differently. "I mean, he's with Grace and Levi."

"Oh. Sorry." Summer scrambled to her feet. "I didn't mean to keep everyone waiting."

"You're not keeping anyone waiting. They're taking him for the day."

Summer blinked at him, brow furrowed. "We can't ask them to do that."

Benjamin shook his head. "I didn't. It was Grace's idea. She thought maybe we'd like to have a— A honeymoon."

"Oh." Summer's mouth opened, and her cheeks went pinker than they already were from the wind.

"I thought we could go mini golfing," he added quickly, before she could think he was expecting anything she wasn't ready for. "And take a walk on the beach. Maybe climb a lighthouse. Honestly, I don't care what we do. As long as we're together."

Slowly, Summer's lips stretched into a smile. "That sounds nice."

"Yeah?" Benjamin stepped closer, sliding his arms around her.

"Yeah." Summer lifted her face, and he brought his lips to hers in a kiss that was wild and free, like the tugging of the wind at his shirt or the surging of the waves on the shore below.

Chapter 46

"Are you happy?"

Summer looked up in surprise as Benjamin led her across the sand at the water's edge. The sun had fallen beneath the horizon, making water and sky blend into one. In the inky dusk, she couldn't read his expression.

"I'm . . ." Oh, she was so many things. Sad about TJ. Scared about the feelings for Benjamin she was having a harder and harder time fighting. And happy. Yes, she was definitely happy too.

Today had been . . . incredible. Probably the best day of her life, if she was being honest.

Benjamin stopped and turned to face her. "I know we never expected to get married. And I know things have been . . . crazy ever since we did."

Summer laughed, but Benjamin didn't. He took both of her hands in his. "But I really do want you to be happy. Because I love you."

The words were barely louder than the waves, but they brought Summer back to her senses faster than being submerged by the icy water could have. She pulled her hands out of his and took a step backwards. "Don't say that." Her words sliced the air, and she saw the force of their lash against him.

"What? Why not?"

She wrapped her arms around herself, suddenly aware of the chill in the air. "Because you don't mean it." She could feel the tears building in her throat, but she was determined not to let them escape.

"Why would you say that?" Hurt clung to his words.

"It's like you just said. We never expected to get married. You did it to help me and Max out, and I'm grateful, but it's not like you ever—" She had to stop, or she'd lose the weak grip she had on her emotions.

"Not like I ever *what*?" Benjamin asked softly, stepping closer.

She turned her head to look out over the waves. They moved back and forth, a constant rhythm against the shore. "Not like you ever wanted me," she managed to whisper as a rogue tear trickled down her cheek.

"What?" Benjamin's laugh was incredulous. "Summer, I've wanted you since . . ." He let out a breath. "A long time. Since our first date, at least. Maybe sooner."

She shook her head adamantly. That she knew wasn't true. "You wanted to take Christine to prom. You only asked me because she said no and then she told you to ask me, as a joke."

Surprise sprang to Benjamin's expression. "Maybe it was a joke to her," he said. "But it wasn't to me. We were friends, remember?"

She pointed a finger at him. "Exactly. We were friends. And that's all you wanted. You even asked me to go 'as a friend.'" She made air quotes around the words. "But I was stupid enough to— to—"

"Kiss me?" Benjamin supplied with a grin.

"It's not funny." Summer crossed her arms tighter. "You only went out with me because you felt obligated after that."

Now Benjamin outright chuckled. "I didn't feel obligated, Summer. I felt like . . . like my eyes had finally been opened to this amazing girl who had been standing right in front of me all along." He lifted his hands, running them up and down her arms. "Just like she is right now."

She shook her head and slipped out of his grasp. She couldn't let herself believe that. She turned and started up the beach toward the bed and breakfast. It was time they rescued Grace and Levi from Max anyway.

Benjamin jogged to catch up with her. "Summer, wait. Talk to me."

"There's nothing to talk about," she tried to sound flippant. "It was a long time ago."

"But clearly you're still upset. Which, to be fair, I think *I'm* the one who should be upset, since *you* broke up with *me*."

"You said we needed to talk about what was going to happen when you left for school." Summer bit the inside of her cheek. It had been clear from his tone that a breakup was coming. He didn't get to be mad at her for doing it first.

"And the next thing I knew, you were telling me that you didn't want a long-distance relationship." A hint of frustration leaked into Benjamin's words. Well, good, then he'd stop saying crazy things like he loved her.

"Because I knew you didn't want one. I was setting you free. And anyway, you didn't say anything to make me think otherwise. The next thing I knew, you were storming out of there. And then you left town without saying another word to me."

Benjamin blew out a breath. "I'm sorry about that. I regretted it as soon as I got to school. But I was too stupid and proud to call you and apologize. Why do you think I came over to game with TJ whenever I was home?"

Summer shrugged. "Because he was your friend."

"Well, yeah. But it didn't hurt that I knew you'd be there too. Not that you'd give me the time of day." He grabbed her hand. "You have no idea how happy I was when I moved back home, and you actually started talking to me again. I finally thought we were at a place where maybe I could ask you out and maybe you would say yes, and then you started dating Nick."

Summer made a disbelieving sound. There was no way he'd been planning to ask her out.

"It's true." He tucked a piece of hair gently behind her ear, looking pensive. "Do you wish— Would you rather still be with him?"

"No." Summer didn't even have to consider the question.

"Good." Benjamin looked genuinely relieved.

"Would you rather still be with Jasmine?" she asked quietly.

"Jasmine?" His eyes registered surprise, but he shook his head. "Nope."

"Come on, Benjamin." Summer started walking again. "She's clearly perfect for you. You could be married to *her* right now if I hadn't gotten in the way."

Benjamin laughed, but Summer wasn't in the mood for his levity. "It's not a joke, Benjamin. I'm serious."

They had reached the path that led from the beach up to Grace and Levi's property, and Summer started up it. But Benjamin caught her arm and held her fast.

"So am I. Jasmine and I wouldn't be married, even if you and I weren't. That ended before any of this"—he gestured between them—"happened."

"No it didn't." Summer very clearly remembered. "You were on a date with her the night TJ died."

"Yes." Benjamin spoke slowly. "And on that date, we agreed it wasn't working out. *Before* I ever knew about TJ or the guardianship or any of that. Why?" He sounded suddenly sharp. "Did she say something different to you?"

"No. No. She thinks it's very noble, what you did."

"There you go then." Benjamin smiled as if that erased any doubts.

But Summer shook her head, trying unsuccessfully to pull away before he could see the tears dropping onto her cheeks.

"What is it?" he asked, gently wiping them away.

"I don't want you to be with me because you're noble," she whispered.

"I'm not," he whispered back, slowly bringing his lips to hers. "I'm with you because I love you." He kissed her again. "And I want you more than I've ever wanted anything else in this world."

Summer's breath caught on the words and on the barely contained longing in the kiss that followed them.

She could feel it in his lips, in the way he pulled her closer, in the way his hands traveled her arms and her neck and her hair—he really did want her.

When they finally pulled apart, he asked through ragged breaths. "Should we go back to our cabin?"

"We should— Ah—" Summer's head still spun with the power of that kiss. "We should get Max first."

"He's having a sleepover at Grace and Levi's tonight."

"Oh," Summer breathed.

Benjamin nodded. Then he bent his knees and scooped her into his arms, pausing to kiss her again before carrying her up the path and into their cabin.

Chapter 47

"Good morning." Benjamin smiled as Summer's eyes fluttered open. He was pretty sure he was never going to stop smiling again.

"Good morning," she murmured. "Do we really have to go home today?"

"We do." He kissed the tip of her nose. "But that means we get to sleep in our own bed tonight."

"Mmm. Well, when you put it that way." She kissed him long and slow, and it was only by supreme effort that Benjamin made himself get out of bed to get ready for church. They packed their bags, so they'd be able to start on the long drive right after the service. Then they met up with Max and Grace and Levi at the bed and breakfast.

Max greeted them both with a hug and spent the entire drive to church telling them about all the fun he'd had with his aunt and uncle.

"Can we come back again sometime?" he asked.

"I think we can *definitely* come back sometime." Benjamin squeezed Summer's hand, and she squeezed his back with a soft smile that made him certain everything was going to be perfect forever.

At church, they sat close to each other and nodded together over Pastor Dan's sermon about how God was in control in all things, even when his people couldn't see it.

But when they said their goodbyes after church and climbed into the car for the drive home, he noticed her eyes cloud over. And by the time they were halfway to River Falls, he could feel her withdrawing into herself, despite his best efforts to keep up a cheerful banter.

"Tired?" he finally asked, praying that was all it was.

She smiled faintly. "A little. I'm not sure I'm going to be much good at work tomorrow."

"Do you ever miss teaching dance?" He wasn't sure where the question came from, but he wondered how he had never thought to ask before.

She looked at him, clearly surprised. "I . . . Yeah, I guess I do. I miss the kids, mostly."

"Have you thought about doing it again?"

Summer shrugged. "There aren't any other dance studios in town, so . . ."

"What if you opened your own?"

Summer snorted. "That takes a lot of money."

"We could take out a loan. You could make your princess parties part of the business too. I'm sure those two things would feed into each other perfectly." Excitement built in Benjamin's chest at the possibilities for her.

But Summer shook her head. "I don't want to go into debt. And anyway, I'm sure no bank would give me a loan."

"We could at least meet with a banker," Benjamin insisted. "See what—"

"I said I don't want to." Summer crossed her arms over her seat belt and closed her eyes.

Benjamin suppressed a sigh. He was not going to let her pull away from him again. But he supposed he could let this rest for now. Besides, the seed of an idea had started to form in his mind, and he needed to see what would happen if he let it sprout.

Chapter 48

Summer steeled herself as she stuck her key in the lock of Mama's front door, her other hand clutching the prescription she'd stopped at the pharmacy to pick up.

If anything said she wasn't on vacation anymore, it was coming here.

At least she only had a few minutes before she had to be at work. And maybe spending time with Pastor Calvano over the past few days had mellowed Mama out a bit.

Summer snorted to herself. Her father-in-law was a wonderful pastor—but he wasn't a miracle worker.

She pushed the door open, calling, "It's me. I brought your pills."

"About time." The grumble came from Mama's recliner. "I thought you said you were only going to be gone a couple of days."

"Sorry, Mama. Benjamin surprised us with a trip to visit his sister in Wisconsin."

Mama knew this, of course. Summer had texted her, and she was sure Pastor Calvano had mentioned it as well.

"Maybe you should have told him you have responsibilities here."

"He knows that, Mama. And so do I." Summer kept her tone even. "But he thought, after everything we've been through . . ." She tried to ignore the hurt that Mama hadn't even asked how their doctor appointments went. She hadn't expected her to.

"I hope you had fun," Mama's voice dripped sarcasm. "Gallivanting all over while I was here by myself."

"You weren't by yourself." Summer picked up a stack of dirty dishes from Mama's TV tray. "Pastor Calvano came over." She started toward the kitchen, but then, feeling a little sassy, threw over her shoulder, "And yes, we did have fun."

She ducked into the kitchen before Mama could see the way her face heated at the memory. She'd spent the whole drive home yesterday and all night last night fighting the fear that it had all been a mistake, that Benjamin was going to regret that they couldn't get an annulment now, and she wasn't about to let Mama add fuel to her doubts.

She moved to the sink, where a pile of clean dishes was neatly stacked in the drying rack—she'd have to thank Pastor Calvano for that—and made quick work of the dirty ones in her hands. She knew Ruth wouldn't be upset if she was late for work—her boss had texted yesterday to say she should take a couple more days off if she needed them—but she really couldn't afford more time off. She was barely contributing to the family income the way it was.

The word *family* sent a throb of joy through her as she headed back to the living room. Her own family—that was something she'd thought she'd never have.

Not that any of it is real, a little voice tried to argue, but Summer pushed it away. She was done listening to that voice.

"I need more toilet paper," Mama called as Summer reached the front door.

Summer paused, gritting her teeth. "You should have texted me. I would have picked it up while I was at the pharmacy."

Mama didn't say anything, and Summer sighed. "I'll stop and get some after I pick Max up from school." She pulled the door open but jumped back at the sight of a man on the doorstep, his hand poised to ring the doorbell.

"Sorry." Summer pressed a hand to her heart. "You startled . . ." She trickled off as she read the logo on the man's shirt: *Liquor Lounge.* Her eyes tracked to the paper bag he held.

"What's in there?" she demanded.

The man opened the bag. "One bottle of whiskey. One vodka. I've got your beer in the van yet. I just need you to sign and—"

"Take it back." Summer barely recognized her own voice. It was like someone bold and icy had taken control of her vocal cords.

"Excuse me?" The man glanced at the phone in his hand. "This is 302 Walker, right?"

"I said, 'Take it back.'" Summer started to close the door, but something got in the way. She looked over in surprise to find Mama holding onto it.

"I'll sign." Mama stepped past Summer and took the man's phone, scribbling something illegible on the screen. The man took the phone back and handed Mama the bag, shooting Summer an odd look.

"I'll be right back with your beer." He fled to his van, and Summer whirled on Mama.

"Oh, get down off your high horse." Mama scowled.

Summer could only stare at her, speechless.

The man returned with a box of beer that Mama could barely lift, but Summer didn't offer to help her. It wasn't until Mama had taken the beer to the kitchen and returned with a bottle in her hand that Summer found her voice.

"Why?" It was the only word she could manage.

Mama lifted the bottle with a smirk. "Liquid happiness."

"That's killing you."

Mama shrugged. "Not like there's any reason to prolong this miserable life."

"Whose fault is it if you're miserable, anyway?" Summer knew the moment she said it that she should have held her tongue, but the words had burned their way right out of her.

Mama looked up, her eyes filled with malice. "I had plans, you know. Big plans. And then you and your brother came along, and your daddy left, and who had to give up all of their plans? Not *him*. Not you or TJ. *Me.*"

Summer's throat burned and her eyes stung, but she stood her ground. "You know what, Mama? I feel sorry for you."

Mama snorted. "You think you're so much better? You think your life is going to be so different? With your *husband*." She made the word a mockery. "Mark my words, someday you're going to be sitting in your chair, looking for your whiskey, and asking yourself what ever happened to your dreams."

Summer opened the door with a shaking hand. "You can order booze, Mama? Then order your own toilet paper too." She stepped outside, slamming the door behind her and angrily swiping away the tears that had found their way onto her cheeks. Mama didn't deserve them.

Chapter 49

"I guess your trip was good then." Ireland grinned at Benjamin as she passed through the kitchen, where he was inspecting the day's meat and vegetable delivery before the rest of the kitchen staff arrived. "You're always cheerful, but the humming is over the top, even for you."

"Was I humming?" Benjamin couldn't banish the smile from his face. Ireland laughed. "Loudly."

He chuckled. "I'll try to keep that under control. But, yes, it was an amazing trip." He had already updated his family on the good news from Summer's and Max's cardiac screenings. "I think going to Hope Springs was just what we needed."

"I'm glad." Ireland stopped and watched him examine a bushel of carrots. "I like Summer."

His grin grew. "Me too."

She laughed. "Yeah, I kind of got that from the fact that you married her." She patted his shoulder and continued on the way to her office.

"See," Benjamin muttered to himself, "*she* knew I liked Summer." He was still baffled by the fact that Summer hadn't believed it. But hopefully the surprise he'd spent the morning finalizing would be one more way to show her.

He continued working, handing out instructions as his staff filtered in.

"Someone is chipper today," Chloe said when she arrived. "Good trip?"

He felt like jumping up and down and shouting about how amazing it had been. But he simply nodded and said, "The best. I owe you for covering here."

"Trust me. You'll be paying me back." She cackled and rubbed her hands together, sending him what he imagined was supposed to pass for an evil grin, though she was about as evil as a puppy.

The next few hours passed in a blur as Benjamin fell back into the familiar rhythm of the kitchen. His grill master had called in sick, so Benjamin was manning the grills tonight—one of his favorite jobs. His phone buzzed in his pocket a few times, and he planned to check it during a lull in the cooking, but the lull never came.

"Chef." A hostess stepped gingerly into the kitchen, careful to dodge a server on his way out. "Your wife is on the phone."

Benjamin grinned at the phrase. He would never get tired of hearing those words, *your wife*. But he couldn't walk away from the grill right now. "Can you take a message?"

"Um. She said it's an emergency." The hostess looked distressed.

"What kind of emergency?" He was already crossing the room, and out of the corner of his eye, he saw Chloe take up his spot at the grill.

"She didn't say." The hostess led him into the dining area and gestured to the phone next to her podium.

Benjamin picked it up, stretching the cord so he could duck behind the low wall that stood behind the podium.

"Summer? What's wrong? Are you okay? Is Max hurt?" When he paused for a breath, he could hear sirens in the background.

"It's my mom." Summer's voice sounded strange, but Benjamin let out a breath and leaned heavily against the wall.

"What happened?"

"She . . . We . . . We had a fight earlier. About toilet paper. And alcohol. And I stormed out. But I came back with Max just now because— Well, I don't even know why— She couldn't catch her breath and she was confused and didn't seem to know where she was. She kept saying I should call TJ, and . . ." Summer broke off on a little gasp.

"Where are you now?"

"The ambulance just pulled away," she said. "Max is with me, and I don't know what to do."

"Hang tight. I'll be there in ten minutes, and we'll go to the hospital, okay? I'm calling Mia to watch Max."

He handed the phone to the hostess, then strode into the kitchen and straight to the grill. He couldn't believe he was going to ask another favor of his sous chef.

"Go," Chloe said before he could ask. "I've got this."

"I didn't even tell you what happened," Benjamin protested weakly.

Chloe shrugged. "It's your family. Besides, I'll just add this to the pile of things you owe me for."

"Deal. Thank you." Benjamin shed his apron and made a quick dash to the parking lot.

But when he got outside, he froze. His Gremlin was nowhere in sight.

And then he laughed at himself. Of course it wasn't.

Not when he'd sold it this morning.

He pulled the keys for his new car out of his pocket and hit the key fob, heading for the sensible hatchback with the flashing headlights. He jumped into it and pulled out of the parking lot, calling Mia and then saying a prayer for Mrs. Ellis—and for Summer and Max, who had already lost so much.

When he reached his mother-in-law's house, he left the car running and jogged to the door, opening it without knocking.

Inside, Max and Summer were both perched on the edge of the couch. Summer jumped up with a start when she saw him, and he strode straight to her and pulled her into his arms. "It's going to be okay."

She nodded against his shoulder. "She was really awful today," she whispered. "The things she said. But I shouldn't have left like that."

"It's not your fault," Benjamin said firmly. "Come on. We'll drop Max off at home on the way. Mia is going to meet us there."

He scooped Max into his arms and led Summer to the door.

"Should we take my car?" she asked as they passed it.

"That's okay. We'll come back for it later."

"But you don't have a—" They stopped at the passenger door of the still-running car, and she blinked at it as if coming out of a fog. "What's this? Where's your car?"

"You're looking at it."

Summer turned to him, her mouth curved in confusion.

"Surprise." He patted the vehicle. "This wasn't exactly how I planned to tell you, but I sold the Gremlin."

She stared at him. "You can't do that."

He chuckled. "I already did." He opened her door. "Come on, I'll tell you my plan in the car."

She got in slowly, as if afraid the car might swallow her whole.

Benjamin buckled Max into the car seat he'd picked up this morning, then got into the driver's seat.

Summer sat stiffly next to him, and he reached for her hand. "It will be okay," he reassured her again as he pulled out of the driveway.

She nodded. "Why did you sell the Gremlin?" She sounded almost angry, and Benjamin glanced at her in surprise.

"It wasn't exactly a family car," he said easily. "We couldn't even put Max's car seat in the back."

"My car was fine for that."

"Sure." Benjamin turned down the next street. "But now we have two cars for that. And I got a really great offer on the Gremlin. It was enough to buy this car, and I thought we could use the extra—" He took a breath, his excitement building to share the good news. "Toward getting your dance studio up and running."

Summer inhaled sharply, and Benjamin looked over, expecting to see her wide, beautiful smile. Instead, she wore a sharp frown. "No," she said flatly.

"No, what?" Benjamin tried to keep the hurt out of his voice at her less-than-enthusiastic reaction.

"No, I'm not going to use the money for a dance studio."

"You don't want to open a dance studio?" Had he let his own imagination run away with him after she'd said she missed teaching dance? Maybe he should have talked to her about it more. But he had just been so excited about helping make her dream come true.

"Maybe someday." She was staring out her window. "But not with your money."

"Summer." He didn't try to hide his exasperation. "We're married. It's *our* money."

"I didn't ask you to give up your car for me." She shot the words at him, hot and angry, and he turned to her in bewilderment.

"I know you didn't. I *wanted* to."

"Well, I didn't want you to." She crossed her arms in front of her as he pulled into the driveway. "You're only going to regret it."

"Of course I won't." He wanted to add more, but Mia was already there, and he got out to let her and Max inside.

Then he climbed back into the car and drove Summer to the hospital. He tried to bring up the Gremlin once, but she shut him down, and he decided it was a conversation for another day.

She was clearly upset about things with her mom. But when all of this was past, he would make her see that he wanted to do this for her.

Chapter 50

Summer stifled a yawn and opened the driver's window a crack. Chill air rushed past her face, but she yawned again. A week of traveling back and forth to visit Mama at the hospital in Brampton was starting to take a toll on her. She rubbed her eyes and turned up the volume on the radio, wishing Benjamin could have come along today. But he had to work—and besides, if he had come, they would have taken his new car, and it still made her sick every time she rode in it, to think of him giving up his Gremlin for her.

He'd tried a few times to convince her to use the money for a dance studio, but there was no way she could do that, not when that car had been his pride and joy. She wasn't going to be responsible for taking that from him. He would only resent her for it one day.

Wearily, she pulled into the hospital parking lot and found a spot near the door. The moment she turned the engine off, she let her head fall back on the seat and closed her eyes.

She didn't realize she had drifted off until she startled awake. Heart pounding, she grabbed her phone to check how long she'd been asleep, then let out a relieved breath. It couldn't have been more than ten minutes.

She opened her door and marched toward the hospital. The doctor had said yesterday that he might discharge Mama today, and Summer hadn't yet decided if she should hope for that or not. It was certainly easier not to have to travel to the hospital every day. But Mama had been so much more . . . not pleasant, exactly, but restrained, while she was here. Plus, at the hospital, she didn't have access to the alcohol that was killing her.

Inside, Summer headed for the elevator, sneaking in right before the door closed. A woman who might have been in her late thirties offered Summer a tired looking smile, and Summer returned it, feeling a sudden sense of solidarity. The elevator jolted to a start, and Summer grabbed at the railing as her stomach lurched.

"This thing is awful, isn't it?" the other woman said.

Summer nodded, though she wasn't sure if the woman meant the elevator or the whole experience of being at the hospital.

The elevator dinged, and the doors opened. The woman disappeared in the opposite direction of where Summer needed to go.

A nurse greeted her cheerfully when she reached Mama's room. "We've got your mama almost ready to go. I'm going to help her into a wheelchair, and if you want to grab her bag, I'll walk y'all out."

Summer braced herself for a big to-do from Mama as the nurse moved to her side, but Mama remained quiet and meekly let the nurse wrap an arm around her and support her into the chair. It struck Summer suddenly how frail Mama looked. She picked up Mama's bag and followed the nurse back to the elevator. There was no one else on it this time, and the nurse kept up a friendly chatter about the weather on the way down. But Summer remained as silent as Mama.

Outside, she pulled the car up to the door, and the nurse helped her get Mama tucked inside. The drive home was blessedly quiet, and Mama only grunted her assent when Summer said they'd stop to pick up her new prescription on the way home.

By the time she pulled into Mama's driveway, Summer felt like she needed another nap. But first she needed to get Mama settled.

She walked around to the passenger side of the car and opened the door, reaching in to help her mother.

"I can do it myself," Mama snapped, and Summer stepped back.

But halfway to the house, Mama looked like she was about to topple over, and Summer wrapped an arm behind her, taking Mama's elbow with her other hand. Mama grunted but didn't say anything as she leaned into Summer.

It took Summer a moment to fumble with the keys, but as soon as she had the door open, something putrid hit her nose. "What's that smell?" she choked.

"I don't smell anything." Mama stumbled toward her chair, and Summer tried to help her, but her eyes fell on something green and gray and fuzzy on a plate that still sat on the TV tray next to the chair.

"Oh." She clapped a hand over her mouth as her stomach turned over.

She got Mama into the chair, then snatched up the plate and rushed to the kitchen with it, careful to avert her eyes from the moldy blob in the center of it. But she couldn't escape the smell, and she gagged a few times until she managed to drop it into the garbage and cinch the bag tight. Breathing roughly, she held the bag as far in front of her as she could and carried it out to the trash can behind the house.

She stood outside, sucking in deep breaths of fresh air, until her stomach was settled and she was pretty sure she wouldn't gag anymore. Then she went into the kitchen, washed her hands, and brought Mama's pills and a glass of water to the living room.

Mama eyed her as she took the offering. "You pregnant?"

Summer startled. "What? No."

Mama pressed her lips together. "Never saw you get so squeamish over a little mold before."

"A little mold? That—whatever it was—was foul. And the smell—" She shuddered.

"I didn't smell anything," Mama said again.

"Then you should get your nose checked. I have to go pick Max up. Mia has class tonight." She made sure the remote was within Mama's reach, then headed for the door. "Call if you need anything. And please don't drink."

As Summer pulled the door open, Mama called, "I hope you're not. For your sake."

"Not what?" Summer hovered in the doorway.

"Pregnant," Mama said, as if it were obvious.

Summer rolled her eyes. She wasn't going to give Mama the satisfaction of asking *why* she hoped that. Instead, she said, "I'm not," and closed the door.

Chapter 51

Benjamin could not stop bouncing his leg against the couch as they waited for the video call with Judah to start. Even Summer's hand on his knee wasn't enough to calm him. It had only been two weeks since they'd gone to Cleveland, and the genetic test results had come back much faster than they'd expected. He couldn't decide if that was a good sign or a bad sign.

Next to him, Summer sat completely still, but he could tell by her clenched jaw that she was nervous too.

"Whatever happens—" He turned to her suddenly, and she jumped. "We're going to be okay."

Summer nodded, but she looked so tired, and Benjamin had to work hard to push down the lump of worry. Of course she was tired. She'd been with her mama almost every spare moment since bringing her home two days ago.

But he was going to be strong for her, whatever they found out.

"Can you hear me?" Judah's voice suddenly burst into the room, and they both spun toward the laptop that rested on the coffee table.

"We hear you." Benjamin adjusted the screen so that they were both in the frame.

"Good. How have y'all been?" Judah looked tired too, and a little bit sad, and Benjamin's heart clenched painfully.

"We're good," Summer answered when Benjamin couldn't. "How are you?"

"I'm ... fine." His hesitation made Benjamin sure his heart was going to stop altogether. Judah was going to give them bad news, Benjamin could feel it.

"Dr. Fowler is sorry she couldn't be here today. She's at a conference, but we've gone over everything together, and we didn't want you to have to wait for the results."

"Thank you," Benjamin croaked.

"Of course." Judah cleared his throat. "Let's start with the good news."

Benjamin closed his eyes.

If Judah was starting with the good news, that meant there was bad news too.

"Max's testing reveals that he does not have any copies of the gene variant that TJ had. So he neither has nor can pass on the disease."

"Thank you, Lord," Summer gasped, dropping her head to her hands. Benjamin rubbed a hand up and down her back, his relief over Max's clean bill of health warring with dread over what Judah was going to say about Summer.

"What's the bad news?" The words found a way out of his mouth.

Summer lifted her head, as if it hadn't occurred to her that there might be bad news as well.

"It's mixed news, actually," Judah said slowly, his face grave. "Summer, you do have one copy of the gene variant."

"What does that— I don't—" Summer looked to Benjamin as if he could explain, but all he could do was shake his head over and over again. This couldn't be happening.

"It means that though you don't have the disease yourself, you are a carrier of the gene."

It took a moment for the words to penetrate Benjamin's brain. "You mean—" He hardly dared to believe it. "She's okay? She's not going to— She's okay?" He couldn't seem to form any other words.

"She's okay," Judah confirmed.

Benjamin turned and snatched Summer close to him, burying his face in her hair. He held her, letting her apricot scent envelop him, until Judah cleared his throat.

Benjamin eased back. "Sorry. I just— Thank you."

Judah's expression sobered. "We should talk about what this means for your children."

"Okay." Benjamin tried to make himself sober too, but his heart was bouncing around too joyously for that.

"If you also happen to be a carrier of the gene variant," Judah said. "There's a twenty-five percent chance that any of your children would have the disease."

Summer pressed a hand to her mouth, but Benjamin wasn't worried. "I can get tested before we have kids, right?"

Judah nodded. "I would recommend that, yes."

"And we can always adopt if I do have it. Simeon and Abigail adopted a little girl last year, did you know that?"

Judah shook his head.

"And Ava and Joseph have a little boy who was born the same day. And Asher and Ireland have a little girl, and they're expecting again." They'd just told everyone after church on Sunday.

Judah looked a little overwhelmed by all of the news, and Benjamin stopped. "You should come visit sometime."

"Yeah," Judah said vaguely. "Listen, I have to run, but if you have any questions at all, give me a call or text. And make sure you go get that testing done." He said goodbye, and the meeting ended.

"Well," Benjamin turned to Summer. "That's the best news I've ever gotten in my life."

She nodded, but worry still darkened her eyes.

"What is it?" He slid his hands through her hair.

She seemed to shake herself. "Sorry. Nothing. I was just thinking about what he said about you getting tested."

"We have plenty of time for that." He brought his lips softly to hers. "But for now, I say we celebrate."

Chapter 52

Summer sat on the edge of the bathtub, trying to work up the courage to walk over to the sink. The three-minute timer had been beeping at her for at least a minute, but her feet seemed to be welded to the floor. She glanced toward the door, needlessly closed, since Max was at school and Benjamin had left yesterday for Atlanta. He hadn't wanted to go, but Summer had insisted, both because she didn't want to keep him from a chance to see his friend and because she knew she needed to take this test.

She'd tried to dismiss Mama's offhand question about whether she was pregnant. But from the moment they'd gotten the results of her genetic test back last week, fear had gnawed at her from the inside out. And then she'd missed her period.

It's only three days late, she reminded herself.

Except she'd never been three days late before.

With a rough breath, she forced herself off the tub. She reached first for her phone, careful to keep her eyes on the screen as she turned off the timer, so she wouldn't catch a glimpse of the results.

But then she set the phone down, and she couldn't avoid it any longer.

With a quick resolve, she snatched the test off the counter and held it up in front of her.

She'd already memorized the directions, so she knew exactly what the two lines meant.

The hand holding the test began to shake, and she pressed her other hand to her mouth. Tears rolled down her cheeks, but she couldn't tell whether they were happy tears or devastated tears.

This wasn't supposed to be happening. Not yet. Not until Benjamin was tested. What if he had the gene variant too, and they passed the awful disease that had killed TJ on to their child?

And yet . . .

What if he didn't have the variant and this baby was perfect? Part him and part her.

Summer moved her hand to her stomach, trying to take in the fact that there was a new life growing inside of her.

She bit her lip, considering what to do next. She had to leave to pick up Max from school in a few minutes. But should she text Benjamin or call him or wait until he got home tonight? Or maybe longer?

She tried to picture how he would react. He was great with kids, and he loved Max, she knew that. But they hadn't even talked about having children of their own. Maybe he—

Her phone burst into song, and Summer jumped. She didn't recognize the number on the screen, but she answered anyway, in case it was someone calling to schedule a princess party—in which case, she'd have to hope they wouldn't mind a pregnant princess. The thought made her half giggle her "Hello?"

"Hello," a deep male voice replied. "Is this Summer Calvano?"

Summer's smile immediately died at the man's serious, official-sounding tone. Fear clawed at her heart. Had something happened to Benjamin?

"Yes," she scratched out.

"The Summer who is married to Benjamin?" The man sounded a little less serious this time, but Summer barely managed another, "Yes."

"Oh good. I hope you don't mind me calling. I got your number from Benjamin."

"I— Um— Who is this?" Summer stammered.

A chuckle reverberated through the phone. "Sorry. I'm Ian. I just dropped your husband off at the airport."

"Is everything okay? Is he all right?" Summer asked quickly.

"Yes and no," Ian answered, his voice growing serious again.

Summer clutched at the bathroom countertop. "What does that mean?"

"It means," Ian said, "that Benjamin is physically fine. Like I said, I just dropped him off at the airport. But I'm afraid he's making a big mistake, throwing away the biggest opportunity of his life."

"Opportunity?" Summer eased her grip on the counter, her legs weak with relief. She let herself sink to the floor.

"At Kalibre," Ian said, as if that should mean something to Summer.

"I don't know what that is," she said.

"Kendra Hill's restaurant."

Summer still had no idea what he was talking about.

"I'm sure you don't realize what a big deal this is, or you would have said yes already, but we're talking next-level career stuff here," Ian went on. "People are going to flock to this restaurant. And I don't mean like ordinary people. I mean like celebrities, athletes, everyone who's someone. And they're going to be eating *his* food and begging him to cook for their events. I mean, this is unheard of for a chef his age. I wouldn't be surprised if he ended up with a Food Network deal someday. He has exactly the right personality for it. I know it would be hard on you to move to Atlanta, but—"

"Move to—" Summer pressed the phone to her ear. "Are you saying Benjamin was in Atlanta for a job interview?"

"No." Ian laughed.

Summer let out a breath, but Ian continued. "I'm saying the job is his if he wants it. Or, well, if you want him to have it. I *know* it's what he wants. More than anything in the world."

What he wants more than anything in the world. The words rang in Summer's head. That was what he'd said about her.

But it made more sense that this was what he wanted. It was the dream he'd been working toward until she'd derailed his plans by marrying him. And he wouldn't have gone to Atlanta if he didn't want it.

"Did he even tell you about any of this?" Ian's question cut through Summer's circling thoughts.

"No," she whispered.

Ian's laugh was hard and unamused. "I should have known. He's too . . . too . . ."

"Noble," Summer filled in.

She heard the sound of fingers snapping through the phone. "Yes, that's it," Ian said. "He always has to be the one to make the sacrifices. But if he doesn't do this . . ." Ian paused. "He's going to regret it for the rest of his life."

Regret. The word set Summer's stomach rolling again. It sounded an awful lot like *resent.*

"I know you don't want that for him." Ian's voice became quiet, coaxing.

Summer shook her head. Never that.

"You should tell Kendra that Benjamin will do it," she said past the acid burn at the back of her throat.

There was silence on the other end and then, "Are you for real?"

Before Summer could answer, Ian broke in again, "No, don't tell me. I don't care if you're for real or not. I'm telling Kendra that it's a done deal."

Summer lowered the phone from her ear, staring at the blank screen.

Then she forced herself to her feet and picked up the pregnancy test. She buried it under a pile of tissues in the garbage, then tied up the bag. She'd toss it in the trash can waiting at the curb to be picked up on her way to get Max. And then she'd come home and start packing.

Chapter 53

Benjamin sighed as he steered through the dark streets of River Falls. His flight had been delayed, and he couldn't wait another minute to get home. It had been nice to catch up with Ian, and he had left with no doubt that the new Kalibre would be a success—but also no doubt that he had made the right choice in turning down the job. It was a flattering offer, and had Ian made it six months ago, he might have taken it. But what he wanted had changed so much since then. It had required an extraordinary effort to convince Ian that he was serious about not taking the position, and he knew his friend still thought he was crazy—but at least Ian had finally accepted Benjamin's decision, and they'd parted as friends.

Just turning onto his own street made Benjamin's spirits lift, and his eyes eagerly sought out his own house. He had missed Max and Summer every moment that he was gone, and he hoped maybe Summer would still be awake, so he could tell her how happy he was to be home. And even if she wasn't, he could climb into bed with her and greet her first thing when she woke up in the morning.

But the house was completely dark, not even the porch light casting the welcoming glow that always filled his heart with joy when he came home from work. He brushed aside the sting of disappointment. Summer was probably exhausted from two days of taking care of Max on her own. But now that he was home, he was going to make sure she got all the rest she needed. At least after getting the results of the genetic tests, he didn't have to worry anymore that the reason for her fatigue was that she was ill.

He jumped out of the car and grabbed his bag, the cool night air washing over him. He lifted his face to the starry sky and breathed out a prayer of thanksgiving for the way God had worked everything out. Then he bounded up the porch steps and slipped silently into the house. He headed straight for the bedrooms, pausing first to check on Max.

The room was completely dark, and Benjamin frowned, peering toward the spot where the night light should be glowing. Maybe the bulb had burnt out. He tiptoed closer to check it, but his eyes fell on the bed, and he realized it was empty.

Benjamin shook his head with a soft laugh. If he had to guess, Max had probably climbed into bed with Summer. Fortunately, once he was asleep, the boy rarely woke, so Benjamin could carry him back to his own bed and then take his place next to Summer.

The door to the master bedroom was open, and Benjamin nodded to himself—a sure sign that Max had come in.

But halfway to the bed, his heart stopped.

It was empty—still made up.

"Summer?" Benjamin fumbled for the light switch. "Max?"

Where were they? Had something happened to them?

The only answer was the quiet hum of the furnace.

Benjamin stumbled into the hallway, turning on the light and pushing into Summer's former room. It was empty too. He made his way back to Max's room and flipped on the light in there too. Was it messier than usual? Had the room been ransacked, or was that only Max's usual clutter?

"Max?" he called again, pulling out his phone and checking for messages from Summer.

But there were none.

He tapped to call her number, but it went straight to voice mail.

He hung up, then realized he should have left a message, so he called again and left one he wasn't sure made any sense. Hopefully she would get the gist and call him.

"Oh Lord, where are they? Please let them be safe," he muttered as he dialed Zeb's number next.

"Everything all right?" Zeb answered immediately, his voice somehow conveying calm and concern at the same time.

"I can't find Summer and Max." Benjamin scrubbed a fist against his chest. He couldn't breathe.

"What do you mean you can't find them?"

Benjamin looked around wildly, as if they had been playing a game of hide and seek and he had given up too soon. "I mean, I just got home from Atlanta, and they're not here. The beds are empty. Max's room is a mess, like maybe someone—"

"Let's not jump to any conclusions." Zeb's voice was firm. "Did you check if Summer's car is in the garage?"

Benjamin shook his head and bolted through the kitchen to the door that led to the garage. He yanked it open and stopped himself short.

"It's not here." He glanced around, as if they might have hidden it wherever they'd hidden themselves.

"That's good."

"That's good?" Benjamin asked wildly.

"It means wherever they went, it was probably by their own choice." Zeb's matter-of-fact answer calmed Benjamin a little.

"Okay, yeah, that's a good point. But Summer didn't call, and she's not answering her phone."

"Maybe she had to take her mom to the hospital." Again, Zeb sounded certain and reassuring, and Benjamin let out a breath.

Why hadn't he thought of that?

He turned back toward the kitchen. "Yeah, maybe. Is there any way you could—" His eyes fell on a piece of paper on the counter, Summer's loopy handwriting curving across it. "Oh, you know what? She left me a note."

Zeb made a sound somewhere between exasperation and a chuckle.

"Sorry I over-re . . ." Benjamin trailed off as his eyes scanned the note. Queasiness rolled through his stomach, and he dropped the paper back to the counter.

"So, is it her mom?" Zeb asked.

"It's . . ." Benjamin stared at the words of the note again. *So we'll stay at my mama's for a little while until we find somewhere else.* "Yeah. Sorry I woke you."

"I wasn't sleeping," Zeb said easily. "Do you want me to give you a ride or anything?"

"No." Benjamin's throat was almost too dry to get the word out. "Thanks."

He hung up, then reread the whole note. But the words refused to make sense.

He shoved it in his pocket, then strode toward the door and grabbed his keys.

Chapter 54

What are you doing here? Summer asked herself for the millionth time as she tossed and turned on the small couch, trying to avoid the springs poking at her through the fabric no matter which way she flipped. *Go home.*

But she couldn't do that. She'd been living in a fairy tale, convincing herself that she and Benjamin could have a happily ever after, when it turned out that she'd already stolen his from him. She'd already cost him a car and a girlfriend. She wasn't going to cost him the job he wanted more than anything too.

Well, he wasn't the only one who could be noble.

She'd set him free, and he could go to Atlanta and have the life he'd always wanted.

You don't really want that, the little voice that had been plaguing her all day argued.

But Summer ignored it. It didn't matter what she wanted. This was what she had to do. For Benjamin's sake.

And for hers and Max's and the baby's.

She wasn't going to keep Benjamin tied to them so that he could grow to resent them all someday.

He wouldn't resent you, the voice whispered. *You've never seen him resent anyone.*

But she had. He had resented her after they'd broken up the first time. He'd stormed away without speaking to her.

If anything, he's going to resent you for this, the voice chimed in again.

But Summer shook her head against the couch. Then let him resent her. It was better than resenting Max and the baby. She couldn't bear to think of them having the kind of childhood she'd had.

Her hand splayed across her stomach.

He's going to find out about the baby. That stupid voice was relentless.

She knew that. She'd have to tell him eventually. But if she could put it off long enough, he would be settled in Atlanta already, and he would see that it was better this way. That he really was happier without them tying him down. She wouldn't ask for child support or alimony or any of that stuff. He could be free to start his life over.

The thought brought back the nausea she'd been fighting all day, but she pushed it down.

At least Mama hadn't gloated when she and Max had shown up with bags in hand. All she'd said was, "I ain't giving up my bed," to which Summer had replied, "No one's asking you to."

Summer flipped over again, staring out the window at the deserted street and trying not to think about the comfortable bed she could be sharing with Benjamin right now. Was he home yet? Had he found her note? She'd deliberately left her phone in the kitchen so she couldn't be tempted to answer if he called. She'd have to talk to him sometime, of course, but she didn't trust herself to do it tonight. Not when everything in her ached to be in his arms.

Stop it, she commanded herself. She was going to go through with this, and that was all there was to it.

Outside, headlights slid slowly down the street, and Summer squinted against the too-bright lights, waiting for them to pass.

Her breath caught as the vehicle slowed and then turned into Mama's driveway. Less than a second later, the lights went out and a car door closed.

She heard that sound every night, and it always brought joy pattering into her heart.

But tonight . . . Tonight it only brought heaviness.

She briefly considered hiding under the light blanket that covered her and pretending she wasn't there, but she knew Benjamin well enough to know he would knock until she answered the door. It had to be close to midnight, and the last thing she needed was for Mama or Max to wake up.

Silently, she slipped across the room and out the door. Benjamin paused for a moment at the bottom of the small stoop, his eyes raking over her. And then he leaped past the steps and crushed her to him. "When I got home and you weren't there . . ." He held her back a little and sought her eyes. "What's going on?"

Summer shrugged out of his grip, the bite of the night air cutting through her t-shirt. She hugged her arms close, letting her eyes skirt away from his. "You shouldn't have come."

"I shouldn't have . . ." Benjamin sounded confused and maybe a little angry.

Summer shivered. It was good if he was angry. It would make this easier.

"I don't understand what's happening right now," he said.

"I told you in my note. Max and I are staying here for a while."

"Because you're leaving me?" Benjamin's anger gave way to hurt. "But I thought everything was . . . I thought we were . . ."

Summer bit her lip but shook her head, still not looking at him. "You should go."

"Summer." Benjamin's voice was ragged. "Why are you doing this?"

His brokenness sliced at her, and she had to hug her arms tighter around herself so she wouldn't wrap them around him.

He blinked at her for a moment, then wriggled out of his jacket and hung it around her shoulders.

The warmth that cloaked her almost made her break down. But she couldn't. It wouldn't be fair to him.

He reached for her, but she sidestepped him, and he let out a frustrated breath. "So, what, we're not even going to talk about it? You're just going to up and decide you don't want to be with me anymore, and that's that?"

"There's nothing to talk about." Her voice nearly cracked, and she had to pause to take a breath. "I think it's time we stop pretending this is a real marriage. I'll go on and live my life and you go on and live yours."

"This *is* a real marriage. You *are* my life." His voice was thick in the dark. "You and Max."

She shook her head. "No. You had a life and then we came along and interrupted it. You should go to Atlanta. Take the job with Kalibre."

"I— What?" he sputtered. "How do you know about that?"

"Ian called me today." She watched his expression as it changed from shock to anger.

"I'm going to kill that guy," he muttered.

But Summer shook her head. "It sounds like an amazing opportunity. And you didn't even tell me about it. You were going to sacrifice your own happiness for us."

Benjamin shook his head. "I'm sorry I didn't tell you. I didn't want you to worry that I might actually consider the job. The only reason I went to Atlanta was so I could tell Ian that in person. He's not great at taking no for an answer." He laughed humorlessly.

"But it *is* a once-in-a-lifetime opportunity," Summer persisted. And then she made herself repeat Ian's words that she hadn't been able to chase out of her head. "It's your dream. What you want more than anything in the world."

Benjamin caught her arms. "It's what I wanted once, yes. But it's not what I want anymore."

"What you wanted when?" Her voice was quiet. "Before Max and I came along?"

He hesitated. "That's not the point."

"It's exactly the point." Her voice grew firm. "If it weren't for us, you would take this job, and we're not going to keep you from it. You would only resent us."

"How could I ever resent you?" Benjamin's hands slid up and down her arms. "I love you. Don't— Don't you love me?"

Summer closed her eyes, willing the tears behind her lids not to fall. Of course she loved him. That was why she was doing this.

She made herself shake her head.

Then she reached behind her and opened the door.

"Summer, don't do this." Benjamin's grip on her arms tightened, but she pulled away and propelled herself inside.

"I have to."

"I'm not going to give up on you, you know I'm not," Benjamin said as she closed the door.

It wasn't until she sank to the floor and wrapped her arms over her head that she realized she was still wearing his jacket.

Chapter 55

Benjamin stared at the nearly empty closet in Summer's room. She and Max hadn't been in church this morning, and now he knew what she'd done while he was gone. The absence of her princess costumes made all of this a little too real. At least while they'd still been here, he'd had some hope that she'd be back. But now . . .

He scrubbed at his face.

He'd gone to see her at her mama's before and after work the last three days. He'd brought her flowers and pie. He'd told her a thousand times that she wasn't making him give up his dreams—that she *was* his dream. But none of it seemed to make a difference to her.

At this point, he didn't know what would. But he wasn't going to give up on her. Not until she presented him with divorce papers. And probably not even then.

She was what he wanted, all he wanted, and he was going to make her see that—somehow.

He scanned her closet again, then checked the drawers. But the prince costumes were gone too. She'd told him last night that she didn't need him for today's princess party after all. But she was getting a prince, whether she liked it or not.

He strode to his own room and pulled out the closest thing he could find to a princely costume: a pair of dress pants, a white button-down shirt left open at the top, and a vest. He pried on a pair of dress shoes and surveyed the effect in the mirror. Well, he wouldn't win any awards for best-dressed prince, but it would have to do.

He grabbed his keys and ran out to his car, lifting a hand to wave at his neighbor, who gave him an odd look but waved back. Fortunately, he knew the family having the party, so he didn't have to text Summer for directions. He was pretty sure she wouldn't have sent them.

Although the drive was short, by the time Benjamin got there, parents were already walking their kids to the door. He got out of his car and hurried after them, ignoring a fresh slew of strange looks.

Mrs. Sherman was welcoming the kids inside, but when Benjamin reached her, she did a double take. "Benjamin?"

He grinned. "Actually, it's Aladdin today."

She eyed his clothing and gave him a dubious look. "I thought Summer said we weren't going to be able to have a prince?"

Benjamin shook his head. "Summer didn't think it would work out. But I was determined to make it happen."

"Okay, well, great." Mrs. Sherman still looked uncertain, but she stepped aside and gestured him into the house. "Summer is setting up in the family room." She pointed to a wide set of stairs. "Some of the girls are already up there."

"Perfect." Benjamin rushed past her to take the stairs two at a time. At the top, he stopped, his eyes traveling straight to Summer. She wore a silky blue top that fell off her shoulders and a pair of flowing blue and gold pants with a gold band around her waist. A turquoise headband circled the top of her head, and her long, dark hair flowed down her back.

She was already surrounded by a group of eager girls, who chatted excitedly.

"Jasmine, you're my favorite princess," one of them said, and Benjamin winced. Of course she had to be Jasmine today.

But Summer smiled sweetly at the girl. "Thank you."

"Is Aladdin coming?" another girl asked.

"Uh, no, he couldn't—"

Benjamin cleared his throat and stepped forward, keeping his eyes on Summer's face as she looked up, her cheeks going first pale, then flushed. Her lips worked up and down, and he couldn't tell if she was fighting a smile or a growl.

"What are— How did—" she stammered.

"I couldn't miss the party of the year, could I? I told Genie to keep an eye on things for me."

"Benji," Max's little voice called out, and Benjamin spun around in surprise as Max charged toward him.

"Maxerooni." Benjamin scooped the boy into his arms and swung his feet into the air. He'd missed this little guy terribly.

"Who's Benji?" one of the girls asked as Benjamin set Max down.

"That's my nickname," Benjamin offered smoothly. "I'm going incognito today. That's why I'm dressed like this too. I couldn't let everyone know I'm a prince. Otherwise, they'd all stop me to ask for an autograph, and then I'd never get here on time."

His gaze sought Summer again. She was shaking her head, but he didn't miss the slight upturn of her lips. Hope surged through him. "So, are we ready to get this party started?"

For the next hour, they played games, made crafts, ate cake, and opened presents. Max seemed to love it all, but Summer was tense, though Benjamin doubted anyone else noticed. He could only tell by the stiff way she held her smile in place—and by the careful distance she kept from him. The one time their hands bumped as he handed her a glue stick, she pulled hers away as if she'd been burnt.

Finally, she announced that it was time for the sing-along. She passed Benjamin her phone so that he could run the music while she led the singing, and he eagerly scanned the playlist she had put together, grinning as his eyes fell on the last song.

He sat on the floor with Max on his lap, the girls gathered around them, as they listened to Summer sing. He even joined in with the girls' voices for the parts he knew. But when they got to the last song, he moved Max to the floor and stood up, making his way over all of the little legs to stand next to Summer.

She eyed him. "Was there something you wanted to say, Aladdin?"

He shook his head. "Nope." Then he pressed the button to begin the final song: "A Whole New World." He waited through the introduction, then at the cue, stepped forward and took her hand, singing the first words of the song loudly and clearly.

Summer's eyes grew wide, and the kids cheered—Max loudest of all.

Benjamin grinned and kept singing, not taking his gaze off of Summer. Her lips pressed into a tight line, and her eyes shone with unshed tears. Benjamin faltered a little, wondering if he'd made a mistake. But when they got to her verse, she came in with her strong, steady soprano. She didn't look away from him, and her lips curved into a smile that set his heart flying higher than any magic carpet could have.

He pulled her closer as they came in together on the final refrain, wrapping an arm around her waist and resting his palm on her cheek. Their voices mingled and then faded away, and still they stood like that.

There was silence for a moment, but then the kids broke into wild applause and Summer seemed to come back to herself. She unwound his arm from around her waist and moved into the crowd of girls, hugging them.

Benjamin recruited Max to help him start cleaning up, and once all of the girls were gone, Summer silently joined them.

"I think we can chalk that up as another success," he said cheerfully.

Summer nodded tightly. "You shouldn't have come."

Benjamin sighed. He was getting a little tired of hearing those words every time he saw her.

But before he could say anything, Mrs. Sherman bustled into the room and started gushing to Summer about how wonderful the party had been. Benjamin continued to clean up, grinning as Mrs. Sherman added that she was so glad he had come, even if his costume was a little "unusual."

By the time Mrs. Sherman wound down, Benjamin had everything packed up, and he carried it out to Summer's car for her. He loaded it into the trunk while she buckled Max into his seat. She must have raced through the job because she was already opening her own car door by the time he shut the trunk.

"Summer, wait." He hurried to catch her, half afraid she'd jump in and squeal away like a criminal in a cop movie.

But she paused with her hand on the open door. "What is it?" She sounded so weary and worn that it was all he could do not to pull her into his arms.

"Can we talk?" he asked quietly.

She shook her head. "There's nothing to talk about."

He gave a disbelieving laugh. "We could talk about the fact that I love you, for starters."

Again she shook her head, and he fought the urge to growl out loud.

"I do, Summer. I've tried to show you every way I know how. What more can I do? What more proof do you need from me? Tell me, and I'll do it."

"I don't need anything. You've already given up too much for me."

"And I would give it all up again," he said fiercely. "I would give up my life for you."

She closed her eyes, and he thought for a moment that he'd convinced her. But then she opened them, her expression blank. "But I don't want you to. There's only one thing I want you to give up."

"Name it."

She looked away, toward the orange and gold trees dotting the mountains. "Me."

All of the breath escaped Benjamin faster than if he'd been tackled by an entire football team.

"I can't do that," he managed to gasp. "I love you, and I know you love me." She kept denying it, but he could see it in her eyes. She loved him, but she was afraid. "I know you're scared but—"

"I'm not scared. I'm tired. I need to go home."

"Yes." He seized her hand. "Come *home*. With me. Where you belong."

She shook her head and pulled her hand back. "You know I'm staying at my mama's."

"Are you really telling me that's where you'd rather be?"

She grimaced but nodded.

Benjamin scrubbed his hand through his hair. This woman was more stubborn than anyone he'd ever met.

"Okay," he finally relented. "Go get some rest. But I have off tomorrow, and I thought we could—"

"I have an appointment tomorrow," Summer interrupted. She looked away, then inhaled quickly and met his eyes. "With a divorce lawyer."

The blow made Benjamin stagger backwards. He grabbed at the roof of her car to keep from falling over his own feet.

He wanted to say something, to scream, to protest—but it was a fight just to pull in a breath.

"I'll bring the papers over afterward," Summer added.

"I won't sign them."

"You don't have to. Only one person has to want it for it to go through."

"What about Max?" Benjamin pressed a hand to the car window, as if that could keep her from taking Max from him. "I'm his guardian too."

"I can take care of Max. He was never supposed to be your problem."

"My problem— Summer— I *love* Max. I *love* you." Was there no getting through to this woman?

"Then we'll work something out." Summer wrapped her arms across her stomach, and he wondered if this conversation was making her as nauseous as it made him.

"This is what you want." He meant for it to be a question, but it came out as a flat statement.

If she didn't really want it, she wouldn't have gone so far as to make an appointment.

"Yes," she answered, her voice cool and steady.

Benjamin watched her for another moment, then spun on his heel and strode toward his own car.

He hesitated a moment, waiting for her to tell him to stop, to say it was all a mistake. But she remained silent.

He turned and let his eyes meet hers one more time. She didn't blink, didn't waver.

He yanked his car door open, dropped into his seat, and drove away.

Chapter 56

Summer pressed a hand against the pain in her stomach, lowering herself heavily to the couch. She'd woken up in the middle of the night with a sharp pain behind her belly button, and it had only intensified as she'd taken Max to school this morning.

She leaned her head back against the couch, letting out a long breath. She didn't close her eyes because if she did, she'd only see the look on Benjamin's face when she'd told him yesterday that she was going to the divorce lawyer. That look had haunted her all night. But at least she seemed to have succeeded in finally driving him away. He hadn't come over this morning—and she knew he wouldn't.

Her whole chest burned, and she pressed both hands into her stomach, leaning forward to try to find a comfortable position. She told herself that it was just stress or nerves or maybe even the flu.

That it wasn't the baby.

She pulled out her phone to check the time, but it was only nine o'clock. Which meant she still had three hours before her appointment with the lawyer.

She'd taken the day off of work because she'd known she wouldn't be any good to anyone—but that meant she had nothing to keep her occupied until the appointment, except her thoughts.

And she couldn't let herself dwell on those or she'd never do what needed to be done. It had been so, so hard not to lose her resolve yesterday when he'd shown up at the party with that ridiculous costume and that enticing grin and that incredible song. When he'd said he would give up anything for her.

But that was the thing. She knew he would. And he might even be okay with it for a while.

They might all live happily ever after—for a time.

But eventually, Benjamin would realize how much he'd given up for them. Just like her father had. Just like her mother had.

And he would want out—but he'd be trapped. Living a life he hadn't wanted—and resenting them for it. She couldn't do that to him. To any of them.

"What's wrong with you?" Mama shuffled into the room and dropped into her recliner with a grunt.

"Nothing. Just a stomachache." She hadn't told Mama yet that she was pregnant, although by the shrewd look Mama was giving her, she had likely guessed it already.

"When are you going home?"

"I need a few more weeks to save up, and then I should be able to put a security deposit on an apartment." Summer tried not to picture Benjamin's cozy house as she said it.

Mama blinked at her. "Why on earth do you want to do something stupid like that?"

"Well, we can't stay here, and—"

"So go home," Mama said again. "Then I won't have to listen to my doorbell ringing at all hours of the day and night."

Summer shook her head. "It's not my home, Mama."

"What, because you had a little fight?"

"We didn't have a fight. We're getting divorced."

Mama snorted. "The way he keeps showing up would seem to indicate otherwise."

A fresh pain pulsed through Summer's stomach, and she leaned forward with a little moan.

"You should go to the doctor," Mama said flatly.

"I'm fine."

"Anyway," Mama continued, as if there'd been no interruption. "I've heard there are couples who are happily married. I suppose you all could be one of 'em."

"He was asked to run a restaurant in Georgia, Mama. And he didn't take the job because of me and Max. I can't let him make that kind of sacrifice. He'll resent us. And I've had enough resentment to last a lifetime." She refused to look away from her mother's eyes, but Mama's shrug was slow, maybe indifferent.

"Suit yourself." She turned to click on the TV.

Summer wanted to scream. Just once in her life, couldn't her mother have some kind of wisdom to offer her? Some motherly advice? Or at least some comfort?

She tried again to get comfortable, but only succeeded in shifting the pain to her lower right side. She closed her eyes, but there was Benjamin's face again. So she turned on her phone instead, and scrolled through her social media feed, barely registering what any of the posts were about.

A picture of a man sitting at the edge of a cliff with his head bowed caught her eyes, and she stopped scrolling. That was how she felt right now. Like she was at the edge of a cliff. And she had nowhere to go but down it.

Her eyes went to the text, and she realized it was a post from Beautiful Savior with a video of yesterday's sermon. She'd missed being at church, but there was no way she could have sat with Benjamin and his family—or worse, without them—and kept her composure, so she'd stayed home, despite Max's protests.

She clicked on the video, and the image of the man on the cliff faded to reveal the front of Beautiful Savior, with Pastor Cooper in the pulpit. Summer's eyes greedily scanned the backs of the heads in the frame. She touched the screen, accidentally pausing the video, when she spotted Benjamin.

She hit play again, and the camera readjusted to zoom in on Pastor Cooper. His warm voice rang from her phone. "Y'all aren't going to believe this," the pastor began, "but I wasn't a perfect child." A smattering of chuckles sounded offscreen.

"Turn that down," Mama demanded.

Summer made a face to herself but complied.

"Good to know that doesn't come as a surprise to you." The pastor grinned. "But I still remember one time that I did something truly terrible. I was probably about eight years old, and I was mad at my parents about something or other. I can't even remember what now. But I decided that they must not want me anymore. So I grabbed my backpack, and I packed it with about twelve pairs of socks and a book, and I ran away."

He took a breath. "Well, you might know my daddy served with Pastor Calvano at a youth camp when I was a kid, so we lived in the woods. I knew them pretty well. Figured I could live off the land. I'd be fine. So I walked and I walked and I walked some more—farther than I'd ever gone into those woods on my own before. When I thought I had gone far enough, I built myself a little hut out of branches. And then I sat in it and pulled out my book. It was summertime, so I wasn't cold. And I wasn't afraid." He paused. "Until the sun started to set. But I was determined to stay out there, alone—well, forever."

The camera panned again, and Summer caught sight of the back of Benjamin's head. It was bowed, and she wondered if that word, "alone," hurt him as much as it hurt her.

"Just as it was getting too dark to see, I started to hear shouting," Pastor Cooper went on. "I recognized my daddy's voice—he was a big bear of a man and had a voice to match." The pastor drew in a deep breath, then bellowed, "Aaaaarrrrrrooooooonnnnnn."

There were a few gasps in the background of the video, but all Summer could think was that her mama never would have come after her like that.

"I knew his voice," Pastor Cooper said quietly. "And I knew he was calling for me. But I didn't want to hear him. So I covered my ears. But every few seconds, I heard the voice again, right through my hands." He mimicked covering his ears, then shook his head and lowered his hands.

"Finally, when I didn't hear it anymore, I took my hands off my ears. I figured he had given up—and I'm not gonna lie, I was hurt. I might not have wanted to be found—but that didn't mean I didn't want him to keep looking." Pastor Cooper's gaze swept the congregation—spending, it seemed, an extra second on the camera. Summer held her breath and pressed her hands to the pain in her stomach, feeling a desperate need to know what happened next.

"And then," Pastor Cooper said quietly. "I heard it. Just the faintest, gentlest whisper: 'Aaron.'" He shook his head, and Summer could see the emotion on his face. "And in that moment, I knew what I had been trying to ignore all along. My daddy loved me. He wanted me back. He would do anything to find me."

Pastor Cooper leaned forward in the pulpit, his gaze searching. "Does that sound familiar?"

He picked up the Bible. "It should. Because this book is full of the same story. Of a Father who loves his children so much, who wants them so

319

much, that he pursues them relentlessly. That he has done anything and everything to save them."

Summer closed her eyes, letting the pastor's words wash over her.

"Sometimes he calls us with a big voice, with power and with might, like my daddy's shouts. But we don't always see it, do we?" Pastor Cooper continued. "We don't always listen. Like Elijah. Granted, God called Elijah to be a prophet when it wasn't an ideal time to have that job. King Ahab and Queen Jezebel were not big fans of God or of his prophets. They wanted to worship their idols in peace, so they were hunting the prophets down and putting them to death. But God was with Elijah. He sent Elijah into the desert to keep him safe from the king and queen and then sent ravens to bring Elijah bread and meat. Later, God brought Elijah to a widow and her son and then blessed them with an unending supply of flour and oil. When the son died, God even allowed Elijah to restore him to life. And if all of that wasn't enough, he also brought Elijah to a showdown with the prophets of the false god Baal. It was 450 prophets of Baal against one prophet of God. But hard as they tried, those 450 prophets of Baal couldn't rouse their god to light even a spark on their sacrifice. But Elijah's God—our God—he answered with power and might, burning up the sacrifice, the altar, the stones, the soil, and even the trench of water Elijah had ordered dug around it all."

Pastor Cooper shook his head in amazement. "Wouldn't you have loved to see that? If that's not a sign that God is with Elijah and that he loves him, I don't know what is. But the very next time we see Elijah, he's fleeing into the mountains. Queen Jezebel has promised to kill him, and he's sure there is no one left in all the world to help him. He's so forlorn that he tells God, 'I've had enough. Take my life.'"

The pastor shook his head. "If I were God, I would have been like, 'Really, man? How much more could I have done to show my love for you? What more proof do you need from me?'"

Summer sucked in a breath. Those words. Wasn't that the same thing Benjamin had asked her yesterday?

"Fortunately," Pastor Cooper continued with a smile, "I'm not God. His response was much better. Instead of shunning Elijah, instead of giving up on him, God tenderly took care of him. He provided Elijah with food and water. Then he led him to a cave in a mountain and promised to show Elijah his presence. Elijah stood on that mountain and waited. He waited through a great and powerful wind. He waited through an earthquake. He waited through a fire. All pretty loud shouts. All pretty clear proof of God's power. But the Bible tells us that the Lord wasn't in any of those shouts."

"Elijah must have been wondering what could possibly come next. If I were him, I'd have been plenty scared. I mean, y'all, if God wasn't in the wind or the earthquake or the fire, he must be coming in something really terrifying. So imagine Elijah's surprise when the Lord's voice came to him not in a shout." He lowered his voice. "It came in a gentle whisper. And in that whisper, Elijah heard God's love."

The church had fallen into absolute silence, and Summer closed her eyes, letting the statement wash over her.

"Now, maybe you're thinking that's all well and good for Elijah." Pastor Cooper's voice went back to its normal volume. "But you haven't heard God's shouts *or* his whispers in your life. Well, first of all, let me assure you that you have. In here." He held up the Bible. "God has called you to be his own. He has given you his Word. He has worked in your life, for your good. I mean, what more could he do to show his love for you? Only this." Pastor Cooper opened the Bible still in his hand and read, "But God demonstrates his own love for us in this: while we were still sinners, Christ died for us."

He let out a low whistle. "That's a powerful demonstration of love, isn't it? God didn't wait for us to clean up our act. He didn't wait for us to transform into perfect people. He didn't wait for us to stop sinning. Because we *couldn't* do any of those things. Not without him. Instead, he looked at us. He saw sinners who did nothing but sin against him. And he *loved* us. He *wanted* us. He sent his Son to *die* for us. The godly for the ungodly, the righteous for the unrighteous, the perfect for the sinful. Jesus for *you*. Jesus for *me*."

Summer's stomach squeezed, and she groaned, trying to readjust her position but giving up when the movement made the pain worse. She bit down on her lip, attempting to ignore the ache so she could focus on the video.

"You know, that day I ran away, my daddy was supposed to leave for a fishing trip to Canada. And because of me, he missed his flight and didn't get to go at all. I felt guilty about that for years. But it wasn't until I was a teen that I had the courage to confess that to him. I realized how much he must have regretted missing that trip, and I told him I understood if he resented me for it. And do you know what he said? 'How could I regret finding my child, the most precious thing in the world to me? A fishing trip is nothing. I would give up my life for you, son.'"

Summer swallowed roughly. That was what Benjamin had said to her.

Pastor Cooper ducked his head. "I think of those words every time I think about what Jesus has done for me. He *did* give up his life for me. And not just to spare me for this world. To give me the promise of eternal life. He probably should regret it, honestly. He has a right to resent me. After all, the punishment he faced was *my* punishment. I deserved it. Not him. But you know what?" Pastor Cooper looked right at the camera, and

Summer felt like his eyes were on her. "He has never once stopped wanting you. He has never once stopped loving you. Instead, 'For the joy set before him he endured the cross, scorning its shame, and sat down at the right hand of the throne of God.' Jesus considered it joy to suffer for you. Not because he didn't feel it—he felt every blow of the hammer, every tear of the nails through his flesh, every labored breath on the cross. He felt what it was to be forsaken by his father. But he considered it joy because he would give up everything—he *did* give up everything—to make you his child. Whether you shout it or whisper it or anywhere in between, that is a truth you can trust all the way to eternity. Amen."

Summer lowered her phone slowly, tears overflowing her eyes and splashing onto her cheeks. *God* wanted her. *That* was what mattered. *He* had given up everything for her because he loved her. Loved her even though she didn't deserve it. Loved her even though she couldn't do anything to pay him back. Loved her even though she had allowed herself to get caught up in so many doubts.

Knowing that meant it didn't matter whether mama loved her and wanted her. Or whether Benjamin did.

Except . . . Oh, how had she not seen it? He *did*.

Wasn't that what he'd been showing her all along? He had been a living example of God's love. He'd willingly given up everything for her. He'd pursued her even when she pushed him away. He'd loved her even when she didn't deserve to be loved.

And she was about to throw all of that away.

Her hand shook as she picked up her phone again and dialed.

It only took a moment to cancel her appointment with the attorney. Then she dialed again, moaning a little as she waited for a sound on the other end. The phone rang three times and then went to voicemail.

"Hi, you've reached Benjamin. I'm not avoiding you, I promise—unless you're a telemarketer. Otherwise, leave a message, and I'll call you back."

Summer laughed a little at the familiar greeting, pressing a hand to her stomach as the motion sent a shot of pain through her. The phone beeped, and she tried to open her mouth. But she had no idea what to say. She waited a few moments, thinking, then hung up.

She would find him later and tell him in person. Just as soon as this stomach pain passed.

And in the meantime, she would close her eyes and let herself dream of being in his arms again.

Chapter 57

"Are we going to talk about it or what?" Zeb spoke around steady breaths as he ran next to Benjamin.

"Talk about what?" Benjamin's own breaths came harder than usual, his whole body crying out for rest after his sleepless night. Around dawn, he'd given up and texted his brothers that he was driving into the Smokies to make an impromptu final training run on the trail where Saturday's race would be held.

He'd been relieved that Zeb was the only one who could make it. He wanted to run today, not talk. And Zeb was good at not talking.

"About that phone call from Summer you ignored in the car."

Benjamin huffed. He should have taken into account that Zeb may not be a talker—but he was an observer.

Benjamin had stared at his phone, watching Summer's name, his finger hovering over the button to answer. He wanted so badly to hear her voice. To try one more time to convince her not to go through with the divorce. But when his finger hit the screen, it was to send the call to voicemail. He'd been too afraid that he'd answer, and she'd say it was already done—that she already had the paperwork in her hands. And the fact that she didn't leave a message only solidified his fears.

"So?" Zeb prompted.

Benjamin shook his head. "If I wanted to talk, I would have run with Simeon."

Zeb snorted but didn't push.

They ran side by side, the weight of what he wasn't saying—what he hadn't told anyone—punching at Benjamin with every footfall.

Finally, he couldn't go any farther. His feet stopped, and he bent in half to catch his breath, wrapping his hands over the top of his head.

Zeb's footsteps continued past him for a few beats, then stopped and doubled back.

"You okay?" His brother's hand landed on his back. "Leg cramp?"

Benjamin shook his head and forced himself upright, still fighting to regain his breath. "I'm fine."

Zeb inhaled and exhaled, watching him, not saying anything.

The weight pressed on Benjamin again, and he couldn't do it any longer. He couldn't pretend. "She left me. She wants a divorce."

Zeb didn't flinch, didn't react, and Benjamin wondered if that was a result of years of training or if it was because he wasn't surprised. Maybe everyone else had seen it coming.

"Do you want one too?" Zeb finally asked.

"Of course not." Benjamin lifted his shirt to his face to scrub away the sweat.

"Did you tell her that?"

"A thousand times. But she refuses to believe me, no matter what I say or do."

"Why?" Zeb asked simply.

Benjamin threw his hands in the air. "I have no idea." But then he considered the question again. "She keeps saying that none of this was part of my plans. We got married so she would get guardianship of Max. Now that we have it," he continued, the truth smacking him like a branch to the face, "she thinks I'm going to resent her for what I gave up." He looked at his brother. "But I don't feel like I gave up anything. I feel like I *gained* everything I didn't even know I wanted."

Zeb smiled a little. "She's probably the one you should tell that."

Benjamin laughed, then hit his brother on the arm. "I'm going to do more than *tell* her. Come on." He started off in the direction they'd come, checking the distance on his fitness watch. They'd run eight miles in. That meant they had to go eight miles out. Plus the drive home was almost an hour.

He picked up his pace, his feet eating up the trail as he formulated his plan. When they got into the car to head back to town, he had too much pent-up energy to sit still. He tapped the door to the rhythm of the song on the radio until Zeb sent him a quelling look.

"Sorry." He breathed out a heavy sigh of relief. If everything went well, this whole nightmare would be over by tomorrow. And Summer would *know* that he wanted to be with her all the rest of his days.

His phone rang, and he pulled it out of his pocket, his heart leaping as Summer's name appeared on the screen.

"What a difference a few hours can make," Zeb muttered with a grin as Benjamin eagerly answered.

"Summer, hey. I'm on my—"

"Benji."

Benjamin froze at the fear in Max's voice.

"What's wrong, Maxerooni?" He worked to keep his own voice steady even as his heart slammed to a stop.

Out of the corner of his eye, he saw Zeb reach to turn the radio down.

He pulled the phone away from his ear and put it on speaker.

"Aunt Sunny has a tummy ache. And grandma tried to get up to help her but then she fell down." The boy's words ran together in one long string.

"Hey, Max. Slow down. Who fell down? Sunny or Grandma?"

"Grandma. Her eyes are closed, and she won't get up."

"Can you talk to her, Max?" Zeb asked calmly. "Does she say anything?"

"No." Tears filled Max's voice. "Is she dead?"

Benjamin closed his eyes, praying the boy wouldn't have to witness his grandmother's death on top of everything else he'd been through.

"Everything is going to be fine, Max." Zeb's voice exuded calm even as he grabbed his own phone and hit the emergency call button.

"Max." Benjamin sought the same calm tone as Zeb but didn't achieve it. He forced himself to take a breath. "Where's Sunny? Can I talk to her?"

"She's in the bathroom," Max answered. "I think she's throwing up. She keeps making weird sounds."

Benjamin let out half a breath. At least it was nothing life threatening. "Can you let me know when she comes out?"

"Yes." Max's voice sounded so small and helpless, and Benjamin hated that he wasn't there to take care of them. He never should have run away this morning.

"An ambulance is on the way," Zeb said quietly.

Benjamin nodded. "Listen, Maxerooni. An ambulance is going to come help Grandma, okay? If Sunny isn't feeling well, you'll have to let them in. And then stay out of their way. They might have to take Grandma to the hospital, but that's okay. Everything is going to be fine."

"Can you come over?"

"Yeah, Max. I'm on my way." He glanced at the landmarks out the window. They were still a good forty-five minutes from home.

"Text everyone," Zeb said, as if reading his mind.

"I'm going to have someone come hang out with you until I can get there, okay? One of my brothers or sisters or maybe my dad or Mia. You can let them in when they get there."

"Okay," Max whispered. "I'm scared."

Benjamin's heart twisted. "I know Max. But you're a brave boy. You did such a big boy thing to call me. I'm going to stay on the phone with you the whole time, okay?"

Benjamin clicked over to his texts while he talked, quickly scrolling to the family group chat.

"How was school today, buddy?" Zeb asked as Benjamin typed.

Can someone go over to Summer's mom's house to check on them? Her mom fell. An ambulance is on the way, but Summer is sick too, and Max is scared.

"It was good." Max's voice was strained. "We went on a leaf hunt. I found a big red one."

"That sounds neat." Zeb kept talking to the boy, drawing him into conversation, and Benjamin was in awe of his brother's calm. He knew it was his job, but it was more than that. It was a steadiness of character. He never lost his cool. Never lost his faith.

Benjamin wished he could be like that. *Please give me strength, Lord. Help me to trust in you.*

Sirens sounded in the background, and Benjamin breathed out.

"The ambulance is here," Max shouted.

"Okay, buddy, I need you to go open the door for them, all right?" Zeb's jaw was tight, but his tone was encouraging.

"Yes, I'm go—" Max's voice suddenly disappeared, and Benjamin glanced down at his phone.

Call lost.

"No, no, no." He hit the screen to dial again, but the call refused to connect.

"Signal always drops here. It'll come back in ten miles or so." Zeb's continued calm irked Benjamin.

"Yeah, well, I don't have ten miles. That's my wife and kid—" As soon as the words were out of his mouth, a wall of regret slammed into him. "Zeb, I'm sorry. I didn't mean—"

"I know what you meant, Benjamin. And I know how you feel. I'm getting us there as fast as I can, I promise."

Benjamin nodded tightly.

"Would you like me to pray?" Zeb's question was quiet, and Benjamin looked at him in surprise. Though all of the Calvanos had grown up praying out loud as a family, Zeb was rarely the one to volunteer to do it. Benjamin knew that wasn't because of a lack of faith but because he wasn't a naturally outspoken man.

"Yeah." Benjamin's voice was hoarse. "I'd like that. Just don't close your eyes."

Zeb snorted as Benjamin bowed his own head.

"Heavenly Father." Zeb's voice was quiet but strong. "You are everywhere at all times. Help us to trust that you are with Summer and Max and Mrs. Ellis, even when we can't be. Help us to trust that you know exactly what each one of them needs and that you will provide it. Be with the paramedics and the doctors and give them wisdom. Be with Max and give him courage. Be with Summer and her mother and give them healing. Be with Benjamin and give him hope. Be with our family and help us to be there for all of them. Surround them with your love through us, Lord. In Jesus' name we pray. Amen."

Benjamin opened his eyes slowly and lifted his head, blinking a few times to clear his vision. "Wow, Zeb," he finally said. "I had no idea you were so . . ." He almost said sweet, but that wasn't the right word. "Eloquent," he finally settled on.

The side of Zeb's lip lifted in a half-smile. "Carly used to tease me that she could only find out how I was really feeling about something by listening to my prayers."

Benjamin laughed, his heart aching for his brother and the wife and child he had lost.

"I miss her," he said without thinking.

"Me too." Zeb's voice was wistful.

"I'm sorry. I shouldn't have—"

Zeb shook his head. "It helps to know that other people miss her too." He nodded to the phone in Benjamin's hand. "Try again. You might be able to get through now."

Benjamin tried with both his phone and Zeb's, but he couldn't get a call to go through. Which didn't stop him from reattempting it every ten seconds.

Finally, when they were thirty miles from River Falls, Benjamin's phone buzzed with a text from Ava.

They're taking Summer and her mom by ambulance to the hospital in Brampton.

He read it out loud, then muttered, "Why would they take Summer in the ambulance too?"

"She probably wanted to ride along with her mom." Zeb's answer made complete sense. And yet a strange uneasiness filled Benjamin.

He texted Ava back, *Is Summer okay?*

She's in a lot of pain. They think it might be her appendix. They're afraid it might have ruptured.

"Oh." The word came out of him with the force of a punch. "They think her appendix ruptured."

His phone dinged with another text. *We're halfway to the hospital now. Max is with us. I hope that's okay.*

He stared at it, then his fingers somehow managed to type, *Yes, thank you.*

"Keep praying," Zeb said firmly as the car surged forward.

"I'm trying," Benjamin clutched desperately at his phone, but there were no more messages. "I don't know how you did this, Zeb. How you got through losing Carly and the baby without losing your mind. Or your faith. I don't think I'm strong enough for that."

He felt his brother's eyes on him. "Of course there were days when I thought I was losing my mind. And my faith. Still are."

Benjamin turned a sharp eye toward him. "It never seems like it."

Zeb shrugged. "Doesn't make it any less true."

"But how?" Benjamin asked.

"How do I get through it?" He glanced at Benjamin, who nodded.

"God's Word. You all." He sent Benjamin a pointed look. "That's one of the good things about having such a big family, you know. You never have to go through anything alone."

Benjamin swallowed. He'd been trying so hard to prove that he wasn't too young and foolish—that he could handle things on his own—that he'd lost sight of that. Which only proved that he was the most foolish of them all.

They fell silent, and Benjamin knew Zeb was praying as fervently as he was. When they finally pulled into the driveway of the hospital, Zeb drove straight up to the emergency room doors. "Go in. I'll park and be there in a minute."

Benjamin sprinted toward the building, a sharp breeze kicking up and trying to steal what little breath he had.

He pushed through the doors, nearly plowing into a group of people. It took a moment to realize that they were *his* people as arms surrounded him from every side.

For a second, he couldn't speak. It wasn't only Joseph and Ava here with Max. It was Dad and Simeon and Abigail and Lydia and Mia.

"The others are on their way," Lydia said as she gripped him tight.

Benjamin nodded, blinking back his emotion that they had all come to be here with his wife.

"How is she?" he rasped.

"They took them both straight in for tests. We haven't gotten any updates yet."

The group settled around him, and Benjamin had never felt more keenly what Zeb had said about the blessings of a big family.

It felt like six years before a doctor finally approached them. Benjamin meant to stand up, but Max was on his lap, and he couldn't get his legs to work anyway.

"I'm Dr. Duma," the petite woman said. "I'm the physician treating Summer." Her face was grave, and Benjamin heard himself swallow.

Lydia gripped his hand.

"I'm afraid she has appendicitis. The good news is her appendix hasn't ruptured."

Benjamin let out a breath so big he was surprised it didn't blow the doctor away.

"The bad news," Dr. Duma continued, and Benjamin's lungs seized before they could pull in another breath. "Is that the surgery is always trickier during pregnancy."

On either side of him, Ava and Lydia gasped. But Benjamin could only gape at the doctor.

Had she said *pregnancy*?

"You should know that there is a chance of fetal loss during or after surgery. But if we don't do the surgery, there is a much greater risk of losing both mother and baby."

Benjamin stared at her. Losing them? He couldn't lose them. He'd only just found out about the baby. And he and Summer still had a whole life to live together.

"Do the surgery," he said hoarsely.

The doctor hurried off, promising to update them as soon as she could.

Benjamin watched her go.

"I guess congratulations are in order." Joseph reached across his wife to clap Benjamin's shoulder.

Benjamin was too stunned to answer. But he bowed his head gratefully as Dad offered to pray for Summer and their baby.

Their baby.

Benjamin shook his head. He had never known it was possible to be this elated and this terrified at the same time.

Chapter 58

The world came back in soft waves, and Summer sighed sleepily, listening to the gentle murmurs around her, trying to place where she was and what she was doing.

It was dark wherever she was. And quiet.

Except for a muted whispering sound, soothing and sweet, and yet heart-rending.

Her eyes fluttered open to search for the source.

It took a moment for everything to come into focus, but once it did, Summer's heart shattered and healed again a thousand times. Somehow, some way, Benjamin was here. He sat at the side of her bed, his forehead braced against clasped hands, and she realized the whispering sound was him praying. For her.

"Benjamin." The word came out as barely a whisper, but his head shot up as if she had shouted.

"Hey," he whispered back. "How are you feeling?" His forehead was creased with worry as his hand came to her face, his fingers grazing her cheek.

"I'm . . ." A sudden memory swept over her, and her hand shot to her abdomen. She winced as it hit a strip of bandages.

"The baby is okay," Benjamin said quietly.

"Oh." Tears sprang to her eyes. She tried to blink them back, but a sob tore through her.

Benjamin's arms were instantly around her. He kissed her forehead and smoothed her hair back from her face. "It's okay."

She shook her head. "I'm sorry I didn't tell you," she choked into his shoulder.

"I know," he soothed. "And I forgive you."

"No, but Benjamin—" She started, but he gently shook his head.

"We can talk about it later, Summer. I promise. But right now, there's something else I need to tell you." He looked grave, and she stilled.

"Mama?"

Benjamin nodded. "The doctor says it's not looking good." He squeezed her hand. "If you're up to it, we should go see her before . . ."

Summer closed her eyes, trying to work up the strength.

"I'll be with you the whole time," Benjamin promised.

Summer nodded, and he called for a nurse, who brought a wheelchair. Benjamin carefully helped her into it, and she clutched her hands in her lap as he steered her through the hospital's winding corridors into the elevator.

"Benjamin?" she said as it started upward. "I have to tell you something." And she knew it couldn't wait another moment.

"What's that?" He sounded sightly wary, but he stepped around the wheelchair and squatted in front of her, resting his hands on her lap.

"I know this might not be the best time or place but—"

"If you're going to try to tell me to leave," he interrupted, "you should know it's not going to happen."

"I'm not going to tell you to leave." She wrapped her hands around his. "I'm going to tell you to stay. I'm going to tell you . . ." She took a quick breath. "That I love you." The words felt so good that she couldn't suppress a little, joyful laugh.

Benjamin's smile could have lit up the whole city. "It's always a good time and place for that." He raised himself enough to lean in and kiss her, long and slow and deep.

Vaguely, Summer registered a ding and the sound of someone clearing their throat.

Benjamin pulled back, still grinning at Summer, then scooted around the wheelchair and pushed her out of the elevator with a cheerful, "Sorry about that" to the nurse who was waiting to get on.

Summer couldn't stop smiling as he pushed her down another maze of corridors. But then he stopped in front of a closed door.

Summer felt her smile fade, and a prickle of fear went through her stomach. What were they going to find on the other side of that door?

Benjamin's hands came to her shoulders. "Are you ready?"

She let herself lean into him for a moment, gathering strength from his presence, then nodded. He leaned past her to push the door open and wheeled her inside.

Mama lay in the hospital bed, monitors and tubes flowing into her like a maze. She didn't move as Benjamin pushed Summer closer to the bed, and Summer closed her eyes.

Maybe it would be better to turn around and leave. To remember Mama like this. Rather than by the hurtful words that were bound to come out of her mouth if they stayed.

"So you're all right." Mama's voice was thin and raspy, nothing like the voice that had cursed Summer out a thousand times in her life.

"I'm okay." Summer gestured for Benjamin to wheel her to the side of the bed.

Mama looked from Summer to Benjamin, whose hands rested on her shoulders, still imparting his strength to her.

"I'll give you this," Mama said to Benjamin. "You don't quit easy."

"No, ma'am." Benjamin chuckled.

"Hmm," was Mama's only reply as she turned her head to stare at the ceiling again.

"Do you need anything, Mama?"

Mama grunted. "I'm dying, Summer. What could I possibly need?"

Me, Summer's heart cried out. *You could need me, your daughter, to be with you.*

"Do you want us to go?" she asked quietly.

Mama's head shake was barely visible. Benjamin pulled a chair up next to Summer's wheelchair and sat, reaching over the armrest to take her hand.

She smiled at him, but she could feel her lips wobble. The doctors hadn't been able to give them a timeline other than "not long." She should say goodbye to her mama. But what could she possibly say?

"I— Um— *We* have news," she finally managed, smiling weakly at Benjamin, who nodded his encouragement. "We're going to have a baby."

Mama snorted. "Well, no kidding. Didn't I tell you that weeks ago?"

"You asked, but that wasn't— I mean it was too—" Summer stopped. There was no point in arguing.

"You'll be a better mother than I was." Mama's voice was quiet.

Summer wanted to say she sure hoped so, but instead she remained silent.

After a while, Mama said, "I could have done things differently. Probably should have. I don't know why you . . . stuck around."

Summer blinked. "Because . . . I love you." She'd wondered a thousand times if it was true—had even been sure she hated Mama plenty of times—but when it came down to it, she couldn't deny that she loved her mother.

Mama squinted at her, as if trying to detect a lie. "How can you? I don't deserve that."

"Maybe not." Summer wasn't going to give her mother empty reassurances on her deathbed. "But I do anyway."

Mama grunted and fell silent, and Summer tried to think of something comforting to say.

"I'm scared." Mama's whisper was barely audible, but it cut through Summer's heart.

"Oh, Mama, I know." Summer leaned forward to clutch her mother's hand, the movement sending a slight ache through her middle. "But you don't need to be."

Mama shook her head. "I've done such horrible things. And now I have to pay the price."

For a moment, Summer was tempted to agree. But she couldn't let Mama die without knowing the beautiful promise that had changed her own life. "No, you don't, Mama. Jesus paid that price for you. So you could go to heaven."

Mama grunted her disbelief. "It may be a long time since I was in a church, but even I know there's no place in heaven for me after everything I've done."

"But there is." Summer glanced to Benjamin, and he nodded his encouragement. "Jesus died for your sins." She clutched Mama's hands tighter. "He died for them, Mama. He took them away. He forgives you. For all of them. Do you believe that?"

Mama shook her head. "I don't deserve that."

"No one does," Summer said gently.

Next to Summer, Benjamin pulled out his phone, and then his clear voice rang out, filling the room, "At one time we too were foolish, disobedient, deceived and enslaved by all kinds of passions and pleasures. We lived in malice and envy, being hated and hating one another."

Summer glanced at him. She wasn't sure this was the message Mama needed right now.

But he kept reading: "But when the kindness and love of God our Savior appeared, he saved us, not because of righteous things we had done, but because of his mercy. He saved us through the washing of rebirth and renewal by the Holy Spirit, whom he poured out on us generously through Jesus Christ our Savior, so that, having been justified by his grace, we might become heirs having the hope of eternal life. This is a trustworthy saying."

"I don't— What does that mean?" Mama whispered.

"It means—" Benjamin leaned forward to rest a hand on her arm. "That all of those horrible things you did—"

Summer winced, but Mama didn't flinch.

"Are gone," Benjamin continued. "Like they never happened. Because Jesus washed them away with his blood."

"Oh." Mama turned toward them, and though her face was stretched and gaunt, hope shone from her eyes. "That's good news."

"That's exactly what it is," Benjamin agreed.

A sob burst out of Summer, and she leaned forward as much as she could to circle Mama in a gentle hug. Mama's hand on her back was frail and feeble, and yet nothing had ever felt so comforting.

When Mama let go, Benjamin gently settled Summer back into her wheelchair. Her abdomen throbbed from the movement, but it was worth it just to feel Mama's embrace—the embrace Summer had spent years longing for.

Mama blinked a few times, and Summer was astonished to realize she was trying to hold back tears. "I . . . love you," she said, her hand weakly squeezing Summer's. "I know I stopped saying it, if I ever did say it, but I do."

Summer nodded, pressing her lips together against the tears. Those were words she had never expected to hear.

"Not as good as that man loves you, though." Mama nodded toward Benjamin. "You stop being my foolish and stubborn daughter, and you let him love you."

Summer laughed as Benjamin said a soft, "Amen."

"I will, Mama."

"And you." Mama turned her gaze on Benjamin, and Summer felt him sit up straighter. "You take care of her. Don't let her push you away in her stupid hardheadedness."

"I won't," Benjamin promised.

"I only wish . . ." Mama's words came in rough gasps. "That I would have seen sooner. That I would have . . ."

Summer shook her head and patted her hand. "It's okay, Mama. We'll have eternity together for all of that."

Mama nodded and closed her eyes, and Summer knew even before the alarms on the monitors went off that she was gone.

Chapter 59

"How are you feeling? Do you need anything?" Benjamin sat next to Summer on Dad's couch and studied her face anxiously, but she laughed and shoved his arm.

"I'm fine. You have to stop worrying."

"I can't help it. I love you."

"And I love you too." She'd said it probably a hundred or more times in the past week, but it still electrified him every time. He leaned closer to kiss her.

"Benjamin." Summer's cheeks pinked as she glanced around the room at the rest of the family, all in various states of chatter and laughter. Max was showing little Caroline his dinosaur.

"What?" he asked innocently. "They don't mind if I kiss my wife."

"I don't mind," Liam agreed, approaching the couch. "As long as you make room for me."

"And get closer to my wife?" Benjamin asked. "All right, if I have to." He closed the gap between himself and Summer, tucking his arm behind her.

"Every muscle in my body hurts," Liam groaned as he sat.

Benjamin grinned at his brother-in-law. "You did good yesterday."

Liam grimaced as he readjusted his position. "Twenty-ninth is better than I thought I'd do, but it's no fifth-place finish."

Benjamin shrugged. He was happy with his finish in the trail race—but even happier that his brothers had run the race with him. And happiest of all that Summer had been well enough to be at the finish line. Because of the baby, they'd kept her in the hospital an extra day for observation, but she'd been able to come home on Thursday, and they'd had a small funeral for her mama on Friday, and then they'd had the race yesterday.

And now they were all gathered at Dad's after church, and Benjamin had something he wanted to say. Something he wanted to *do*.

He was about to stand and call for everyone's attention when Dad popped into the room and announced lunch was ready. There was a stir, but before anyone could leave the room, Summer got to her feet.

"Um, y'all?" she said quietly.

No one else seemed to notice, so Benjamin stood too and yelled, "Hey, y'all, pipe down. My wife has something to say."

Summer hit his arm, but everyone laughed and then grew silent.

"I just wanted to say thank you." Summer cleared her throat again, blinking a few times, and Benjamin wrapped an arm around her back. She gave him a wobbly smile, then continued. "Thank you all for running in memory of TJ yesterday. And . . ." She drew in a breath. "Thank you for welcoming me and Max into this family. I used to be afraid of y'all because I thought you were so perfect. But now I see that you're not."

"Some thank you speech," Joseph protested.

Summer laughed sheepishly. "That's not what I mean. What I mean is that you're all so *real*. And you're always there for each other. And you've been there for me and Max and Benjamin. And just . . . You're the perfect family for us."

There was silence for a moment, and then, in true Calvano style, everyone started talking at once.

But Benjamin called out, "Hold on. I have something to say too." He waited for his family to quiet again, then turned to Summer and took both of her hands in his. She gave him a questioning look, and a wave of nerves swept through him. Which was ridiculous, given that they were already married. But he needed her to know—needed everyone here to know—how much he loved her. How much he wanted to be with her.

"The last time I did this, I may have been a bit hasty," he said, his voice a little shaky. "I may not have thought things through all the way. And I don't regret that for one moment because it has brought us here. But I want you to know that I've thought about this now. In fact, I do nothing but think of you—"

He heard someone say, "Aw," but he couldn't take his eyes off of his wife, who still had an eyebrow raised, as if she wasn't quite sure what he was doing.

So he would make her sure.

"And I am so deeply in love with you." Emotion suddenly blocked his throat as tears filled her eyes. He cleared his throat so he could continue. "And I don't want you to ever doubt that. I don't want you to ever doubt that you are loved and wanted and treasured."

Tears spilled from Summer's eyes, and Benjamin gently wiped them away. Then, slowly, never taking his eyes off of hers, he pulled a small box from his pocket and lowered himself to one knee.

"Benjamin," Summer protested weakly.

But he shook his head. "I know we're already married. But I want to give you the wedding you should have had. One that says to the whole world that I, Benjamin Calvano, am the most fortunate man in the world to have you, Summer Calvano, as my wife. So will you renew your vows with me?"

"I don't need a wedding," Summer said softly.

"Well, we do," Lydia's voice chimed in with a tearful laugh. "We want to celebrate y'all."

Summer bit her lip.

"Say yes," Asher called.

Benjamin looked hopefully up at Summer, and when she nodded, he jumped to his feet and pulled her into a kiss as the family all cheered.

When he finally let her go, he opened the ring box and held it out to Summer. "I hope you don't mind that it already has the wedding band.

"No," she laughed, wiping at her tears with one hand and holding out the other for him to slide the ring onto. "I don't mind at all."

The family surrounded them with hugs and congratulations, and then everyone moved to the kitchen to eat. But Summer dropped to the couch, and Benjamin looked at her in concern.

"Are you okay?" He sat next to her, gathering her hands in his. "Do you need to lie down?"

She shook her head. "I think I need to wake up. It feels too much like a fairy tale to be real. I never expected to get my own happy ending."

"Well." He brought her hands to his lips. "I'm going to spend the rest of my life making sure you do."

Epilogue

"Good morning." The low rumble of Benjamin's whisper in her ear made Summer smile, but she didn't open her eyes, allowing herself a minute more to savor being in his arms.

"Wake up, sleepyhead," he teased. "We don't want to be late for our wedding."

"We're already married," she reminded him.

"And I'm very glad about that." He kissed her forehead and her cheeks and her nose and finally her lips. "But we still don't want to be late. Besides, I have a surprise for you."

"You do?" Her eyes sprang open, and she couldn't help smiling at the look of boyish anticipation on his face. "You know I don't like surprises."

"That's all talk." Benjamin kissed her again, and she had to smile. She certainly had grown to like his surprises.

"What is it?"

He grinned. "A *surprise*. You can see it after we get ready."

She pouted. "That's too long to wait."

"Now who's being impatient?" He tapped her nose, and she rolled her eyes. Wanting to see a surprise right away was a little different from wanting to hold your vow renewal the day after proposing it.

Summer honestly would have been fine with that. But Benjamin's sisters and sisters-in-law had convinced him that they needed a couple of months to plan everything so that she could have the kind of wedding he wanted for her.

He had finally agreed to right after Christmas.

At first, that had seemed too long, even to Summer, but with the terrible morning sickness that had kicked in only days after the proposal, she was grateful they'd waited.

Fortunately, the morning sickness seemed to have mostly passed now that she was at the beginning of her second trimester, and today all she felt in her stomach was a wild fluttering of excitement.

Maybe it was silly—after all, they had already been married for four months—but it felt like today was big. Like they were saying that they may have gotten married to get guardianship of Max, but they were *staying* married because they loved each other. A fact that still took her breath away.

"Stay right here." Benjamin rolled out of the bed. "I'll bring you breakfast."

"You don't have to—" But he was already darting into the hallway.

She shook her head but laughed and pressed a hand to her stomach. Could the baby feel the excitement too?

The results of Benjamin's genetic tests showed that he didn't have the gene variant for cardiomyopathy. Which meant that the baby couldn't have it. And they'd had an ultrasound only last week that had shown everything was normal—although Summer could hardly believe that the little bean on the screen was going to be a baby in her arms in six more months.

"Here we are." Benjamin breezed back into the room, a tray in his hands, Max at his heels. "I found someone who wants to join us."

"Climb on up." Summer sat up and scooted over to make room for both of them as Benjamin settled the tray heaped with muffins and crepes and fruit onto the bed.

"When did you have time to make all of this?"

He raised his eyebrows. "I'm very sneaky."

"I saw it on the porch," Max said, stuffing a big bite of blueberry muffin into his mouth.

"Tattletale." But Benjamin laughed. "Chloe brought it over. But I put it on the tray."

His eyes twinkled, and Summer shoved his arm. "Are you ever going to be serious?"

"Only about you." He leaned across the tray to kiss her.

They finished eating, and then he sent her to the room she'd slept in when they were first married—which they now planned to convert to a nursery—to get ready.

"What do you say to a race?" he asked. "I bet Max and I can get ready faster than you."

"Boy oh boy!" Max sprang down from the bed. "We'll win for sure."

"We'll see about that." Summer jumped out of the bed, grabbing Benjamin's tie off of the dresser on her way past.

In the other bedroom, she quickly pulled on the simple white satin empire waist wedding dress her sisters-in-law had helped her pick out. She brushed her long hair into soft waves that she had decided to leave down and put on a light layer of makeup.

Then, not even taking a moment to survey the complete effect in the full-length mirror, she wrapped Benjamin's tie around her wrist and rushed into the hallway. But both of the other bedrooms were empty, and Benjamin's and Max's voices carried to her from the living room. She followed the sound, her breath catching as she stepped into the room to find them bent over the new train set they'd gotten Max for Christmas. They wore matching gray suits, although Benjamin's was missing the tie.

Summer cleared her throat, and they both looked up at the same time.

"Oh boy!" Max yelled. "We beat you."

But Benjamin stood speechless, his eyes shining in that way that made Summer feel like the most treasured person in the world.

"Technically," she told Max, "you didn't beat me. Benji doesn't have his tie on." She unwrapped it from her wrist and held it up.

Benjamin laughed, and then he sped across the room, pulling her into his arms. "Now who's the one who's not serious?"

"Ah well. I may have learned a thing or two from being married to you." She slipped the tie around his neck and tied it, then brought her lips to his. "Now, where's my surprise?"

"Oh boy! I know!" Max barreled out of the room, through the kitchen, and out the patio door.

Summer gave Benjamin a questioning look, but he just smiled. "Go see."

She followed Max's path to the door. But when she stepped into the chill but bright December morning, the boy seemed to have disappeared.

"Max?"

A little giggle came from somewhere in front of her, and Summer followed the sound to the edge of the deck.

"Oh!" She laughed in surprised delight as her eyes fell on the hammock that rested in front of the deck, Max nestled inside of it.

"Do you like it?" Benjamin slid his arms around her from behind, resting his chin on her head.

"I love it."

"It made me think of that night, after TJ . . ."

She nodded, blinking back tears. "He would be happy about this. About us."

Benjamin nodded. "I'm pretty happy about it too."

He kissed her again, and then they called Max out of the hammock and headed for the church.

Beautiful Savior's parking lot was already half-filled with cars, and Summer laughed. "I guess we *were* almost late for our wedding."

"Don't worry. I don't think they'd start without us."

Benjamin and Max got out of the car. Then Benjamin came around to her side, opening her door and bowing low with a hand outstretched, the same way he had done in Hope Springs. "My princess."

This time, she didn't call him ridiculous. Because she had never *felt* more like a princess.

Even the sky was glowing with happiness, and Summer didn't notice the winter chill until she felt Benjamin's warm suit coat settle over her shoulders.

Then, hand in hand, the three of them made their way to the church. Inside, Benjamin's family tackled them all in hugs. Grace and Levi had made the trip from Hope Springs and had revealed last night that they were expecting too, and Summer had been so deliriously happy to see their joy.

The only one who wasn't there was Judah. Summer knew Benjamin was disappointed that he hadn't been able to convince his brother to come home and visit yet, but if she wasn't wrong, Judah seemed to be softening toward the idea. She almost thought he would have come to the wedding if he weren't out of the country right now. And he had promised to think about coming when he got back—which should be right around the time the baby arrived.

Max ran to Mia, who had offered to keep him occupied until he was needed for his ring bearer duties.

"Hi, Miss Summer." A little girl walked up to Summer shyly.

"Hi, Nadia." Summer smiled down at the girl, who had been the first to sign up when she'd begun offering private dance lessons last month. Eventually, she hoped to turn it into a full-fledged dance school, alongside her party business, but she and Benjamin had agreed to take things slow until after the baby was born. "I'm glad you could come."

"I'm glad you're marrying Prince Charming." Nadia giggled, then skipped off to join her mother, who waved to Summer.

"Hey, man, I'm glad you could make it," she heard Benjamin say, and she turned to find him shaking hands with a man with platinum blonde hair and a convincing smile. "I want to introduce you to my wife, Summer." Summer started to reach for the guy's outstretched hand, just as Benjamin said, "Summer, this is Ian."

She hesitated, almost pulling her hand back, but Ian laughed lightly. "I don't blame you if you hate me. I'm sorry for anything I messed up, I really am. Trust me, Benjamin put me in my place. And I see why now. Clearly what he has going here is better than any job I could offer. No hard feelings?"

Benjamin sent her a beseeching look, and she nodded, setting her hand in Ian's. "No hard feelings."

"Good." Ian's grin was wide, as if he'd never doubted she would agree, and she shook her head as he went to sit down.

The lobby emptied as their guests all headed for the sanctuary, and Pastor Calvano strode toward them, beaming. He'd spent the past two months taking them through premarital counseling, and Summer had loved the opportunity to grow closer not only to her husband but also to her father-in-law.

"Are you two ready?" he asked, setting a hand on each of their shoulders.

"Absolutely." Benjamin hugged his dad, and then Pastor Calvano hugged her too, and Summer squeezed back for all she was worth. Then he slipped into the sanctuary, and Mia appeared with Max at her side.

Benjamin squatted so that he was at eye-level with the boy. "Are you ready to be our ring bearer?"

Max nodded solemnly.

"Good." Benjamin pulled a velvety red bag out of his own pocket. He opened it and held it out to Summer. Carefully, she slid her ring off of her finger and slipped it into the bag, her hand feeling suddenly bare.

Then she reached into a seam of her dress and came out with her own velvety blue bag.

Benjamin's eyes widened. "Where did that come from?"

She grinned. "My dress has pockets."

"But— But— Where did— How did— What is—"

She laughed. "You think you're the only one with surprises?"

The processional music started, and she quickly tucked the bag into Max's pocket. Then Mia led Max to the door and pointed down the aisle. Max glanced over his shoulder at them, grinned, and then sauntered into the church.

Benjamin chuckled. "He's eating this up."

Summer nodded, but the significance of what they were about to do had suddenly hit her, and she couldn't say anything.

Benjamin looked at her, his face concerned. "Are you nervous?"

She shook her head and threaded her arm through his. "Not with you at my side. I'm just . . . so happy."

"Good." He kissed her lightly and wrapped his hand over hers.

They'd decided not to have a wedding party since it would have been impossible to choose among Benjamin's siblings—and if they'd asked them all, there wouldn't have been many people left in the pews.

So when Max was halfway to the front of the church, Benjamin stepped confidently into the aisle with her on his arm. The whole way to the front of the church, all Summer could think was that this was everything she'd ever dreamed of.

When they reached Pastor Calvano, he hugged them each again, then began the ceremony. Summer soaked up the words as he talked about how marriage was a picture of Christ's love for the church and how Christ loved his bride so much that he had pursued her and given himself to make her his own. She could only smile through her tears as she realized again what a beautiful truth that was and how Benjamin had been—and was still—an example to her of that kind of love.

When it was time for the vows, Benjamin took her hands in his and said, with a little laugh, "It's probably bad form to contradict the pastor at your own wedding, especially when he happens to be your father, but . . ." He paused as the congregation laughed—and so did Pastor Calvano.

"But," he continued, "it's not that I disagree with what he said. Marriage is a picture of Christ's love for the church. And I would absolutely give up everything for you, Summer, including my own life. But you should know that I didn't give up anything when I married you. I *gained* everything I ever wanted."

Tears spilled onto Summer's cheeks, but she wasn't about to let go of his hands to wipe them away.

"I confess that I thought I was taking control of the situation when I married you. I thought God had fallen down on the job." He laughed a little. "It turns out that he was taking care of things all along. He knew exactly what I needed when he gave me you and he gave me Max and he gave me our baby—" His voice cracked, and his smile wavered as he cleared his throat. "In ways I can't even fathom, he has given me a richer life than I could have ever imagined, and I look forward to spending every day of it with you."

His smile was back, and it wrapped itself around Summer's heart as Pastor Calvano invited her to say her vows.

She took a breath, then said apologetically, "They're kind of the same as Benjamin's."

Benjamin laughed and looked at their guests. "We didn't even plan that."

Their light laughter, combined with the gentle pressure of Benjamin's hand around hers, gave her the courage to start. "When TJ died, I thought I had lost everything." A sob almost overtook her, but she swallowed it down. "I thought no one else in the world would ever love me." She licked her lips and whispered, "Would ever want me."

And then, her voice stronger, she said, "But you were there the whole time. You didn't once leave my side, except when I made you." There was a gentle chuckle from the church, and Summer smiled too. "You even went so far as to *marry* me, and still I didn't see it." She shook her head at her own foolishness. "I tried to push you away. I tried to tell myself you didn't really want me, but you kept coming back, you kept being there for me, you kept whispering that you loved me and shouting that you loved me and *showing* me that you loved me. I don't know how you never gave up on me, but I'm so thankful you didn't. Because the day we married, I gained so much." The tears started falling again, but her voice remained steady. "I gained you, and I gained this incredible family." She looked around at them all, smiling and wiping their own eyes. "And I gained this *love*. I never could have imagined being surrounded by *so much* love, and I am so grateful that I get to spend the rest of my life with you."

She let out a shaky breath as she finished, and Benjamin swiped a quick hand under his eyes.

Then they both repeated the vows they'd made at the courthouse. This time, Summer didn't hesitate for even a moment to say, "for as long as we both shall live."

Pastor Calvano called for the rings, and Max marched proudly forward and held out the bags. Summer took the blue one and Benjamin the red one.

She held out her hand for Benjamin to slip the ring back on it, sighing with contentment to feel it on her finger again, though it had been off for less than an hour.

Then she slid the ring she'd bought Benjamin out of her bag. She held out the gold band engraved with interlocking circles, and Benjamin lifted his hand for her to slide it on. He made a choked sound and then gripped her hand and pulled her to him in a crushing hug as his dad declared them husband and wife.

Over the applause of their wedding guests, Benjamin whispered into her ear, "I love you."

Summer nodded, pressing her cheek to his and marveling at the truth one little whisper could hold.

Thank you for reading WHISPERS OF TRUTH! I hope you loved Benjamin and Summer's story! Join them (and their baby!) and the whole Calvano family in the next River Falls book, Promises of Mercy, as Judah finally returns to River Falls! Will the estranged Calvano brother finally reconcile with his faith and his family—and find love?

Also, be sure to sign up for my newsletter to get Asher and Ireland's story, REFLECTIONS OF LOVE, as a free gift.

Visit https://www.valeriembodden.com/freebook or use the QR code below to sign up.

And if you love the River Falls series, you'll find more uplifting stories of faith, family, and forever love in the Hope Springs series, featuring Grace and Levi and their friends in Hope Springs, Wisconsin. Read on for an excerpt of the first Hope Springs book, Not Until Forever!

A preview of Not Until Forever (Hope Springs Book 1)

Prologue

Spencer paced behind the park bench, tipping his head toward the gray clouds swirling above him. His nerves swirled faster. He patted at the pocket of his hoodie for the eighth time, letting the solidity of the little box there reassure him. Even if some parts of his life were falling apart right now, this was the one thing he was sure of.

He squinted toward the parking lot, watching for the flash of Sophie's bright red Camaro. But the lot was empty, aside from his battered pickup truck, already packed with the few things he needed from his apartment. It was hard to believe he was going to walk away without his degree with less than a semester to go. But this was what he had to do. His family needed him.

He scrubbed a hand over his face and made himself sit down. He should be on his way already. But he couldn't leave without doing this. Without telling Sophie what he wanted for the future. Their future.

Finally, the rumble of the Camaro's engine caught his ears. Spencer fumbled at his pocket again as Sophie whipped into the parking lot. The wind unfurled her golden hair behind her as she stepped out of the car. Spencer shoved a hand roughly through his own hair and swallowed hard. What had he been thinking, doing this here?

He should have picked somewhere more romantic. More elegant. More Sophie. But this park had been their place since their first date three years ago. It was where they came to talk, to laugh, to share everything. Doing this here, now, felt right. Spencer forced himself to take a slow breath as Sophie hurried toward him, her strides long and sure in her heels and slim black skirt.

Just the sight of her lightened his heart. He had no idea what a woman like her saw in a man like him, but he'd learned not to question it. For whatever reason, they worked. And for that, he thanked God.

Spencer sank his face into her hair as his arms tugged her closer. This was what he'd needed. Whatever he was facing, holding Sophie made everything right in the world.

She pulled back a few inches and slid her fingers over his unshaven cheek. "You look tired. You sure you want to make the drive back to Hope Springs yet tonight?"

Not now that he was with her, he didn't. But he nodded. "I have to, Soph."

He'd only been home a couple of days—just long enough to sit with Mom through the worst of the waiting at the hospital. Through the hours of not knowing if Dad would make it.

Sophie looked away, but not before he caught the flash of disappointment in her eyes. "How's your dad?"

Spencer disentangled from her embrace and grabbed her hand, leading her around the muddy patches toward their favorite spot at the edge of the park's little pond. A family of ducks quacked at them and shuffled out of the way.

"He's stable. Should be out of the hospital in a few days, but he's not going to be back in the orchard anytime soon." He couldn't push away the image of Dad's gray face. His slow movements. How could a heart attack have transformed his powerhouse of a dad so drastically?

Sophie bit her lip in that way that made it almost impossible to resist kissing her. "It's just so close to graduation. It seems like a waste to throw away everything you've worked for."

Spencer sighed. He'd had this argument with himself all the way here. But he couldn't see any way around it.

"The work won't wait, Soph. The seasons keep changing, no matter what's going on in our lives." He squeezed her hand. "Anyway, it's not like if I don't finish my degree now I can't ever do it. I have my whole life." *Our whole life.* But he was getting ahead of himself.

"I know." Sophie offered a half-hearted smile. "I just hate the idea of saying goodbye sooner than we planned."

He pulled her to a stop next to the bench they'd spent so many hours on. "Me too. That's actually why I asked you to come here."

He gestured for her to sit, and she did, giving him a curious look as he remained on his feet. He drew in a shaky breath. He'd been so busy thinking about everything else that he hadn't prepared what to say.

"There's something I have to ask you."

A wind gust blew her hair in front of her face, and she swept it behind her ear as he dropped to one knee. Hands shaking, he pulled the ring box from his pocket, opened it, and held the small diamond solitaire toward her.

Sophie gasped, lifting a hand to her mouth. "Spencer, don't—"

"Sophie, will you—" Spencer stopped as her words slammed into him. "What?"

Sophie sprang to her feet and practically leaped over the bench, as if trying to construct a physical barrier between them. "You're emotional right now. You're not thinking clearly."

Spencer pushed slowly to his feet and moved closer to the bench, reaching for Sophie's hand across its back. "I'm not doing this because I'm emotional. I already had the ring. I was planning to wait until graduation, but with everything going on, I wanted you to know that I want a future with you."

He squeezed her hand and tried to pull her around the bench so he could try again and this time do it properly. Leave it to him to screw up the proposal the first time.

But Sophie pulled out of his grasp and looked past him, toward the pond.

Spencer's heart crumbled. She didn't want to marry him.

"I'm leaving for Chicago in two months, Spencer. You know I can't pass up this job offer."

He wanted to tell her it didn't matter. That he'd go with her. Or he'd find her a job that was just as good closer to home. Anything.

But admitting his need would only lead to more hurt. Would only remind him that he'd never be worthy of her.

"I'm sorry," Sophie whispered.

And then she turned and walked away.

And he let her.

Chapter 1

Five years later

Sophie stepped off the L, deftly dodging the enormous puddles on the sidewalk from last night's rain so she wouldn't ruin her new Jimmy Choo heels. She inhaled deeply, trying to catch a hint of spring. But spring in Chicago smelled nothing like spring at home in Hope Springs. There, the season carried the heady scents of ice melt and earth and fruit blossoms. Here, all she could smell were exhaust fumes and the overripe garbage bins that had been set out on the sidewalk for pickup.

It didn't matter—she'd likely be inside all day and long into the night anyway. This new development was the biggest deal she'd worked on yet, and with any luck, it was the one that would secure her promotion as the firm's youngest VP. It didn't matter how much time she had to spend indoors or how many hours it took. She'd make it happen.

She pushed through the doors of the sleek glass tower on North Clark and hurried across the lobby, relishing the sharp click of her heels against the polished marble floor. She still couldn't believe sometimes that she'd landed a position with Heartland, one of the most prestigious development firms in the country.

"Good morning, Sophie," the white-haired security guard greeted her as he did every morning.

"Morning," Sophie mumbled as she hurried past and jabbed at the elevator's up button.

At the twenty-eighth floor, she stepped out into the posh lobby of Heartland and made her way to her office. As always, her eyes were drawn immediately to the breathtaking view of the city and the Lake Michigan shoreline. There was a slight chop on the water today, though the waves winked in the sun.

Not that she had time to stand here and admire the view. Sophie settled into her leather chair and grabbed the project she'd been working on for two weeks. She leafed through the papers. This was her first project as lead developer, and she had a lot riding on it. But if she could pull off the purchase and development of the combination apartment, shopping, and entertainment complex she'd envisioned . . .

One step at a time, Sophie. When you get ahead of yourself, you get sloppy. How many times had her mom used that reprimand on her growing up? It seemed to apply to everything from math tests to ballet recitals. Somehow, nothing she did had ever been good enough for her parents.

She shook herself. She'd never earn her promotion if she focused on the past instead of the task at hand. She pulled out the latest renderings from the architect and dove in.

An hour later, a rap on her door made her jump.

"Staff meeting, three minutes." Her assistant Tina passed her a fresh cup of coffee.

"Ah, thanks." Sophie smoothed her hair and shuffled the papers she'd spread across her desk into a neat pile. Then she gathered the whole bunch and hurried to the conference room.

The firm's six other developers were already gathered around the room's large mahogany table. This room was definitely the most intimidating in the office, with its oversize table and chairs that seemed to swallow her, but Sophie kept her chin up as she entered the room and grabbed a seat next to Chase. He gave her a warm smile and a subtle wink.

She ducked her head to hide her blush. Not that it was a big secret that the two had been casually dating. But Sophie felt awkward when he acted like that at work—especially in front of his father, who also happened to be one of the partners.

"Glad you could make it, Sophie." Mr. Davis's joke barely masked a hard edge of irritation.

"Sorry, I got caught up in the Hudson project."

Mr. Sanders, who'd always been the friendlier of the two partners, turned to her. "How does it look? Everything on track?"

Sophie patted the folder in front of her. "I think so. But—"

"Excuse me." All eyes swiveled to Tina as she poked her head into the room.

Sophie gestured for her to step back outside. Heartland had a strict policy about interruptions during meetings. As in, you didn't do it. Ever.

"I'm sorry." Tina motioned to Sophie. "You have a phone call. It's your grandmother."

"My grandmother?" She hadn't talked to Nana in months—and never at work. A slice of fear cut through her. It must be an emergency. Her mouth went dry, but she pushed her chair back and mumbled an apology, not sure if her words were audible.

Once she was out of the conference room, she sped across the common area to her office.

She lunged for her phone and snatched it off the desk, hitting the flashing button. "Nana?" The word came out breathless, as if she'd just finished a marathon cardio Pilates session.

"There's my Sophie." Her grandmother's voice rasped through the phone.

"Nana, is everything okay? Of course it's not okay or you wouldn't be calling me at work in the middle of the day. Is it Mom? Or Dad?" What if it was both of them—a car accident, maybe, on one of the rare occasions they were actually together.

"I knew you'd make time for me." Nana's words sounded garbled, and Sophie felt as if she'd been dropped into the middle of a foreign movie.

"Make time for you? Nana, what's the emergency?"

"I just wanted to hear your voice."

Sophie held the phone away from her ear and gave it an incredulous stare. Nana had interrupted her meeting to hear her voice? She rubbed at her temple as she pulled the phone back to her ear. "It's so good to hear from you, Nana, but I'm actually in the middle of a meeting." She glanced at the clock above her door. "I'll call you back in an hour or so, okay?"

She was met with silence.

"Nana?"

"Do me a favor, Sophie."

Sophie drummed her fingers on her desk. Now wasn't the best time for favors. "You got it, Nana. Whatever it is, I'm on it. Just as soon as my meeting is over. I'll—"

"Remember that I love you and so does God." Nana's voice was getting fainter, as if she was holding the phone too far from her mouth. Sophie strained to hear. "If you remember that, then I've done my job. Okay, Sophie?"

"Okay, Nana." Sophie didn't really have time for Nana's philosophical musings right now. "I have to go. I'll call you—"

"That's okay, Sophie. You don't have to call back. I just wanted to hear your voice one more time before I go."

"Go?" A brainstorm about the Hudson project hit Sophie, and she reached for a pen and a sticky note to jot it down. "Are you taking a trip?"

Nana was always going somewhere or other.

"I'm going home, Sophie."

"Hmm." Sophie finished her note. "Where are you now?" Probably the Mediterranean or somewhere in East Asia. She'd probably forgotten the time difference.

"I'm in the hospital, dear."

Sophie dropped her pen and straightened. Nana had been battling cancer for a couple years and had ended up in the hospital more than once in that time. Still, Sophie knew how much she hated being cooped up.

"But you get to go home soon? That's good news."

"Not that home, dear." Nana's voice was overly gentle, like it had been the first time Sophie came to her with a broken heart.

"What do you mean, 'not that home'? What other home do you have?" Sophie frowned. She hadn't noticed any decline in Nana's mental ability, but much as she hated to face it, Nana *was* getting older.

"I mean, I don't think I'll see that home again. I'm going to my true home."

"True home?" This conversation was making less sense by the minute.

Nana sighed, and Sophie felt like she'd missed something important, but she couldn't for the life of her think what it could be.

"Heaven, dear. I'm going home to heaven."

Sophie's head jerked up as she sat hard in her desk chair. She opened and closed her mouth a few times before she could get any words out. "You don't know that, Nana. I'm sure you have lots of time left. You—"

"You can't argue my way out of this, Sophie." Nana's chuckle grated against Sophie's nerves. How could she deliver news like this and then laugh?

"How long—?" Sophie swallowed the boulder that had lodged in her throat.

"A couple of days, the doctors think. Maybe a week."

"I'm sorry, Nana." Her voice was barely a whisper. She fought off the sharp sting gathering behind her eyes. If she didn't cry, she wouldn't feel. It was a skill she'd perfected over the years.

"Don't you be sorry for me, child." Nana's voice was firm. "I know where I'm going. And I got to say goodbye to my Sophie. That's all I asked. God is good."

Sophie chewed her lip. A phone call was no way to say goodbye to the woman who'd been almost a mother to her. Who had loved her unconditionally her whole life, even when her own parents hadn't.

"I'll be on my way in ten minutes. Do you think you could—" Sophie sucked in a breath. "Could you wait for me? Before you—" But she refused to finish that sentence.

"It's in God's hands, dear."

It wasn't the guarantee Sophie had been hoping for, but it would have to do. She hung up and took a minute to steel herself. Then she pushed slowly to her feet and walked to Mr. Sanders's office, taking a steadying breath before she knocked on his door.

Chase was already in with his father, but Mr. Sanders invited her in as well.

She waited for one of them to say something about the phone call, but when neither did, she pushed forward. "I need to request a few days off. That was my grandmother who called—" Sophie cut herself off. No need to remind them of the interruption to the meeting. "Anyway, she's not doing well. The doctors only give her a few days." She didn't let herself dwell on the words. "I'd like to go home. To say goodbye."

Chase toed the floor, not meeting her eyes.

"Are you close to your grandmother?" Mr. Sanders's voice was neither compassionate nor judgmental. It was a solid neutral.

"I am. Or, well, I was. I haven't been to visit her in a while . . ." Sophie cleared her throat.

"You understand how important this project is? To the firm as well as to your career?" Mr. Sanders folded his hands in front of him on the desk.

Sophie bit her lip, nodding.

"Then—" Mr. Sanders stood, and Sophie understood the move as a dismissal. "I'll leave it up to you. If you stay, you keep the project. If you go, I'm going to put Chase on it. We can't afford to lose out on this one, and if you can't dedicate yourself to it one hundred percent . . ."

Sophie blinked at the unfairness. He was going to make her choose between her family and her career?

She ducked out of her office, her insides roiling. How was she supposed to make a decision like this?

Halfway across the lobby, Chase caught up with her. "Sophie, wait. What are you going to do?" She couldn't tell if that was eagerness in his voice or compassion.

"I guess I'm going to—" The word stay almost came out. It's what she should do. For her own good. But the image of Nana, alone in her hospital bed, pushed into her head. Could she really forgive herself if she let Nana die alone like that? "I'm going to go. I'll get you the plans."

To his credit, Chase didn't gloat or even smile. "For what it's worth, Sophie, I'm sorry. I know how much you wanted this project."

She shrugged. "There'll be others." Of course, she could kiss that VP position goodbye. If Chase hadn't been a shoo-in before, he certainly would be after this.

She stepped around him and into her office, grabbing the stack of plans for the Hudson project off her desk. She passed it to Chase. "I should get going."

He gave her hand a quick squeeze. "Don't be gone too long. Maybe you can help me put the finishing touches on the project plan."

Sophie nodded and stepped out of the office toward the bank of elevators.

She had no intention of staying in Hope Springs a moment longer than she had to.

The lowering sun lit the water on fire as Sophie crested the hill above Hope Springs five hours later.

She pulled down the Camaro's sun visor and rubbed at her weary eyes.

As the road dropped into the town, she slowed, letting herself take in sights she hadn't seen in more than five years.

It was odd how everything looked the same and yet different. It wasn't yet tourist season, so most of the shops were closed for the evening, and the streets were mostly empty, aside from the occasional local walking their dog.

Memories piled up and slammed into her as she passed the Hidden Cafe. The Chocolate Chicken. The post office. Sophie tried to beat them back. She wasn't here to reminisce. She was here to say goodbye to Nana and then get back to her real life.

She accelerated, trying to leave the memories behind as she passed out of town. Her stomach tightened into double knots as she pulled into the long, winding driveway that led up the highest bluff overlooking the lake. Bare trees pressed in on her from all sides, until her parents' over-large house finally came into view, all hard lines and sharp angles.

She parked in the large section of the driveway her parents reserved for guests and sat for a minute, gazing toward the now-dark waters of the lake. Was this really the same lake she'd been looking at hours ago from her office in Chicago? It was the one thing that connected her two lives. That and the memories. But those she tried not to think about.

She forced herself to push her car door open. To grab her suitcase out of the trunk. To follow the slate path to the front door.

She reached for the doorknob but then thought better of it and pressed her finger to the doorbell.

When no one answered after a minute, she let herself in. "Hello?" She felt oddly like an intruder as her voice echoed around her childhood home.

"In here." Mom's voice carried from the kitchen.

Sophie left her suitcase in the foyer and followed the sound.

Mom was seated at the long granite breakfast counter, poring over a design magazine. She barely glanced up when Sophie entered. "I told you, you didn't have to come."

"I wanted to come." Sophie gave her mother an obligatory kiss on the cheek.

She knew better than to ask where her father was. If her mother was home, her father was likely at the club. The two had barely been in the same room together, aside from at church and when brokering real estate deals, in the past fifteen years.

"How's Nana?" Sophie went to the refrigerator and grabbed a bottle of water.

"Call her grandmother." Sophie's mom gave an exaggerated huff. "You know I hate when you call her Nana. Sounds like that dog from that movie."

"Peter Pan?" Sophie wrinkled her nose. She'd been calling her grandmother Nana since she was seven. She wasn't about to stop now. "Have you been to see her?"

"I called earlier. There's no change." Mom flipped the page of her magazine. "I don't know what you think being here is going to accomplish. You should have stayed at work."

Sophie took another sip of her water to keep from striking back. It was the same old story. Her parents would never be satisfied with anything she did.

"I wanted to say goodbye." She focused on keeping an even tone.

Her mother nodded, eyes fixed on her magazine. "I'm thinking about redoing the kitchen. What do you think of these cabinets?"

Sophie set her water on the counter and walked out of the room without looking at the magazine. "They're nice, Mom."

She grabbed her suitcase and trudged up the staircase before her mother could infuriate her any more. Not that Mom had ever been emotionally available, but planning to redecorate the kitchen while her own mother was dying was too much even for her.

At the end of the hallway, Sophie pushed open the door to her old room. It'd been completely redone as a guest room almost the moment she left for college. All her old posters had been stripped from the walls. The poppy orange she'd painted the room when she was fifteen had been replaced by a soft lilac. She had to admit that the room was more to her taste now, but seeing it stripped of her former self stung.

Oh, well. It's not like she could ever go back to who she used to be.

Sophie hefted her suitcase onto the overstuffed chair in the corner and collapsed on the king-size bed. That was new, too. She longed for the twin-size canopy bed she'd gotten from her grandmother—it'd been the one place that always felt cozy in the cold house.

After a few minutes, she grew restless. She'd had way too much coffee on the way up. She wouldn't be able to sleep for hours yet, but the thought of returning to the kitchen and doing another round with Mom turned her stomach. She crossed to the room's built-in bookshelf. When she'd lived here, it'd overflowed with books. Mysteries, mostly. Romance. Some classics.

Now, it held mostly knickknacks, but a few books were sprinkled here and there. She ran her fingers over the spines until they landed on *Pride and Prejudice*. Had this really been her favorite book once? Had she really believed that two people who were so different, who came from such different backgrounds, could make a life together? Well, Jane Austen may have been that naive, but she wasn't. Not anymore.

Still, she couldn't resist pulling the worn copy off the shelf. A bookmark stuck out about a third of the way through the book.

As she flipped to the page, something small and white fluttered out and drifted to the floor.

She bent to pick it up, and her breath caught.

It was a pressed cherry blossom, in pristine condition.

From Spencer. When he gave it to her, he said it reminded him of her—strong and delicate at the same time.

She gently lifted the blossom to her face. A faint scent of spring lingered on it. Or maybe that was just wishful thinking.

She replaced the blossom in the book and stuck it on the shelf. That part of her life was over.

Besides, Spencer likely had a wife and family of his own by now.

A pang sliced through her belly. What if she ran into him while she was home? Worse, what if she ran into his new family? Could she handle seeing him with another woman?

She shook her head and flopped onto the bed. She was being ridiculous. It wouldn't matter if she saw him and his family or not.

She had a highly successful career, an upscale apartment, a casual boyfriend who didn't expect anything long-term from her. She had everything she had ever wanted.

Which didn't explain the hollow feeling that had taken up residence in her chest.

KEEP READING NOT UNTIL FOREVER

Also By Valerie M. Bodden

More River Falls Books

While the books in the River Falls series are linked, each is a complete romance featuring a different couple.

Pieces of Forever (Joseph & Ava)

Songs of Home (Lydia & Liam)

Memories of the Heart (Simeon & Abigail)

Whispers of Truth (Benjamin & Summer)

Promises of Mercy (Judah & Faith)

River Falls Christmas Romances

Wondering about some of the side characters in River Falls who aren't members of the Calvano family? Join them as they get their own happily-ever-afters in the River Falls Christmas Romances.

Christmas of Joy (Madison & Luke)

The Hope Springs Series

While the books in the Hope Springs series are linked, each is a complete romance featuring a different couple.
Not Until Forever (Sophie & Spencer)
Not Until This Moment (Jared & Peyton)
Not Until You (Nate & Violet)
Not Until Us (Dan & Jade)
Not Until Christmas Morning (Leah & Austin)
Not Until This Day (Tyler & Isabel)
Not Until Someday (Grace & Levi)
Not Until Now (Cam & Kayla)
Not Until Then (Bethany & James)
Not Until The End (Emma & Owen)

Want to know when my next book releases?

You can follow me on Amazon to be the first to know when my next book releases! Just visit amazon.com/author/valeriembodden and click the follow button.

Acknowledgements

First, a confession: I've started and restarted writing these acknowledgements half a dozen times. Not because I don't know what to say but because there are *so many* things I could say. I could talk about how I wrote this book at a time when our family was facing some big decisions and nothing felt certain, and how I needed Benjamin's prayer, *Please show me how to surrender to you*, more than ever. I could mention that between Benjamin's impulsiveness and Summer's stubbornness, I didn't think they would ever let me give them a happy ending. But most of all, what I think I want to tell you is what Summer learns: "*God* wanted her. *That* was what mattered. *He* had given up everything for her because he loved her."

Those words weren't written only for Summer. They were written for you. And for me. What an amazing God we have, who loved us so much, who wanted us so badly, that he gave up his Son for us. He sent Jesus to pay the price for our sins. As always, my first and highest thanks and praise go to him for that incredible truth. For that amazing love. And I thank him for giving me the honor and privilege of sharing his love through my stories.

I thank him also for the amazing family he has blessed me with. If you want to know a little secret, Benjamin is probably the most like my husband of all my heroes. Oh, Pastor Calvano and Pastor Cooper (and Pastor Dan from my Hope Springs series) are very much like my husband in their warm, friendly preaching style (and their ability to make people chuckle in church), but personality-wise, my husband is Benjamin all the way. In fact, it wasn't long after I finished writing the book that he said to me, "Me serious? Never," in exactly the same tone of voice I pictured Benjamin saying it in. But, like Benjamin, he is also unwaveringly steadfast and supportive. He leads our family with strength and love—all while making us laugh—and for that I am eternally grateful. I'm also so thankful for the four children with whom the Lord has blessed us. Somehow, pieces of them seem to make it into every single book I write. Max's enthusiasm for his dinosaurs and bugs and sticks and volcanoes comes from my own boys and all of the science experiments and explorations we did together. And Summer's princess parties are a tribute to my girls, who loved both to dress up as princesses and to meet princesses. What a blessing to know that all four of you are real-life princes and princesses—for you are sons and daughters of the King of kings!

As always, I am thankful for my parents, sister, in-laws, and extended family. You all are the reason I love to take characters like Summer, who have never experienced the kind of supportive, encouraging family I have, and bring them into the arms of a loving family like the Calvanos.

I also can't give enough thanks for my incredible advance reader team, for your enthusiasm, for your encouragement, and for your prayers. Special thanks to: Sandra M, Sandy Golinger, Patty Bohuslav, Laura Polian, Margaret N, Michelle, Vickie, Pam Williams, Diana A, Connie Gandy, Julie Mancil, Carol Witzenburger, Rhondia, D'Anna Helms, KBH, Jeanne Olynick, Trista, Seyi, Bonny Rambarran, Alison Komm, SuzieMc, Darla Knutzen, Lincoln Clark, Judith, Judith Barillas, Sharon, Korin Thomas, Jan Gilmour, Jennifer Ellenson, Kathy Ann Meadows, D.S., Sandy H, Maxine Barber, Connie G, Evelyn Foreman, Jayne L. Campbell, Lynn S, Kelly Wickham, Becky C, Ellen B, Melanie Tate, Julie Miller, Chinye Ukwu, G Durr, and Josie Bartelt.

And finally, thank *you* for reading Benjamin and Summer's story and becoming part of the Calvano family. I know there are a lot of ways you could spend your time, and I hope your hours in this story have uplifted and encouraged you with the reminder that God loves you. He wants you. He has made you his own. May his peace and blessings be with you always.

About the Author

Valerie M. Bodden has three great loves: Jesus, her family, and books. And chocolate (okay, four great loves). She is living out her happily ever after with her high-school-sweetheart-turned-husband and their four children. Her life wouldn't make a terribly exciting book, as it has a happy beginning and middle, and someday when she goes to her heavenly home, it will have a happy end.

She was born and raised in Wisconsin but recently moved with her family to Texas, where they're all getting used to the warm weather (she doesn't miss the snow even a little bit, though the rest of the family does) and saying y'all instead of you guys.

Valerie writes emotion-filled Christian fiction that weaves real-life problems, real-life people, and real-life faith. Her characters may (okay, will) experience some heartache along the way, but she will always give them a happy ending.

Feel free to stop by www.valeriembodden.com to say hi. She loves visitors! And while you're there, you can sign up for your free story.

Made in the USA
Columbia, SC
22 July 2024

39180052R00228